THE AUCTION

CLUB INDULGENCE DUET
BOOK ONE

MAGGIE COLE

PULSE PRESS INC

PROLOGUE

Riggs Madden
Seven Years Ago

"*R*iggs?" Hugh Gallow nudges me, pulling me out of my trance. I've barely heard a word of my business partner's stifling conversation for the last few minutes.

It's his daughter Blakely's fault. She stepped into the garden wearing a nude slip dress and matching four-inch designer stilettos. Her blonde hair cascades along her shoulders in long curls, and when her blue eyes met mine, she quickly broke our stare as if she were caught with her hand in the cookie jar. Since then, I've been too captivated to tear my eyes off her, pleased every time I catch her gazing my way and trying to pretend she's not looking at me.

The attraction between us started three years ago. She turned eighteen and was no longer Hugh's little girl. It didn't take long for me to notice the little flush in her cheeks when she glanced at me or her nervous finger tapping on whatever she could find to torment. Her usual victims consist of a table or her thighs, the latter of which I'm dying to get between. Right now, her champagne flute is taking a beating.

Hugh demands, "Riggs, confirm my numbers."

I clear my throat, recover from my absence, and answer, "That's right. We're up over thirty percent." I down the rest of my scotch and add, "Excuse me. The men's room is calling." I escape Hugh and the circle of his stuck-up friends he's always trying to impress, hightailing it to the restroom, glad to exit their presence.

Blakely's father and I have been partners for over a decade, and while his mentorship influenced many things in my life, there's one thing he couldn't change about me—I just don't care about impressing people like Hugh does. I couldn't give a shit about what anyone thinks unless I need to impress them to sell one of our companies for a huge profit.

After growing up on food stamps in Compton, where most adults didn't have a job and addiction was rampant, you'd think anyone with business acumen would have impressed me. I'd escaped the gangs and pitfalls of poverty in the absence of anyone molding me into a successful young man. Yet most of the entrepreneurs I came across didn't strike me as anything special.

Then I met Hugh. I was in my late twenties and he was in his forties. Our first discussion led to a six-hour meeting. I impressed him for my age, and I was craving a business mentor even though I didn't realize it at the time.

Hugh was different. He would speak of things I hadn't heard of or show me new ways to manipulate others to get deals done.

When I told him the story of how I got scholarships and put myself through school to get my MBA in finance, he instructed me to never speak of it again. He claimed successful people— rich people—wanted to know you were born with money. So I listened to him, and he created a backstory about me growing up in Northern California, which was just far enough away that no one ever questioned it.

Within a few months, we created an investment capital firm. Hugh had money and I had grit, along with an unquenchable work ethic. Slowly, I've earned my shares and we're now fifty-fifty partners. And even though I've always done more work than Hugh, including finding and closing almost all the deals over the last five years, I wouldn't be here without him. You have to have money to make more, and Hugh had plenty at a time when I had none. The combination of his start-up resources and my overzealous determination to be the best allowed us to create a dynamic partnership. Our start-up firm is now the largest in the country and a global name.

It's the exact reason why nothing can happen between Blakely and me. I'll forever be loyal to Hugh for giving me the chance and knowledge to create my life. So she's off-limits. And the last thing I need is to have daddy's little girl run to him, crying about how I broke her into submission and didn't marry her afterward.

Plus, she's sixteen years younger than me. I don't normally even think about women who aren't at least thirty years old. The things that quench my appetite are considered a bit taboo. Full consent is required, and I don't need a woman claiming she didn't know what she was getting into. You go below thirty, and you're asking for a wishy-washy woman who's still trying to find herself and can't be relied on to understand what she's dipping her toes into.

But my rules aren't helping my predicament every time I see Blakely. The desire to have her at my fingertips only gets harder to ignore. Hell, I knew before I arrived at the party and laid eyes on her that I would be in agony the entire time. And every time she sneaks a glance at me only reiterates that I should have given Hugh an excuse about why I couldn't attend tonight. So my time here is up and I need to go before my partner realizes his daughter is giving me a hard-on.

I do my business in the bathroom and make my way through the mansion, determined to return to the backyard and say my goodbyes. Halfway there, I turn the corner and run into Blakely.

Her champagne splashes on my shirt, and she frets, "Oh my gosh! Riggs, I'm so sorry!" A pink flush crawls up her cheeks, her doe-eyes widen, and she swipes at my shirt.

I grab her hand, and she freezes, her palm an inch from my pecs. My heart pounds harder in my chest and I curse myself for reacting like a teenager. It's another thing that's been happening when I'm with her, and it makes me feel exposed, instead of my normal controlled self. I state, "It's okay. It's only champagne. It'll dry."

She stays silent, her cheeks growing hotter, and I can only wonder if her ass would turn the same color after a good slapping.

I have to stop these thoughts.

Blakely lifts her chin, and the remaining room in my pants disappears. My cock painfully strains against my zipper. I scold myself again, but it's pointless. Her expression is another reminder how different she is, yet exactly what I look for in my conquests.

She doesn't have the snotty Beverly Hills air about her that most women at this party have. Her little gesture is a confident stance. It indulges my cravings further. I love nothing better than dominating a woman with a backbone, and Blakely's always had one. It drives Hugh and his wife Madelyn nuts. I'm one of the few they don't put on a show for when it comes to their daughter. Over the years, I've heard them complain too many times to count about their daughter's stubbornness, or how she forged ahead with something they forbade her to do.

Attempting to regain some control of this situation, I nod to her half-empty glass, questioning, "So you're legal now?"

She glances at it, then locks eyes with me again. Her lips curve into a small smile. She answers in a low voice, "Yes. Totally legal as of today." She inhales deeply then licks her lips, and her cheeks turn redder.

I clench my jaw, keeping my breathing controlled, trying to convince myself she doesn't mean anything by that admission, but I can't. There's a tornado of lust and hope swirling in her blues, and no matter what lie I tell myself, it's impossible to ignore.

Christ, she's young.

I bet she's tighter than any woman I've been with in years.

She'd look good on her knees, with her hands bound and those plump lips around my cock.

She opens her mouth, then snaps it shut. She glances behind her, then refocuses on me.

More visions of her in positions I can never have her in assault my brain. Several moments pass before I state, "Happy birthday."

Her face lights up even more as her lips curve into a bigger smile. She shifts on her feet. "Thanks."

"Twenty-one is a big occasion. I assume you're going out and getting crazy with your boyfriend later?" I question, prying for information.

It doesn't matter. She's Hugh's daughter.

She shakes her head, and a blonde curly tendril falls over her eyes. She replies, "I don't have a boyfriend."

Thank God for that.

Not that he'd have anything over me.

Mesmerized, not thinking clearly, and unable to stop myself, I reach for the lock. She holds her breath as I slowly drag my fingers over her forehead, then even slower over the side of her head, pushing her strands behind her ear. Just as I suspected, her hair's soft, unlike the typical overprocessed blondes roaming all of L.A. I've always known she's a natural blonde, but finally feeling it only adds fuel to my thoughts. I have to stop myself from wrapping all of it around my fist.

She arches her eyebrows, waiting for me to answer, the heat from her cheeks radiating past the inch of air between her skin and my hand.

We've never been this close, nor have I touched her before. Now that I breached my self-control, I step closer, studying the flecks of blues in her eyes. I admit, "Your eyes remind me of the favorite part of my morning surf."

Her voice falters as she inquires, "How so?" She swallows hard but doesn't flinch or retreat.

Her ability to stand in front of me and not break our heated gaze challenges me. It stokes a deep-seated craving I can't seem to shake. I contemplate taking her to my house—not the club—which is another surprise. I don't bring my play things home. They stay at the club and out of my private life. Yet the thought of breaking her into submission in my personal environment, somewhere she can't come and go from, with no one else around, takes root.

I trace the edge of her ear, and she shakily inhales, her lips parting enough I could slip my tongue between them if I attempted. My blood heats to the point I might sweat, and I curse myself for putting myself in this position. Yet I can't stop. Now that I have her attention, I need to keep going. I answer, "When the sun rises over the water, and the light hits it just right, there's calm chaos."

She furrows her brows. "Calm chaos? That's an oxymoron. It doesn't make sense."

I clench my jaw, trying to contain my pleasure that she's not just a pretty face. She has a brain and uses it, which is another thing I don't often see with many beautiful women in L.A. I flip my hand and lightly graze my fingertip over her chin, enjoying how her eyes quickly shut then reopen. I answer, "When the tide's rolling away, barely giving way to any waves, and the water looks like it's full of sparkles trying to jump into the air, that's calm chaos."

She ponders my statement for a moment, her expression morphing into a soft smile I assume she'd make after I wore her out with my demands. She asserts in approval, "I suppose your oxymoron works."

It's all too much. I might as well be a reckless teenager unable to control his urges instead of a sexually experienced, normally always in control thirty-seven-year-old man. I reach behind her, grab a fistful of her hair, and firmly tug her head backward. It's nothing like what I've done to women in the past, but it's enough to make her gasp and get an idea of what I'd do to her if I had the chance.

Whatever her perfume is flares in my nostrils. It reminds me of the surf, along with something else I can't put my finger on besides the combination of sea salt and driftwood. I lick my lips, studying hers, then pin my gaze to her widened one, murmuring, "There are many things I do that perception would claim don't work but do."

Her bottom lip quivers, but she catches it and takes a deep breath. Her chest rises higher, and I give it a lewd glance, then pin my most challenging stare on her. She opens her mouth, tries to speak, but nothing comes out.

I tug her head farther back, leaning so dangerously close to her mouth her breath hits mine.

She whispers, "What kinds of things?"

I don't hesitate, taunting, "Things that would make your father despise me."

Her plump lips part again, but her mother's voice calls out, "Blakely!"

Goddamn it!

I release her and step back just as Madelyn turns the corner.

She beams. "There you are! We're about to cut the cake." Then she turns to me, bats her eyes, and puts her hand on my bicep. Vodka overpowers Blakely's sea salt and driftwood scent, and Madelyn coos, "Riggs. I didn't know you'd arrived."

I groan inside. Madelyn and Hugh are no saints. They both fuck whatever walks, and for years, she's made it clear she's into me. But I'd never do her for two reasons.

One, she's my partner's wife. I don't need that kind of drama in my life.

Two, I'm not interested. She's another product of Beverly Hills, overindulging in alcohol and prescription pills, and void of anything interesting. The only difference between her and the people I grew up with is she has money. She's as predictable as they come and might as well be a junkie on the corner.

All of it bores me.

I step out of her grasp and nod. "Madelyn. Good seeing you. Please give my regards to Hugh. Something's come up." I high-tail it down the hallway, ignoring her questioning calls after me. I move to the front door, step outside, and get into my Porsche, racing out of the subdivision and driving directly to Club Indulgence in L.A.

Something has definitely come up.

Yet it's not anything the Gallows would expect.

As I pull into the club's secret parking garage, I already know I'll be here well into the night, trying to get Blakely out of my head. It won't be the first time I've dealt with my frustration here, but this time, I curse myself for stepping over the line that I know I can never cross.

1

Blakely Fox (Formerly Blakely Gallow)
Seven Years Later

"*I*nto you," I belt out in a long, smooth note.

The few people in the dark lounge clap, but the lights Jarrod has positioned on the stage don't let me see any of their faces.

"Thank you. I'm Blakely Fox. Have a great night," I state. I smile, put the microphone on the stand, then get off the stage as the next act takes my place. I go behind the bar, grab the envelope Jarrod left with my name on it, then stuff it in my purse.

It takes thirty minutes with traffic to get to my next gig, which isn't as fun but pays the bills better than the Lizard Lounge. I pull into the parking lot, then slide the plastic keycard into the slot. All the girls who work at Cheeks have one. I still have to load it with money to park, but it's better than walking ten blocks at four in the morning. Traffic in L.A. is a nightmare no matter where you go, and parking is a luxury. Plus, it's not safe. Muggings happen a few blocks over too often to keep track of. There have even been a few murders over the years. So I make sure my parking card always has funds on it.

I step out of my car, make my way across the dimly lit lot, then nod to Troy, the bouncer who stays in the back alley.

He opens the door the strippers, bartenders, and servers use, then booms, "Blakely! You got any new notes?"

"Working on some," I reply.

"Hit me up when you're ready," he orders.

I give him a tiny salute, replying, "You know I will."

Over the last few years, Troy and I have gotten to know each other. He heard me singing when I was cleaning up tables one night after a shift, and one question led to another.

He has a friend in the music industry and said when I'm ready, he'll slip him my demo. The only problem is I'm far away from creating a demo. Shortly after my twenty-first birthday, I moved out of my parents' house. Living in L.A., even as frugally as I do, doesn't make saving money easy.

My father always told me my head was in the clouds. No daughter of his was going to live the seedy life of a singer. I didn't understand why he thought that, but then I realized I could have wanted to do anything, and he would have given me an excuse about why I shouldn't pursue it. It didn't matter that I graduated early from Berkley with honors in Arts & Humanities. My degree was strictly for his bragging rights and to show the world I could accomplish something. In my father's mind, I was to become a wife and follow in my mother's footsteps.

I'd rather die.

Her life of charity committees, day drinking with friends at the country club, and having too many affairs to count doesn't appeal to me. It's not that I don't like to support charities, but it baffles me how people rationalize spending way too much money on dinner and entertainment in the name of those less fortunate. It doesn't make any sense. If they really cared about the charity, why wouldn't they donate the money it takes to pay for all the amenities of their over-the-top events?

So not only don't I agree with luxury charity events, but I would die of boredom if I had to spend my life planning them. The housewives in Beverly Hills on those committees are as fake as they come. Plus, I want my life to mean something.

Since I was little, all I've wanted to do was sing and write songs. My parents used to think it was cute, but then I entered high school. That's when the comments from my father that I needed to focus on what was important started.

Once I turned twenty-one, I couldn't take it anymore. My parents began inviting men to our house. They claimed they were eligible for me to marry. The last thing I wanted was to get hitched, especially to one of the stuck-up guys they deemed appropriate.

When I moved home after graduation, my future became clear. The only way to follow my dreams was to leave. So I moved out.

At first, I stayed in contact with my mother via phone calls. My father wanted nothing to do with me, stating he would speak to me when I returned home and chose to follow his wishes.

My mother would call and beg me to return, telling me about different committees she wanted me to join or what was happening at the country club. She'd always have a list of their social committee events and try to convince me to sign up to plan them. I always refused. Then one day, my father sent two of his men who run security during our parties to bring me home. It took me by surprise when they showed up at my apartment, and I went kicking and screaming.

My father locked me in my room for a week, reiterating every night how my behavior was embarrassing to him. Toward the end of the week, he came in and told me to get dressed. A team of makeup artists, hair stylists, and a fashion designer came into my bedroom. They fitted me into a cocktail dress, spent an hour on my makeup and hair, and reported to my father I was ready.

He ordered me to go downstairs, and I've never felt so sick. Six men were waiting for me, each drooling to get access to my father's fortune. He took me aside and demanded I pick who I wanted to marry.

It was horrifying. As the night went on, and my parents drank more, I managed to escape. I grabbed any cash I could find in my room, packed a small backpack of clothes, then hid in the catering van until the next morning.

I spent a few nights on the street. I couldn't return to my apartment and finally found a shelter. I showered, went to several bars and lounges looking for work, and finally ended up in front of Cheeks.

A strip club wasn't where I anticipated working, but they had a server position open, and I was desperate to find work. The manager tossed me a black leather thong and a blingy black bra. He told me to put them on and then come to his office.

It was the most embarrassing job interview I'd ever had. Three men assessed every part of my body. And I don't consider myself a tiny girl. Sometimes I feel as if everyone in L.A. could be a cover model. While I'm not fat, I'm more voluptuous, which doesn't make me fit in with the skinny standards of the city.

They discussed my body parts, tossing out phrases like "thicker thighs," "nice rack," and "round booty." Their comments made me believe they would send me on my way, but they offered me the job. So I filled out my paperwork as Blakely Fox, which I had wanted to use for my stage name since I was a child. And since my parents weren't ever super active in raising me— leaving the nannies to deal with me while I grew up—I've never told them what I wanted to call myself. So I figured it was safe to use.

When the manager asked me for my documentation, I tried to bluff, telling him I was mugged and didn't have any. He called Troy to the room, who helped secure me a fake ID and social security card. I've been using Blakely Fox ever since.

Then, I stayed in the shelter until I could afford an apartment with several women I met at work. Slowly, I secured some lounge gigs singing during the day or early evening.

Now, Cheeks is like a second home to me. Nothing shocks me anymore. I'm used to hustling around the club half naked, seeing the strippers do all sorts of things my sheltered life kept me in the dark about, and fending off comments and offers men make.

The naive girl I walked into Cheeks as is no longer in existence. And not a day goes by that I regret leaving my cushy old life behind. I may not be the definition of successful yet, but I'm living my life in a way that makes me happy. The people around me are real. And every time I get to take the stage and sing, it refuels my desire to keep going.

And I could earn more, but I can't seem to bite the bullet and take the management up on their offer to change my position. I don't judge the strippers. I admire their ability to do what they do. They excel at it, and I don't believe I could. I may wear barely any clothing during my shift, but it still gives me a thin layer of protection.

"Blakely, can you handle two sections tonight? Cindy called off again," Savannah, the night manager, asks in an irritated tone.

"Sure," I reply, happy to be offered the extra tables. I'll have to work my butt off, but it'll pay off at the end of the night when I'm counting my tips.

"Thanks." She pats me on the shoulder and cries out, "Phoenix! What are you doing?"

The bartender freezes in the middle of pulling a fifth out of a new case. "What did I do now?"

"We have six open. Did you check the cabinet?" she questions.

"Oops," she says.

"Yeah, oops," Savannah mimics.

I go into the dressing room, toss my purse in my locker, then remove my jeans and top. I've found it's easier to wear my Cheeks clothes than take the time to get changed. The sooner I get on the floor, the more I can earn. I exchange greetings with several girls, then go to the main room.

Some of the regulars are at their usual tables. Within an hour, more customers fill the room. I hustle between the two sections, doing whatever I can to keep the men happy and earn higher tips.

It's after midnight when two beefy white men I've never seen sit down in my section. One has salt-and-pepper hair and the other is bald. They're wearing expensive suits, which isn't out of the ordinary. Cheeks is a higher-end club, and many rich men from around the world frequent it when they're in town.

I approach the table, set two drink napkins down, and chirp, "Welcome to Cheeks. I haven't seen you two in here before. Are you in L.A. traveling for business?"

The bald one firmly answers, "No."

They both study me, and a chill runs down my spine. It's not the first time I've experienced it, but it rarely happens.

"Are you enjoying your shift, Blakely?" the salt-and-pepper-haired man asks.

Goose bumps pop out on my skin. I blurt out, "Sorry, have we met?"

The bald one replies, "Not exactly."

My mouth turns dry. I question, "What does that mean?"

They stay quiet.

"How did you know my name?" I inquire.

"Lucky guess," the salt-and-pepper man states.

We all study each other for a moment, and I suddenly feel extremely exposed. I lift my chin, asking, "Can I get you something to drink?"

"Two waters," Baldy replies.

"Coming right up," I say, then go to the bar, punch the order into the computer, and motion for Savannah.

She steps next to me. "Everything okay?"

"Table fifty-five. They knew my name. I've never seen them before, and when I asked them if we've met, they said not exact-ly," I relay.

She glances behind us and then leans closer to me, muttering, "They're watching you."

My gut drops. I gaze at them, then turn back toward the machine. "I don't know them."

Savannah offers, "Let me see if the bouncers told them your name. I'm sure that's how they know it and they're only inter-ested in getting into your pants. You know how these men are when they're let out of the house for the night."

"Both of them?" I question, not convinced.

She shrugs. "Maybe they're into threesomes."

I cringe at the thought of doing anything with one of them, much less both at once. I'm not a virgin, but I haven't had too many experiences. I spend most of my time working and trying to get on new stages to sing. And those two are definitely not my type.

Phoenix calls out, "Blakely, orders up!"

Savannah hightails it to the front door, and I pick up the tray of drinks. I drop off orders at several tables, trying to ignore my flipping gut. I return to where Baldy and Salt-and-Pepper are, then set down their bottles of water. I force a smile. "Can I get you anything else?"

"Nope," Baldy replies.

I nod, then leave, trying to focus on the rest of my customers.

Savannah joins me when I'm adding another order into the computer and informs me, "No one told them your name."

The hairs on my neck rise. I fret, "Then how do they know it?"

"No idea, but they could have been in here before. You've worked here a long time," she suggests.

Worried, I shake my head. "I don't think so. I have a great memory. I rarely forget a face. Besides, why would they remember my name?"

"Honey, when a man wants to screw you, he'll remember your name," she states.

"I would have remembered at least one of them," I insist.

"Maybe only one's come into the club before," she proposes.

I'm not convinced.

She snaps her fingers. "I know! They've probably seen you sing!"

"And they just happen to know I also work here? I don't exactly get on stage, sing, then announce I'm running off to my job at the strip club," I say, then add, "No offense."

She laughs, then teases, "That would leave quite the impression. Maybe you should? We could get some new clientele in here."

"Ha ha," I reply.

She slides her arm around my shoulder. "Listen. Go work your sections. I'll have the bouncers keep an eye on them, but as long as they don't do anything, they're probably just two horny men trying to get you to go home with them. No different than any other night."

I take a deep breath. She's probably right. Plus, I'm safe as long as I'm inside the club. Out of caution, I'll make Troy walk me to my car tonight. It's not the first time I've had him do it. "You're right."

She releases me. "Of course I am. Now, go work those tables."

"On it," I say, then try to focus on my other customers. I try to treat the two men like all my other tables, but I can't shake my nerves. Plus, they don't seem interested in any of the strippers. They shoo them away whenever one comes over to try and grab their attention.

About an hour before the club closes, they disappear. Relief hits me that they left. I finish my shift, go into the locker room, and put on my jeans and top.

I step into the main room and walk over to Troy. "Hey, do you mind walking me to my car tonight?"

He furrows his eyebrows. "Did someone bother you?"

I admit, "Not anything I can report. But two guys that were in here creeped me out."

He slings his arm around my waist and leads me to the door. "Best to keep you safe, then. I got you."

I sigh. "Thanks."

"Sure." He guides me to my car and waits until I pull away.

I'm halfway home when I get the chills again. I could be wrong, but I swear someone is following me. There's an SUV that stays far enough away that I can't see who's driving it.

I debate about what to do, then I gun the engine and go through a red light. The SUV disappears, and I continue on to my place. I pull into my apartment complex lot, and a car with a group of my neighbors in it parks next to me.

"Blakely," Tim calls out, sounding intoxicated.

I laugh. "I take it you had a good night?"

His girlfriend Sarah shakes her head and then points at him. "He needs food to soak up his shots."

I wince. "That great of a night, huh?"

She rolls her eyes.

Matt, who also lives with Tim, sings, "Blakely, Blakely, Blakely!"

"He drank more than Tim," Sarah announces.

I smile bigger and say, "Sounds like—"

Floodlights glow around us. Tim puts his hand over his forehead and squints. "Dude, turn your brights off."

I spin, and bile rises in my throat. An SUV is pointed right at us.

"Let's go inside," I say, then take one step toward the building.

"Turn your lights off, assholes," Matt shouts.

"Matt, don't!" I warn, then tug on his arm.

Sarah asks, "Do you know who's in that SUV?"

I shake my head, not sure what I would tell her. Is it the guys from Cheeks or someone else? And maybe I'm assuming they're following me but it's really some drunk idiot from our complex. I answer, "No, but I think it's best we go inside. We don't need any altercations."

"Agreed," she says, then links her arm through Tim's.

The four of us get to the entrance. The SUV doesn't turn off the lights or move. I punch in the code, and the lock unlatches. We step inside, and I shut the door.

As quickly as possible, I make my way up the stairs to the second floor, helping Sarah goad Tim and Matt to follow me.

I finally get inside my apartment. Both my roommates' bedroom doors are shut, so I assume they're sleeping out or have company since neither had to work tonight. I go to the living room window and peek through the blinds.

The SUV is still there with its brights on, except the bald man from the club is standing next to the passenger door, looking up as if he knows which unit I live in.

My heart beats harder. I stare at him until he gets back inside the vehicle and it takes off. I have no clue who the men are, but I'm officially freaked out.

2

Riggs

*C*alm chaos is all around me, but it doesn't relax me today. It still reminds me of Blakely's eyes after all these years. God only knows where she is, and I used to feel sorry for Hugh and Madelyn that she disappeared into thin air, but now, I'm beginning to enjoy that they have a family issue.

I don't know that he's screwing me.

It's pretty clear.

Wait for the evidence. It's Hugh.

The clawing in my gut has only gotten worse. No amount of surfing can eliminate it, including the last wave I caught, which might be the biggest one I've ever ridden.

The red flags started rising about a month ago when I noticed Hugh was taking longer and longer to send me numbers. Last week, my personal accountant called me.

I never liked Hugh's guy, George. Something about him gave me bad feelings. A few years ago, I met Rachel. She instantly impressed me with her level of expertise, so I tested her with a few personal projects and quickly saw she's one of the best in her craft. It wasn't long before I turned all my accounts over to her.

I wanted to hire her for the business, but Hugh refused to let his guy go. It was the first time he utilized his power to override me in the business. We may both own the company in equal shares, but he's always held veto power.

I agreed to it when we formed the company. I had no money, and Hugh gave me an opportunity I would never have had otherwise. But it burned me when he used it. I can account for over eighty percent of the growth of our firm. I've brought in more business than Hugh, and lately, I'm confident he no longer knows more than me. If anything, he's become a tad outdated. And my decade-plus of experience no longer makes me anything less than him.

Although I'm sure he'd beg to differ. One thing I can always count on is Hugh's ego. He thinks his family money will always trump me since my wealth is new. I'm not naive to it, but I've accepted it over the years. It's just how he's wired.

When I told Hugh I was keeping Rachel for my personal accounts and firing George, he did everything he could to try and change my mind, but I refused.

Now, I'm glad I listened to my gut and brought Rachel on board. She works for me and only me. And while I must be careful to keep things strictly professional since she has the hots for me, she's brilliant.

It's not that Rachel isn't good-looking, but I'm not interested. She was a tad flirty the first time we met, but it quickly got a bit more intense. After that, I made her call me Mr. Madden and not Riggs. That little adjustment made it clear this arrangement was strictly business. I only discuss our accounts with her and never mention anything about my life outside of work.

Rachel called yesterday and insisted I meet in person with her. I don't know what she plans on throwing at me, but I assume it's not good.

A week ago, I asked her to audit the business accounts even though it's George's job. If Hugh knew I'd shared our information with Rachel, he'd have a fit. But my gut said something wasn't right, and I couldn't sleep until I either squashed the nagging feeling or discovered what was off.

I've never allowed Rachel—or anyone else, really—to come to my home. The only people who typically are allowed inside are my cleaners. I bought the Malibu beach house a few years ago, and for some reason, I've kept it my secret gem. Hugh doesn't even know about it.

I have a condo in L.A. where I stay if I need to be in the office multiple days in a row or if I'm frequenting Club Indulgence. Besides that, I spend my time here, waking up every morning to surf the waves and feeling at peace.

Not that I love to be around a ton of people anyway. I do it for business, but ever since I was a kid, I've always been more of a loner. Maybe it's because I've never really trusted the people around me, whether it's the slums or the most expensive suburbs of L.A.

Hugh's the exception. The notion I might have been wrong about him all these years makes me feel ill. Perhaps it's because I never second-guess myself or my decisions. I've always trusted my gut, which makes the idea of him screwing me over even more painful.

He hasn't.

Then what did Rachel find?

I catch a final wave, ride it toward shore, then carry my board up the sandy path to my house. I put it away, go to my outside shower, and strip out of my wetsuit.

The hot water cascades over my body, but no matter how much soap I use, I can't wash the feeling of grime off me.

What has Hugh done?

I turn off the shower, secure a towel around my waist, and go into my house. I get dressed, debate about making my daily green smoothie, then decide to opt out. The clawing in my stomach only grows more intense the closer I get to eight A.M.

The doorbell rings two minutes before, and I let Rachel inside.

She glances around my open floor plan. "Wow. Nice place."

"Thanks. Let's get started," I order, motioning for her to sit at my oversized table.

She straightens her shoulders and obeys, sitting, then opening her briefcase. She pulls several manilla folders out, then lays half a dozen highlighted spreadsheets on the wood.

I hold my breath, wondering what the highlights mean.

She hesitates, then locks eyes with me. "These accounts all have money missing. There are transfers throughout the last few years that tally over one hundred million dollars."

I grind my molars, trying to calm my rage. Quite a bit of time passes before I can muster, "Where is the money going?"

Sympathy fills her expression, and I hate it. She answers, "Some offshore accounts in the Caymans."

"Is it George?" I question.

She shrugs. "Him. Or Hugh. But I have a hard time believing Hugh could do it without George. My guess is the accounts are layered so they're untraceable."

Bile rises in my throat. I swallow it and stare through the glass, watching the waves crash and white foam hit the shoreline.

He stole from me.

He stole from our clients.

Rachel clears her throat and sets another piece of paper in front of me. "I've made a summary so you can turn it over to the FBI."

I glance at the cheat sheet, my stomach diving further. The FBI will have to call in the SEC. The investment firm I've spent my life creating will have a stain on it forever. Trust will be lost, and that's hard to earn back.

I firmly state, "I'm not calling the FBI."

Rachel furrows her eyebrows. "But—"

"I'll handle it. As always, you're under a strict confidentiality clause," I assert.

Her eyes turn to slits. Irritation fills her voice, and she seethes, "You don't need to remind me."

I ignore that I just offended her and inquire, "Is there anything else I should know?"

Her jaw twitches. She rises, slings her briefcase over her shoulder, and dryly answers, "No, boss."

I don't miss the attitude. It's the first time I've ever heard it from her, but her feelings are the last things I'm worrying about right now. I've got bigger problems. She can put on her big girl panties and deal with my usual bluntness or cry like a baby. Either way, I don't care. I walk toward the entrance, and she follows. I open the door and state, "Thanks for bringing this to my attention."

She crosses her arms and glares at me.

I wait her out, giving her my most challenging stare. The last thing I'm going to be is intimidated by my employees.

She finally asserts, "A little kindness would go a long way."

I keep my tone flat and reply, "I'm sorry. Did I hire you to be friends?"

She glares at me.

"Well?" I push.

"No," she answers.

"That's right. I hired you because you're the best accountant I know. And I appreciate you for your talent. That's also why I pay you what I do and give you huge bonuses. Have I upheld my end of the deal?" I arch my eyebrows.

Her face hardens. "Yes."

I nod. "Good. You've always upheld yours as well. Now, is there anything else we need to discuss?"

She leers at me another moment, then steps outside. I wait until she's next to her car, then close the door.

For over two hours, I pace my house. From time to time, I reread her summary and revisit the numbers on the spreadsheets, still unable to believe Hugh would do this.

I've seen him do some unscrupulous things, but I never thought he'd screw me.

I need to call the FBI.

My reputation will never recover. I'll be associated with his embezzlement.

The SEC will have a field day.

I can't notify them.

But I can't let him get away with this.

Most people would turn the evidence over to the FBI and SEC, let Hugh rot in jail, and try to recover from the fallout.

Not me.

The longer I stew over it, the clearer it becomes. I grow more and more determined to make his life ten times worse than if the FBI and SEC went after him.

Hugh doesn't deserve a white-collar penitentiary.

Instead, I vow to destroy him, take anything close to his heart, and burn it to the ground until there's nothing left except ashes.

But how?

I spend another hour pacing, my mind spinning with questions about how to take him down. Then it hits me.

I pick up my phone and type in Jones. My time in Compton wasn't a total waste. Only a few people I know got out. Jones is one of them. And over the years, he's come in handy for some of my top-secret jobs. Plus, Hugh has never met him.

Something told me not to disclose my relationship with Jones to Hugh. I assumed it was because he was from my neighborhood, and I know how Hugh looks down on anyone not raised in

Beverly Hills or a similar suburb. I was the exception. However, maybe it wasn't about that. Perhaps I kept Jones a secret because I knew deep down not to fully trust my partner.

Yet I did.

Did I?

I push the disturbing questions to the back of my mind and hit the dial button.

Jones answers, "It's been a long time, Riggs."

I run my hand through my hair, studying the waves, replying, "Indeed."

He continues, "I assume you have a job for me?"

He's always straight to the point. It's another reason I respect him. "Yes. It's extremely sensitive. Can you meet in the next hour?"

"I'm in Compton," he informs me.

I groan inside. One place I hate returning to is the old neighborhood. Jones may have survived, but he can't seem to leave it in the past. He owns an entire block, has fixed up the houses, and often uses one to do his work.

I don't get it. He could go anywhere. The guy's a millionaire and works off his laptop. Whenever I've asked him about it, he claims he likes to stay true to his roots.

I inquire, "Is your garage free? I'm not parking on the street."

He chuckles. "Maybe you should get an average car."

"Maybe you should do business somewhere else," I retort.

He snorts. "Still driving a Porsche?"

"Is there any better car?" I reply.

"That's debatable," he answers.

"Not to me. You got an open space or what?"

"Yeah. Come on over. I'll lock it up nice and tight," he states.

"On my way." I hang up and grab my keys. I go into the garage, slide into my Porsche, and make the trip to my old neighborhood.

My chest tightens as it always does whenever I come here. A trip down memory lane is the last thing I'm ever interested in, but desperate times call for desperate measures. The only way to take Hugh down is to access his offshore accounts and the funds inside them. Once I have that, the rest is going to be fun.

Now that I know what he's done, I look forward to watching his demise. It's something I never contemplated before his betrayal.

Hugh should have known not to fuck with me. One thing I don't do is forgive and forget. Revenge isn't something new to me. He's seen the extent I'll go to right a wrong done to me. He's witnessed me take others down before. It's why I don't understand why he'd even attempt this. He has to know I'd find out and come after him.

He's too arrogant.

I deal with the pileup on the expressway, inching through traffic, with my thoughts racing. By the time I get to Compton, my desire for revenge grips me tighter than ever before.

I reverse into the driveway and text Jones.

> Me: I'm here.

The cedar door, which looks too upscale for Compton except for this block Jones fixed up, opens. He takes a final drag of his cigarette, then tosses it on the ground. He grinds it out with his sneaker.

I back up the Porsche until I'm inside, get out, and he closes the garage. He slaps my back, then opens the entrance. "You made good time."

I step into the house and grunt. "It's a mess out there like always."

He leads us into the biggest room. It's dark, aside from the green glow from the dozens of monitors secured on one wall. Blackout shades cover the window, and Jones rolls a second chair next to his.

I sit and say, "I need you to hack into Hugh Gallow's network."

Shock fills his expression, then he mutters, "Always knew you shouldn't trust that rich bastard. What's he done?"

If I hadn't just discovered my partner's been fucking me, I would have called him out for his stereotyping and stuck up for Hugh. Jones is a self-made millionaire, but he's never trusted anyone who came from money.

My gut dives. I stay quiet, not even wanting to speak the words.

"I need to know what I'm looking for," he asserts.

My pulse pounds harder in my neck. I confess, "He's stealing funds from the firm. My accountant said the money's going to some offshore accounts. I need the account details and the ability to get into them and move the money."

Jones whistles, then mutters, "Sorry, man."

"How long do you think it'll take?" I ask.

He scratches his head, then answers, "Not sure. It depends on how encrypted everything is, and the banks will take more time. But once you have access, you need to be smart. If you move that money, make sure it disappears."

"That's why I have you," I declare.

He sits back in his chair and crosses his arms over his chest. His eyes turn to slits.

"Is there a problem?" I ask.

"You're talking about money laundering."

"So? Since when do you do anything on the up-and-up?"

He clenches his jaw.

I push, "What's the issue?"

"It's a bigger risk for me," he claims.

"But you can do it, right?" I challenge.

He nods. "Sure. But if I'm going to take a bigger risk, the fees are going to double."

"Jones, I don't care what you charge me. I need to know that you can get this done and it'll be a priority on your list. The clock's ticking," I state.

He picks up a clipboard, flips through a few pages, then tosses it back on the desk. He declares, "I can start tomorrow. I've got several projects I need to wrap up."

"Then you'll focus exclusively on this? Right?"

"Yeah."

Relief fills me. "Great." I rise.

Jones points to the chair. "We aren't done."

I take a seat. "What else is there?"

He turns to his computer. "I need to know information on him. The more I have to go on, the quicker it'll be."

It's close to one when I finish answering all his questions. Then I get back into my Porsche and head toward Malibu. The traffic is just as bad, and I'm at a complete standstill when I get a text.

> Club Indulgence: Charity auction tonight. Monthly terms. New subs on the list. Starts at 2 A.M.

For the first time all day, I grin. This is just what I need after the shit I've discovered today. Lately, I've had a hard time feeling satisfied at the club. It's the same faces, and I'm bored.

A new woman, preferably one I get to break in, is exactly what I need to get my mind off this situation. It'll help relieve my stress, and since it's an auction, I'll have all month to train her accordingly.

It won't be the first time I've participated in an auction. The club has them a few times a year. Both parties agree to terms. Then the sub gets to choose a charity and the Dom writes the check. I could give a shit about the charity, but the prospect of developing a newbie sub heats my blood so hot, I veer off the exit and head toward my condo in the city.

I spend a bit more time stewing over all the deceit, then change my focus on what's ahead of me tonight.

Patience is a virtue I've worked on over the last decade. I lacked it as a child but learned to embrace it as a businessman. Until Jones gets me the information I need, there's nothing I can do about Hugh. So while I'm waiting, I'll see to my other needs. And there's nothing more perfect than a fresh face to be at my mercy—especially for an extended timeframe.

3

Blakely

*I*t's a busy night at Cheeks. I've not stopped moving since I stepped on the floor. As soon as one table clears, more men fill it.

"Blakely, Snake wants to see you," Cindy informs me.

I glance toward the front door. "Why?"

She shrugs. "I don't know. Ugh! What does Savannah want now," she whines, running off.

I roll my eyes. Since Cindy called off the previous night, Savannah's been all over her. I'm glad I've never done anything to get on her bad side.

I push through the crowd and step into the small corridor the club uses to charge the cover fee. Snake, one of the newer security guys, grasps my elbow and leads me outside.

"What's going on?" I question, and the muggy night air hits my skin.

He leans down and says, "Don't worry, Savannah approved."

"Approved what?"

"For you to talk to my friend. He's an agent and heard you sing at the Lizard Lounge."

Shock and excitement fill me. "Really?"

He chuckles. "Yep. But he doesn't want to talk inside. He'd rather speak with you out here."

"Okay. But... I should change!" I fret, glancing down at my leather thong and blingy black bra.

"Nah, you're fine," Snake says and guides me around the corner, and I freeze.

Baldy and Salt-and-Pepper from the other night stand outside of their SUV.

"What the hell!" I exclaim, trying to get out of Snake's grasp, but it's too tight.

Baldy opens the back door, Salt-and-Pepper reaches for my other arm, and before I know it, they shove me into the backseat.

I scream, but no one's around. Within seconds, Baldy's next to me, and the SUV takes off. Baldy puts a silk scarf around my eyes and more panic fills me.

"Let me go!" I yell. My heart races and I attempt to hit him, but he pins my wrists to my lap.

"Stop it!" he commands.

My hands flail in the air.

He grabs the scarf off my eyes and winds it around my wrists.

He mutters, "You need to plan better next time, Roy."

"What did I do wrong now?" the man now known as Roy grumbles.

"Tape would be better. Like an entire roll," Baldy states.

I scoot to the other side and reach for the door handle, but it won't budge.

"Child lock. There's no point hurting yourself," Baldy announces.

My insides and voice quiver, "Wh-what do you want from me?"

Baldy's eyes travel down my body, and I cringe. He locks his lewd gaze on mine and replies, "Daddy isn't going to like this outfit of yours."

Daddy.

He found me?

Of course they work for him!

I attempt to open the door again, but Baldy just laughs.

There's a loud pop, and the SUV veers to the curb.

"Fuck!" Roy cries out.

"What was that?" Baldy asks.

The SUV stops. Roy opens the door, gets out, then goes around the hood. He curses again.

Baldy knocks on the window and Roy opens the passenger door, saying, "Flat."

I try to follow Baldy, but he shuts the door too fast.

I have to get out of here.

I can't go back home.

No, no, no!

I try to free my hands, but the silk is tight around my skin. I stare out the front window. Badly and Roy are assessing the damage.

Baldy walks to the trunk, pops it open, then opens a floorboard. He pulls a tire out and carries it to the front.

I glance around the vehicle, trying to find something sharp, but I don't see anything.

Think!

I gaze down at my feet and then get an idea. I put my wrists as close to the floor as possible, then lift my legs between my arms, pushing my stiletto heel on the silk fabric, hoping I don't slice my hand.

It takes a few moments, but it finally cuts through the material. My pulse increases, and I debate about going through the driver's door or trunk.

I finally decide that the trunk is the easiest. I take off my shoes and hold them by the ankle straps. There's no way I can run in them.

I wait for both men to bend down and then I slide over the seat, taking my shoes with me. I step onto the blacktop.

"She's out!" Roy yells.

I take off, running across the street, unsure where I am or where I'm going. I turn the corner and slide past groups of people out for the night. Several of them yell at me, but I don't stop.

"Get back here!" Baldy orders.

I turn another corner, run past a valet stand, and then up to a bouncer-looking man. There's a red rope in front of the door.

"You here for the auction?" he asks.

I have no clue what he's talking about, but I'm not about to ask. I reply, "Yes."

"You're late," he states.

"Sorry." I glance behind me. Baldy and Roy are fifty feet away.

The bouncer lifts the red rope and opens the door, motioning for me to go past. He shouts, "Maureen. The last girl is here."

I slide inside, and a sign states *Club Indulgence. Members Only.*

A woman with fire-red hair grabs my arm and tugs me through a hallway, claiming, "You don't have a lot of time."

I say nothing, following her, my heart still pounding and hoping the Members Only statement on the sign is true. Surely Baldy and Roy aren't part of this club?

Maureen leads me down several dark hallways until we get to the end. She opens the door on the right. A dozen women wear risqué outfits. Excited chatter fills the room, and Maureen points to another woman holding a clipboard. Maureen states, "The last one showed up."

The woman looks at the list and asks, "What's your name, darling?"

"Blakely Fox."

She peers closer at the paper, then states, "You aren't on the list."

Panic hits me. I don't know what this list is, but I can't go back outside. I blurt out, "Is that an issue?"

She glances at me, then shakes her head. She writes it in and adds, "Must be your lucky night. Number twelve hasn't shown up. You can take her spot."

"Great," I reply.

Maureen leaves, and the woman asks, "Is there anything you're not willing to do?"

My stomach flips. *What exactly am I getting myself involved in now?*

Anything is better than what my father might have in mind.

"Can you expand on your question?" I inquire.

She eyes me over. "Are you unclear on the charity auction specifics?"

I lift my chin. "Yes. Could you review them with me, please?"

She assesses me again, then answers, "Whatever Dom bids the highest, wins. He'll supply your secret living arrangements for a month. Assuming you agree to their contract."

Secret living arrangements?

A month?

Contract?

And what does she mean by win?

Her voice drops. "Honey, you look like you have more questions than before I spoke."

I clear my throat. "Sorry. I'm... I'm new to this."

She smiles and nods. "Yes, they all are. That's the point. You don't bring any bad habits the Doms have to correct for their tastes."

Dom? What is a Dom?

She steps closer. "Have you chosen your charity?"

"My charity?" I utter.

"Yes. The Dom writes a check for the amount he bids to whatever charity you direct."

A bleached-blonde woman cuts in, "It's how this isn't prostitution. It's for a good cause."

Prostitution?

Oh God. The man who bids on me will want to sleep with me.

"You get to negotiate though. So contracts are only signed after all parties agree to the terms. If you can't agree, then you're still free to go after the auction is over," the blonde adds.

"Number one, you're up," a man calls out.

A brunette wearing a white, barely there lace teddy and silver collar steps through the curtain. The room erupts in cheers, and an auctioneer states over a microphone, "Linda's ready to allow her Dom to get dirty. She's open to all activities, including multiple partners of either sex, public humiliation, and being recorded."

The bidding starts, and the woman with the clipboard nudges me and orders, "Put your shoes on."

I glance at my stilettos and realize I'm still gripping them for dear life. I relax my fingers and step into them.

"Wait until you see the shoes these Doms buy their subs," she states.

I continue processing all the information. My inner voice tells me to leave, but then it screams that anything a Dom wants to do to me isn't as scary as having to go back and live under my father's control.

Plus, I get to negotiate. It buys me time, and I can figure out my next steps after I don't sign whatever contract this bidder puts in front of me.

I can't leave right now.

They know where I live.

The girls get bid on one by one until the auctioneer states, "And now we have number twelve, Ms. Blakely Fox."

I freeze, staring at the auctioneer and the lights, which remind me of the Lizard Lounge.

The woman with the clipboard pushes me, and I step forward. Cheers fill the air, and the auctioneer says, "Ms. Blakely Fox prefers to keep her desires secret between her and her Dom. As she just reiterated to us, she's new to the lifestyle. Do I hear a hundred thousand?"

The bids are shouted throughout the room, and it gets to over a million dollars.

I gape, unable to see any faces, wondering why these men are so eager to toss their money to a charity when they don't even know which one I'd pick.

"Sidebar," a voice calls out. It sounds familiar, and something deep in my core aches. Yet I still can't see any faces.

The room turns silent. Several men whisper off to the side and then approach the auctioneer. He tells him something, and the auctioneer turns toward me. "It seems you've grabbed one of our most sought-after Dom's attention."

I open my mouth, but nothing comes out. What would I say anyway? I'm still confused about what's happening and how I'm even in this auction.

The woman with the clipboard steps next to me. Her eyes light up with excitement. She slings her arm around my waist and ushers me behind the curtain.

"What's happening?" I ask, my stomach dancing with nerves.

"Oh, this is so good," she whispers, then guides me to a private room.

"What's going on?" I inquire.

The auctioneer comes into the room and states, "The Dom who bid on you wants a longer contract."

"I'm...I'm sorry?" I ask.

He announces, "He doesn't want a month. He wants a year. The same provisions exist. He'll house you in secret where he sees fit and pay for all your living needs while you're under his care."

Shock continues to ripple through me.

The auctioneer continues, "He said to tell you that he'll allow you to pursue whatever your passion is during your time with him."

I swallow hard. "My passion?"

"Maybe you call it a hobby?" the woman suggests.

So I could still sing and write songs.

What am I doing even contemplating this?

I square my shoulders. "Who is this man? Why isn't he here with us?"

The auctioneer smiles. "He's very private. If you are open to a year, he will have you blindfolded, escorted out of the private exit, and taken to his house several cities over. Once you are there, you can discuss the contract terms and negotiate. Our driver will stay. He will bring you back to the club if you opt out of the deal."

I'd get out of L.A. in secret. That's far enough away from my father's thugs.

Am I really going to do this?

"You should say yes. He's our most sought-after Dom, but he's extremely picky when it comes to his subs," the woman chirps.

I'm still ignorant about this Dom and sub talk, but it seems like my only option. Once I get out of L.A., I'll decide where to go next.

"It's a once-in-a-lifetime chance," the auctioneer claims.

I turn toward the woman. "He's safe? This Dom?"

She nods. "Yes."

I don't know why I trust her. She's a complete stranger, but my gut says she wouldn't lie to me.

I add, "And I can tell him no and leave if I don't like the contract?"

"Yes. We will provide transportation back here," she reiterates.

I take a deep breath, then make a decision. "Okay. I'll go and listen to his terms."

She claps her hands and then leans into my ear, whispering, "I can't wait to see you back here with him."

Once again, I'm clueless about what she's referring to, but I definitely won't be returning. Everyone's treated me well here, but I'm pretty sure this isn't my scene.

Plus, I can't live with a stranger for a month and definitely not a year. Especially one who wants me to sleep with him.

Nope. I'll hitch a ride to wherever this secret hideaway is, then go on my way.

The auctioneer pulls a black satin scarf out of his pocket, and I have a flashback of less than a few hours ago.

I wince, asking, "Why do I need the blindfold?"

"Like I said, the Dom is extremely private. He doesn't allow anyone at his house. To be honest, I'm surprised he's allowing you," the auctioneer claims.

My stomach flips again, but I allow him to blindfold me.

I'm led to an SUV. I know because I have to step up to get into the back seat. The door shuts, and the sound of the engine starting fills my ears.

I spend the long ride tugging on my fingers or tapping my thigh, trying not to freak out. When the car finally stops, the driver says, "We're here."

I wait, and he opens my door, reaches in for me, and leads me over a driveway and into a house.

A man orders, "You'll wait outside."

Goose bumps break out on my skin. *Why does that voice sound familiar?*

The sound of the front door shutting hits my ears. The man steps forward and a woody-spicy scent laced with orange peels

45

flares in my nostrils. My skin prickles with electricity. There's only one man who's ever smelled like that.

But it can't be.

His hot breath hits my ear, and I shudder as his tongue touches my lobe. He purrs, "Blakely, it's been a long time."

I gasp, holding my breath, my insides quivering with too many emotions.

For years, I've thought of him. I've wondered what he's doing, what it would be like to be with him, and if he remembered me.

He removes the blindfold, and my mouth turns dry.

I whisper, "Riggs."

His dirty-blond surfer locks are exactly how I remember, with one side curling close to his crystal-clear blue eyes. He's more filled out than I recall. He must have removed his suit jacket because the white designer shirt strains against his pecs. Several buttons are undone, and his cuffs are rolled to the middle of his thick forearms, displaying his arm sleeve tattoos I never knew existed. Thinking back, he always wore buttoned-up, long-sleeve shirts like my father and his friends. I gape at the inked artwork, sprawling across him. And it all makes him sexier than I remember.

"Sit down, Blakely," he orders.

A new fear hits me as I get over my shock of seeing him. I beg, "Don't take me to my father."

His lips twitch, and he claims, "It'll be a cold day in Hell when I turn you over to Hugh Gallow."

His statement doesn't make any sense. My father and Riggs have always been tight. I've never seen him have anything but respect for my father, yet now, all I see is disgust in Riggs's expression. So my gut says he isn't lying.

"Sit down," he repeats, pointing to a chair.

I obey, unsure what else to do.

He sits next to me, and his scent teases my nostrils. I barely notice the stack of papers until he slides them toward me and demands, "You have to sign if you want to stay with me. And there's only one way this goes, Blakely, and that's my way."

My butterflies flutter so strong I put my hand on my stomach. I glance between him and the contract, then swallow hard. I inquire, "What does that mean?"

He doesn't hesitate, answering, "It means for a year, I own you. Your body. At times, your mind. And all the breaths you take."

A shiver runs down my spine. I wonder if this is a dream. Riggs Madden has haunted enough of them ever since I turned eighteen.

He drags his knuckles over my cheek, studying me.

I close my eyes, trembling, trying to decipher what he means. I finally ask, "What do you want to do to me?"

"Whatever I feel like at the moment," he states in his normal, confident tone.

I lock eyes with him until my gaze drifts to his lips, a tad puffy from all the sea salt only a hardcore surfer would have. They're the same lips that I couldn't shake. I even wrote a song about those lips and what it would be like to have them on mine and other parts of my body.

He continues, "A year, Blakely. You live here with me. No one knows about this place, not even your father. You only leave when I'm with you and allow you. I'll take care of you." His hand slides between my thighs, and tingles explode in every cell of my body.

My breath turns ragged. I gaze between his hand and mouth, debating if his lips could possibly come near creating the buzz his palm currently is bestowing on me.

He adds, "I'll fulfill all the deep-rooted desires that made you step on that stage tonight."

He thinks I went on the stage knowing what all this is about?

Just sign the contract and let him do whatever he wants.

What am I talking about? I can't do this.

Why not?

"Wh—"

He puts his fingers over my lips. "You want to focus on your music?"

I stay quiet.

"Answer me," he demands. "Isn't that what you love? Or is that no longer your dream?"

I sit straighter, trying to appear confident. "Of course it's still my dream."

"Then you can do that here. I'll never stop you from pursuing your music," he claims.

Unsure why his statement surprises me, I question, "You won't?"

"No. I'm not your father." His hand slides higher, and electricity in the air intensifies all around us.

I shift in my seat, pushing my hips toward him, unable to stop myself.

He curls my hair around his fist, then tugs my head back. It's the same way he did it on my twenty-first birthday. Ever since that moment, I've wondered what could have happened had my mother not interrupted us. Riggs had never touched me or been so forward before then. But I knew his loyalties were with my father. At this moment, his actions disintegrate all the questions I want to ask him about what changed, because something has.

His face hovers over mine, challenging me in the same manner as all those years ago, yet now, no one is here to interrupt us. For some unknown reason, he's no longer worried about me being my father's daughter, or my age, or whatever it was that stopped him from pursuing me when I was younger. His deep voice rolls through the air as he demands, "What's it going to be, Blakely?"

4

Riggs

I thought my eyes were playing tricks on me when she walked on stage.

Blakely Fox.

So that's what she's been going by.

I like it better than Gallow, but I can only imagine what Hugh will say when he finds out the one thing he's been searching for all these years was right under his nose.

What were the chances of her being here?

Never in my wildest dreams did I peg her to have hidden submissive tendencies. Sure, I'd thought about how I'd turn her into one if given a chance, but for her to be so curious about it, she's willing to let herself be bid on...

Jesus, help me.

And the outfit she's wearing. I didn't think she'd have it in her to prance around in the cheap bra and thong.

Her blonde hair is now dark, with blueish-purple highlights weaved throughout her thick locks. I would have said it's a sin for her to have done it since there are few natural blondes in L.A., but she pulled it off. It gives her an edgier look, and I know damn well the Gallows would hate it.

It makes me love it even more.

The irony of it all has me almost giddy. I couldn't have planned for the timing of this to be any better. In all the things I plotted in my head about how to take down her father, this was never an option.

I had it on my list to seduce Madelyn, not because I'm interested in the drunk floozy but just to irritate Hugh. Once his friends found out, he'd be more pissed than when he discovered the other men he found her with over the years.

But his little girl...the one who embarrassed him by running away and showing all his cronies he couldn't control her...

This is too perfect. It's better than fucking Madelyn. And it'll be the final nail in the coffin to take Hugh Gallow down.

Plus, I'm going to enjoy every second of breaking his long-lost daughter and training her to be my perfect little pet.

My cock's never been harder. The girl I couldn't forget, the one I've wanted to defile for almost a decade, is sitting in my house and staring at me, debating about signing my contract.

At least, she wants me to think she's debating, but I know she's not. She stepped on that stage begging for this. Now, I'm offering her everything she could ask for on a silver platter.

And she's going to be mine for a year. Long enough to have my fun and destroy Hugh in every way possible.

Blakely doesn't answer me about my offer, so I give her an ultimatum. "I need an answer, Blakely. Are you signing or walking?" I graze my index finger over her wet slit.

She inhales sharply, her eyes widening.

"Calm chaos," I mutter, watching her blues dance in the dim light.

Her lips curve, and she softly replies, "Your oxymoron."

I point to the darkness, claiming, "When you wake up, you're going to look out that window, and you'll see it. Every morning you're here, you'll watch the ocean morph into it."

"Did you ever think of me?" she blurts out, then her cheeks turn to fire. She glances at the ceiling, takes a deep breath, then pins her focus on me again. She adds, "When you were surfing and realized it was calm chaos." A mix of hope and anxiety fills her expression.

I answer honestly, "Yes." I tap the papers. "Now, sign the contract, pet."

"Pet?" she asks, her lips parted.

I groan inside. That mouth of hers has haunted me. I reach for her and slide my hands under her body, lifting her onto my lap.

"Riggs! What—" She bites her bottom lip.

I drag my finger between her cleavage, then slip it under the cheap material, stating, "Pets learn to be obedient and get rewarded. They're also mine to touch...to stroke...to train. They get taken care of, but I guarantee you that you'll feel more pleasure than you ever thought you could, even when I mix it with pain." Her nipple hardens under my finger, and I pinch it.

She gasps, jumping slightly. Her breath turns to shallow intakes.

I keep my fingers pressed firmly around her, and she squirms on my lap, her skin turning hotter. I press my forearm over her thighs.

"Stop moving, Blakely. You don't have permission," I state.

She furrows her brows, her defiance growing.

And it's just where I want her. She's always been independent. Hugh's biggest problem was not being able to control her. He'd only admit it to me after several rounds of drinks. So it'll be even sweeter when he learns that his daughter will listen to any command I give her. Of course, it'll be when he's at his lowest point, having already lost it all.

Yes, I'm going to turn Blakely into the submissive she's dying to be, only this will be different from all the other women I've broken and trained. She won't only be for my pleasure. She's a weapon, and I'll use her to my full advantage.

She murmurs, "I don't want to be told what to do, Riggs."

I drag my eyes down her body, homing in on the only parts covered by her scant clothing. When I meet her eyes again, I retort, "Oh, but you do."

She shakes her head. "No."

I softly chuckle. "You don't know what you want. But you were on stage, willing to be bid on by strangers."

She opens her mouth, then shuts it and turns away.

I move her chin, forcing her to look at me. "A year, Blakely. Whatever you've been doing to survive, stop doing it. Focus on your music. And me."

"You?" she asks.

"Yes. Me. And I focus on you. Isn't that what you wanted all those years ago?" I taunt.

Her cheeks deepen to a maroon.

I quickly add, "What we both wanted."

My admission seems to momentarily appease her, but then she continues to contemplate the situation.

I switch gears and put her on her feet. I rise and state, "Okay. I guess I read the situation wrong. You're not interested. Your ride's outside."

She swallows hard and doesn't move, not flinching or retreating.

"Time to go, Blakely," I claim and point toward the front door.

I wait for a minute, expecting her to tear her gaze off mine, but she doesn't. It only makes me want her more. I slide my arm around her waist, moving her toward the door, and say, "It was nice seeing you. Our trip down memory lane is now over."

She pushes away from me. "Riggs! Wait!"

My pulse quickens. I keep my neutral expression and cross my arms over my chest. "What is it? I don't have time to waste, Blakely. And I'm not into teases."

"Teases? I'm not—"

"Let's not act like there's nothing between us. You aren't in your father's house anymore, and I don't give a damn what he thinks," I admit.

"Why?" she cries out.

Her question takes me by surprise. I stay quiet.

"Tell me why you don't care about what he thinks anymore," she demands.

I contemplate telling her the truth, but I never lay all my cards on the table. Plus, the less anyone knows, the better. Even my accountant and Jones knowing the truth are two too many people who know. I reply, "I have my reasons."

Her expression hardens.

"Let's say your father and I have a different opinion on how to do things."

"Meaning?"

"It involves business. That's all I'm saying, and it's more than I should have admitted."

She takes an anxious breath, then lifts her chin. "Do you promise my father will never know where I am? If I sign the contract."

I grunt. "I thought I made that clear already."

In a firm tone, she orders, "Promise me, Riggs. Swear to me he will never find me here."

"I vow upon my life that he'll never know you're here. I meant it when I told you he doesn't know about this place," I state, having no intention of ever revealing my Malibu house to anyone. Even the driver from the club had to sign a nondisclosure.

She adds, "And you'll protect me from him?"

A sick feeling fills my gut, surprising me. *What kind of father does a daughter want protection from?*

I nod, making another declaration I mean to keep. "At all costs."

She stares at me for another moment, and I do everything I can to wait her out. I think she's going to cave, but she surprises me again and opens the front door.

My insides tremble. I don't want to lose this opportunity, but I'm also not a beggar. I thought I had her sold on our little deal, but apparently, I don't.

I'll find out where she lives from the club.

One way or another, she's going to be mine.

She steps outside into the dark night.

I watch her walk away from me, frozen and unable to chase her but racking my brain with how to stop her from leaving.

Blakely strolls to the SUV, taps on the driver's window, and waits for him to roll it down. She says something, then steps back.

He reverses out of the driveway, and the hairs on the back of my neck rise. She returns to the house, walks past me, then sits down at the table. She picks up the pen, initials all the pages, and signs the final one. She holds the pen out. "Your turn."

I don't think I've ever worked so hard to maintain my cool. I sit next to her, scribble my initials and signature, then toss the pen on the contract. It makes a loud thud. I lean into her ear and murmur, "Didn't your father teach you to read contracts before you sign them?"

Her lips twitch. "Yeah, he did. I try not to do most of the things he taught me though."

I can't help my growing smile. That's the Blakely I know. Defiant and confident. Fearless in some ways. And I'm going to enjoy every moment of getting into her mind and breaking her until she trusts only me.

She adds, "Besides, you already made it clear."

I'm so fascinated with her I can't remember what she's referring to or tear my eyes off her calm chaos fighting with a brewing storm. I question, "What did I make clear?"

Something dark enters her storm. It broods in a way that sends adrenaline shooting through me. She leans closer, her sea salt and driftwood scent I've tried to erase from my memory but couldn't, floating in the air around us. She traces my skin around the opening of my shirt and states, "You stated that you were going to do to me whatever you felt like at the moment. Is that not true?" She pouts, batting her eyes.

I need to fuck her.

No. She needs to learn what this is about, not what she thinks will happen.

If I fuck her now, there's no going back.

Patience gets rewarded.

She needs to learn who's in charge.

I grab her hands and pin her wrists behind her back so hard, her chest arches into my pecs. Her breath hitches, and shock fills her delicate features.

I reply, "That's right, pet. You're going to see sides of me you never knew existed. But before we start, what is it you think I want to do to you right now?"

Confusion replaces shock. "I-I..."

I tighten my grip over her wrists.

"Riggs," she whispers, scrunching her beautiful face.

I put my mouth an inch from hers, wanting to kiss her but knowing if I do, it'll mess everything up. And there's no do-overs in my world. I have one chance to break her. There won't be any way of using her to destroy her father if I act like a little boy and give in to my raging hard-on.

Her gaze drifts to my lips.

My erection strains against my zipper and I fight the debate.

No, I can't afford either scenario to blow up, just to give in to the temptation of coming inside her.

I ignore my aching cock and release her, demanding, "Stand up."

She hesitates.

I reach down, grip her armpits, and lift her to her feet.

"Riggs?"

I spin her, push her over the table, and splay my hand across her spine.

"Riggs, what are you doing?" she cries out, turning her head to look at me, her cheek pressed against the wood.

I palm her ass, then lean over her, asserting, "This cheap, fake leather, along with this gaudy bra, is to never again be on your body. Do you understand me?"

She stays silent.

"When I talk to you, I expect answers," I warn.

She nods, blinking hard. She manages, "I understand."

"You will never wear anything unless I approve it. Are we clear?"

Her lips quiver. She closes her eyes.

I slam my hand on the table next to her face.

She jumps, and her eyes glisten.

"Answer me," I threaten.

"Y-yes," she replies.

"Good girl," I praise, dragging my knuckles down her spine. I step back and demand, "Turn over."

She slowly spins, her expression both defiant and fearful, with confusion increasing by the second.

I make a circular motion with my finger, ordering, "Take it off."

She hesitates.

"I won't tell you again without imprinting my hand on your ass," I warn, even though when I eventually spank her, she'll love it so much she'll beg me to do it some more.

She swallows hard.

I cock an eyebrow, taunting, "Ah, you're already craving my handprint branded on you, aren't you? Tell me, Blakely, did you think about it when you stepped on that stage tonight?"

She stays quiet.

I grind my molars, studying my new plaything, reminding myself that everything comes with time. "Off. Now," I command.

Taking a deep breath, she slowly reaches for her bra. She moves one strap at a time off her shoulders, not tearing her gaze off me, then reaches behind her and unclasps the hooks. She drops it on the table and lifts her chin higher.

I hold in my groan and don't push her to remove her panties. I count to sixty, staring at her pink nipples, watching them get harder with every passing second as her breasts move up and down faster.

Real breasts.

So un-L.A.

But it's her vulnerability that almost makes me come in my pants. I finally point to her lower body, commanding, "Keep going."

A small tremble in her finger is the only indication she's nervous. Other than that, she appears as cool as a cucumber as she slides them under the thin material and drops the thong to the floor. She steps out of it and continues to give me her exposed stare.

Minutes pass while I fixate on her bare body. Then I motion to the bar. "Go get me a scotch."

She glares at me.

There's the Blakely I know.

"Did I stutter?" I ask.

She clenches her jaw and huffs at the ceiling, then spins and goes to the liquor counter. She fills a crystal tumbler to the top with scotch and returns.

I go to the kitchen, pour it into the sink, then hand the glass to her. "Two fingers. Never more. Now, try again."

She tilts her head. "Why are you doing this?"

"The sooner you learn not to question me, the better your time here will be," I inform her.

She puts her hand on her hip and throws daggers at me with her glare. It's nothing I didn't expect. In fact, she's playing right into my hand the way I figured she would. "I'm not going to be bossed around by you, Riggs."

"Is that so?" I challenge.

"Yes. I don't know who you think—"

I grab her wrist and tug her down the hall.

"Riggs! Let me go!" she shouts.

I push open my bedroom door, go to the dresser, and take out a pair of handcuffs.

"Riggs! I said to let me go!" She tries to escape my grip but can't.

I take her to the bathroom and position her in front of the mirror. I sling the handcuffs over the towel rack and secure one of them to her wrist.

"What are you doing?" she cries out, trying to free her arm from the restraint.

I spin her so she's facing the mirror, pin her other wrist behind her, then secure the second cuff. Her eyes dart between me and her reflection. Her voice turns fearful, and she meekly asks, "Riggs?"

I graze my fingers over her thigh, slowly sliding up over her torso, then breasts, until my hand is around her neck. I don't squeeze, but her breath hitches. I kiss the curve of her neck, then murmur in her ear, "I'm in charge, pet. You don't question me. You never defy me. If I say to do something, you do it the right way. And you never touch me without permission. Understand?" I flick my tongue on her lobe and inch back to study her.

There's no calm in her expression. It's pure chaos on a tidal wave, which only fuels my fire. The defiance I saw earlier still brews underneath the fear, and it's so perfect, endorphins are zinging all through me.

"Let me go," she quietly begs.

I cup her pussy and slide my finger inside her.

She arches her back and closes her eyes.

"You sure you want me to let you go?" I question.

She opens her mouth, and I circle my thumb over her clit, slowly pumping my finger in and out of her wet heat. She whimpers, and her knees wobble.

"Tell me to stop," I taunt, curling her hair around my fist and tugging her head backward harder than in the past.

Her body trembles against mine. The defiance in her blues grows stronger.

"Tell me to stop, Blakely."

Heat radiates from her glistening skin. Her whimpers grow louder and longer as I continue manipulating her body, Neither of us tears our gaze off the other.

I insist, "You can't have it both ways, Blakely. You either want what I give you, or you don't. Which one is it going to be?"

She tries to look away, but I won't let her.

"Tell me to stop," I restate, then curl my finger inside her.

Her knees buckle, and her eyes roll.

I hold her tight to my waist, not letting up, keeping her shuddering and whimpering. I lower my voice further, more to maintain my control than for her benefit, and warn, "The next time you defy me, you won't get this. Good pets get rewarded. Naughty ones get punished."

The metal handcuffs jangle against the towel holder, making a loud clang. I release her hair, and she buries her face into the curve of my neck, riding out her orgasm and tormenting my cock even more.

When her body calms and she regains the strength in her legs, I step back, assessing my flushed, spent pet. I enter the bedroom, open a drawer, and pull out a gold collar. I return to the bathroom and secure it around her neck. Then I step next to her so we're both facing the mirror.

She furrows her forehead, her questioning glare reappearing and pinned on my reflection.

I assert, "You're mine, Blakely. I'm in charge. It's best if you don't forget it. Last chance to change your mind about the contract. You can yell at any time and I'll let you go. I'll tear up the contract and send you on your way. But if you don't leave tonight, you won't hear me give you any more outs. So decide if you're in or out."

She glares at me but stays quiet.

I cup her chin and nod at the mirror, murmuring, "If you stay, I own you, Blakely. All of you. Games are over. You're in or out." But I know the games are only starting. I peck her on the lips even though I don't kiss my subs on the mouth. But I know her already and, just as I suspected, she turns her face away from mine.

"Ah, that's my defiant little pet," I taunt, then add, "Yell at any time and it's over."

If she could, she'd be shooting darts at me with her eyes.

Feeling giddy, I walk out of the room and leave her cuffed to the towel rack and collared, with the only place to look being directly at her reflection.

5

Blakely

The heat begins to fade as my body cools from Riggs stepping away and leaving me. I stare at my naked body, restrained to the wall, still red-cheeked from how Riggs touched me, with a thousand thoughts attacking me.

A debate flares inside me. Common sense tells me to yell for Riggs to release me. This is already out of my comfort zone. No one's ever been so aggressive with me. It should scare me, but if I'm being honest, it wasn't fear that raged throughout me.

It was excitement.

I'm unsure if it's because it's Riggs, and I've harbored too many feelings for him for way too long that I don't believe he would ever hurt me, or if it's something else. But if anyone else had done to me what he did, I would have been petrified.

Something deep inside me that I didn't know existed rears its head, making me question if I've lost my sanity. It's a craving to see what else Riggs will unleash upon me. There's a desire to prove to him that I can handle whatever he wants to do to me better than any other woman he's done it to.

Maybe I'm crazy. When I was eighteen, I wondered what he did with other women. I pretended I was one of them, but I knew I never could be. He was too tight with my father. Then he cornered me on my twenty-first birthday. It was the last time I ever saw him.

That night, I vowed that if he ever touched me again, I would prove to him I was worth taking the risk and getting past whatever loyalty he felt toward my father.

Now, whatever is going on between him and my father seems to have allowed him to get past the barrier that used to be between us. So while one part of my brain screams at me to get out of here, the other won't let me. It reminds me of the ache I've never lost all these years, wondering what it would be like to have Riggs as mine. So even though he's into things I'm too naive about, the memories won't let me run.

A long time passes. I start to shiver from the cold, with goose bumps breaking out on my skin. My teeth chatter, and I grow tired of my body being in the restrained position. Sleepiness sets in, and I fight the urge to doze off.

The physical agony almost makes me break my resistance. And then the real questions come.

Is this what it'll be like if I stay with Riggs? I'll be tied up and collared like a dog?

I stare at the expensive gold band around my neck, wondering why Riggs even has it.

Was it on another woman?

Jealousy ripples through me, making me shiver harder. Something about the possibility wakes me up. I don't take my focus off it as the cold continues to sear through me.

The only thing that tears my eyes off it is when I hear Riggs state, "You look cold, pet."

I jerk my head toward him. "How many women wore this before me?"

Amusement fills his blue eyes. He leans against the doorframe and crosses his arms, pointing out, "You've been in here three hours, and that's what you want to know?"

Anger suddenly replaces my anxiety. I seethe, "Was there something else I was supposed to think about? Did I not pass your test?"

His lips twitch. He steps forward, turns on the oversized tub, and adds bubbles. Then he moves in front of me and slips his fingers under the collar, grasping it, so his knuckles press into my neck. He reaches around my body. His warm palm grips my ass, and he tugs me tight against his frame.

A deep-rooted quiver rips through my core. He shifts his body, and his erection presses into my stomach. He murmurs, "Why didn't you yell for me to release you?"

Defiance floods me. I ignore the zings bursting through my cells and square my shoulders, hating and loving his arrogant expression in equal measure.

He slides his knuckles over my neck, and the tension grows, creating the same nervous anticipation I felt when he put his hand on my neck earlier. His lips move an inch in front of mine, and he challenges, "Is my pet a jealous pet?"

More humiliation fills me. I curse myself for asking him about the collar, but then I reprimand myself. I assert, "I don't care what's in the contract, Riggs. If I'm here, with you, no other women."

A mix of surprise and approval takes over his expression. He stays quiet, assessing me.

"I mean it. Promise me, or I'm going," I threaten.

"What did I tell you, Blakely?" he questions, lifting his thumb and tracing my lips.

I close my eyes, suddenly exhausted beyond anything I've ever felt and getting a new adrenaline wave brewing in my veins. I admit, "I don't know. I'm so tired."

He leans into my ear, and tingles burst where his breath hits my skin. He claims, "You're my pet. I'm in charge. You don't make demands."

My eyelids fly open. I turn to him, snarling, "It's not negotiable."

He chuckles, releases my collar, and slides his hands over my wrists, unlatching the cuffs.

"It's not funny," I reprimand.

He spins me, massages my wrists, then arms, and I close my eyes again, feeling the rush of exhaustion once more. His arm slides around my waist and pins me against him. He murmurs, "Relax, Blakely. I'm a one pet owner."

I glare at him in the mirror.

"What? You don't want to be my pet?" he taunts, cupping my pussy and arching his eyebrows.

I stay quiet, torn between wanting him to repeat what he did to me earlier and wishing I could go to sleep.

He chuckles again, then swoops down and picks me up so I'm fully in his arms.

I gasp, then stare at him in question.

He states, "You need a bath, Blakely. Your feet are black."

Embarrassment floods me. "Oh. Sorry."

He pecks me on the lips and then sets me in the warm bubble bath.

I sink into it, and a tiny moan flies out of me. The water feels like heaven.

Riggs picks up a washcloth, pours soap on it, then lifts one of my feet out of the tub and questions, "Why are your feet black?"

I open my mouth and then snap it shut. Maybe it's best if he doesn't know about my father's men. If he has his secrets with my father, then perhaps I should too?

"I asked you a question, Blakely," he demands.

I decide a half-truth is best and reveal, "I was late to the auction and didn't want to run in my stilettos."

His piercing gaze never leaves mine as he scrubs my feet. He asks, "Why were you late?"

"I came from my job."

"And where is that?"

My stomach flips. I'm not embarrassed by where I work, but Riggs is my father's partner. Surely he'll look down upon it?

"Just tell me the truth. Don't ever lie to me," he orders, as if he can read my thoughts.

"I'm a server at a place called Cheeks," I confess.

Riggs doesn't flinch. "The strip club?"

"Yes. You've been there?" I inquire.

"No."

"Oh," I say, suddenly feeling super exposed.

He glances at my foot, lowers it, and picks up the other one. He asks, "You're a server or stripper there?"

"Server. I just said server," I angrily answer.

"Easy," he says in a low voice.

"Don't judge other women or me for what we do to survive," I chastise.

His tone stays neutral. "Who said I was judging?"

I glare at him, crossing my arms over my chest under the bubbles, pointing out, "I know you'd never understand what it's like since you grew up with a silver spoon in your mouth, but there's a lot of hardworking people trying to make ends meet. It's not right to judge them."

He freezes. The washcloth stays pressed against my foot. He scowls. "I just told you I wasn't judging. And before you get all defensive, get your facts straight."

"My facts? About what?" I question.

He clenches his jaw and glances at the ceiling. He takes a few breaths, then returns to cleaning my foot. He releases it and pushes a bottle toward me. "Wash the makeup off your face."

His tone makes me think he doesn't approve of it. I ask, "Is there something wrong with my makeup?"

He studies me, then replies, "When did you start wearing so much?"

"It's not that much," I claim.

"No? Seems like a lot more than what you used to wear," he comments.

I pour the facewash in my hand, and note, "I'm on stage a lot."

His disapproval intensifies. He adds, "So? You don't need it."

My heart swoons. I don't doubt Riggs means what he stated. He isn't a bullshitter. It's one of the things that annoyed my father. He would declare Riggs needed to learn how to schmooze his friends better. Riggs would always claim otherwise.

I wash my face and rinse it with fresh water, then Riggs unplugs the bathtub, asserting, "Time for bed."

"Are you going to answer me about what facts I got wrong?" I push, not wanting him to ignore my inquiry.

He rises, reaches for my armpits, and lifts me to my feet. He moves me onto the mat, grabs a towel, and wraps it around my body.

"Riggs?" I demand.

He takes another towel, diligently dries me off, fists my hair, and tugs on it. I gasp as he positions his face over mine. In a no-nonsense voice, he claims, "It's bedtime. You need your rest."

"What about you? Don't you need rest?" I hurl.

"Sometimes."

"You don't sleep?"

"No more questions, pet." He spins me, leads me to the bedroom, pulls the covers back, and motions for me to get in.

I slide in, and he tugs the blankets over me. "Go to sleep," he orders, then disappears into the bathroom, and the sound of the shower hits my ears.

I fight the urge to sleep, and after several minutes, the glow of his naked body is next to the bed. Butterflies erupt in my belly and then I glance down and gape at the most beautiful cock I've ever seen.

It's long and girthy, complete with a perfectly smooth head that instantly makes my mouth water.

"Like what you see?" he arrogantly asks.

Embarrassed, I curl into the pillow, wondering what it would feel like to have Riggs inside me.

What if he doesn't fit?

Oh God!

"Open your eyes, pet," he demands in his commanding tone.

I obey, unable to defy him.

He pats the mattress. "On your knees, ass on your calves."

I swallow hard, my pulse kicking up several notches.

"Don't make me repeat it, or you'll be punished for the rest of the night," he threatens.

I obey, positioning my body as instructed. He steps in front of me, positioning his cock right in my face. My breath hitches. I glance up at him.

He reaches for my chin, caressing it with his thumb, stating with approval, "Good girl. You always wait for my directions, understand?"

I stay quiet, my chest rising and falling faster.

He commands, "Sit on your hands."

I arch my eyebrows at him.

He returns my stare with a challenging look.

I slide my palms under my ass.

He strokes my hair, tucking a few locks behind my ear, his erection in front of my face growing harder by the minute.

My mouth waters so much that I have to lick my lips.

"How many men have you been with, Blakely?"

I tear my gaze off his dick and stare at his six-pack, feeling super vulnerable. Nothing I've done with anyone has prepared me to be with Riggs. They're all boys compared to him.

He softly says, "Look at me and tell me."

I slowly glance up, admitting, "Three."

Arrogant satisfaction explodes on his face. He quizzes, "Were any of them past their twenties?"

I shake my head.

He continues, "Did they have cocks like mine?"

I swallow hard and shake my head again.

He leans down and murmurs in my ear, "Do you know what I learned tonight when I slid my fingers inside you?"

Heat rolls through me, and I don't know why. I barely whisper, "What?"

He drags his knuckles over my bare breast, then traps my nipple between two of his fingers. He admits, "I assumed you'd be tight, pet. But you're tighter than I thought."

My cheeks flush with fire. I turn away, but he moves my chin back so I'm facing him.

He locks eyes with me. "Why are you embarrassed?"

I take a deep breath. My insides quiver, but I don't know if it's from lust or humiliation.

"Are you on anything?" he questions.

"I don't do drugs. Well, I've had some weed, but that's it," I blurt out.

He bites on his smile and shakes his head. "No. I meant birth control."

More embarrassment fills me. "Oh jeez. Umm...no. I'm, umm... I don't take it unless I'm with someone."

"That's what I thought. Roll over on all fours and stick your ass in the air," he instructs.

"What? Why?"

"You really do have an issue with questioning authority figures. We're going to need to work on this," he declares.

"I'll do what you want but...umm...you'll put a condom on, right?" I fret, reprimanding myself for not even thinking about birth control once tonight.

He grinds his molars, then reaches for me. He flips me so quickly onto my stomach, I gasp. His hard frame presses against my back, and his erection slides between my thighs.

I turn my cheek and press it to the mattress.

He brings his lips to my ear and says, "I told you I'd protect you, right?"

"Yes," I answer, shifting my hips so the tip of his cock hits my entrance.

"I meant it," he states.

A sharp pain shoots through my ass cheek, and I yelp. My back arches, but Riggs's frame holds me steady.

"Shh," he coos, kissing my neck.

"Riggs? What...?"

"It's just a birth control shot. It's okay," he informs me and rubs my ass cheek. He adds, "But for your information, there's no way I'm using a condom with you. My bloodwork was attached to the contract for your review, so you don't have to worry about my status. If you looked at it, you would have seen it."

I close my eyes, suddenly so tired and overwhelmed by everything, I just want to sleep.

Riggs rises, and the loss of his body heat makes me want him to lie back on me. He pats the mattress. "Bedtime."

I don't argue and slide under the covers.

He goes into the bathroom—I assume to dispose of the needle—and then returns. He gets in bed next to me, and I curl into him.

His body freezes.

"What's wrong?" I mumble.

"Did I say you could touch me?" he questions.

I lift my head and look at him to see if he's serious.

"Well?" he asks.

Something about it makes me emotional. Maybe it's too much, or I'm taking it as rejection, but my bottom lip trembles. I blink and roll away from him, curling into a fetal position and hugging the pillow.

He slides down, turning toward me. He doesn't touch me, but I can feel his body heat permeating my skin. It's like torture. I want to curl up in his arms and don't understand why I can't. He asks, "Where have you been all these years?"

"Living," I answer, then yawn.

"Meaning?" he pushes.

I contemplate how to answer his questions. I finally mumble, "Singing. Trying to make my dream happen."

"Where do you sing?"

I shrug. "Wherever I can."

"Want to be more specific?"

I blurt out, "Want to tell me what's going on with you and my father?"

Silence fills the air. The longer it lasts, the thicker the tension gets.

I finally spin and realize he's way closer to me than I thought. I quietly ask, "Why do you care?"

He doesn't hesitate, answering, "I've always wondered where you went. You've been here this entire time, and your father couldn't locate you. I know the resources he's spending. So I find it amazing that you were able to still work on your dream and avoid him."

Until tonight.

I keep my thought to myself and admit, "I mostly sing at the Lizard Lounge. But there are other venues from time to time."

"I'm surprised an agent hasn't picked you up. I remember you singing. You have talent," he says.

Pride fills me. Something about Riggs saying that to me hits me hard. "Thank you."

"You do. So why do you think you haven't gotten an agent yet?"

"Who said I don't have one?"

He arches his eyebrows. "Do you?"

I wince. "No. I need a demo tape. I've been saving, but it's expensive if you do it right. And you definitely want to do it right so they take you seriously."

He studies me for a while, then says, "I'm sorry about your father."

"What do you mean?" I ask.

"He drove you away. I'm sorry you got a bum deal in the father department."

I shrug, then yawn again.

Riggs kisses me on the forehead, then says, "Get some sleep, pet."

I reach up and touch the collar. "Can I take this off to sleep?"

"Is it too tight?" he asks.

"No."

"Then why do you want it off?"

I shake my head. "I don't know. Why do I need it on?"

He slides his hand under it and curls his fingers around the gold.

My pulse quickens. I squeeze my thighs together.

His lips curl, and a sinister expression fills his face. "Because of that, right there."

"What?"

He slides his hands between my legs and slowly circles my clit with his middle finger. His other hand pulls on the collar, adding more tension to it.

I shift my hips, and my breath shortens.

"You like it, pet. You enjoy knowing who you belong to. And when this collar is on, you're mine. So your collars will stay on at all times until our year is up, understand?" he states.

More surprise fills me. "Collars?"

His lips twist, and butterflies ignite in my belly. In a low voice, he adds, "You'll soon understand. Go to sleep, pet." He releases my collar and removes his hand from my thighs, then comes toward my face. I hold my breath, thinking he's going to really kiss me this time, but he gets an inch from my lips, stares at them, then turns away from me.

Suddenly, I'm no longer tired. All I can think about is what it'll be like to kiss Riggs. And my mind is racing with too many questions that only Riggs or time can answer.

6

Riggs

*I*t's still dark when I wake up. I've barely slept, but I never require a lot of sleep. I blame it on my childhood. I always had to be aware of what was happening in my household.

My mother had me when she was fifteen. Prostitution was how she put food on the table. When she brought her johns home, I was supposed to stay in my room. Many of them were violent, and I'd often hear and see them beating my mother. So I never really slept well. When I got old enough to jump in and fight them off, it only pissed my mother off. She didn't like me defending her. She saw it as losing clients, which would only anger me further. It still haunts me when I think about it.

Today's no different. I had maybe an hour of sleep. I lay next to Blakely, turned away from her, listening to her breathe. It took her longer to fall asleep than I anticipated. When the pattern of her breaths changed, I slowly turned over and stared at her.

It's about a half hour before sunrise. The sky is changing into a brilliant shade of pink. I grab my phone and rearrange the sheet to showcase Blakely's creamy shoulders. It's clear she's naked, so I snap a few photos.

Daddy's going to love these.

I quietly get up, go into my closet, and pull a burner phone from its box. I always have at least a dozen on hand. You never know when one might come in handy. It's like the collar, numerous toys, and birth control shots. While I always take those things to one of my L.A. apartments where I house my auctioned subs, for some reason, I keep my stash here.

When Blakely came on stage last night, the thought of bringing her to Malibu consumed me, just like it did on her twenty-first birthday. There was no way I could convince myself to keep her in L.A., hidden away, while I was back in Malibu. Unlike my previous subs, I want her at my beck and call all the time.

I take the phone out of the box and set up the network. It's a secure one that Jones created for me years ago. I've used it a dozen times over the past few years.

I text the picture from my cell to the burner and send it to her father with a caption.

> Me: What should I do with your princess first?

Satisfaction fills me. I turn off the phone and hide it in my closet drawer, knowing he doesn't get up early like I do. It'll be hours before he reads the message.

As quietly as possible, I go out of the house, naked, and grab a wetsuit in the closet near the shower. I put it on, grab my board, and go down to the water. The cool water feels refreshing as I paddle far enough out and wait for the right waves.

My adrenaline won't stop pumping harder than normal. Since I saw Blakely on stage, it's like it's on overdrive. Buying her was the biggest break I could have gotten. I can destroy Hugh without her, but it'll make the process so much sweeter.

And Blakely... Jesus, I'll have more fun breaking her and turning her into my pet than I ever anticipated. All the years of waiting for her and imagining her under my control were grossly underestimated. She'll please me more than I could have ever thought possible.

A swell of waves rolls in, and I ride several of them, but I never take my mind off Blakely. Everything about her is mysterious. It shouldn't be, I've watched her grow up, but there's so much that's happened over the last few years, and I don't know any of it.

Also, I know she wasn't telling the full truth last night. I plan on getting it out of her. Whatever happened, she needs to divulge it.

Several hours pass, and I ride until I'm exhausted, catching one final wave and riding it to shore, surprised and pleased when I see Blakely sitting on the sand.

She hugs her knees to her chest, wearing one of my white button-down shirts. Her dark hair blows wild in the morning breeze, and a couple of the purple highlights glow in the morning light. None of the makeup she wore the night before can be seen, which makes me happy. She's too beautiful to have that crap on her face. Her barely visible freckles dot her cheeks, which are normally covered by her foundation. The gold collar gleams around her neck.

Everything about the vision in front of me makes my dick hard. She's pure perfection, and now I own her.

As much as I like her dark hair with purple highlights, I'm still not totally used to it. I toss my board on the sand and sit next to her. I twirl a lock of purple around my finger, asking, "When did you change your hair?"

She shrugs. "A few years ago. I'm kind of tired of it though. I've been thinking of going back to blonde."

I make a mental note to take more pictures of her to send to Hugh before she changes it. Everything about her hair color with the purple streaks will send him into a tailspin. He'll hate that she's with somebody he doesn't know, but it might bug him more how she changed her hair to something he deems inappropriate.

She takes my silence as disapproval, but her lips twitch. "Is that okay? Or do I have to get your approval to do my hair?"

I struggle with my inner demon, who wants total control of her, and the part of me that suddenly wants to see her back to her natural state. I finally reply, "You're beautiful either way. If you want to change it, I'll make an appointment for you."

She shakes her head. "There's no need for that. I can do it myself."

I snort. "No, you're with me, Blakely. That means you get the best."

She declares, "That's not necessary. I've learned to do a lot of things for myself. It saves money."

I know all about scrimping and saving money. But the last thing I'm about to do is return to that situation. I respond, "Yeah, well, I have lots of it, so you don't need to worry about that."

She hugs her knees tighter to her chest and stares at the ocean. I can't tell if my answer pissed her off, but I can see that she has a lot more questions. Instead of asking her what's on her mind, I decide I'll ask later, and now is the time to push. I want answers that I didn't get last night, and she's going to tell me.

I turn her chin toward me, demanding, "Blakely, why were you running on the L.A. streets last night?"

She freezes, then slowly answers, "I told you, I was late to the auction. I didn't want to run in my stilettos. They're not exactly easy to trot around in."

"You could have stepped on a needle or some other dangerous thing. I'm not buying it, Blakely. Why were you running?" I ask again.

Nervousness fills her expression, and I know it's true. She didn't tell me everything. Yet she also isn't ready to come clean.

I interrogate her further. "Something happened, Blakely. I know it did. So, either tell me, or I'll find out on my own. And if I do that, you won't be happy with the consequences."

She tilts her head and pins her eyebrows together. "What does that mean, Riggs?"

"You don't want to find out," I threaten.

She exhales deeply, glancing back at the water.

I repeat, "Now, tell me what happened."

She groans, scrubbing her hands over her face, confessing, "My father's men were chasing me."

Confused, I ask, "He knows where you're at?" Hugh never told me that he had any idea he knew where she was, not that I should put anything past him. There's obviously a lot he's not informing me on.

She answers, "No, I didn't know he did. His men showed up at Cheeks the other night and followed me to my apartment. Last night, I was at work, and the new bouncer named Snake lured me outside. He claimed his friend was an agent who heard me sing over at the Lizard Lounge. When I went outside, the two men my father hired were there. They tossed me into an SUV, then got a flat tire. I jumped out of the trunk and ran when they were fixing it. It's why I had to take my shoes off. And that's how I ended up at the club."

I remain silent, processing everything. My gut churns as I ask, "So, you weren't on stage at the club to find a Dom? You were clueless about the auction?"

Her face turns red. She nods, admitting, "Yes."

"And you went with a stranger to sign a contract?" I question, getting angrier but trying to stay calm so she can't see it.

She claims, "I didn't know what to do. They know where I live. I figured I could go wherever the club's driver took me. The people at the club said it was a few towns over from L.A. I don't..." She glances around. "Where are we, Riggs? I don't even know where I'm at."

"You're in Malibu," I inform her.

She glances around again. "Malibu. Okay."

More anger fills me, not at her, but that she was in this situation because of her father. Based on what she's telling me, she had no right to be on stage. I ask, "So you were going to show up at my house, not knowing it was me, and do what, Blakely? Give yourself to some man when you didn't even know what you were getting into?"

"Don't judge me. Especially when you're the one buying women on stage at a sex club," she reprimands.

I take a deep breath. "I'm not judging you. I'm trying to understand what's going on here."

"They told me that I didn't have to sign the contract. They said they would bring me back if I wanted. I figured I'd go to wherever they were taking me to get out of L.A. Then I could figure out my next move. And I wasn't planning on signing the contract."

This is bad. So bad. My blood pounds between my ears. I question, "Blakely, do you know what a sub is?"

Embarrassment fills her cheeks. She quietly says, "No."

"Do you know what a Dom is?"

"No," she admits again, her face turning a deeper maroon.

"Yet you signed a contract with me, not knowing anything?" I'm unsure how I feel about this. Part of me is happy because she did it because it was me. But the other part doesn't like this one bit. What I'm into requires full consent, and if she's not on board, that changes the entire situation.

She declares, "It was you. I trust you, Riggs. I..."

"You what?"

She blurts out, "You said you'd protect me from my father. I don't know what else I'm supposed to do. I don't want him to... I don't want to return to him! He'll make me marry some guy. I don't want to lose my life!" She blinks hard, her eyes glistening with tears.

I sternly claim, "I'm not turning you over to your father. I promised you, and nothing has changed regarding that."

She sniffles and asks, "But why, Riggs? Tell me what happened between you two."

"Your father screwed me over. He doesn't know that I know. But that's all I'm going to say, Blakely. So stop asking me about it," I order.

Her eyes widen.

I add, "You don't have to feel sorry for me. I'm handling it."

"He's a horrible person," she softly states.

I stay quiet.

She turns back to the ocean, digs her feet in the sand, and takes a deep breath.

I inquire, "What did you think you were doing when you got on stage?"

She avoids looking at me, and her head bobs side to side. "I don't know. I couldn't go outside. They were waiting for me. I barely made it into the club. I just... I thought it was better to take this chance than to go back outside."

My insides fill with anxiety, and the calm chaos in the water does nothing to alleviate it.

This changes everything.

I rise and pull her to her feet, announcing, "I have errands to run. Today, you'll read the contract while I'm gone. You'll list all your questions, and we'll discuss it over dinner tonight."

Confusion fills her face. "Are you kicking me out?"

"No, I'm not kicking you out. Why would you think that?"

"I... I don't know. You sound upset with me."

I sigh. "I'm not upset with you, Blakely, but you need to know what you're getting yourself into. And for God's sake, I know you want to disobey your father on everything, but don't ever sign a contract again unless you read it. There's a reason you read contracts," I reprimand.

She closes her eyes, squeezing them tight. "Why can't my father just be normal? I wouldn't have to act like I do."

"How do you act?" I question.

She shrugs. "Never good enough for them; him or my mother."

I place my hands on her cheeks and tilt her head up.

She opens her eyelids.

"Blakely, you've never done anything wrong. Your parents are who they are. That's not your problem. That's their problem," I insist,

She grabs my arm, pleading, "Please don't make me return to them. Please."

"Have you not been listening to me? I thought I made it clear there's no way I would ever turn you over to your father or mother."

She nods, but something tells me she doesn't completely believe me.

I add, "I told you I would protect you. Nothing has changed, Blakely."

She looks at me silently.

I lead her toward the house, claiming, "I have things I need to do today. You're not to leave the house. And you are to make sure that you read the contract. Do you understand me?"

She nods. "Yes, I understand."

"Good." I guide her onto the deck and to the door, then add, "I'm going to get ready. Go inside and help yourself to whatever you want for breakfast."

I go over to the shower and strip with too many emotions running through me. Never in a million years would I have thought that she would have done something like this and not had any idea what she was getting herself into.

I wish it didn't matter, but it does. This changes everything. But no matter what, she's going to be mine. When she reads the contract, we'll go through her questions.

I know she's a sub. I saw it in her last night. She can obey. But I don't know if she'll freak after reading my contract. Knowing these new facts, everything about that makes me feel really uneasy.

And that's one thing I don't like in my sex life—wild cards. Right now, Blakely's in control, and I don't like it one bit.

7

Blakely

I'm making coffee when Riggs walks into the house, naked, except for a towel around his lower body. The tattoos on his torso glow in the morning light, and I wonder if I've ever seen anything so majestic.

He quickly disappears into the bedroom, forcing me to tear my eyes off his backside, which is just as toned from surfing as the rest of his body. I return to focusing on brewing the coffee. I'm pouring my first cup when he returns to the main room.

He's wearing khaki shorts and a pink linen shirt with the sleeves rolled up, displaying his ink. I could look at him all day, clothed or unclothed, and when he gives me an arrogant expression, I realize I've been staring.

I clear my throat and ask, "When did you get all those?"

He glances at his forearm and shrugs. "Over the years. I got my first one when I was sixteen." He points to the big swell on his arm.

I trace my finger over it, questioning, "Did you always surf?"

"I stole a board when I was thirteen. Been obsessed ever since," he confesses.

I laugh. "You stole it?"

He nods. "Yep."

"Why didn't you just have your parents buy one for you?" I ask.

His face darkens. He answers, "They weren't into surfing." He turns and grabs his keys off the counter.

I point out, "You've never shown your tattoos when you were at my parents' house. You've always worn long sleeves, even when it was hot. Why is that?"

He grunts. "Your father looks down upon them. He believes that the people we deal with look down on tattoos. He claims they don't give off the impression we should make. When we started our business, I agreed to always keep them covered during events or business meetings."

I mutter, "Sounds like my father."

"You know him well," Riggs says with disgust in his voice, making me wonder again how my father screwed him over. Riggs tosses a notepad and pen on the table, then points to the contract. "You're to spend all day going through this. Do you understand, Blakely?"

I roll my eyes. "Yes."

"Don't do that when I tell you to do something," he warns.

"You've told me several times," I remind him.

He ignores my statement, demanding, "Sit down."

His tone annoys me but also gives me butterflies. It happens every time he orders me around. I don't understand why I like it, but something in me does. So I oblige him and sit down.

Riggs asks, "What do you need to work on your music?"

Surprised he's asking, I recover and tap the notepad. "Only this."

He peers at me, then asks, "That's it? Didn't you used to play the piano? You need an instrument or something, don't you?"

A wave of frustration passes inside me as I think of the grand piano my parents bought only for looks. It wasn't meant to be played, except at high-end parties when my father hired what he referred to as "the talent." I question, "How do you know I used to play the piano?"

Riggs admits, "Your mother told me."

I shift on my feet. "I only played it when no one was home. She caught me a few times. My father didn't like me using it. He claimed it encouraged me to keep my head in the clouds."

Riggs stares silently for a moment with a look of disapproval on his face. He finally asks, "What have you been using to create your music since you left home?"

I admit, "A keyboard I bought at a resale shop. It's not perfect, but it works. A few of the keys are damaged, but I manage to make it work for what I need. I'd ask you to get it for me, but I don't think you should go near my apartment. I'm sure my father's men are watching it, and if you go in, they'll see you. So I'm fine with just a notepad."

Another emotion passes across Riggs's face, but I'm not sure what it is. I'm about to ask him when he says, "No music today, Blakely. Your entire focus is on this contract. Do you understand?"

I give him a tiny salute. "You've already made it clear, boss."

His lips twitch. He states, "It's Sir. But you'll see that in the contract." He winks.

I arch my eyebrows. Last night, I didn't worry about what the thick stack of papers said. Now, I'm getting a bit curious. He's making it sound detailed, which isn't something I ever thought people were, regarding sex. In my experience, you just get at it, and within a few minutes, things are over.

Not that I've had any mind-blowing encounters. My past boyfriends were okay. I enjoyed them, but even last night showed me Riggs is on a different level, and we haven't even had sex yet.

Not that I ever doubted he would be different. Even at eighteen, I knew it.

He asserts, "Help yourself to anything in the kitchen. I'll be back soon."

He's almost to the door, when I call out, "Wait!"

He spins, inquiring, "What's wrong?"

Something about not having access to him panics me. I fret, "How do I get ahold of you if I need to?"

He stares at me for a moment.

I add, "I also need to call work and the lounge."

A flash of nervousness appears on his face but quickly disappears, so I think I imagined it. He goes into the bedroom.

Several minutes pass, then he comes out with a throw-away phone. He reiterates, "Read the contract. If you're good with the terms, call work and tell them you quit. My number is programmed on this. You're only allowed to use this to call them to quit or to contact me. That's it. You don't call anyone else, Blakely. If your father's men are looking for you, it's extra important no one knows you're here."

I don't know who I would call, although I could tell my room-mates or a couple of my friends I'm not dead. But Riggs is right. I also don't want anybody to find out where I am. What if I told them and my father's men tried to interrogate them?

Yet my stomach flips at the thought of quitting. I argue, "It was hard to find work and earn a recurring spot to sing. Can I keep my gig at the lounge? I promise it won't interfere with whatever you want me to do here."

Riggs shakes his head. "No. You can't. But I promise you that you'll be ahead in your career by the time this year is up."

He makes it sound so easy, but I know how much competition there is in L.A. It's nearly impossible to make it. I claim, "I need exposure. How can you promise me that?"

"Pet, you need to trust me. If you can't trust me completely, the deal's off between us," he threatens.

My eyes widen from shock. Riggs is so all in or all out. It's pretty extreme, and I'm still trying to wrap my head around this entire situation. But then again, Riggs has always been blunt and straightforward. It's no secret he's a control freak. It's a miracle my father and he got along as well as they did for almost two decades, not that I knew the ins and outs of their business.

I start to argue, "But—"

He cuts me off. "The only way this works is if you fully trust me, Blakely. There's no room to be wishy-washy. And not just with your body. You need to always trust me to make the right decisions for you. Do you understand?"

I've always been independent, which is why my parents and I never saw eye to eye. So giving the power to Riggs to make decisions for me isn't easy.

He steps closer, lowering his voice. "I'm not them, pet. I want what's best for you and for your career. I promise you."

I take a deep breath and slowly nod. "Okay. I'll trust you."

He briefly studies me, then says, "Good girl."

I hesitate, not wanting to sound needy, but ask, "Will you be gone long?"

"You're going to miss me, aren't you?" he teases.

Fire flames on my cheeks. "I just want to know."

He smirks. "It's okay to admit it. But to answer your question, I'll be back by dinner. I'll bring something home for us to eat. Read the contract, and write down your questions." He gives me a chaste kiss on my forehead, then leaves.

I take a sip of my coffee, move the contract in front of me, and start reading.

THIS CONTRACT IS BETWEEN RIGGS MADDEN (KNOWN IN THIS contract as Dom), and Blakely Fox (known in this contract as sub) for the term of one year. At the end of this agreement, the Dom and sub will part, releasing each other of all prior commitments. No further assistance or terms will be granted unless a new agreement is signed.

. . .

SOMETHING ABOUT THAT STATEMENT HURTS, BUT I TAKE A DEEP breath. I guess it's better to know I have an expiration date than not, so I can prepare myself.

THE SUB AGREES THE DOM IS THE RULING PARTY, AND HE WILL MAKE all decisions at all times.

The sub will tell the Dom which charity she requires him to donate funds to.

The sub understands the Dom is in complete control over her body and will do as he sees fit.

At times, the sub may wish to leave the premises or be alone but will only do so with the Dom's permission.

BE ALONE? WHAT IS THAT ABOUT? I SCAN MORE OF THE CONTRACT, bypassing the legal jargon and focusing on the section titled *Rules of Engagement During Playtime.*

RULE 1: THE SUB WILL KNEEL AS INITIALLY DISPLAYED BY THE DOM and not break the position until instructed.

HE WANTS ME TO KNEEL ON THE MATTRESS IN FRONT OF HIS COCK *like I did last night?*

Okay, no biggie.

RULE 2: THE SUB WILL ADDRESS THE DOM AS SIR, NOT BY HIS NAME, during playtime.

. . .

WHAT IS PLAYTIME? I WRITE ON THE PAD TO GET CLARIFICATION.

RULE 3: THE SUB WILL ONLY COME WHEN PERMITTED BY THE DOM.

MEMORIES OF RIGGS GIVING ME MULTIPLE ORGASMS WHILE restrained to his towel rack flood me.

How am I supposed to control that?

I reread it, then write on the pad, *Only come when permitted?*

RULE 4: THE SUB WILL ALLOW THE DOM TO ENGAGE WITH HER IN ANY sexual positions he desires, at any time he desires, and at any place he desires. Penetration will include vaginal, oral, and anal, sometimes simultaneously.

MY MOUTH TURNS DRY. I STARE OUT THE WINDOW, HAVING NEVER done anal and unsure how I feel about it. I always thought it was a no-go zone, but since it's on Riggs's list, something makes me rethink my hesitation. I watch the waves crash on the sand but barely see them. All I can think about is Riggs's size. I write, *anal and size*, then stare at the waves some more, wondering if I could do it.

RULE 5: THE SAFE WORD IS "STOP." IF THE SUB SAYS STOP AT ANY time, the Dom will cease activity. However, the sub agrees to this contract knowing the Dom will push her limits. It's only to be used if she truly needs the activity to end. If she does utilize the safe word, all play is over for the next seventy-two hours.

. . .

95

I ADD TO THE LIST, *PUSH MY LIMITS. WHAT LIMITS?*

RULE 6: *TOYS, RESTRAINTS, AND OTHER ACCESSORIES WILL BE utilized when the Dom wishes. Video and/or audio recordings are at the Dom's discretion.*

I FIGURE RIGGS WANTS TO USE A VIBRATOR OR SOMETHING ON ME, which isn't too crazy. And I didn't dislike being handcuffed last night. *But what does accessories mean?* I add that to the list. I also add, *recording,* not sure how I feel about that possibility.

RULE 7: *THE SUB WILL NOT TOUCH THE DOM UNLESS GRANTED permission. Failure to obey will result in a punishment.*

I ROLL MY EYES, NOT UNDERSTANDING WHAT THAT RULE IS ALL about. I would have thought if he's as attracted to me as he claims, that he'd want me to touch him.

RULE 8: *DEPENDING ON THE SUB'S REACTION TO CERTAIN techniques, bruising may occur. The sub agrees to use the skincare products the Dom provides to heal faster.*

MY CHEST TIGHTENS. I WRITE ON THE PAD, *BRUISES? HEAL?*

Will Riggs hurt me?

RULE 9: *THE SUB AGREES TO ALL FORMS OF HOT OR COLD PLAY.*

. . .

THOUGHTS OF BEING BURNED HORRIFY ME. I ADD TO MY LIST, *What does hot or cold play mean? Will I have scars?*

RULE 10: *THE SUB WILL AGREE TO BIRTH CONTROL AND THE METHOD determined by the Dom.*

GUESS HE MADE GOOD ON THAT. CHECK THAT OFF THE LIST.

RULE 11: *CONDOMS WILL NOT BE UTILIZED. SEE APPENDIX A FOR A comprehensive report on the Dom's medical records. The sub will provide her updated records, or the Dom will order the proper testing. The sub will not engage in any play with anyone besides the Dom unless the Dom determines it's in her best interest. At any time, the Dom can allow an audience.*

MY STOMACH DIVES. *WOULD RIGGS MAKE ME HAVE SEX WITH someone else? And what does "in her best interest mean"? How can it be in my best interest to have sexual relations with someone else? And why does it only talk about me? What about him not being with anyone else?*

And what does "allow an audience" mean? Is Riggs into letting others watch him have sex?

I write all of it down, flip through the contract to Appendix A, and review the extensive STD lab work. According to the reports, Riggs is clean as a whistle, and it's only a week old. I won't have any issues passing the same tests, and it makes me more comfortable to know Riggs doesn't have anything I could get. I've always been a stickler for condoms after my friend in high school contracted a few STDs. They were curable, but it was horrible for her.

I return to the contract.

RULE 12: *THE DOM WILL PROVIDE FOR ALL BASIC NEEDS OF THE SUB.* *This includes, but is not limited to, shelter, food, clothing, transportation, etc.*

Rule 13: The sub will not abuse substances in any way. This includes alcohol as well as street and prescription drugs.

Rule 14: This contract will not be broken unless the Dom finds the sub unsatisfactory for his sexual needs. If the Dom wishes to break the contract, he will provide shelter at his chosen place for the remainder of the contract.

MY HEART POUNDS HARDER.

Unsatisfactory for his sexual needs.

A new fear of rejection takes hold of me.

What if I'm not good enough?

I read the rest of the contract, which is a lot of legal mumbo jumbo. My stomach growls, and I realize I haven't eaten since lunch the previous day. I go into the kitchen and make a turkey sandwich, eat half of it, and stare at my list of questions.

For several hours, I reread the contract, adding to my list as new concerns pop up. The legal jargon makes my head spin, but there are a few things I'm not sure what they mean, so I write those down as well.

It's late afternoon when I finally push the contract away and forbid myself to read it anymore. My stomach is a frenzied mix of anxiety and anticipation. I've never been so unsure of what I'm getting myself into.

The rational part of me tells me to run. Yet deep down, I already know that however Riggs answers my questions, there's no way I won't agree to what we already signed.

I tell myself it's for his protection from my father, but it's another lie.

I've wanted Riggs since before I was eighteen. That year, I saw the flames burning in his eyes when he looked at me. It was as if he finally saw me as more than a kid.

Everything about that moment is etched on my mind, just like our encounter on my twenty-first birthday. I've never forgotten how it felt when he pinned his seductive gaze on me or tugged my hair, cornering me against the wall.

Back then, my father stood in our way. Now, it's like the universe wants us together. And I'm not looking to tempt fate. There's no other person in the world I would do this with and feel safe. If anyone else had bid on me in that auction, I would have left last night. So whatever this is between us must be something meant to be, even if only for a year.

Besides, it's Riggs. What's the worst that could happen?

8

Riggs

*a*s soon as I pull out of the driveway, I call my personal shopper, Isabella. She handles all the wardrobes for my subs.

She chirps, "Riggs, to what do I owe the pleasure?"

"Isabella, I need a full wardrobe," I state.

She softly laughs. "Right to the point. Can always count on you for that. What size is your girl?"

"Her shoe size is seven and a half. Clothes are a six, maybe an eight. I don't know. Get me an assortment," I demand, not sure what size Blakely is, but pretty sure she's a six or an eight.

"Got some meat on her, huh?" Isabella says.

I groan inside. The L.A. standards of women being a size double zero drives me insane. Blakely's got curves in all the right places, and boney women don't do anything for me. Still, I'd reprimand her if Isabella wasn't so good at what she did. But she's my go-to for clothing, so I reply, "She's curvy, not a stick."

"No problem. I'll have a bunch of choices for you. Are you coming here, or do I need to meet you?" she asks.

"I have some things to take care of. I can text you when I'm on my way, but my guess is it'll be early afternoon. Is that enough time?" I inquire.

"Definitely," she replies.

"Great. I'll pull up, and your staff can bring it out to my car," I instruct, not wanting to deal with parking issues.

"No problem. Talk soon," Isabella states and hangs up.

I continue battling traffic on my way downtown. I park in a lot and walk into the music store. It's the best in L.A.

Within seconds of walking in, a middle-aged sales guy approaches me. He pushes his glasses up his nose and says, "Welcome. My name is Kyle. Can I help you, sir?"

"What's the best piano you have?" I question, knowing hardly anything about pianos but convinced Blakely needs one. I've promised her she can work on her music the next year and she'll be better for it when she leaves, so I need to keep my promise.

A look of excitement appears on his face. He leads me through the store and stops in front of a crystal piano. It's completely transparent, and I have to admit, it looks like a masterpiece. I'm sure the price tag is as well.

Kyle states, "This is a Heintzman & Company. They're made in Canada."

"Not a Steinway?" I inquire, throwing out my limited knowledge of pianos.

He shakes his head. "We have Steinways if you want one, but this is a top-of-the-line, rare item."

"What's the price tag?" I ask.

"3.2 million, plus tax. It includes shipping anywhere in California," he states.

I whistle.

He adds, "If you want something a little bit more economical—"

"No, that's not necessary," I state. It really is a beautiful piece. I can imagine it in the beach house, and I can picture Blakely sitting on the matching crystal bench with her fingers dancing over the keys.

Kyle's face lights up. "Fantastic! It's a great choice!"

"Better be for the price tag. When can it be delivered? I'm out in Malibu," I inform him.

He motions for me to follow him, answering, "Let me look at the schedule."

It takes twenty minutes to check out and arrange for next-day delivery. Satisfied with my purchase, and convinced Blakely will love it, I get back in my car and head toward Skid Row.

It's another area of L.A. I hate as much as Compton. It's not quite as bad, but over the years, it's gotten worse and worse. Plus, I'm not comfortable leaving my Porsche there.

I call my contact Chainsaw when I'm outside of his house. Rumor has it he got his nickname because he cut off his father's legs with a chainsaw when he was eight. I don't know if I believe the story, but I wouldn't put it past him. He's one of the meanest sons of bitches I know. We met when I was living in Compton. Over the years, he's done several jobs for me.

"Riggs," he answers.

"I'm outside. You here?" I ask, wondering why I didn't call before I got here.

Because all I can think about is getting home and breaking Blakely.

"Yep," he replies.

I order, "Come meet me outside."

"I see you're still demanding," he teases.

"Not leaving my car outside, man. You know how I am," I claim.

He grunts. "Maybe you should get a beater for the hood."

"Not a chance."

He adds, "I'll be out in a minute."

I wait, watching my mirrors, only semi-confident that no one would try anything on Chainsaw's doorstep. Relief hits me when he finally steps outside.

He opens the passenger door and slides in. We slap hands, and I notice he's added three more tear tattoos under his eyes. It's common with gang members, which I'm sure Chainsaw is. Which gang, I don't know or care, since I don't ever mess with him. Each tear is a sign that he's killed someone and proud of it. I assume the tears represent rival gang members since he's probably killed way more than only three people since I last saw him.

Chainsaw questions, "What's the job?"

It's why I like him. He's straight to the point, like I am. I state, "I have a guy I need you to pick up. He works security for the front door of Cheeks. His name is Snake. Make sure it's him you pick up and no one else."

"Yeah, of course," Chainsaw says, as if I've insulted him.

I ignore his tone, adding, "Take him to my warehouse."

"Will do. Do you know his schedule?"

I shake my head. "No. I'm assuming he'll be there tonight, although I could be wrong."

"I'll call you when it's done," Chainsaw states.

I hand him a yellow envelope of cash. "Call me when he's at the warehouse."

Chainsaw arches his eyebrows.

I continue, "Don't finish him off. I want to make sure I'm there."

His lips form into a sinister smile. "I love it when you like to jump in and play."

I grunt. The warehouse is only for these types of situations. It's not the first time Chainsaw's handled business for me. I normally like to have him do everything so my hands are clean, but Snake messed with Blakely. This is personal.

"I'll text you when he's there," Chainsaw states, then gets out of the car with the yellow envelope.

I peel out of the neighborhood. I'm heading toward Malibu when another call comes in. I hit the answer button on my dashboard screen and say, "Jones, what's going on?"

He relays, "There's movement in the US accounts going into the offshore ones."

"Fuck," I mutter. Hugh is really testing my patience. I can't wait to take him down. I add, "I need you to hurry up and get me access to the Cayman accounts."

"I'm on it, but I thought you should know," Jones says.

"Thanks, man. Keep me posted of any other activity," I demand, then hang up.

Traffic's bad like always, and it's later than I anticipated when I pull up to the boutique. The staff loads my trunk, and I fight more traffic on the way back to Malibu.

I make another stop to pick up dinner at a local farm-to-table restaurant. I down a beer while I stare at the waves crashing into the rocks, waiting for the food to be made. For the millionth time today, I wonder what Blakely is thinking about the contract.

By the time I get home, it's almost dark. I don't realize how anxious I've been all day about leaving her on her own until I walk in and see her standing at the window.

Her arms are crossed, and she's wearing one of my flannel shirts. She has the sleeves rolled, and her hair is tied into a loose bun.

It's another thing I really like—seeing her in my clothes. Knowing she's naked underneath and waiting for me to come home gives me such a hard-on. I consider going against my rule and fucking her tonight even though her birth control won't be effective yet.

I can pull out.

I push the thought to the back of my mind, knowing it's a bad idea. If you give a sub too much too soon, it can backfire on the training process.

She's drinking red wine, tapping her finger against the glass. My heart beats harder. She's so lost in her thoughts that she doesn't realize I'm there.

I glance at the notepad on the table, but it's shut. The contract's neatly stacked and sitting in the middle of the table where I left it.

I'm not sure how to take things. Is she lost in thought because she wants to back out, or is she lost in thought thinking about all the things in the contract that I'm going to do to her?

I creep up behind her, inhaling her sea salt and driftwood scent, wondering how she always manages to smell so good and the same. She has no perfume here, so it has to be her natural scent. I slide my arm around her stomach, tugging her into my frame.

She jumps and gets flustered, turning her head to pin her blues on me, admitting, "Riggs, you scared me."

I glance at the wineglass. "Sorry. You drink red now?"

"You said to help myself," she reminds me, then smirks. "Don't worry, I didn't break rule thirteen. I'm not abusing it."

I'm pleased she memorized what rule it was, but I also have to make sure she remembers that I'm the boss. I warn, "You're begging for a punishment with that tone."

She spins into me and tilts her head, giving me a look I can't decipher. Is it apprehension and nerves? Is it disappointment?

My stomach flips again, and my fears race through my mind.

What if she's not down with the contract?

I'll convince her.

It will never work if I have to convince her. I've tried to do that before with women, and it's a disaster. I end up having to enforce rule fourteen, and all it does is cost me money.

Blakely knows how to submit. She did it last night. She's defiant, but I know she has it in her.

I decide to only show confidence and ask, "Did you call and quit your jobs?"

She shakes her head, not flinching, as if challenging me.

My nervousness increases. I ask, "Because you wanted to disobey me and see how I'd punish you or for some other reason?"

She hesitates and answers, "I don't have to work until tomorrow. I thought it would be best if you answered my questions first, before I upend my entire life."

I don't like her answer. That means there's a possibility she's not okay with something and might decide to walk.

No, she wouldn't.

Maybe she would. She walked away from everything that her family offered her. She had the whole world of riches at her fingertips, yet she did everything she could to stay away.

What if I somehow get added to that category?

I release her. I point to the table, pull out a chair, and motion for her to sit. "Let's eat dinner and talk."

She obeys, and I grab two plates, the bottle of wine, and another glass. I refill hers, pour one for myself, and make two plates of salad, sea bass, and couscous.

I sit across from her and nod for her to begin eating.

Her lips twitch. "You're making me nervous."

"That so?" I question, hiding the fact that I'm also nervous. I don't want her to know that.

She takes a few deep breaths and continues staring at me.

"Eat," I order, pointing at her plate.

She takes a few bites, as do I, but I'm no longer hungry. She puts her fork down and asks, "Can we start the conversation?"

Relief hits me. I can't handle the suspense anymore. I coolly state, "If you'd like."

"I would."

"Okay. Ask me anything."

She opens her notepad, and I glance at the page full of ink. She pulls it closer to her so I can't see it, furrows her eyebrows, and her cheeks grow redder.

I reach across the table and grab her hand. "No need to be embarrassed. I expect you to have a lot of questions."

Surprise fills her expression. "You do?"

"Yes. You're new to all this. If you didn't have any, I'd be worried," I assure her.

A nervous smile appears, and she glances back at the page, then asks, "Why can't I be alone if I want?"

I don't hesitate. "Because I'm in charge and know what's best. If I feel you shouldn't be, then I won't allow you to be."

"Why wouldn't it be best for me?" she questions.

"I'm going to push you past your limits as you know them," I claim.

"What does that mean?"

"I can't answer that. You'll discover what it means through our sessions."

"Sessions?"

I reply, "When we're together."

She taps her finger on the table and stares at me.

"Next question?" I ask.

She picks up her pad and studies it, then says, "So whenever we do anything sexual, it's called playtime?"

I shrug. "For the purpose of this contract. You can call it whatever you want. Does that word bug you?"

She thinks a minute, then shakes her head. "No, it's okay."

"Great. What else is on your list?"

She hesitates, then clears her throat. "Ummm... It says I can only come when you permit me."

I can't help the curve forming on my lips. "That's correct."

I can see the confusion in her eyes. "How do I stop it if you're touching me?"

I work hard to keep from smiling so she doesn't think I'm patronizing her. I answer, "You'll learn."

Moments pass with tension filling the air. "Next concern," I assert.

She looks at the paper, then questions, "Can you give me an example of an accessory?"

I keep it light and easy so I don't scare her off. "Sure. A blindfold is an example."

Panic fills her face. She turns toward the window and taps the wood faster.

"Is something wrong with that?" I ask.

She reaches for her neck and grasps her collar, admitting, "They put one on me last night."

"To bring you here?"

She shakes her head. "No. Yes, they did, but I meant my father's men. It was just briefly."

Anger rages through me, thinking about what her father's done to her. And I'm not thinking straight because I should have asked her this morning what the men look like or if she knows their names. They're going to see my wrath as well. I file it in the back of my mind for another discussion and soften my tone, asking, "But you allowed them to blindfold you to come here?"

She looks at her list, lifts her chin, and asserts, "Yes. It's fine. Umm..." She swallows hard.

I wait for her to continue, not sure if I should push the blindfold issue or not. I need to know if she's got some sort of PTSD from it. I don't want to trigger her.

Her face turns maroon as she blurts out, "What if you don't fit?"

"Sorry? I'm not following. Can you be clearer?" I ask.

"In me." She looks down at her finger, which is tapping like she's a master typist. She adds, "You're pretty big."

I do everything I can to not laugh. I put my hand over her finger and demand, "Blakely, look at me."

Mortified, she obeys but winces when her eyes meet mine.

I firmly state, "I assure you that you and I will fit together."

"How do you know?"

I can't control it anymore and smile. "I just know."

My assurance doesn't seem to convince her. She asks, "Are you going to hurt me?"

"When I penetrate you? No."

She points out, "The contract discusses bruises. And hot and cold play. I don't want to be lit on fire."

I lose all sense of control and chuckle.

"It's not funny!" she reprimands.

I neutralize my reaction. "Sorry. I will not be setting you on fire. Promise."

"No?"

"No. And I assure you, any pain you feel will result in a high you've never felt before," I claim.

She stares at me.

"What else is on your list, pet?"

"Where do I go for the lab tests?"

"Have you been tested before?" I question.

She nods.

"When?"

She ponders my question a moment and replies, "Maybe two years ago."

"Okay, so you'll need a new test," I claim.

"But I haven't had sex since then," she blurts out.

I gape at her, unable to hide my shock.

Her cheeks burn again, and she asks, "Why are you looking at me like that?"

"Sorry. Why haven't you had sex?"

She shrugs. "I'm not dating anyone. So where do I get the test?" Her finger starts to move under my hand.

I pick it up and run my thumb over the back of her hand, stating, "You don't have to."

"Why?"

"Your tests were fine two years ago?"

She nods. "Yes."

"Then there's no need to do it."

She peers at me closer.

"What did I say now?" I ask.

"Do you take everyone's word?"

I lean closer. "No. But you aren't everyone, are you?"

She holds her breath, and I can't figure out whether it's good or bad.

I motion to her list. "Anything else?"

She hesitates. A mix of fear and hurt fills her expression.

I get up and walk around the table. I sit next to her and slide my arm around her. "What is it, pet?"

She scrunches her face, and the emotions intensify. I wait her out until she reveals, "How long does it take before you know if

I'm unsatisfactory for your sexual needs? Is it right away or months into this?"

Shock fills me that she's worried about rule fourteen. I gather my thoughts to try to assure her, stating, "You don't need to worry about rule fourteen."

"I don't?"

"No."

"How do you know? We haven't really done a lot," she asks.

I slide my hand over her cheek, tracing her lips with my thumb. She briefly closes her eyes, and I reply, "That, right there."

She opens her blues in question.

"You react to me, pet. You did when you were eighteen, and you do now. And my body responds to yours."

"It does?" She takes a deep breath.

I grab her hand and put it between my legs, torturing my cock with her touch, declaring, "That's because of you. And it's been like that since I saw you on stage last night."

Her lips twitch.

I add, "So rule fourteen doesn't apply to you."

Her smile grows.

I remove her hand and point to her plate. "Eat. You're going to need your energy."

9

Blakely

*R*iggs keeps the conversation light over dinner, asking me about my songs and avoiding more talk about the contract. When I finish everything on my plate, he gets up and clears the table.

I rise to help, but he pours more wine into my glass and says, "Relax, Blakely."

My nervousness reappears as I watch him put the dishes in the dishwasher and toss the takeaway containers in the trash. The cleared table only has the contract, my notepad of questions, and my wineglass on it. I tap my fingers on the wood, staring at the thick stack of papers.

Riggs must sense my anxiety. He steps behind me, places his hands on my shoulders, and rubs his thumbs over the curve of my neck where it meets my back. He quietly says, "Pet."

I lift my head toward the ceiling, glancing up at him.

"Come sit on the couch with me," he orders.

I rise.

He grabs the contract and my notepad, leads me to the couch, then sits. He takes my wineglass, sets it on the coaster, tugs me onto his lap, and inquires, "Do you have any more concerns?"

My nerves tap dance in my belly as I ponder the question, mentally reviewing the long list I created on the notepad. I reach for my neck and slide my finger back and forth over the smooth gold collar. I'm unsure why, but something about the collar soothes me.

"Is that a no or yes?" he pushes.

"I, umm..." I deeply exhale and glance at the paperwork.

Riggs opens the side table drawer and drops the items in it. He closes it and asserts, "If you have more things you'd like to discuss, then now's the time, Blakely. If not, why don't we keep the contract out of sight and forget about it."

I blurt out, "Easy for you to say. You don't have fourteen rules to memorize."

His lips twitch. "Thirteen. I got rid of fourteen for you, remember?" He wiggles his eyebrows.

I softly laugh, relaxing a bit.

His grin falls, and his tone turns serious. "I do need an answer from you though. Do you have any other concerns?"

I start to shake my head, then stop.

He peers at me closer. "What is it?"

I hesitate, trying to gather my thoughts. Tension thickens in the air, and I open my mouth, but nothing comes out.

Riggs pushes my hair behind my ear, demanding, "Whatever it is, just say it."

I take another moment, then say, "Rule eleven."

He arches his eyebrows, asserting, "I already gave you my medical records and told you I won't require you to be tested. What's the problem?"

"Not that part of the rule," I quietly add.

He furrows his eyebrows, then his expression changes. "Ah. I see. I assume you are referring to 'The sub will not engage in any play with anyone besides the Dom unless the Dom determines it's in her best interest.'"

I nod.

He grinds his molars, then asks, "Are you telling me you want to engage with others?"

"No! Not at all."

"Then what is it?"

My pulse pounds hard against the choker. "Are you going to want me to do things with other people?"

He studies me, and my gut flips faster. He finally answers, "I haven't thought that far. But I have no desire to share you. However, I would arrange it if it were in your best interest."

I'm glad he doesn't want to share me, but his answer also confuses me. I ask, "Why would it be in my best interest?"

"Some people need it," he states.

"What do you mean?"

He doesn't tear his gaze off me, drags his knuckles down my arm, and claims, "Every sub has different needs, pet. It's my job to figure out what those are, and often, we aren't aware of what we need the most."

I tilt my head, letting his answer sink in, but I still don't understand it. I ask, "How can screwing someone else be something someone needs?"

His confidence only grows. He asserts, "It just is. Unless you need it and then do it, you probably won't understand it."

My heart pounds faster. I lower my voice and ask, "And you? Is this something you need?"

"To fuck other women?"

I nod, blinking hard, not trusting myself to speak without showcasing the emotional roller coaster I'm on. The thought of Riggs with anyone else is too much to bear. I might only be his for a year, but I don't want to share him. The jealous streak in me would probably kill me.

He slides his hand on my cheek, leans forward so his lips are an inch from mine, and announces, "There's something you should know about me."

My voice cracks, "What?"

He declares, "I'm not a Dom who plays around. When I signed that contract, my focus was on you and only you. And as long as we're in this arrangement, it'll stay that way. Do you understand?"

Relief washes over me. My pulse lowers a few notches, and I nod. "Okay."

He asks, "Are there any other things we need to discuss?"

I contemplate for a moment, then shake my head. "No. I think I'm clear on things. Well, as much as I can be with my limited knowledge of certain aspects." My face heats again.

The corners of his mouth curve up. He replies, "Good." He glances at my wineglass and questions, "Are you buzzed?"

"No."

He stares at me.

"I'm not," I insist.

"You'd tell me if you were?"

"Yes. Why?"

He clenches his jaw and drags his knuckles down my neck and breast. I shudder as he asserts, "I need you alert when we play, Blakely." He traces my nipple with his finger.

I squeeze my thighs tighter together. I assure him, "I'm alert."

"What's the safe word?" he quizzes.

"Stop."

"And when can you say it?"

I arch my eyebrows. "Is this a trick question?"

"No. I assure you it's not."

I slide my hands over his shoulders and lace them around his neck, reciting from the contract, "When we're playing and I want you to cease the activity."

His voice turns stern. "Not want. *Need*. You use it if you *need* me to stop."

Confusion fills me again. "What's the difference?"

He fists my hair and tugs my head backward. It's not gentle, but it's also not hard. I gasp in surprise and shift on his lap. He asserts, "I'm going to push your limits, Blakely. Want will often be there. Want is a primary defense mechanism that makes us weak. A need is different. There's no other choice because you're breaking, and the world collapses around you. It's so unbearable you'd rather die than continue to go on."

My chest tightens. I hold my breath, trying to imagine what he could possibly do to me to make me feel that way.

He continues, "I need to know you understand the difference. Giving in to want cheats us of our full potential. It keeps us weak and stagnant instead of growing into the person we're meant to be."

I nervously chirp, "Gee, I thought sex was just sex."

He reprimands, "This is about more than sex, Blakely. This is about learning to submit so you can fully understand your power."

"If I submit, I don't have any power," I mutter.

"Ah, quite the opposite. And one day soon, you'll grasp what I'm saying. Your inner soul is begging to fully submit. Once you do, only then will you thrive," he claims.

I stay quiet, unsure how that would ever be possible. I'm only playing his game where I have to do what he says because I want to be with him. I'm too independent and headstrong to ever be a person who thrives on submitting, even if it's to Riggs.

He softly chuckles. "You don't believe me." It's more of a statement than a question.

I choose my words carefully, claiming, "I think we both know I'm not one to conform or follow the rules."

The blue flecks in his eyes sparkle. He inquires, "Then why did you agree to this?"

There's only one answer, and I tell him, "It's what you want."

Satisfaction and arrogance appear on his face. He challenges, "And it's what you want."

"No. I—"

He puts his fingers over my lips. His other hand slides under my collar and he presses his palm into my beating pulse. His voice is low, seductive, and so full of confidence, my lower body throbs as if trying to prove to me I'm wrong and he's right. He argues, "We're wasting time, pet. The rules of engagement begin now."

My butterflies go crazy. I open my mouth, then snap it shut when he arches his eyebrows at me.

He asks, "Did I not answer your questions and concerns?"

"You did," I affirm.

"Then are you in or out?"

My blood turns to lava burning in my veins. I lift my chin, declaring, "I'm in."

He smiles, then asks, "What charity am I writing the check to?"

My stomach flips. I raise my chin, stating, "The L.A. Center for Addiction."

Riggs arches his eyebrows. "Interesting choice. Why that charity?"

I try not to be ashamed, but I can't fight it. I tell the truth, "I have a few friends who got clean after going there." My gut flips. I add, "And I wish my mother would check into the facility."

Something passes in Riggs's eyes, making me think he understands how I feel about my mother. Then again, he's met her and knows her well. He softly replies, "That's a good choice, but don't get your hopes up. Addiction runs deep."

I stay quiet, turn away, and blink hard.

A few moments pass, then he orders, "Let's see how well you can follow the rules. Stand up, pet."

I swallow my pride and rise, tapping my fingers on my thighs.

"Strip," he commands.

Fire races to my cheeks. I stare at him.

"Do I need to repeat myself?" he questions.

I swallow hard, slowly unbutton his flannel, and slide it over my shoulders. It falls to the ground at my feet, baring my body.

He assesses me, slowly running his leering gaze over every inch of my skin for longer than necessary. He locks his blues on mine and twirls his finger in the air. "Spin."

I obey, turning so my backside is in front of him, with my heart thumping harder into my chest cavity.

He rises and steps behind me, close enough that I can feel his presence looming yet not touching me. Chills break out along my spine. I shiver as he orders, "Go to the window and kneel, pet."

I turn my head in objection, but he anticipates my reaction. He grabs my chin and provokes, "You will not look at me when I give you an order unless given permission. I'll take you over my knee the next time you defy me. Now, I said to go kneel."

I take a deep breath, attempt not to glare at him, and wonder why I agreed to this.

I have nowhere else to go.

That's a lie. I did it because it's Riggs.

I concede and kneel in front of the glass.

He follows me, crouches down, and instructs, "Hands folded on your lap unless otherwise instructed. Head bowed. Back straight with your butt resting on your calves."

I reposition my body and try to look at him with my peripheral vision.

"Don't do that. You'll get punished," he warns.

Frustrated, I stare at my hands, twisting my fingers.

"Stop fidgeting," he demands.

I freeze, wondering how long I'll have to stay in this position.

His shadow falls over me. He continues, "You will not speak unless spoken to, or I permit you. It includes when I touch you. Do you understand?"

I roll my eyes. "Yes."

"Yes, who?"

I sigh. "Yes, Sir."

He crouches in front of me again. "Do you think you're allowed to display an attitude toward me?"

"I'm not," I claim, turning toward him.

His eyes darken so much that it freaks me out. "Did I tell you to break your position?"

"Sorry," I add and look back at the floor.

"Sorry, who?"

I swallow more pride. "Sorry, Sir."

He leans closer, and his hot breath hits my ear. I close my eyes, trying not to shift, and he states, "You have two weeks."

"Sir?" I ask, not understanding.

"To learn proper etiquette. You will not embarrass me in public."

"Where are we going?"

"Not the right way to ask," he declares.

I stay quiet, unsure what I did wrong.

He continues, "The proper way is to ask, 'Sir, permission to ask where we are going.'"

I look up and gape at him, muttering, "You have to be kidding me."

Anger flares on his expression. "Do you think this is a joke?"

My stomach flips. I quickly answer, "No. Sorry."

"Ask me the correct way, and stay in position," he commands.

I take a deep breath, tighten my grip on my fingers, and say, "Permission to ask where we are going, Sir."

He waits a minute, then replies, "Permission not granted."

"What?" I ask, glancing up again, then quickly look back at the floor when I realize what I just did.

His tone changes as he practically sings, "Oh, Blakely, Blakely, Blakely," while tracing the edge of the collar.

I resist the urge to mimic him, wondering how I'll ever get used to this. Maybe I made a huge mistake and should tell him the deal's off and I can't do this. It's just not me.

"Don't move," he says and leaves the room.

The sound of the clock ticking is the only thing I hear. Too much time passes. My knees hurt, and I'm tired of keeping my back straight. He finally returns and holds out his hands. "Rise."

I take them, happy to stand and glad he's helping me since my knees feel locked. He leads me to the kitchen, then puts his hand on the back of my neck, murmuring in my ear, "Arms out straight, breasts and cheek on the counter."

I do as he says and shriek, "Oh my gosh, that's cold!"

He slides his hands over my arms and curls my fingers over the edge of the quartz, instructing, "You don't have permission to speak. And don't you dare move out of position." He takes his foot and pushes against my ankles until my legs spread farther apart. His warm palms caress my ass.

Zings assault me. I press my ass against his erection, wondering if this is how he'll finally take me. The sound of his belt hitting the floor echoes in the air, and I close my eyes, suddenly appreciating the contrast between the cool countertop and my hot skin.

His ripped torso hits my back. Tingles burst near my ear from his breath. One hand curls around my neck, and the other cups my pussy from behind. He locks eyes with me and murmurs, "I own you, pet."

In a normal situation, I'd get upset about that statement. But here, at this moment, with Riggs's body caged over mine, his seductive, bad-boy expression pinned on me, and his hands where they are, my brain is mush.

"Tell me I own you," he demands, slipping a finger inside me.

My breath hitches. I close my eyes and roll my hips into his palm.

He pulls his finger out of me, and a sharp sting, as hard as it sounds, erupts on my ass.

"Riggs!" I scream, my eyelids flying open.

He smacks me again, barking, "What is my name?"

"Sir!" I call out.

"Say it," he grits between his teeth, rubbing my cheek, then thrusting his finger in and out of me.

My hips automatically shift into him. I whimper and close my eyes again.

Another sharp sting bursts on my ass. I arch my back, but he's holding my neck down, keeping me against the counter.

He growls, "I didn't permit you to move any part of your body, did I?"

"No!" I cry out.

"No, who?"

"No, Sir!"

He swirls his finger on my clit, and I groan, attempting to keep still and taking more shaky breaths.

"Say it! Tell me I own you," he orders, shoving his thumb inside me and circling his finger faster.

I cave, shouting, "You own me!"

"And why do I own you?" he pushes, drilling his blue flames into me.

"I-I don't know!"

"Bullshit! Tell me, pet!"

Tears well in my eyes. "Riggs, I-I don't know!"

"Who?" he snarls.

"Sir!"

"You want to submit. To me! Admit it!" he demands, manipulating me to the point I'm about to come.

My vision turns blurry, adrenaline pools in my cells, ready to explode, and he removes his hand. He leans closer, kisses my cheek, and murmurs, "I want to hear you say it, pet. You want this because it's with me. So say it!"

It hits me like a lightning bolt, and I can't deny his statement. It's the only reason I'm here. I admit, "I want to submit to you."

His mouth pulls into an arrogant grin. His ragged breath merges with mine. His thumb slides over my forbidden zone, and I clench. He orders, "Relax."

"Riggs," I whisper, suddenly scared.

His voice turns softer. "Relax, Blakely." He pushes his pointer finger inside my pussy, swirls it against my throbbing walls, and kisses under my earlobe.

I close my eyes.

"Look at me, pet," he quietly demands.

I open my eyes, and he tilts his head, intensely watching me. He praises, "Good girl," then slides his thumb past the tight ring of muscle.

I gasp, blinking hard, arching but unable to lift off the counter due to his continued grip on my neck and torso over me.

"Shhh," he coos, then slides his thumb in farther. "Breathe, sweetheart." He demonstrates how he wants me to breathe.

I do what he says, mimicking him until I'm fully relaxed and nothing feels bad.

"Everything is okay, pet," he claims, slips another finger inside me, then slowly creates a twisting pattern.

I whimper, unsure why I'm enjoying what he's doing.

He keeps his eyes locked on me, calmly asking, "Who owns you, Blakely?"

I don't think about it and answer, "You do, Sir."

He nods. "And who do you submit for?"

"You, Sir."

"Who else?"

I try to shake my head, but it's still pressed against the quartz.

"Who else?" he gently repeats.

"No one."

"No one, who?"

"No one, Sir," I affirm.

He kisses my cheek and adds a third finger.

"Oh God!" I moan.

"Shh. No talking, pet."

I swallow hard, trying to be quiet, but it's impossible, and I whimper loudly.

"We have a lot of work to do," he claims.

I can't even contemplate what he's referring to. The sensations moving through me, I've never felt before. It's a rush of endorphins I never expected, not because I'm coming. It's from the taboo of his actions and how I want him to continue.

He removes his fingers, and I instantly feel empty. I press my ass toward him. He chuckles. "Greedy girl," he says, then slides something else into me.

I don't know what it is, but it's not his fingers. My voice cracks. "Riggs?"

He smacks my ass, and a sting spreads across my cheek. I yelp, and he says, "Who?"

"Sir!"

He warns, "The sooner you learn, the better." He rubs the sting and asks, "You're surprised, aren't you?"

I remain silent.

Cockiness flares all over Riggs. "Admit you love everything I've done to you, Blakely."

For some reason, defiance reignites inside me.

He smirks. "No? I guess I'll stop, then." He backs away from me.

"No! Wait!" I blurt out before I can even think about what I'm doing.

He purses his lips and traces the edge of whatever is inside me, commanding, "Confess you like it and don't forget the 'Sir.'"

There's no way to hide from him. I cave again, stating the truth. "I love everything you do to me, Sir."

A wicked grin appears on his lips. He licks the back of my ear and states, "It's time to practice some more things, pet."

10

Riggs

Q uestions fill Blakely's eyes, mixing with all the confusion and desire I've seen in too many other subs I've broken.

My pet's no different from the others in that regard, yet nothing about her is the same. I'm aware of it and how I'm in dangerous territory. I want to give her too much, too soon. I have urges I normally don't get until I'm in full control. And the rules I follow, I'm struggling not to break.

She's not ready.

I'll make sure she handles it accordingly.

Don't do it.

I don't normally react to flushed cheeks, potent eyes, or naiveté. Usually, it's just part of the gig. Seeing those traits on Blakely tortures me. And it's too early in the process for me to be this revved up. Now, it's causing me to make decisions I shouldn't. The moment I put my hand back on her neck to hold her down, I know better.

I slide inside her, silently cursing myself, grunting loudly. Her hot, wet, tight little cunt is more than I bargained for, and I should have had more self-control. Yet I didn't. So I continue thrusting as deep as I can until I'm fully inside her.

"Riggs!" she cries out, gripping the edge of the counter, her back arching but not much, due to how I have her pinned down.

Every time she says my name, I want to forget about the Sir rule. Then she says it, and it's another thing throwing me off and screwing with my head.

Calling me Sir has to become second nature to her. I realized within a few minutes of our engagement that I enjoyed her calling me by my name. So I cursed myself over that too.

I grit my teeth and slide backward, then forward, then do it several times, reminding her, "Sir."

"Sir," she breathes, closing her eyes and taking shallow breaths. Her walls squeeze around me, and a quiver runs through her body.

I fist a handful of her hair while still pressing on the collar, warning, "If you come on me, I'm impregnating you. So don't you dare clamp your pussy on me."

Her eyes glisten with fear and need. More tremors roll through her, and she claims, "I-I can't stop it."

"You can," I insist, knowing this is too soon in her training to expect her to have mastered it. And the pregnancy issue is real.

Her shot isn't effective for seven days. The last thing I want is a baby ruining my life.

This is beyond reckless on my part. I should stop now, but you can't get out once you get into bed with the devil. And I've officially challenged Satan.

Sweat coats our skin. I thrust harder, fully aware I'm doing it all wrong but too obsessed with how it feels to be inside her, finally taking her as mine.

Her lips tremble harder, and she begs, "Riggs! Please! I-I can't...oh...oh God!" Her eyes roll, and her walls begin spasming on my erection.

"Fuck!" I bark, slide out of her, and flip her over. I tug her to the floor, ordering, "Kneel."

She glances up at me, breathing hard.

I grab her armpits, helping her in position, and fist her hair, holding her mouth in front of my dripping-wet dick.

My chest heaves with adrenaline and chaos, matching the look in her eyes. I demand, "Swallow all of me." I nudge her head forward.

Her mouth inches around me, teasing me too slowly for the pent-up tension I've been fighting.

"Look at me," I demand, then take control, moving her head at the pace I need. She gags a few times, then gains control. I pick up the speed until I'm grunting and spewing my seed down her throat.

My little pet handles me the best she knows how, a few tears escaping down her cheek, swallowing multiple times the contents of my orgasm that seems to go on and on.

It's another thing we'll work on. Before I take her out to show her off, she'll learn to drink me without any spillage and swallow me whole.

When I'm spent, I wipe the corner of her lips, assessing her reaction. I'm at a point I should stop. It's early into our arrangement, and she's not ready for more. But I'm playing with Satan now. The rush I'm feeling is borderline crazy, and I have no more control left. I can't convince myself not to keep pushing her. It's a place a Dom should never be and one I've never been to before.

That's the thing about Blakely and why I never touched her in the past. Deep down, I knew she was different. Maybe even then, I knew I wouldn't have control over my actions.

Hatred and confusion swirl in her expression. Defiance slowly fights its way through, challenging me in my crazed state, digging deeper into my desire to push her past the limit I know I should.

"Say thank you, Sir," I demand.

She glares at me and turns toward the window, blinking hard.

I crouch down and tug her chin in front of me. "I'm waiting."

Her lips tremble harder, and her voice cracks. "Thank you, Sir."

I pick her up off the floor and sling her over my shoulder.

"Riggs!" she cries out, slapping my back.

"Stop it, pet, or there will be consequences," I threaten.

She stills but digs her nails into my ass.

I carry her to the bedroom, then place her on the bed.

She looks at me in question.

I cage my body over her, stating, "We need to work on your self-control."

"My self-control?" she questions in an angry tone.

"Were you trying to end up pregnant?" I accuse.

She gapes at me.

"I told you not to come," I hurl.

"Then you shouldn't have stuck your dick in me," she states.

My lips curl, and another wave of obsession and power rolls through my veins. I lower my voice, trying to feign that I'm in control, but I know I'm not. "When I say there's no coming, you don't disobey."

She clenches her jaw, throwing daggers at me with her eyes.

I reach for the nightstand, pull out the handcuffs, and restrain her wrists to the headboard.

She tugs on them. "Let me out, Riggs!"

"There's only one way out, pet. And you know what that is. Now either say your safe word, or put on your big girl panties," I order.

Her chest rises and falls heavier.

"No coming," I mutter and drag my tongue over her breast.

She stays quiet, other than the sound of her breaths.

I roll my finger over her clit, and she squeezes her eyes shut. I demand, "Open your eyes, Blakely."

She obeys, hardening her features.

I chuckle, enjoying how my pet has hatred all over her and directed at me. That look drives me to continue, and I kiss her neck, moving closer to her mouth. As much as I want to, I don't allow myself to break my kissing rule.

She inches forward, trying to make contact with my mouth, but I don't let her, which only frustrates her more.

I continue manipulating her body, quickly taking her to the edge, then pulling back when she's about to come, reprimanding her when she doesn't call me Sir or cries out without permission to speak.

Exhaustion wears on her face. Her body's a wet, quivering mess, but I'm just getting started. I slide my face between her thighs and taste what I've craved for years.

My tongue hits her pussy, and she lifts her hips in the air, whimpering. I take my time, slowly torturing her, licking and sucking her until she's sobbing and begging me to let her come.

It adds fuel to the fire raging inside me. I scold, "You have to learn, pet."

"Please! Riggs! I-I can't do this," she claims.

"Don't you dare come. You can do anything you want," I insist, then suck her while flicking my tongue on her clit, retreating when quivers overpower her.

I'm insatiable for her and the power she's agreed to give me over her. My cock turns hard again. I cage my frame over hers, gliding my hands through her hair, holding her face in front of mine, and thrusting inside her once again.

"Riggs, please!" she pleads.

I ignore her, kiss the curve of her neck, slowly thrust, and murmur, "You don't like me inside you, pet?"

Tiny moans fly out of her.

I bring my mouth closer, and she sticks her tongue out, grazing my bottom lip. I retreat out of her reach.

Her eyelids flutter. She whispers, "Why won't you kiss me?"

I'm so damn tempted, but I resist, ignoring her question. I pound into her until her walls clamp over me, then I pull out of her, coming on her stomach and growling, "I said not to come."

Both of us are breathing hard in the aftermath, challenging each other with our pinned gazes and a thousand thoughts plaguing us. I leave her restrained, shower, then bring a washcloth to the bed. I sit next to her and wipe my fluid off her stomach.

She doesn't look at me, and I love it and hate it at the same time. It's another way I know I'm in over my head. I'm on my way to breaking her. There should be nothing but adrenaline pounding through me right now. But for the first time ever, I do something I shouldn't.

I release her from the cuffs, tug her into my arms, and stroke her hair.

Within seconds, she begins to sob. It's a win for me, yet nothing feels further from it. Guilt eats at me. I pushed her too far, too soon. A good cry after what I put her through would be normal, but I rushed things, unable to control my demons.

"Shh. Everything is okay, pet," I calmly state. I tighten my hold around her, kissing the top of her head while her hot tears run down my chest.

She eventually quiets, the only sound being her choked-up breaths. She slowly lifts her head, locking her wet blues on mine. The tension rebuilds, and she reaches for my cheek, then tries to kiss me.

Everything crashes around me. I flip her on her side, turn away from her, and order, "Go to sleep, Blakely."

"Why won't you kiss me?" she asks in a desperate voice again.

"I said go to sleep," I repeat in a firm tone.

It's a long time until I can tell she's asleep. I never fall prey to it, and when the darkness turns to dusk, I sneak out of the room and go outside. I suit up for the waves and take my board down to the surf.

It's rougher than normal, and I spend the sunrise fighting the waves, unable to shake the look Blakely gave me. I crossed too many lines last night. I'm in new territory and need to get a grip on it before I do something I can't erase.

A wave swells, and I ride it halfway in before it violently throws me into the salty water. I fight the current and finally make it to shore, still feeling as off keel as when I first stepped foot in the tow.

I sit on the sand for at least an hour, vowing to be better and get things on track. I have to slow down. If I don't, it could backfire on me.

I make my way to the house, feeling more confident I can change the course of our arrangement. After all, Blakely doesn't know what she doesn't know. Everything is new to her. Today is a new day, and I'll back down a bit.

I strip out of my wetsuit and step under the shower. I finish rinsing my hair and open my eyes.

Blakely stands in front of me in nothing but her collar. Her expression tells me she's not okay. Emptiness fills her usually sparkling eyes.

I silently curse myself, step out of the water, and tug her into me. "What's wrong, pet?"

She tilts her face up. Her lips tremble, and tears fill her blues.

Panic shoots through me. I grab her ass cheeks, pick her up, and pin her to the wall, repeating, "What's wrong?"

She glances at my lips, swallows hard, then locks her sad gaze on mine. Her voice shakes, and she whispers, "I want you to want me."

"I do want you," I honestly declare.

Tears fall down her cheeks. She shakes her head. "You won't even kiss me."

Every rationale I have about why I don't kiss subs or how I'm moving too fast and need to back off flies out the window. My tongue wraps around hers so fast she gasps, then hers molds against mine with urgent fury.

It's once again too soon. But my control is nonexistent. She squeezes her legs tighter around my waist and lifts her hips over my erection.

As much as I want her, I can't keep risking her getting pregnant. Last night was reckless, and I promised to protect her, not ruin her life.

So it's too soon, but I tug the plug out of her ass and toss it on the ground. I reposition my cock under her cheeks and pull out of our kiss for a brief moment, pausing to wait for her to make the next move, which isn't something I'd normally ever do.

She takes a few breaths, not tearing her gaze off mine, then whispers, "Don't stop."

Another tense moment passes, then another dam breaks, washing all my thoughts about what I should or shouldn't be doing with her right now down the drain.

My lips attack hers, and as I push past her hard ridge, she sinks her hips, digging her nails into my skull, whimpering with fluttering eyelids.

I press her closer to the wall, exerting the control I should have had the previous night, thrusting at a pace she's comfortable with while slipping my thumb between us and circling her clit.

In the glow of the pink morning sky, there are no orders, or Sir, or controlling agenda. It's an animalistic urge to show her a different side of me, one that only wants her.

I barely feel the spray of the water on my back. I'm lost in her, consumed by how she clings to me, obsessed with how her tongue seems to crave mine.

I have no urges to stop her from coming. A desire to get her there and keep her there festers within me.

An earthquake explodes within her, and the tremors continue like aftershocks, as violent as the initial eruption, driving me to the point I can't continue.

Only this time, I don't retreat. I bury my head into the curve of her neck, convulsing inside her with force.

When it's over, I slowly retreat, lifting my face in front of her, firmly warning, "Don't ever doubt again how much I want you."

As the words come out of my mouth, I know I've crossed another line. Yet I'm unsure how to save myself from what's sure to be my downfall.

11

Blakely

*R*iggs washes my hair and body, then turns off the shower. He reaches for a towel, wraps it around my head, then uses another to diligently dry off every inch of my skin.

I'm still shaking, holding on to the wall so I don't lose my balance. He rises, tightens the towel around his hard frame, and avoids looking at me. He leads me into the house, steering me directly to the bathroom inside his suite, and declares, "There's a hair dryer under the sink and a comb and brush in the drawer. Help yourself." Before I can respond, he kisses the top of my head and disappears.

I find the comb, untangle my hair, then locate the dryer. It's a top-of-the-line European one, and I doubt Riggs uses it. Even the comb and brush scream they're for a woman. I peer closer at them, wondering if any other women he's been with have used them or the dryer.

Why am I worrying about this?

There's no hair on the tools, making them appear new. Relief fills me, and I turn on the dryer and don't turn it off until my locks are no longer wet.

I study my reflection, wondering if I appear any different, reminiscing about what I just did with Riggs in the shower.

Kissing him was more than I bargained for. It was an explosive mix of passion and something I've never experienced before. I can only describe it as euphoria out of control.

Our bodies fit seamlessly, proving he was right and all my worries were in vain. And he controlled every moment of it, even when he was waiting for me to sink down on him. I felt his dominance as much as I felt myself give in.

I don't know if that's the submission Riggs has been talking about, but if it is, I want more of it. Something about letting Riggs be in control feels right.

Maybe I've gone crazy. Perhaps it's his experience that gives him the right to be the one in control. Either way, I want more of him.

I stare at myself harder.

Riggs's voice flares in my head, *"Don't ever doubt again how much I want you."*

My butterflies take off again, and I take a deep breath, feeling in my heart that we've turned a corner.

Can this be real between us? Can this year-long contract just be a catalyst for our future together?

What am I doing? I need to stop these thoughts.

My face flushes, thinking about what I just did with him—something I thought I would never do with anyone.

I didn't like it.

I loved it.

Every moment of Riggs inside me, holding me close to him, kissing me like I was his possession and he couldn't get enough, was beyond my expectations. I never came close to imagining what he was capable of doing to me or how every sensation in my body would come to life in ways I didn't know were possible.

It has to be real between us.

Or is he like this with everyone?

Is being with me similar to what it's like for him to be with other women?

Muffled voices tear me out of my disturbing thoughts, which is good. I don't need to go down this road.

I leave the bathroom. Two sets of identical outfits are on the bed. One is a size six, and the other is a size eight. Each set is a designer pair of white silk shorts and a thin cashmere sweater. A delicate gold lace bra and matching thong sit next to it.

A pair of flip-flops and a pair of stilettos sit on the bed. A note is next to them.

Pet,

Which one do you think I want you in right now?
Choose wisely.

Riggs

I STARE BETWEEN THE NOTE AND SHOES, MY BUTTERFLIES KICKING off in nervousness and anticipation, unable to decide which pair to choose.

Plus, I haven't worn anything luxurious or designer since I left my father's house. Everything I buy is from thrift stores or no-return clearance racks, as I was just trying to survive in L.A.

I drag my fingers over the silk, then the cashmere, and finally the lace. I put on the size eight and leave the other set on the bed.

Which shoes?

More anxiety fills me, but a fire in my core can't be ignored. I reach for the stilettos, feeling ridiculous since we're in his beach house but wanting to feel sexier for him.

I can do this.

I can be better than anyone he's previously been with.

I step into Riggs's huge closet, perfectly organized with a row of designer suits on one side and casual clothes on the other.

I stand in front of the full-length mirror and assess myself, deciding I look hot and the stilettos are a good choice. The material of the shorts and sweater is thin, so the gold shows, but it's the current fashion trend and is meant to display a woman's undergarments and skin. I normally think see-through material looks trashy, but something about this outfit makes me feel sexy and empowered.

What will Riggs think of me in this?

I turn in the mirror and study my booty. I might be imagining it, but I swear I can see his handprint on it, with the gold separating the red marks on each cheek. I tug my shorts down and swallow hard. My heart beats faster as I assess Riggs's faint handprints and the gold lace glittering between them.

My cheeks were tender during our shower encounter. Riggs's fingers gripped me, controlling the speed of his thrusts, reminding me of how he spanked me the previous night. I loved it all. If anything, it added to my pleasure.

How can that be?

I gently touch my cheek and wince.

Why does it feel good if Riggs touches it but not me?

Men's voices break my thoughts once more. I walk out of the bedroom and freeze.

A piano sits in the corner of the room, perfectly positioned so the person playing can either view the water on the left or the living space on the right.

And it's not just any piano. It's a Heintzman & Company crystal piano. It sells for over $3 million. I know it well.

Well, I've never seen one. I've only heard about its beauty and seen it online. But it's my dream piano. I never thought I would get anywhere near one, much less be staring at one at a beachfront house I'm staying in.

Two delivery men and Riggs stand near the piano, talking, but I hear nothing. I continue gaping.

Riggs's firm voice snaps me out of my trance. He orders, "Pet, come look at your new piano."

Heat fills my cheeks. I've almost gotten used to him calling me pet. In some ways, I prefer it. The endearment makes me feel more like his. I'm unprepared to hear him call me it in front of others, and something feels unsettling about it.

He locks eyes with me as if he's waiting for me to dare to defy him.

One of the delivery guys shifts on his feet. The other ogles me, assessing my body, then stares at my collar until my cheeks are on fire.

Riggs sees it all, and his arrogant expression grows while his challenging gaze never falters. He sternly repeats, "Pet, come look at your new piano."

Wanting to get the delivery man's eyes off me, I lift my chin and step next to Riggs.

He protectively slides his arm around my waist and locks eyes with the guy who was inappropriately looking at me.

The man squirms as tension builds in the air.

"What do you think about the piano, pet?" Riggs questions, glancing down at me.

I smile, answering, "It's gorgeous."

He slides his hand on my ass cheek. "Not as much as you. Aren't I right, gentlemen?" Riggs questions, not taking his eyes off me.

Embarrassed, I hold my breath, unsure why Riggs is asking them.

Ogler blurts out, "She sure is."

Riggs's jaw twitches.

He slowly looks at the ogler, then questions the other man. "And what do you think?"

He nervously agrees, "Yes. She's very beautiful."

Approval fills his expression until he turns back to the ogler. He doesn't say anything for a few moments.

Tensions mounts, and the man looks like he's going to break out in a sweat under Riggs's dark glare.

I start to feel bad for the guy. I place my hand on Riggs's bicep and declare, "It's amazing but too much."

He waits another tense moment, then turns to me and replies, "I told you that in a year, you'll be way ahead of where you are now."

My heart swoons, and I blink hard. I'm not used to anyone supporting my dreams.

"Do you write music or just play?" the ogler asks.

Riggs's jaw twitches. In an authoritative tone, he asks, "Is there anything else you need?"

The other delivery guy clears his throat, stating, "We just need you to sign here." He pushes a clipboard in front of Riggs.

He scribbles his name and then points to the door. "Please wait outside for me. I'll be just a moment."

Confusion fills both men's faces.

"Sure," the one with the clipboard replies.

The ogler gives me a final glance and follows his co-worker outside.

Riggs steps over to the kitchen island. He reaches for a black leather notepad and crystal pen, then returns to me. "These are for you."

I run my hand over the smooth leather and open it. The left side is blank. The right has rows of staves, which are five parallel lines for drawing musical notes. I gape at it, overwhelmed.

Riggs waits for me to speak.

I finally lock eyes with him. "This is too much."

"I promised to take care of you as well as further your career," he states.

"But this...this..."

"What?" he questions.

I blurt out, "I always assumed you'd be a lot like my father."

Riggs's face hardens. He claims, "I'm nothing like him."

I add, "You're partners. I figured you have the same beliefs and would look down on my musical ambitions."

"I gave you that impression?" he seethes.

I shake my head. "No. I-I just assumed—"

"You assumed wrong, Blakely," he snaps.

I gasp, unprepared for his anger. "I'm sorry. My attraction for you should have made me realize you aren't anything like him. I didn't mean it as an insult. I'm grateful for everything. Really, I am."

His face softens, and he nods. "Fair enough."

I glance behind me at the piano, still shocked he bought it. I gush, "It really is beautiful."

He grips my shoulders and spins me toward it, tugging me against his hard body. His hot breath hits my ear, and he murmurs, "You know what's going to be even more beautiful?"

Zings fill my stomach. I tilt my head up, asking, "What?"

A sinister expression explodes across his face. His fingers trace my collar, then gracefully unclasp it. He removes it, then kisses the curve of my neck, murmuring, "Your upgrade."

"What's that?" I question, reach for his head, and slide my fingers through his thick locks, shivering from the touch of his lips.

He retreats, grabs my hand, and holds it to my stomach. I feel naked from the lack of his lips and collar.

He tosses it on the counter and dangles another one in front of me, dipping it between my breasts, then dragging the thick gold metal over each of my nipples until they're hard.

My core lights on fire. I whimper, grasping his thigh to steady myself.

He takes my hand and pins it on top of my other hand, warning, "You have a lot to learn, dear pet."

Confused, I lock eyes with him.

He orders, "Take a good look at your new collar."

I obey, studying it with curiosity. This one is more intricate, with different-sized rings around the entire band. It's at least three inches wide, whereas the other was maybe only two.

He takes my hand and moves it toward the collar, demanding, "Feel it."

I touch the rings, surprised to learn they aren't molded to the band when one lifts.

Riggs traces my jawbone, then turns my chin toward him. His dark gaze lights with fire. He asserts, "What's going to be even more beautiful is you, restrained in this, to whatever I choose, and begging me."

I swallow hard, whispering, "Begging for what?"

His lips twitch. "That depends."

Hot blood races through my veins. I dare to ask, "On what?"

He clasps the collar around my neck and spins me into him, studying me for a few moments, then finally replies, "On whether I'm punishing or pleasuring you."

My mouth turns dry, and I squeeze my thighs together. If his pleasure is like what happened in the shower, bring it on. If his punishment consists of spankings like last night, I'm more than okay with it. But I'm not telling him that.

He steps back and releases me. He picks up the notepad and pen, walks to the piano, and sets them on it. He grabs his keys and says, "Work on your music, Blakely."

I snap out of my shock, and he's almost to the door when I cry, "Wait!" I run over to him and toss my arms around his shoulders. "Thank you! It's my dream piano." I try to kiss him, but he turns his head, so my lips kiss the air. I freeze, and my stomach dives.

Why is he rejecting me?

He removes my hands from his neck and pins my wrists above my head, stretching me as far as possible. His face darkens.

I don't know what I did wrong, but my pulse creeps up, pounding harder and harder between my ears until I can barely hear the waves crashing outside, even though the slider door is open.

Riggs questions, "Did I give you permission to touch me?"

Confusion and hurt fill me. I stutter, "I-I just wanted to show you my gratitude."

Every moment that passes with him scowling makes me feel smaller and smaller.

I inquire, "Why are you acting like this?"

His features darken further. He threatens, "Don't confuse what happened outside with our agreement, pet."

Anger and frustration swirl within me. I blurt out, "What does that mean, Riggs?"

His blues turn to stone. He tightens his grip on my wrists, adding more pressure until I'm on my tiptoes. He grasps my chin with his other hand and leans into my ear, keeping his voice calm yet sharp, stating, "Review the contract if you don't understand what it means and take this as a warning. The next time you break rule seven, there will be consequences." He retreats, leering at me, assessing my reaction as if it's fun for him.

My insides quiver. How can someone be so passionate an hour ago and supportive of my dreams yet sound so hurtful?

He never flinches or releases me, as if daring me to cave and be the first to move. It continues for so long that my toes begin to ache. I'm determined not to show him any weakness, but my legs begin to wobble.

I glare at him, which only makes his sinister smile appear. He chuckles, then declares, "Your defiance will be your downfall."

"Meaning?" I seethe.

He removes his hand off my chin and drags his knuckles over my cheeks, neck, and breasts.

I shudder from the tingles erupting under his touch, reprimanding myself for responding to him.

Arrogance overpowers his features as he claims, "Every moment I give you is my choice, Blakley. I created the rules. I decide what happens here. Don't ever forget it."

My mouth turns dry.

He warns, "I assure you I'll enjoy administering your punishments as much as giving you pleasure." His lips curl tighter as he adds, "And the punishment won't be something you enjoy."

I try not to react, but the shaking in my legs gets more intense. And I'm confident by his expression that I have a horrified look on my face. How can I not?

Once again, I'm being naive. Everything was in the contract I signed and then agreed to after he made me read it all day. It's not the first time he's mentioned punishments, but would he really do something awful to me?

My curiosity about how far he would go grows.

Unable to control my balance, my body bows into his.

He circles his arm around my waist, grips the tender spot on my ass, and uses it to prop me up. He keeps my wrists in the air, not giving me any relief.

He continues studying me, as if he can see deep into my soul and read all my thoughts. It takes everything in my power not to flinch or look away.

"Ah, this is going to be more fun than I planned," he announces.

My breath hitches. I blink harder, wishing I understood every-thing he's referring to and where he's coming from on all of this.

He finally releases me and steps back. "I have work issues I need to attend to. Work on your music."

He spins and reaches for the doorknob. The door opens, and the two delivery men stand near their truck in the driveway.

I shouldn't care that he wants to leave after what he just did. I don't consider myself a clingy person. But something about him leaving after all the different exchanges we had this morning makes me panic. I blurt out, "When will you be home?"

He freezes, and his shoulders tighten. He turns his head, lowers his voice so the others can't hear, and in a stern voice answers, "When I decide."

12

Riggs

*A*nger rages inside me. It's not at Blakley. Nothing is her fault. I shouldn't have lost control in the shower and kissed her.

She's going to want more. I can already see it.

Hell, I want more, and it can't happen again. Kissing leads to attachments. The last thing I need is to take my eye off what's important, which is taking down Hugh. So no matter how much I'm attracted to his daughter, she's my secret weapon. I need to remember that at all times. And I quickly need to regain the power in this relationship.

It's why I had to call her pet in front of the delivery men. I knew it would embarrass her as well as distort her rose-colored view of what happened this morning between us.

Then there's the issue of the delivery guys. Sam gets a pass. He had the willpower not to give my pet lewd looks. On the other hand, Wayne has my wrath coming to him.

I step outside the beach house, intentionally not giving Blakely an answer she wants to hear, and head down the driveway toward the men.

Everything I felt as a child spins inside me, and the monster within me takes off his disguise. I lunge at Wayne, spinning him into the truck and restraining him to the metal with my forearm against his spine. I grab him by the hair, tugging until his face is toward the sky and he's choking for air.

"Easy!" Sam yells.

I jerk my head toward him, feeling the chaos building and knowing I'm at a point there's no calm anywhere, threatening, "Do you want to put your job in jeopardy too?"

He holds up his hands, his brown eyes widening, answering, "No, man." He takes a step back, freezing on the concrete.

It doesn't surprise me. I just bought a three-million-dollar piano, and with that comes the ability to turn men into cowards. It's a hard fact I learned early on in my career. I had just begun making money and saw how Hugh could shut people up or get them to back off by showcasing what he could buy.

L.A.'s upper echelons opened up a different world to me than I knew in Compton. In my neighborhood, street credibility came from guns or knives or fighting your way to the top of gangs. The differences in how Hugh's world worked were eye-opening yet also a hard transition. I had to learn to control my temper, not use violence, and be strategic in how I threatened others.

Most days, I have complete control over my actions. Then there are moments like these. There's a loss of all discipline, fueling a fear that I might totally snap and destroy everything I've built.

In these situations, I can barely control myself. I mix all the lessons I learned from Hugh about how to make people hurt with the ways of my past.

It's a dangerous headspace for me to dwell in, and getting out of my neurotic state as quickly as possible is vital. I know this about myself. I'm one wrong move away from ending up where most of the kids I grew up with reside.

Calling the piano store and getting this guy fired would be easy. It would keep me out of prison. But it's not enough.

Right now, I'm so unhinged from the lack of control I displayed earlier in the shower with Blakely and from watching this piece of shit have the balls to inappropriately check her out, and right in front of me, that I can't see straight.

Wayne's face morphs from red to purple. I sniff hard, reminding myself not to snap his neck off. I lean into his ear, snarling, "Do you always go into other men's houses and lust after what's theirs?"

He sputters some more, and saliva drips from the corners of his mouth.

I tug his head another inch, seething, "If you ever look at what's mine again, you're dead." I lower my voice, warning, "And let me assure you. She's mine."

"He won't," Sam vouches.

Still pissed, I shove my knee into Wayne's back, and something between a choking sound and yelp comes out of him. I glance at Sam, threatening, "If he goes near her, I'm coming after you too."

Horror fills Sam's expression.

I push Wayne into the truck harder, then step back, demanding, "Now, get off my property before I kill you." I stroll over to my Porsche and hop inside it. I make a note to call the piano store and get Wayne fired.

My car's already facing the road, and hence the front of the van. I always reverse into the driveway. Call it a habit from having to watch my back and speed away from trouble too often in my youth.

I watch Sam help Wayne into the vehicle. I rev the engine, and Sam hurries to the driver's seat, sliding in and slamming the door. He backs up onto the street and takes off.

I follow the van, then wait for the wooden gates to shut and secure Blakely from any unwelcome guests. I make my way to the office, unable to get her off my mind the entire ride.

Jesus, that outfit.

I need to give Isabella a bonus.

I picked it out of the wardrobe I brought home, thinking my pet would look sexy wearing it, but I underestimated her. The silk was so thin, I could see a hint of my palm mark on her ass. And the gold strip between her ass cheeks, knowing I was in there only a short while ago... Fuck!

And my pet isn't as naive as she wants me to believe. She wanted me to think all day about what it felt like to be inside her virgin hole. It only took one look at her during our discussion last night over the contract to know she'd never let anyone else go there. All that knowledge did was stroke my ego more.

Today, she could have worn the flip-flops, but she chose those stilettos to tease me. I know she did, and it worked. The way her ass popped just a bit higher made my dick instantly hard again.

I sit in traffic for over forty minutes at a standstill, finding the control to not stroke myself over all the images of what I plan on doing to her over the next year. When I start moving, it's as fast as a baby crawling, so it takes close to two hours to get to the office.

It's one of the curses of living in Malibu and having an L.A. office. I normally set off earlier in the morning, but I wasn't about to leave Blakely on her own with delivery men. Not that I think she'd do anything, but there are few men I trust. No one is getting near her without me present. Now that I saw how Wayne acted with me right next to her, I'm glad I made that decision. Who knows what the bastard would have tried if I wasn't there.

I pull into the parking garage, then briskly make my way through the building, still feeling tense. If I didn't have to close a big merger I've been working on all year, I'd normally go to Club Indulgence and take it out on a sub all day. Since I have my pet now, I would have stayed home and reminded her she's here to submit to me.

When I get to the top floor, my assistant Connie hands me a file and announces, "Cedcon arrived early. They're in the conference room."

I glance at my watch. It's thirty minutes before our meeting time. I snap, "Let them wait."

Connie arches her eyebrows.

Cedcon is a tech company Hugh thought I didn't stand a chance of convincing to sell. Today would normally put me in a good mood—and I never respond to Connie in that tone—but this is what happens when I'm off-kilter. I can't control the tiniest of things.

Regardless of her insulted look, I saunter past her and go into my office, shutting the door.

Tossing the file on my desk, I stand in front of the window, stare down at the L.A. chaos, and take some breaths, trying to calm myself. About ten minutes later, I'm able to glance at the folder.

I review all the merger information, go down the hall, and enter the conference room. Hugh's sitting at the head of the table, telling them how their life will change once they have our money.

Disgust fills me. I force myself to put on a happy face and say my hellos.

Hugh gives me his usual expression, which I used to take pride in. It's his order to close the deal once he finishes schmoozing. My gut churns now, when in the past, I looked forward to that expression.

We were a team, and he trusted me to take over. Now, I know the truth. I'm not only better at this than he ever was, but I also can't stand the sight of him. So I muster all the self-discipline I have to appear normal as he continues his egotistical talk.

I observe him, wanting to find some clue that he's treating me differently or a shred of uncomfortableness in his body language, but there's nothing. It only makes me beat myself up further for falling for his act all these years and trusting him.

I vow again to destroy every part of what he holds dear in his life. Then I decide he deserves to receive another picture of his princess tonight. I debate whether it should be my handprint on her ass cheek or her lips around my cock. Or maybe I'll record her begging me for mercy.

When it finally comes time for me to take over, I spend an hour on final negotiations. Our attorney edits the contracts. Their attorney reviews the changes and then everyone signs.

If I hadn't known my partner was screwing me over, I'd have the biggest hard-on in L.A. right now. This is the largest deal I've ever closed, and it's also international. The merger will attract even more clientele, and we won't be going to them. They'll be knocking on our door, which is something we used to only dream would someday happen.

Yet all I can wonder is how much of this deal Hugh's going to siphon off into his offshore accounts.

The clients leave, and Hugh slaps me on the back, booming, "We did it! Give me a few minutes, and I'll meet you at Bar Fifty-Two. I have an issue I need to handle first."

You mean I did it, you snake.

I shake my head. "Sorry, I have to get out of here in a few."

His face falls. I would have rather died in the past than let him down. The thing Hugh loves most about our business is the celebration scotch and boasting about it to all his cronies at Bar Fifty-Two. He orders, "Just one."

"Sorry. We'll catch up next week. I can't get out of my engagement tonight," I quickly add, then steer him out of the conference room and to his office. I repeat, "Next week, for sure."

"Okay, but you're buying," he states.

His comment would normally not bother me. Now, I can only think about how he's stealing from me and I'm still buying the drinks.

"Done," I say, then nod to two security guys, Roy and George.

"My office," Hugh demands in a firm voice.

The hairs on my arms rise. Why is he pissed at them?

Something tells me to stick around. I grab the door handle, motion for everyone to go inside Hugh's office, and declare, "Nice work, Hugh."

"You too," he replies, then orders Roy and George to sit.

I shut the door but leave it open with a slight crack.

Hugh seethes, "How did you let her escape?"

"We got a flat tire, boss," Roy explains.

"She jumped out the back of the SUV. We followed her, but damn, she's fast," George adds.

Hugh bellows, "Morons! I should fire you now."

Silence fills the room.

Hugh asks, "Where did you lose her?"

"She went into a club. The bouncer wouldn't let us in," Roy declares.

It's like fuel pouring over my rage. I've heard all I need to. It's clear these two are the ones who kidnapped Blakely.

I leave the building and get into my Porsche. I call Chainsaw.

He answers, "Riggs. I should have some news later tonight."

I state, "Hurry up. When you get done, there's a deuce for you."

He chuckles. "I see you're making lots of friends these days."

"Yep. Speed it up," I reiterate and hang up. Snake's going down, but so are Roy and George.

I leave the parking garage and head toward Malibu, anxious to get home to Blakely, but a few minutes in rush hour traffic makes me realize I'm still too out of control. And all I can envision is the new affection she had in her eyes for me when I left her to dry her hair in the bathroom.

Every part of me craves to see more of it. Yet I need to avoid it. At least for now. It's time to refocus. The event at the club is right around the corner.

I mentally go through my schedule to think about what I can push out, but there are too many large deals on the table.

I need reinforcements.

I pick up the phone and call one of my former subs, Aria. I broke her in years ago. She's helped me with a few of my subs in the past.

The phone rings twice, and she coos, "Riggs. Long time."

"Aria, how've you been?" I question.

"I can't complain. You?"

"Good. I need your assistance."

She laughs. "Of course you do. Why else would you call."

"Guess I'm predictable," I claim.

Aria takes a deep breath, which makes me smile. She's like an open book to me after our time together. Every ounce of air she takes displays a different emotion, and this one has pure adrenaline in it. She inquires, "The woman you bid on?"

"Yes."

"When do you want to meet?" she asks.

Calmness enters me. Getting some assistance to train Blakely while I'm at work is the best idea I've had all day. Aria is the best at what she does. She's never let me down with any previous subs.

Since I bought Blakely at the auction, I have to prove she's fully submitted to me at the two-week mark, or the club will revoke our contract. They'll give an apartment to her in the city. It'll be in a discreet location the club chooses for the remainder of the contract period.

The fine print of the club's paperwork states that Club Indulgence has the final say over everything. It's in the members' contracts and the subs who go up on the auction block. Since Blakely didn't even bother to look at my contract until I forced her to, I doubt she paid attention to the details, not that it's clear what it means.

It's why rule fourteen is in my contract. The one Blakely was fretting over. Every Dom must have it in his contract, as well as rule five stating a safe word, and rule twelve about basic needs being provided for by the Dom. The rest of the rules the club allows the Dom to create. And while I added language to rule five, it was approved by the board when they reviewed my contract.

The mandatory rules ensure subs are being taken care of properly and sever the relationships that aren't working.

So while I told Blakely not to worry about rule fourteen because it's off the table, I was telling a half-truth. It won't be due to my boredom if it gets enacted, but if she doesn't fully submit when it's time to present her to the club, I won't have a choice.

And I'll be damned if I allow that to happen.

I ask Aria, "Can you meet tonight?"

She chirps, "Sorry. I have a date."

"Cancel it. I'm on a timeline. And I need you to stay until she's ready. Please," I add.

Another moment of silence passes.

"Aria—"

"Well, don't beg me. It's not becoming of you, Riggs," she teases.

"You know what the rules are, Flower," I remind her.

"Oh, not fair! You know I still get weak-kneed when you call me that," she scolds.

I chuckle. Flower was the nickname I gave Aria. I assert, "Then say yes to tonight, and you'll hear more of it."

"Ugh. Riggs, I like this guy," she whines.

"Bring him. I'll train him for you," I offer.

Another moment passes, and she lowers her voice, confessing, "He's not in the lifestyle."

My pulse pounds quicker. Aria and I are good friends. There's nothing between us except that, and I care about her well-being. I claim, "You know that'll never work."

She groans. "Things change. People can change."

"No. That's not how our lifestyle works. You'll get bored."

"I won't. He's a really great guy!"

I reprimand, "Aria, you can't go backward."

The line turns silent again.

She says, "Riggs, he's different."

"Then you have to convert him," I declare.

"He says he isn't into it."

"Then dump him," I order.

"No."

"Flower, I'm trying to look out for you," I state, then veer left to avoid a semi.

Horns blare, and I give the driver my middle finger. And I'm frustrated with this entire conversation. I can't risk losing my pet, and Aria will realize after tonight there's no backtracking into old lifestyles once you're in ours. So I use my most commanding voice, demanding, "Loverboy will wait. Tonight, Flower."

She sharply inhales, then stays quiet.

I can imagine her squeezing her thighs together and lightly scratching her neck. And this is exactly why she can't be with a vanilla-sex guy. She needs a Dom. One firm order, and I know I have her, but I still question, "Is that a yes?"

She sighs. "Okay, but you owe me."

"But you love reminiscing so much," I remind her.

She snorts. "Don't push it. Apartment Thirteen?"

I grin. "Always. And bring your stud. Let him learn."

"Hard pass," she says.

"Suit yourself. I need blueish-purple highlights put in your hair, and call Isabella. Tell her to rush over the gold heels and lingerie I bought the other day. Wear it tonight. I'll send a driver around six." I hang up and continue to deal with the traffic. I crack my window but within seconds shut it when the smog seeps into my Porsche.

I almost call Blakely but stop myself. It's too soon for her to hear from me. She needs to wonder what I'm doing and when I'm returning.

When I get to Malibu, I roll the windows down and turn the volume up. I get to my driveway, open the gate, and reverse in.

For several moments, I sit in the car, fighting the adrenaline pooling in my cells over the thought of seeing my pet. I remind myself of several things.

I must retain full control over Blakely at all times.

Real submission can only be achieved after one has been broken into pieces and put back together.

Everything must be earned. I'm not entitled to anyone, including Blakely. It all has to be her choice, but she'll have to demonstrate it, or our journey will end before it begins.

13

Blakely

*B*lank pages stare back at me. I've played all the songs I've written in the past on the new piano and belted out the lyrics, trying to find some inspiration, yet nothing comes.

All I can think about are the moments I've spent with Riggs. I even went for a walk on the beach, trying to decipher why he acted like he did before he left.

It didn't help. If anything, I'm more confused about his erratic behavior. What happened between us in the shower should have brought us closer. Now the wedge is between us again.

I'm trying to understand his motivation, but nothing makes sense. And as much as I want to let it go, I'm obsessed with trying to figure it out, which isn't helping me write any new lyrics.

It's almost six when I realize I never called my employers. I cringe and pick up the phone, calling the lounge first.

"Lizard Lounge," Jarrod answers.

I squeeze my eyes shut, knowing I'm about to hear his wrath. I reply, "Hey, Jarrod. It's Blakely."

"Where are you? You're up in five minutes," he frets.

Guilt eats at me. Jarrod was the first lounge manager to give me a real shot. I hate doing this, but I have no choice in my current circumstances. I inform him, "I'm so sorry, Jarrod, but I had an emergency. I'm out of town and won't be back for a while."

"What? You aren't serious," he says.

I tap my fingers on my thighs, wincing. "I'm sorry, but I am."

"You couldn't call sooner?"

"I'm sorry, but no. I didn't have a phone," I lie.

"Since when?" he snaps.

I decide there isn't a way to stop him from being angry with me, and it's best to end this call. I declare, "I really am sorry. I have to go. Thank you for all you've done for me."

"Wait! When are you—"

I hang up and stare out the window. The day begins to morph into the night, and the sky is a beautiful pink, glowing in the fading light. My heart continues racing.

Get it over with.

I force myself to call Cheeks and ask for Savannah.

"Where did you go the other night? Are you okay?" she answers.

I cringe again. She's another person I've never wanted to let down. I should have called yesterday. I never thought about how she would worry. I assure her, "I'm fine. But I have to quit."

Her voice turns into a mix of shock and a snarl. "Excuse me?"

"I'm really sorry. I had an emergency and won't be in town for a long time," I tell her.

"What kind of emergency?" she interrogates.

My chest tightens. I tap harder on my thigh, replying, "I can't get into it. Thank you for our time together."

"Blakely, you can't just—"

I hang up, knowing there's nothing further I can say. Then I pace around the living area, struggling with guilt.

Riggs walks in, asking, "What's going on, pet?"

Relief hits me that he's here, taking me by surprise. I'm an independent person, so why do I keep feeling this when he returns?

He doesn't give me time to process it, closing the space between us. The scent of woodsy spice laced with orange peels flares in my nostrils, calming me while stirring the deepest part of my core. He slides his palm on my cheek, arches his eyebrows, and questions, "Blakely?"

I admit, "I forgot to call my employers earlier. I just did."

"And?"

"I feel horrible for not giving them more notice and letting them down."

He claims, "They'll be fine."

"But—"

He puts his fingers over my lips, asserting, "It's over. They'll figure it out. That's life. Now, come with me." He takes my hand and leads me to the front door.

"Where are we going?"

"To the city."

Nerves fill me. I blurt out, "I don't want to go there. I'm safe here."

He freezes and assesses me. Tension builds, and he cuts through it, questioning, "Do you think I would let anyone hurt you?"

I swallow hard, answering, "No."

"Do you believe I'd let anyone near you who I didn't deem harmless to your well-being?"

I shake my head. "No."

He picks up my hand and kisses it, declaring, "Then you have nothing to worry over. Let's go, pet." He returns to guiding me out of the house and to the passenger side of his Porsche. He opens the door.

I get in, and he shuts the door, then goes around the car and slides next to me, turning on the car. He reaches toward the roof and presses a button. The wooden gates at the end of the driveway open, and he pulls out.

"Why are we going to the city?" I inquire.

His lips twitch. His voice lowers, creating a mysterious yet alluring tone, sending a shiver down my spine. He answers, "You'll see."

I bat my eyelids, slide my hand on his thigh, and lean closer, whining, "Aw, no clue?"

His jaw clenches. He removes my hand, puts it on my lap, and asserts, "Rule seven. And rule two goes into effect as of now. But I can't keep giving you passes, pet. Since we're driving, slide your hands behind the seat and lace your fingers together."

I gape at him. "You have to be kidding. There's barely any room between the door and seat."

"No, I'm not. And you'll fit. Now, don't make me repeat myself. And what did you forget when you addressed me?" he demands.

My gut dives. It's as if everything that happened this morning between us was all in my head. The only Riggs here is the one who needs to be in full control. I huff, then say, "Sir."

"That's right. Now, get in position," he orders.

I tilt my head and glare at him. This is the most ridiculous thing I've ever heard. And what's the point of making me do it?

He pulls the car to the side of the road and slams the gear into park. I gasp as he tugs my chin to face him. In an eerily calm voice, he asks, "Is this not for you, Blakely?"

"Wh-what?"

"The terms we agreed upon. Are you unable to fulfill your end of the deal?"

The hairs on my arms rise. Rule fourteen flashes in my mind, and I panic. "I never said that!"

He studies me until my eyes start to water and I'm blinking hard to stop it from spilling over. I don't want him to toss me aside, nor am I prepared to leave him right now.

In a serious tone, he warns, "If you're unable to stick to our contract, and you can't demonstrate to the club that you've submitted to me, they'll enact rule fourteen."

The air in my lungs turns stale. A quiver erupts in my belly, growing more powerful every second. I blurt out, "What are you talking about?"

He doesn't flinch. "All auctioned subs and buying Doms must demonstrate at the two-week mark their relationship. If you cannot submit to me, they will move you to an undisclosed location for the remainder of the contract period."

Horror fills me. "That's not in the contract I signed!"

"It's on the paperwork you signed with the club," he informs me.

I look away, trying to remember what was on it.

"Did you read it?" he questions.

I squeeze my eyes shut, stuttering, "It-it was chaotic. I-I had my father's men chasing me."

He replies, "It's simple. Members sign that the club is in charge, and so did you. Rule fourteen is in all the contracts for the safety of the subs. It appears to be for the Doms, but it's not. So if you cannot do what you're supposed to, this ends between us. I'll have no choice in the matter."

I glare at him. My voice shakes as I ask, "So that's it? I'll be their prisoner for the rest of the year, and you'll go on with your life like normal?"

"No. You aren't their prisoner. They'll put you in an apartment in the city where I don't know the location. You'll be free to do what you want, but there will be no more communication between us."

My mouth turns dry. No more talking, seeing, or touching Riggs. Do they really have that much control over the situation?

"I won't break their rules, pet. It's a strictly enforced policy. Again, it's protection for the subs."

"Why? What would happen that's so bad?"

His face softens. He answers, "Anything can happen. They're in danger if a sub isn't with the right Dom."

I lift my chin. "And do you think you're the right Dom for me?"

Darkness erupts in his expression. He pins his eyes on me, declaring, "I know I'm the right one. But it's up to you if you want to stay with me. So, in a couple of weeks, you'll prove it, or that'll be it. And once you're gone, Blakely, there's no coming back to me. That's it."

It's a statement mixed with relief and cruelty. He thinks he's right for me, yet he's making it clear that we're done once this arrangement ends. I stay silent, trying to process the finality of not seeing him again.

Now that Riggs is back in my life, I don't want him to disappear again, even though I signed knowing this is only for a year. But the thought of having to separate in less than two weeks...

He swipes a tear from my cheek and reiterates, "This is your call, pet. If you want to stay with me, you must fall into your role."

My reality hits me. I slowly sit back and slide my arms around the seat, lacing my fingers together.

His voice stays firm. "Good girl. Now bow your head."

I take a breath and obey.

"Who are you going to obey?"

The defiant part of me wants to tell him to go fuck himself. But the thought of being ripped away from him stops me. I reply, "You, Sir."

He studies me. I can feel it. He finally puts the gear into drive, and the car moves forward.

It's hard to stay silent with your hands laced behind the seat and your head bowed in a moving vehicle. Riggs shows me no mercy, veering lanes often and speeding whenever possible. The sound of horns erupts several times, and I fight the urge to break my position.

Time isn't my friend, and it seems to go slowly. My limbs begin to hurt. Right when I feel like I can't do this anymore, the car comes to a stop. "Punishment over. You may release your position," Riggs says.

I lift my head first, take a deep breath, and slowly move my arms to my lap. We're at a stoplight, and I realize it's an L.A. expressway exit. I glance at the clock.

Fifty-two minutes he kept me in that position.

Asshole.

"We'll be there in a few minutes," he announces.

I study the landscape, trying to figure out what part of the city we're in, but I can't. It's dark, and the only thing I'm sure of is that this isn't a neighborhood I want to be in alone.

Riggs races through town and then pulls into a parking garage. He places his palm on a screen and a set of concrete walls opens. He steers through them, and they shut behind us.

Whatever we're in moves up. Darkness is everywhere, except for the glow of the dashboard. A nervous apprehension fills me.

"Relax," Riggs demands.

I exhale, wondering how he knows I'm anxious.

The box comes to a halt. A new set of concrete doors open and four parking spots appear. Riggs selects one, reverses into the space, and turns off the car.

I reach for the door.

"Stop," he orders.

I turn my head toward him and freeze.

He declares, "You don't ever get out of the car unless I tell you to or I open your door. Understand?"

I try not to glare at him but must fail.

He shakes his head. "That right there is going to be your downfall."

"What would that be?"

"Sir. 'What would that be, Sir,'" he reprimands.

I smirk. "Sorry. What would that be, Sir?"

His eyes turn to slits. "Maybe I should call you brat instead of pet."

"I'm not a brat," I claim.

"You're acting like one."

"No, I'm not."

"Did you not learn any lessons from your punishment?" he threatens.

I take a deep breath and resist rolling my eyes. The punishment was doable, but I don't care for another, so I answer, "I did, Sir."

He waits another moment, then adds, "Chivalry isn't dead, but I'm sure you think it is after the boys you dated. Don't ever open that door by yourself again unless instructed." He gets out of the Porsche and comes to my side. He opens the door and reaches in for me.

I take his hand and step out.

He keeps me close to his side, leads me to the wall, and presses his hand on another screen. A metal door opens. We go into a small hallway. It has the same security protocol.

"A bit paranoid?" I mutter.

His body tenses.

I add, "Sir."

He glares at me.

I feel small under his disapproval. I square my shoulders and lift my chin, trying not to appear intimidated.

He seethes, "Maybe if you had taken some precautions, you wouldn't have been in the presence of your father's men."

I don't speak, unable to deny his statement.

"There will never come a time when I won't take all measures to ensure your safety. Remember that," he scolds, then places his hand on the screen.

Another set of metal doors opens, and the L.A. skyline lights up against the darkness outside of the floor-to-ceiling windows. He grabs my hand, steering me into the room.

Black leather furniture fills the space. Candles flicker, creating a soft glow. Soft music plays at the perfect volume, not too loud and not too soft.

"Where are we?" I ask.

He arches his eyebrows.

"Sir," I add.

The same expression I saw on him the previous night appears on his face. Goose bumps break out on my skin. He answers, "Apartment Thirteen."

"Which is...?"

He looks at me with disapproval again.

I quickly fix my error. "Sir. Which is what, Sir?"

He takes a deep breath, filling his lungs with fresh air and making his pecs look more powerful. He steps forward, closing the gap between us, and drags his knuckles up my waist, over my breast and neck. He traces my jaw.

Butterflies flood my stomach, fluttering so fast, I reach for his chest to steady myself and realize his heart's beating faster.

He covers my hand with his palm, stares at my lips, then drags his gaze to mine. He answers, "Where you'll stay until you prove your submission to me at the club."

"You're leaving me here on my own?" I fret.

He grunts, then twists a thick lock of my hair around his fist. "No. You'll always be with your trainer, myself, or both of us."

Blood pumps hard between my ears. My voice cracks as I ask, "My trainer?"

Something flares in his eyes, scaring me. It's arrogant, challenging, and something darker than normal. The quivering reignites in my belly with full force, matching the racing of his heartbeat.

His firm voice declares, "I suggest you focus on the end goal. There's no time to waste, Blakely. Starting tonight, commit to throwing yourself into this lifestyle, become the perfect little pet I know you're capable of, and eliminate all the boundaries that keep you from submitting to me."

"Boundaries?" I question.

He tugs my head back an inch, leaning closer to my mouth. His hot breath hits mine, and my mouth waters. He answers, "Your defiance. The self-limiting beliefs you have about what's plea-surable and what's painful. All the things you believe are taboo and even wrong. Let go of questioning things when I give you orders. Accept that your body and mind want to follow me blindly, so much it's an inherent need deep inside your soul. And give in to the fact I own you. Nothing is yours without my approval, and that includes your orgasms, your reactions, and even certain thoughts."

Panic fills me as his statement sets in. His wishes aren't possible. There's no way everything he wants can be achieved. I'm not a robot waiting for him to give me directions.

He softly chuckles, but it's just another challenge. He adds, "You're going to hate me, then love me, then hate me some more. When you get to the club, you'll be so confused over your feelings about me, you won't even know what's about to happen. And it'll be at that moment that you have to decide. Whatever you tell yourself you'll do, you won't be able to count on. That I can promise you."

I don't need a few weeks to pass. I'm already confused over his claims. And I'm starting to get more freaked out.

He releases my hair, steps back, and orders, "Take your shirt and shorts off."

I hesitate.

He crosses his arms, and his face hardens.

I obey, and he takes them, then puts them on a table and steps back in front of me.

Satisfaction fills Riggs's expression. He commands, "Flower. Come kneel."

Flower?

Shock fills me as a woman close to my height, with the same-colored hair as mine and matching blueish-purple highlights, enters the room. She's wearing the same gold thong, bra, and stilettos as me. Her body isn't quite as curvy as mine, and it's hard not to compare us.

She kneels at Riggs's feet, her spine perfectly straight, her butt on her calves, and her head bowed. She folds her hands on her lap and waits.

He crouches and lifts her chin, studying her.

My stomach churns. I told Riggs no others. I meant it. I'm not okay with this. I will not share him.

"Say hello and introduce yourself to Blakely," Riggs states.

She turns her head and smiles, but not before I see the look she gives Riggs. She respects him. She responds to him. She might even love him. Most of all, she trusts him. Completely. I see it.

Her soft voice is friendly, but I already hate her. She offers, "Hi, Blakely. I'm Aria."

I glare at her, fighting the angry earthquake ready to break inside my body.

"What do you say in return, pet?" Riggs questions.

I turn my rage to him, my emotions spinning out of control. Violent tremors fill me, along with more anger and jealousy than I've ever felt. They have a relationship. It's sexual and intimate, and I'm sure she knows how to please him way more than I do. It makes every insecurity I have about my lack of knowing what Riggs needs come to life.

"Don't be shy," Riggs orders.

I keep my eyes pinned on his and snarl, "You're right. I hate you."

A sinister smile curves his lips, mocking me. He steps forward and caresses my cheek, taunting, "Welcome to Apartment Thirteen."

14

Riggs

$\mathcal{M}$ y pet's anger blazes off her, searing into me. Her lips quiver, and she keeps her glare pinned on me.

Her reaction doesn't shock me. I'd be disappointed if she didn't react this way. I know how she feels about involving others in our relationship. I intentionally had Aria dye her hair and wear the outfit to match Blakely's. It's all part of drawing out my pet's insubordination.

She lowers her voice and seethes, "I told you no other women."

Arrogance explodes inside me. I couldn't have predicted this any better. I keep my gaze on Blakely and boom, "Who's in charge, Flower?"

Blakely's hatred grows in her expression, her cheeks turning redder.

Aria answers, "You are, Sir."

I question, "Who decides what happens and with whom at all times?"

"You, Sir."

"Why would I bring someone else into my relationship?" I question, continuing not to flinch under Blakely's death glare.

Aria replies, "For the well-being of your sub, Sir."

"Because...?"

She adds, "They need it, Sir."

I step closer to Blakely and ask Aria, "Am I a Dom who plays around?"

Aria says, "No, Sir."

I continue, "Who is my focus on?"

She answers, "Your current sub."

Blakely's lips tremble harder. She blinks fast, trying to control her emotions, but never tears her gaze off mine.

"Flower, are you my current sub?" I ask.

"No, Sir."

"Who's my current sub?"

"Blakely," Aria answers.

"That's right. So who is my focus on?"

"Blakely."

"And why are you here?"

Aria claims, "To help train Blakely."

I slide my thumb over my pet's trembling lips, asking Aria, "Why?"

"So rule fourteen doesn't get enforced," Aria declares.

Blakely shuts her eyes. A tear escapes, and I watch it roll down her cheek. I swipe over her jaw, wiping it away, and she opens her eyelids.

I lean into her ear and murmur, "You need to learn. I want you with me for the year. Do you still want that?" I retreat and study her.

Her defiance swirls with her desire to stay with me. She stays quiet.

I warn, "There's only one answer here, pet. There are no do-overs. Now, I asked you a question, don't make me repeat it."

She takes two short breaths, her nostrils flare, as she manages to get out, "Yes. I want to stay with you."

"Yes, who?"

Her glare returns to hatred.

I wait.

She spews, "Yes, Sir."

I put my hand on her cheek, wait a few moments for her to calm down, then spin her so her back is against my chest. I slide my hand on her stomach and demand, "Do you see how she kneels?"

Blakely nods.

"Answer me with words at all times," I instruct.

She swallows hard, then exhales loudly. "Yes, Sir."

I hold her closer to me, move her hair over her shoulder, and kiss the curve of her neck. She grips my thigh with her palm. I move it to her stomach and murmur, "Rule seven, pet."

Her body stiffens.

I kiss her neck again, then tug her hair until she faces the ceiling. My lips brush the side of hers as I remind her, "There are rewards and punishments. It's up to you what you get. Now, go kneel next to Aria." I kiss her on the cheek, squeeze her ass, then release her.

She hesitates, pinning her hatred-filled glare on Aria.

"Now," I reiterate.

She finally caves and takes her position, replicating Aria.

My erection twitches. It's almost like having two Blakelys, even though I know it's not. And I'm aware that once Aria looks up, the resemblance will be gone.

I drop my pants, step out of them, but keep my boxers on. Then I remove my shirt. I add my clothes to the pile where Blakely's are, then take a few extra moments to stare at the women kneeling in front of me, heads bowed, waiting for my commands.

I crouch in front of Aria and decide there's no point in easing Blakely into this. She's too defiant and has a long way to go to be ready for the club. I tilt Aria's chin, and the resemblance to my pet disappears just like I knew would happen. My cock softens. It makes me wonder how I used to keep it so hard for all the months I was with Aria, but nothing compares to my pet. Having the two so close together, there's no fooling my cock. I ask, "What do you want for your reward tonight, Flower?"

Blakely's head snaps toward me.

I don't look at her but can see from my peripheral vision. I say to Aria, "Excuse me. I need to deal with disobedience."

The wild look in her eyes grows deeper. I've seen it too many times not to recognize it, and it worries me. She's been away from the lifestyle too long, doing whatever she's doing with this guy she's seeing. I make a mental note to talk to her about letting me train him. I know almost everything there is to know about Aria, and her need to submit isn't a thing she does for fun. It's part of who she is and trying to go backward will only destroy her.

I know from personal experience. Once you've sunk your toes into this lifestyle, there's no returning to a vanilla world.

I rise, and she lowers her head. I ask, "Aria, would you like to be part of the process?"

She meets my eye and breathily answers, "Yes. Please, Sir."

I smile and stroke the top of her head, nodding. "You may take part."

"Thank you, Sir," she states, as if in relief.

I step in front of Blakely and crouch down. She continues glaring at me, and I ask, "Flower, we need to sort something first. Tell me what my pet did wrong."

On cue, Aria answers, "Rule one. She broke her position without your permission, Sir."

"And what happens if a sub does that?" I stroke Blakely's cheek, which twitches under my touch.

Aria replies, "It's a punishable offense, Sir."

"That's right." I rise and reach for Aria, pulling her onto her feet so she's in front of Blakely. I pat Aria's ass and order, "Go into the playroom."

She smiles and leaves the room. I stare at her backside, not because I'm more interested in it than Blakely's but just to make her angrier.

My pet blinks hard and looks away. I hold my hands out, and she refuses to take them.

I command, "When I hold my hands out, you take them."

She stays frozen, except for her quick blinks.

"Your punishment is increasing," I threaten.

She meets my eye with a fresh stream of anger. She whispers, "Please don't do this."

I crouch down, tilt her head, and drag my knuckles over her cheek. "Don't do what, pet? Don't train you? Don't do everything in my power to keep you as mine?"

She closes her eyes.

I lean into her ear and assert, "This only works if you trust me. And listen. It's clear you've not heard a word I've said since we got together."

She inhales sharply, puts her hand on my arm, and insists, "I have."

"Have you?"

"Yes!" she cries out.

I shake my head. "In the last minute, you've broken rules one, two, and seven. And if you trusted me, nothing about this situation would bother you. You'd know that every action I take is carefully constructed for your benefit."

"This is cruel," she claims.

"Cruel is what happens if I lose you. And that will be your choice. Now, I'm going to rise. Decide if you're going to learn or if we should stop everything now. If you want to quit, I'll turn you over to the club and you'll remain under their protection until the year is up. You won't have to worry about your father or his men. You have my word. But I'll be damned if I take you to the club in a few weeks unprepared," I threaten and stand tall.

A moment passes, and I hold my hands out.

She hesitates, then slowly takes them.

"Good girl," I praise and pull her to her feet.

She sniffles.

I wipe her cheeks and question, "Do you remember what I asked Aria?"

Blakely pins her eyebrows together as if confused.

"Let me remind you. I'm not a Dom who plays around, pet. What I do, I do for you because you need it. Now, dig down and find that trust you had for me the night you signed an unread contract after I told you I'd own you."

She takes a few deep breaths, straightens her shoulders, and lifts her chin.

Pride sweeps through me. She's perfect in so many ways. Her confidence at this moment, whether she knows she has it or not, is something I've rarely seen. "Good girl," I commend her and give her a peck on the lips.

She tries for more, but I retreat, guiding her down the hall and into the playroom.

She gasps when we step inside.

I freeze, letting her take in the numerous pieces of sex furniture, wall of toys, floggers, paddles, and different restraints, as well as the fourteen-ringed, steel St. Andrew's Cross. Her eyes grow wider, and a flush creeps into her cheeks until her gaze rests on Aria, who's in the kneeling position in the middle of the room, head bowed. Blakely's body tenses again.

I slide my hand on her ass and murmur in her ear, "This time, learn from your punishment."

She looks at me in question.

I grip her waist, turn my head toward Aria, and boom, "Go pick a flogger, Flower."

Aria lifts her head, her green eyes practically glowing, and rises. She walks to the wall and chooses a black flogger, putting it next to her nose and deeply inhaling. The long, full-grain buffalo leather tassels are perfect for inducing different sensations. It doesn't surprise me she chose it. It's her favorite. She spins and waits.

I move Blakely behind the St. Andrew's Cross.

Her eyes widen, and she stares at me.

I command, "Spread your legs and arms so they're in line with the metal."

She arches her eyebrows.

"Flower, what are the only two correct answers?" I question.

"Yes, Sir. Or, thank you, Sir," she states.

"Let's try this again, pet. Spread your legs and arms so they're in line with the metal," I repeat.

Blakely's jaw twitches. She quietly says, "Yes, Sir," and obeys.

My cock hardens. I stare at the thin gold material across her back and between her ass cheeks. Her pale skin, flush against the metal, is just a bonus. I rip my gaze off her, grab four cuffs, and restrain her to the cross. I move her hair over her right shoulder, drag my knuckles down her spine, then stroke the thin lace over her slit.

She shivers, and her breath hitches. Goose bumps break out on her skin.

I murmur in her ear, "Say thank you to Aria for volunteering to help you."

Her jaw clenches.

I grab the crotch of her thong and tug, ripping them off her.

"Riggs!" she screeches, her back arching into my torso.

I grip her chin and turn her head to the side, demanding, "Who am I?"

"Sir!" she cries out.

I release her and repeat, "Say thank you to Aria."

She takes loud breaths, refusing to obey.

I slide two fingers inside her.

She bucks into my hand, her walls clenching around my digits.

I slowly thrust, taking my other hand and tugging her head back, ordering, "Say it."

Her expression hardens, her chest rises and falls faster, and her cheeks turn redder.

I step to the side of her, keep thrusting my fingers, and slap her ass so loud it echoes in the room.

"Oh!" she cries out.

"Oh, who?" I shout, add a third finger, and slap her again.

"Sir!" she shouts.

I spank her until both her cheeks are red, her arousal drips down my hand, and she's shaking so hard her knees buckle.

I inhale her sea salt and driftwood scent and rub her ass, sliding my fingers in front of her face, ordering, "Suck."

She glances at me with her watering blues, her lips part, and I shove my digits past her teeth.

"Suck, my little pet," I taunt. "Be a good girl and show Flower how much you love the taste of your pussy."

Her eyes dart toward Aria as if she forgot she was there. She moves her head back as if to escape my fingers, but I'm behind her. There's nowhere to go, and all she can do is continue to suck.

Aria's eyes glow like an animal's in the dark. The flogger shakes in her hand, and her eyes slowly move from Blakely's mouth to my gaze, silently pleading.

This is why she can't return to the world of vanilla. I know what Aria needs more than she does. I thought she'd come to accept who she was and what she needed, but I guess she still has some inner work to do.

"Watch and learn, pet," I demand, then pull my fingers out of Blakely's mouth. I move toward Aria and hold my hand out.

She hands me the flogger.

I order, "Take your position."

Like a good little sub, she chooses the bench in front of the cross. She lies on it so her face is toward Blakely. She puts her hands on the legs, and I cuff them. Then I cuff her ankles to the back ones. I crouch in front of her, tuck her locks of hair behind her ears, and lower my voice so Blakely can't hear. "Remember this when you think of this guy you're seeing. This isn't something you can deny anymore."

She shuts her eyes and takes a deep breath.

"Flower."

She locks her tormented gaze on mine.

"Bring him into the life," I state.

She bites her lip and blinks hard.

"Tell me why I should do this to you," I demand.

She looks at me in surprise.

"I want to hear it, Flower."

She licks her lips, then her voice cracks. "I need it."

I decide it's enough for now. I stroke her cheek. "Okay, then."

She lets out a breath, as if she's releasing some sort of pent-up suffering. But I don't doubt she has been. I know Aria's past and what she's been through. I understand why she can't escape her submissive or masochistic tendencies.

I rise and step behind her. I glance at Blakely, whose looking at me in horror. I order, "Flower, what do good girls get?"

"Rewards, Sir."

"Have you been good?"

"Yes, Sir."

"Would you like your reward?"

"Please, Sir," she begs, her voice laced with pain.

I run my hand over her ass cheeks several times, notice Blakely clench her jaw, and keep my hand there longer than I normally would.

"Please, Sir," Aria whispers so quietly I barely hear her.

It tugs me out of my obsession with Blakely. That's the issue with working two subs at once. You have to keep both their needs in mind, and it's easy to get lost in one, which can hurt the other. I step back, raise the flogger in the air, and smack it on Aria's ass.

"Ugh...thank you, Sir," she says.

Blakely's eyes widen.

Knowing what Aria needs, I give her ten strong lashes in a row, watching her body language and listening to changes in her voice. I go to the drawers, select a bullet, and stand above her. I lock eyes with Blakely and state, "The duality of pain and pleasure morph together more than we know in life, becoming one highly charged emotion. You, Aria, even me, we can't escape it." I turn the vibrating feature on and slide the bullet under Aria's panties and into her body.

She moans, then adds, "Thank you, Sir."

Emotions flare on Blakely's face. I've never had a sub show so much jealousy over me touching another sub. Yet I also see the curiosity budding, and I know I've finally made some progress.

I remind myself Aria's in a vulnerable position. I return to my role and resume flogging her. After five slaps, I yell out, "Don't you dare come, Flower."

"Please, Sir!" she cries out, which surprises me. She normally can take more before she begs. It tells me that it's been too long since she had a release.

"No," I reply, knowing the longer she fights it, the more intense it'll be for her. Plus, Blakely needs to see what's possible...what she has to learn to do.

I flog her three more times, and Aria shrieks, "Please, Sir!" Her tears drip on the wood floor, pooling under the bench. Sweat coats her skin in tiny beads.

Blakely studies it all, her eyes darting between us like she can't decide where to focus.

"Pet, watch Flower's face," I demand.

Her jealousy flares again.

"That's an order, and I expect a response," I bark, my crazed feeling beginning to brew.

Blakely jumps but can't go very far since she's still restrained to the cross. She blurts out, "Yes, Sir."

I point to Aria.

Blakely refocuses on Aria.

I hit the button on the remote, so the vibrations intensify, and continue flogging Aria, denying her requests until her "Sirs" are barely audible with her broken voice. I finally crack the leather over her red ass and demand, "Come."

Her body erupts in a spasm, convulsing against the bench, and I rub my hand over her ass cheeks to soothe the sting.

And then it happens. Aria's whimpers turn to sobs, and I know I made an error. I unlatch her from the bench, tug her into my arms, and stroke her hair. I tell her, "Shh. It'll be okay."

She becomes hysterical, and I silently curse her. I warned her she couldn't go back. We've had plenty of conversations. This is what happens when you try to deny your needs after getting in tune with them. When she told me she was head over heels for a guy who isn't in the life, I shouldn't have had her come here. I should have known she'd be too fragile.

Now, I've really messed up.

Aria's so distraught, there's no doubt she's having a breakdown. I leave Blakely on the cross, carrying Aria out of the room.

I take her to the guest bedroom and sit on the bed with her crying on my lap.

She finally calms enough to look up. "I-I'm sorry," she cries out, and fresh tears fall.

"Shh. Everything's fine."

"Riggs, I don't know what I'm doing," she chokes out.

I tug her head to my chest, letting her sob until she calms again. In a firm voice, I say, "We'll talk about this tomorrow. But you have to let me speak to him. He needs to come into the life, or you have to let him go."

"But I love him," she cries out.

"Shh. We'll talk tomorrow," I order, wait until she's sniffling, put her on her feet, and pull back the covers.

She slides onto the bed, and I pull the blankets over her. She says, "I'm sorry, Riggs."

I shake my head. "No sorry. You did well."

"I shouldn't have—" I put my fingers over her lips.

"You were perfect. We'll talk in the morning. Go to sleep." I leave the room, grab my phone out of my pants, and return to the playroom.

"Is she okay?" Blakely asks.

My thoughts spin out of control. My worries and fears take hold. I shouldn't have let so much time pass without checking in on Aria. I should have known something was up when I hadn't heard from her in a while. But most of all, I'm two steps away from losing my pet. There's too much to do and not enough time. It's clear Aria isn't in any frame of mind to properly train Blakely.

I step closer, stating, "What did you learn tonight?"

Horror fills her expression.

She thinks I'm a monster.

Good.

"I expect answers when I speak to you, or I'll leave you on this cross all night," I threaten.

Blakely's lips tremble. Her eyes turn to slits.

All I want to do is kiss those trembling lips. The fact I can't only pisses me off further. I warn, "Is that what you want? To stay on this cross all night?"

"No."

"No, who?"

"No, Sir."

I repeat, "Tell me what you learned. And think before you speak."

She waits a moment, then says, "To follow the rules."

"And?"

She swallows hard. "Pleasure and pain can morph together."

"And how do you know this?" I ask.

Her face turns red.

"Well?" I push.

She takes a deep breath. "From what you did to me."

What I did to her?

Not what I did to Aria but what I did to her.

My cock turns hard again. I try to hide my surprise and ask, "And what did you learn from Aria?"

She licks her lips and admits, "That I have to wait to come until you permit me."

Her answers are so perfect I want to kiss her again. It gives me hope that all is not lost. I nod and walk behind her.

I snap several photos of her, bare-assed with my handprints in red, her gold bra still on, and her juices glistening in a streak down her leg. I'm so disoriented about everything that went wrong yet still right that I feel giddy. I almost send it to her father, then remember it's my personal phone.

I release the restraints and pick Blakely up, carrying her to a bedroom suite. I turn on the shower and order her to get in.

She hesitates, then asks, "Aren't you joining me?"

Every part of my body wants to, but I need to reestablish control.

"No." I turn and leave the room. There's no more sex with Blakely until she passes the test at the club. I can't afford any more mistakes.

15

Blakely

$\mathcal{J}$ step out of the shower, and Riggs orders me to come to bed. To my surprise, his hair is wet.

"Did you shower?" I ask.

"In the other one," he reveals, and motions to the pulled back covers.

I slide under them, and he follows, then turns the light out. Dark silence ensues. He stays on his side, away from me, and I finally can't handle it anymore.

I whisper, "Riggs?"

"Hmm?"

"Is this still considered playtime?"

Tension builds between us. He finally answers, "No."

I move closer and wrap my arm and leg around him.

He freezes, asking, "What are you doing, Blakely?"

"What do you think I'm doing?" I retort.

He turns on his back but keeps his arm around me. He accuses, "Did you forget rule seven again?"

I taunt, "No. Did you forget what the contract states? Or maybe you didn't read it?"

He grunts. "I can assure you I know each word by heart. Are you trying to get punished?"

I take my finger and drag it between his pecs. "Nope. I haven't broken any contract rules."

He grabs my hand and through gritted teeth, demands, "What's rule seven, pet."

I recite, verbatim, "Rule seven. The sub will not touch the Dom unless granted permission. Failure to obey will result in a punishment."

Riggs twists my hair around his fist and asks, "What part of that rule don't you understand?"

"I understand all of it," I claim, sliding my foot against his inner calf.

His body tenses. He releases my hair, stating, "Seems to me like you don't."

"Oh, I can assure you I do. The one who doesn't comprehend what they read is you," I chirp.

He sighs. "Okay, Blakely, I'll bite. In what way do I not understand the contract?"

I slide on top of him and run my fingers over the side of his head. I state, "It's under the section titled, Rules of Engagement During Playtime. You just stated this isn't playtime. So the rules don't exist. I can touch you all I want."

He holds his breath, his eyes turning to dark slits as the whiteness disappears.

I widen my legs so my knees hit the mattress next to his hips. I graze his shaft with my wet pussy, slowly teasing it, leaning into his ear and whispering, "Do you know what I thought about while restrained to the cross?"

His breath turns ragged. His hands move to my hips, and his fingernails dig into my skin. He tries to hold me still, but I still manage to shimmy over his hardening erection.

"Tell me then," he demands.

I lean closer to his mouth, wanting to kiss him but deciding I can play his game. I murmur, "Since you brought another woman into our relationship, tossing in my face your intimacy, we can return to enforcing your rules." I try to roll off him, even though I still need a release after everything that happened tonight. I don't understand why I got turned on by everything in the playroom, but I did. I assumed Riggs would continue whatever lesson he was trying to teach me when he returned from taking Aria away, but he didn't. And I don't know why he refused to shower with me.

He surprises me and flips with me, pinning his body over mine.

My mouth turns dry, and my heartbeat increases.

He shifts his hips so his cock's directly on my clit, sliding back and forth. He scowls at me, grinding his molars, keeping his face two inches from mine. He warns, "You should realize who you're playing with, pet."

"We're not playing right now, remember?" I remind him.

His eyes turn sinister, his lips curving in arrogance. He states, "We play when I say we're playing. It seems to me you want to play."

"I don't," I state.

"I don't believe you," he claims.

I glare at him.

He warns, "If you want to let your jealousy rule your actions, instead of being mature enough to understand why I need to do what I do, then that's your choice."

"Jealous? I'm not jealous," I declare.

He grunts. "Sure you aren't."

"And this isn't about maturity!"

"Yes, it is."

I fire, "I told you no other women!"

"You missed the entire lesson, didn't you?" he seethes.

I continue, "And you didn't bring just anyone. You brought someone close to you. Someone who still has it bad for you!"

"Shh. Keep your voice down," he orders.

"Why? So your piece on the side can't hear?" I accuse.

He covers my mouth.

I shriek, but it's muffled.

"Enough of this outburst," he demands.

I push at him, but he's too heavy.

He doesn't budge, except to lean into my ear. He states, "I'm not telling you this again. I'm not a Dom who plays around. She's here for your benefit...for you to learn. And if you don't trust me soon, your days in my bed are limited, understand?"

Fear fills me. I hate everything about the possibility of what he threatens. Yet I can't stand the thought of him and Aria together.

She's beautiful. Her body is smaller than mine, which normally I wouldn't care about, even though I'm in L.A. and would be considered bigger by many people's standards. Yet it suddenly makes me feel insecure. And the worst thing is that she has something with Riggs I don't. The intimacy between them was undeniable. Watching them together was like taking a knife and stabbing my heart over and over.

Disappointment washes over him. He slowly bobs his head from side to side. "You don't get it, do you?"

I stay quiet, my insides quivering with anger and swirling with hurt.

He traces my lip, admitting, "I kind of like your jealous streak."

"Not funny."

"I'm not laughing."

I claim, "I'd rather not be with you than see you with her."

He holds his breath, studying me, finally saying, "I know you don't mean that."

"I do," I insist, then add, "And that goes for any of your other women."

"It's to help you," he reiterates.

"No, it's not."

"It is!"

"Do not bring her or anyone else in front of me ever again, Riggs. I mean it. If you do—"

"You'll what, pet? What exactly are you threatening? And be very clear before you open that pretty little mouth of yours."

I swallow hard, my eyes locked on his, my pulse beating so hard, it feels like it's going to push through my neck.

He lowers his voice even further, stating, "If you can't see that I'm doing everything in my power to make sure you stay with me, then you're blind."

"By bringing her here tonight?" I seethe.

"Yes. Exactly that. And you admitted you learned a few things tonight, so get off your high horse. Now, go to sleep," he orders, rolls off me, and turns away.

His words do nothing to calm me. I'm more frustrated than before we began. The jealousy never dies, and I toss and turn all night, listening to Riggs breathe, unsure if he's asleep or awake.

When dusk hits, I get up and creep out of the room. I close the bedroom door, walk down the hall, and find my clothes. I put my shorts and sweater on.

"Oh, sorry to disturb you," Aria says quietly. She moves toward the door with a bag slung over her shoulder.

"Where are you going?" I blurt out, my heart racing faster from just looking at her.

She spins, and I suddenly feel bad for her. Black circles darken the skin under her eyes. They're swollen, and she looks super fragile.

Is this what being with Riggs does to you?

I push the thought away and close the space between us. "Aria?"

She keeps her voice low. "I need to go. Tell Riggs I'm fine."

"You don't look fine."

She closes her sad eyes briefly, then pins them on me. "He's right, you know."

My stomach flips. "About what?"

She asserts, "If you don't get your shit together, they'll enforce rule fourteen."

"Wouldn't you like that?" I snap.

Her eyes widen, then she scoffs. "You have it all wrong, Blakely."

Rage builds within me. I cross my arms. "Oh? And what do I have wrong?"

"He brought me here for your well-being and only yours. I'm not here for him."

"Bullshit."

She shakes her head. "The contract between Riggs and me is over."

"Then why are you here?"

"Like I said, because you need help."

"No, I don't," I claim.

We stare at each other, not saying anything until she breaks the silence. "It's not your business, but I'm in love with someone else. Not that you should fall in love with Riggs. He's not long-term. He's a contract."

Her words cut me. I hate that I know she's right. But I don't want her to see that, so I huff and say, "If you love someone else, you shouldn't be allowing Riggs to touch you."

Her face hardens. "Grow up, Blakely. Good luck at the club." She spins and opens the door, slamming it behind her.

I take a few breaths to calm myself, then turn.

Riggs leans against the hallway wall, his arms crossed, scowl pinned on me.

I walk past him, then go into the bedroom. I step into the empty closet.

"What are you doing?" he asks.

I spin. "If you're keeping me here, where are my clothes? I want to put something clean on."

"Maybe that's all you get."

I smirk. "Rule twelve states you have to provide clothing."

His face hardens. "Ah, yes. And I believe that's under the Rules of Engagement During Playtime, isn't it?"

My gut drops.

He adds, "Besides, it looks to me like you're wearing clothes. It seems I've fulfilled my duty."

"Don't be a dick," I hurl.

He lunges toward me, and I step back until I'm against the wall. He slides his hand in my hair behind my head and grasps it tight so I'm unable to look anywhere but at him. His hot breath hits my lips as he states, "Do you think you're the first brat I've broken in?"

My breath hitches, my pulse skyrockets, and the red rage I've felt since he brought me here reignites to an all-time high. I retort, "I'm not a brat."

"No? You sure are acting like one."

"Maybe you should look at your actions."

His eyes turn to slits. "Let's get something straight right now."

I glare at him.

He threatens, "I'm in charge, not you. And you'll speak to me respectfully, or there'll be consequences."

"Respect is earned. Maybe *you* should learn *that.*"

Hot tension escalates as anger flares on his face. His chest heaves with every breath, and he grinds his molars, shooting darts at me with his pinned gaze.

I swallow hard, not wanting to back down but wondering if I've pushed him too far. And every time that thought crosses my mind, I reprimand myself.

He chose to bring Aria into this, not me.

He steps back and sneers, "Let's go."

"Where?"

"Does it matter?"

I don't say anything and don't move.

He steps out of the closet and warns, "Get in the car, or I'll lock you in this apartment for days."

I debate only a few more seconds and realize he'd do it. The last thing I believe is that Riggs bluffs on his threats. I quietly follow him through the apartment and get into the Porsche.

He maneuvers the L.A. streets and then the expressway through the thick smog and traffic. I stare out the window, lost in my thoughts, not sure if I'm overreacting about Aria or if Riggs was right to have her help train me.

As much as I'd like to think I know what I'm doing, I don't. I know nothing about what I've gotten myself into, every day seems to bring up a new issue I never contemplated, and Riggs is so hot and cold it keeps me in a constant state of confusion.

This business with the club should have been explained to me. I feel tricked. Then again, they do it for my protection, according to Riggs. Yet I don't know what to expect when I get there, nor do I know why he thinks I'm not submitting during playtime.

Haven't I?

As upset as I am with Riggs, I still can't fathom having to move somewhere else and not have access to him. No matter how much time passed, I still thought about him over the years. He never just faded away. I doubt after everything that's gone on the last few days he would now.

By the time he pulls through his Malibu gate, I'm more confused than ever. He reverses into the driveway, turns off the car, and pushes the button. The wood closes, and neither of us moves.

He finally turns and states, "There are ten days left. But I don't think anything I do with you will matter."

Panic fills me. "What do you mean?"

"You want to believe what you want to believe, pet. And that's on you, not me." He gets out and shuts his door. He walks around and opens my door but doesn't reach in for me.

I get out, and he motions for me to go inside. My gut says not to fight him. I obey, and he goes into the bedroom.

I sit down at the piano but don't play it. I'm lost in my thoughts when he comes into the room, freshly showered, wearing a suit. A new wave of anxiety fills me. I blurt out, "Why are you dressed up?"

"I'm going to work. Don't wait up," he states, moving toward the door.

I get off the bench and follow him. I grab the back of his arm. "Riggs, what does that mean?"

He shrugs me off him and doesn't look back, answering, "Just what I said."

"Riggs!"

He freezes, still not looking at me. "Work on your music, Blakely."

I step in front of him and slide my palms on his cheeks, which twitch under my touch. "Don't leave like this."

He grabs my hands and holds them away from his face. "Review the contract, pet. From now on, consider every second playtime since you want to get technical."

I open my mouth, but nothing comes out.

He steps to the side of me and says, "Keep your phone on in case I need to get ahold of you." He walks out the door, gets in his Porsche, and opens the gate. He pulls out, and the wood closes once more.

I shut the front door, more perplexed than ever.

And I've always been more of a loner. I normally can get lost in my music, but all day, the loneliness only grows, taking me by surprise. When darkness sets in, he's still not home.

I try calling, but he never answers. I pace until I can't anymore. I try calling again, but it goes to his voicemail.

I text.

Me: When will you be home?

I never get an answer.

Around eight o'clock, I open a bottle of red wine, fill a glass, and take both to the deck. The sound of waves crashing against the shoreline is louder than normal. Goose bumps pop out on my skin from the cold wind, but I don't go inside for extra clothes, letting the wine heat my insides.

I finish my glass and refill it, tug my knees to my chest, and start humming one of my songs. The gust of wind blows harder, and I shiver.

More time passes, but Riggs never shows up. I'm a few sips shy from finishing the bottle when Riggs's voice tears me out of my thoughts.

He booms, "What are you doing?"

Another blast of wind roars across the deck, and the bottle of wine falls and rolls across it.

Riggs lunges, grabs it, and scowls. "Having fun?"

"Oops." I giggle, finding his angry face humorous.

"What's so entertaining?" he seethes.

"You," I state, then finish the wine in my glass.

He studies me, the wind gusts again, blowing his hair to one side, and everything about it makes me laugh harder.

It only irritates him. He snarls, "Want to expand on that?"

"Not really," I say, then put my feet on the ground. I try to get up, but my balance is bad, and I slip.

Riggs grabs me.

"Sorry." I giggle again, pressing my palm against his chest. I add, "You have nice pecs."

His eyes narrow. "You're drunk."

"Nope!"

"Yes, you are," he insists, his voice full of disgust.

I tilt my head, grinning at him. "Prove it."

His jaw twitches. He slides his arm around my waist and leads me inside.

"I can walk," I cry out.

He stays silent, putting the wine bottle on the counter as we pass it, and leads me down the hallway.

"You passed the bedroom," I point out.

He doesn't respond, continuing to move me down the hall.

I lean closer, wiggling my eyebrows. "Let me guess, you have a playroom here too?"

More silence ensues as we get closer to the last door.

I slur, "Are you going to bend me over and do what you did to your girlfriend? I'm sure you loved sticking your fingers up her."

He opens the door to another bedroom.

"Where're the toys?" I tease.

He takes me to the bathroom, turns on the shower, and pushes me into it.

Cold water hits me. "Riggs!" I scream.

His blues turn to flames. He fumes, "You want to act like your drunk mother, do it somewhere else!" He spins, steps out of the bathroom, and slams the door.

I step out of the shower and grab a towel, my teeth already chattering. I open the bathroom door and try to follow him, but the bedroom door won't open.

"Riggs!" I shout, slamming my fists on the door.

But it's useless. Just like the entire day, he never answers. And once again, I'm all alone, with no one to decipher any of my confusion, frustration, or pain. Only this time, I'm confined to the bedroom suite, intoxicated, and wondering if he's ever going to let me out.

16

Riggs
Ten Days Later

"*M*om!" *I cry out.*

Her fear-filled, drugged-up eyes dart over to me. She barely gets out, "Go!"

A man I've never seen before keeps his grip on her throat, pinning her to the wall, and turns his head. He narrows his dark eyes on me, and a sinister smile overpowers his expression. He taunts, "You want to play too?"

"Mom," I say again.

The man laughs, squeezing my mother's throat so hard, her face begins to turn purple.

Something snaps in me. I can't turn around and hide like I normally do. I lunge at him, slamming my fists on his back and screaming, "Get off her!"

She chokes and splutters.

He releases her, spins, and reaches for me, easily picking me up off the ground.

My airway closes. My limbs flail in the air, trying to hurt him, but it's pointless. He's too strong.

He laughs, then tosses me across the room.

"Riggs!" my mother screams.

I hit the ground hard, skidding across the cheap laminate floor and hitting the dirty couch.

He pulls out a knife and holds it to my mother's throat.

"Mom!" I scream.

"Riggs," a voice calls out.

"Mom!" I cry out again.

"Riggs, wake up," a soft voice orders.

He takes the knife and pushes it against her throat. Blood oozes out of her skin.

"Mom!" I yell, tears blurring my vision.

"RIGGS! WAKE UP," BLAKELY DEMANDS, SHAKING ME.

I open my eyes and sit up. My skin's coated with sweat, and my insides rage with hatred. And everything feels out of control.

Blakely's blue eyes are wide. She strokes my cheek and asks, "You okay?"

I snap out of it, realizing where I am, and cringing that she witnessed me having a nightmare.

I thought they had stopped. I hadn't had one in over a year, yet this is the third in the last ten days.

The first nightmare occurred the night I caught Blakely drunk on the deck. The second, a few nights after. Now this one.

I've kept all this away from her. It was easy since I've not allowed her to sleep with me since we returned from Apartment Thirteen.

I snap, "Why are you in here?"

She pulls her hand away and lifts her chin. "I heard you crying."

"I wasn't crying," I claim, then push past her and slide out of bed. I go into the bathroom and turn on the shower.

She follows me. "Riggs, do you always have nightmares? The other night, I thought I heard—"

"Not sure what you thought you heard or saw, but I can assure you it was nothing," I state, stepping under cold water.

She watches me shower, and I ignore her, my irritation increasing since it's pouring down rain. That means surfing's out, which is normally the only way I can work through the aftermath of my past.

Well, that or sex after breaking down a sub for a few hours, but I can't attend the club until tonight. Another rule is that Doms can't play in the club until they've proven they've mastered the sub they bought at the auction.

Not that I would find another sub when I'm in a contract. It goes against my code, no matter what my needs are.

So, until tonight, when I take Blakely to the club, I'm screwed.

Even then, I'm in trouble. I've not touched her since the night at Apartment Thirteen. No matter how much she's tried to make things right between us, I've given her the cold shoulder. After a forty-eight-hour detox, which was extreme even for my standards, I let her out of the guest room, warning her that if she touched any more alcohol, she'd be locked in for a week.

We fell into a pattern. I'd go to work, leave her at the beach house, and come home late at night, well after dark. She tried to make amends the first few days, but I wasn't interested.

She broke rule thirteen. It may be a mandatory club rule, but it would have been in my contract whether they wanted it or not. There's no tolerance on my part for drunks or druggies.

After the fourth night, she didn't try anymore. A few times, I got home and she was already in bed. I hated it, as much as I hated seeing her slurring her speech and barely able to stand.

And now it's time to prove I have control over her and she's able to fully submit to me.

I've never been so unprepared.

The nightmares only add to the unhinged, unstable chaos I can't eliminate inside me. The longer I go without touching my pet, the crazier I feel. The only thing keeping me partially sane is knowing I'm taking Hugh down, but even that has challenges.

Jones hacked into two of Hugh's offshore accounts, but it's like he had a sensor on it. As soon as Jones got in, the money moved. It's a more sophisticated system than Jones has ever seen. While he's confident he'll break the code, it's wearing on my patience.

And Chainsaw hasn't found Snake yet. It seems the thug wised up and fled town. It's another thing bugging me. A good night at the warehouse, dragging the last breath out of Snake would have let me release some energy, but that hasn't happened.

The only saving grace I have in all of this is sneaking pictures of Blakely and sending them to her father.

And I know I'm getting under his skin. It took a while, but I finally got the text messages I'd been waiting for, which means he's starting to crack.

> Hugh: Whoever this is, I'll find you. And once I do, you'll wish you never laid eyes on my daughter or me.

I sent a picture of Blakely in the shower with soap falling down her breasts and a message.

> Me: I'm going to fuck her against the wall now.

> Hugh: You have until midnight to turn her over to me. Otherwise, I'm coming after you.

> Me: I'll keep that in mind when I come in her.

But no matter how much satisfaction I get from sticking it to Hugh, it's only short-lived. The moment I think about Blakely and how long it's been since I touched her, the more unsettled I feel.

I should be training her, pushing her to her limits. She should be broken by now, ready to submit on a moment's notice, and aware of all the protocols.

She's clueless.

For the first time ever, I'm going to fail as a Dom. But the thought of my reputation and ego taking a hit isn't what's bothering me.

I'm going to lose Blakley.

Every night, I make the long drive from the city, reprimanding myself for my inaction. Yet the moment I step through the door and see her, or search the house only to find relief when I discover her safe in bed, my mind plays games with me. Everything I used to feel confident about seems broken. Nothing I would normally do with subs seems like it'll work with Blakely.

She's not intimidated by me. She's able to stand up to me and not even flinch. None of my other subs would have dared to repeatedly argue with me, even the one I nicknamed Brat.

I've always known Blakely was different. I suppose it's what drew me to her, but nothing prepared me for her insubordinate behavior or how out of control it would make me feel.

And the last thing a Dom should ever be is out of control. Irrevocable mistakes can get made, and subs end up hurt. It's irresponsible and dangerous.

So she's got me questioning everything I used to take pride in knowing, but I'm unsure how to stop it.

A bolt of lightning streaks across the ocean, snapping me out of my thoughts. I turn off the cold water, dry myself off, and brush past Blakely. I go into my closet and select a T-shirt and a pair of joggers.

Blakely's glare never leaves me. I can feel it burning along my skin.

I pull my shirt over my head, then step into the joggers.

"Are you going to ignore me all day?" she asks, her voice full of irritation and hurt.

My heart pounds harder. I take a lungful of air and lock eyes with her. "Is there something you need, Blakely?"

She pins her eyebrows together, tilts her head, and crosses her arms.

The defiance I loved at the start now scares the shit out of me. I should have control over it by now, and I don't. Everyone at the club will see it tonight. Only a few hours stand between us, then they'll take her from me, and I'm clueless about what to do about it.

I step in front of her. "I'm waiting for an answer."

She lifts her chin, but all I hear is hurt and fear in her voice when she asks, "Is this your way of letting me go?"

My pulse pounds between my ears. "Meaning?"

"Are we not going to the club tonight?"

"Yes, we are. Be ready to go by six."

She blinks hard, her eyes glistening, and looks away.

Since I'm a dick, I ask, "Do you have another question?"

She meets my gaze. "Are you going to tell me what I'm expected to do tonight?"

Every cell in my body seems to throb with hot blood. Even she knows she's not ready. I hate myself for putting us in this position. I debate how to answer and finally reply, "Do what you're told. Don't argue with me. Trust me and only me."

She stares at me.

My anger at myself flares. I accuse, "But you can't do that, can you?"

Her face hardens.

"Like I told you last week, tonight's in your hands," I declare, then brush past her and go into my office. I shut the door, then quietly bang my head on the wall, hating myself for no longer knowing what direction to lead her.

I take the seat at my desk, open up my laptop, and try to get lost in work. It's Saturday, and while I could have gone to the L.A. office, I didn't want to make the drive twice. But I soon regret it when the sound of the piano and Blakely's emotion-filled voice hit my ears.

I listen to her for hours, unable to leave the room, fearing she'll stop playing. When she finally does, it's past two.

I venture out of the office and find her staring out the window. It's still raining, and the waves are several feet high.

"Have you eaten today?" I question.

She spins toward me. "I'm not hungry."

"You need to eat. It's going to be a long night," I inform her.

"At least I know one thing about tonight," she mutters, then turns back toward the window.

I stop thinking, go over to her, slide my arm around her waist, and step flush against her back.

She freezes.

I murmur into her ear, "If you stiffen up like this tonight, you won't be coming back here."

She slowly tilts her head, pinning her glassy blues on mine. "Do you even want me here?"

Blood rushes to my head so fast that I have to focus on fighting the dizziness. I reply, "Is that what you think? That I don't want you here?"

Her bottom lip quivers. "I might as well have been invisible."

"You're anything but," I declare.

Another streak of lightning bursts through the sky as thunder booms. She jumps, and I chuckle, which feels like the first time I've laughed in weeks.

She takes a deep breath and smiles.

"Come eat. I'll make you lunch." I lead her over to the island and pull out the barstool.

She sits but states, "I really don't think I can eat." She puts her hand on her stomach.

I put my hand on her forehead. "Don't tell me you're sick."

"No. Just nervous."

I nod. "It's normal."

She blurts out, "What else is normal?"

"Nothing," I state.

She glares at me.

I hold my hands in the air. "I'm not lying. Every event is different."

"Tell me one thing, Riggs. Something that when I get there, I know it's always the same," she says.

I try to think, but there's nothing I can tell her.

She takes my silence the wrong way and accuses, "You really can't give me one thing, can you? It's just another way for you to stay in control."

I pull the chair out and sit next to her, confessing, "This isn't about control, pet. I don't know what will happen when we show up. They don't tell me if we'll be in a private room or on the stage. I don't know what tools I'll be provided, if anything at all. The board decides everything, and they feel the element of surprise keeps the process honest."

"Honest?"

"It's for your protection...to make sure subs are with the right Dom," I add.

She closes her eyes, keeping her hand on her stomach. Her face turns pale. I barely hear her beg, "I need something, Riggs. One thing I'm aware of. I don't know why, but something is calming to me about knowing what the normal part is."

I think for a minute, then stroke her cheek and state, "Me. I'm your normal part."

She opens her eyes and softly laughs.

"What's so funny?" I question.

"You aren't normal," she claims.

I shrug. "Maybe so, but I'm your common denominator tonight. Whenever you need to feel calm, you just look at me."

"Except I don't usually feel calm when you're pinning your angry eyes on me, ordering me around," she admits.

"Is that what you think I do?" I tease.

She bites on her smile, arching her eyebrows.

I slide my arm around her shoulders, lean closer, and murmur, "If I recall, your pussy gets pretty wet when I do that."

She nudges me in the chest with her elbow, and her face turns red.

"Ouch!" I cry out, then stare at her. I add, "Seriously. Try not to figure out what will happen tonight. Just go with it."

"Spoken by Mr. Control Freak himself," she mutters.

I pick up her hand and kiss it. "Yep. So if I can do it, so can you. And I need you with me on this if you're going to come home with me tonight."

Her face falls, making my stomach flip. A moment passes and then she nods. "Okay. You're my common denominator."

I rise, kiss her on the top of her head, and announce, "Good. Now let's get some food in your belly."

17

Blakely

*T*here's barely any taste when I eat Riggs's salmon salad and the roll he ordered me to finish. I can only get half the fish down. I'm too nervous about what's going to happen tonight.

Will this be the last time I'm here?

Will I never see Riggs again?

It's all too much to contemplate. I blurt out, "Why do you have to agree to the club rules? Why can't you just break them?"

He grinds his molars, pinning his disapproving gaze on me.

My stomach dives. I add, "If you want to be with me, that is."

"It's not about what I want, pet," he asserts.

"Then what's it about?" I push.

He studies me a moment, then answers, "This is how it is."

"But you can do whatever you want," I insist, in an almost desperate tone that makes me wince inside.

"I won't break the rules," he firmly states.

The doorbell rings, and a new wave of nerves hits me. I glance at him, asking, "Expecting someone?"

"Your people," he claims with a smile.

"My people?"

He nods, then goes and opens the door. The driver who brought me to the beach house, along with two blindfolded women, stand outside.

"Come in and take off your blindfolds," Riggs says.

They slowly remove them and exchange greetings with him. He makes introductions, stating, "Blakely, this is Diana and Nira. They're here to help you get ready for tonight."

"Oh," I say in surprise, then remember my manners. "Nice to meet you."

"I'm your hair girl," Diana states.

"Makeup!" Nira adds.

"They know everything there is to know about the club," Riggs adds.

Part of me feels relieved, and the other part not so much. Both women have a confidence about them, and I wonder if they've gotten Riggs's other subs ready in the past.

Did they help Aria?

I can't dwell on it long. Before I know it, I'm in Riggs's bedroom suite, along with several large black cases.

"Do you have bleach in there?" I ask Diana.

"Sure."

"Can you turn me back to my normal blonde?" I ask, no longer debating about my hair color. Since Aria showed up with locks the same as mine, I've been dying to switch back.

"Umm..." Diana glances at Nira.

Nira smiles. "Why don't we go talk to Riggs first?"

I refrain from rolling my eyes. Of course they'd seek his permission. I insist, "It's fine. I already asked him, and he said I could turn my hair any color I wanted."

They exchange more uncomfortable glances.

"Look, I'm his sub. So it's my fate on the chopping block. I can assure you he's okay with it. Besides, I wouldn't want to get punished, right?" I add.

A tiny laugh comes out of Diana. "You're right."

"Unless you like punishments?" Nira asks.

I shake my head and smile. "Nope. Now, can you turn me blonde?"

Diana relaxes. "Okay."

It takes hours to change my hair color, then style it. Diana tells me that Riggs already instructed her on what he wants done. She puts half my hair up and leaves the rest down in long curls.

Nira creates smokey eyes and adds a silver shadow to my lids. Then she applies a matte red lip stain to my mouth.

A short, black slip dress is on Riggs's bed when I step out of the bathroom. It reminds me of something a woman would wear to bed, not go out in. A pair of black stilettos, with diamonds encrusting the heels, sits next to the dress. They're taller than what I'm used to wearing.

I tell the girls, "I think he forgot my bra and underwear."

Diana's lips twitch.

Nira bites on her smile.

"What am I missing?" I ask in confusion.

"There's no bra and underwear. He just wants you in the dress and shoes," Diana states.

My stomach flips. I've worn less to Cheeks, but something about not having anything underneath the silk material makes me nervous. It's barely going to cover my ass.

Nira unzips the dress, ordering, "Take off your robe."

I hesitate.

Diana adds, "Don't be shy. You're going to the club. I can assure you someone other than Riggs will see you naked tonight."

My chest tightens. I blurt out, "What do you mean?"

She shrugs. "It's normal. Lots of people will be naked."

Of course they will.

I slowly untie my robe and slide out of it. I step into the dress.

Nira zips it, chirping, "You look great!"

"You sure do," Diana adds.

The dress covers a few inches of my thigh. I step into the stilettos, and my legs seem even more exposed.

"Time to go," Diana states, clapping.

"Have an awesome night," Nira says.

I'm too nervous to respond as they lead me out of the bedroom.

Riggs is on the phone. He wears all black. His designer trousers, T-shirt, and sports coat fit his body like a glove. A hint of his tattoos peeks out of the V of his shirt.

My heart stammers. His dirty-blonde surfer hair seems wilder than when he leaves for work. I love it when he wears it like that. Something about it seems a bit taboo compared to his normal buttoned-up work look where he's hiding his ink.

He catches my eye and freezes. His eyes dart down my body, then back to my face. He hangs up. He states, "You look perfect."

"She does," Nira beams.

Diana glances at her watch. "We should get going. We have one more stop tonight."

"Sure. I'll get Luke." Riggs goes to the door and motions for the driver to come inside. He hauls the women's black cases outside, then returns and blindfolds them. He leads them to the SUV, which takes off just as another SUV backs into the driveway.

"Why do you blindfold them?" I ask.

"So they don't know where I live," Riggs replies.

"Isn't that a bit extreme?" I question.

He shakes his head. "No. I like my privacy. They don't even know what town I live in." He pins his blues on me.

I stay quiet as a new burst of anxiety fills my belly.

He steps forward and reaches around my neck. He unfastens my gold collar and states, "This is the wrong one tonight."

"Oh?"

He sets the old one on the counter and picks up a flat box. He holds it out. "This is for you."

"What is it?"

"Open it."

I remove the lid and gape. A new choker glitters back at me. It's a black and platinum mix, with metal rings and diamonds floating around it. "It's gorgeous," I gush.

He picks it up, attaches it around my neck, then adds, "There's something else in the box. Underneath the first layer."

I glance down at the satin and lift it. A matching leash is folded and stuck in the insert.

My pulse skyrockets, and my mouth turns dry. I slowly glare at Riggs, snarling, "A leash? Like I'm a dog?"

His lips twitch. "A dog, no. My pet, yes."

I look away.

He moves my chin so I can't ignore him. "You don't want to be my pet?"

I snap, "Did Flower get a watering can?"

Riggs chuckles, which only infuriates me further. He answers, "No. She got a leash too."

"Well, at least you know how to make a girl feel special," I seethe.

His amusement doesn't falter. He takes it out of the box, unwinds it, and snaps it on my collar. He states, "All auctioned subs will have one tonight. It's a rule, but so you know, you're my only pet."

More anger rolls through me. "What does that even mean, Riggs?"

He wraps the leash around his fist until there's no slack. He tugs so my face moves closer to his, and he says, "It means every sub I have, I give a name to that no one else has ever had. So you know, flowers quickly wither and die. Brats I easily get bored with, and stars eventually fade into the morning sky. And I can go on and on about all the reasons no one was ever my pet until you."

I hold my breath and tilt my head, almost scared to ask, "Why me?"

He glances at my lips, then drags his knuckles from his leash-wrapped fist over my jaw, answering, "Pets are a responsibility. You can't just play with them and run. You must choose wisely, so you pick the one you can't get out of your head, the one you can't walk away from."

Silence grows between us. Like always, Riggs confuses me.

He picks up a lock of my hair and confesses, "I always loved you as a blonde."

I blurt out, "And I don't look like Aria anymore."

He freezes.

My pulse beats loudly between my ears.

"It was only for training. Stop comparing yourself. There's no comparison," he declares.

I stay quiet.

He declares, "It's time to go." He steps back, unwinds the leash, then guides me out of the house and into the SUV.

The divider window is up. The SUV pulls through the gates, and Riggs slides his hand between my thighs.

He leans into my ear. "Let's test how ready you are for tonight."

I arch my eyebrows.

He slides me onto his lap, and I reach for him, but he stops me, asserting, "Rule seven must be obeyed at all times tonight, pet."

"It's a stupid rule," I state.

His lips twitch. "It's not your call." He orders, "Palms flat on the ceiling."

I obey, and he slides his hands over my arms. Tingles burst under his touch. I struggle to keep my hands where they are, and he moves to my breasts, rolling his thumbs over my nipples until they're rock hard and I'm whimpering.

His hot breath hits my neck. He murmurs, "I can already smell your arousal, pet."

Flames burst onto my cheeks.

He chuckles and asks, "What do you want right now, pet?"

"I want to touch you," I blurt out.

"What did you forget?"

"Sir. I want to touch you, Sir."

He moves his face in front of mine and taunts, "Where? And use your manners, pet."

I swallow hard. It's felt like forever since Riggs gave me any attention. Since Apartment Thirteen, I've felt alone, craving him more and more. The longer he ignored me, the worse my obsession to have him touch me got. I admit, "On the lips. I want to kiss you, Sir."

He glances at my mouth, and I think he's going to let me, but then his features harden. "Permission not granted."

I push my hands against the ceiling, trying to somehow rid myself of the angst.

"Where else do you want to touch me?" he asks.

"Your cheek," I admit.

The fire in his eyes brightens. He answers, "Permission not granted."

For the hour ride into the city, he tortures me, never permitting me to touch him, moving me on his lap in different positions, making me kneel on the floor and lie flat on the seat across from him with my ass in the air, and other things. None of which I would have believed I would do only a few weeks ago.

By the time we get to the club, I'm angry, hot and bothered, and unsure if I love or hate Riggs.

The SUV pulls up to the curb and Riggs gets out. He reaches in for me and helps me out. He leans into my ear and asserts, "You obey me and only me, pet. Understand?"

"Who else would I—"

He puts his fingers over my lips. "Only me." He locks his blues on mine and releases his fingers, waiting for me to answer.

I nod. "Yes, Sir."

He smiles and guides me into the club, then past the bouncer. The hostess leads us through a hallway and to a private room. It's dark, with dim lights and one wall made entirely of glass.

On the left, men sit in chairs, drinking and studying the women. On the right are eleven women. I recognize them. They were at the club the night Riggs bid on me. They all went on stage before me.

Now, they kneel with their leashes attached to rings on the wall. Their outfits range from leather to lingerie. Some only wear panties, their breasts fully exposed. Others are bare, their nakedness glowing against the dim light.

It occurs to me that others might see Riggs and me do intimate things. I can't say the thought never crossed my mind, but now, it feels very real.

The need to flee hits me. I spin into Riggs, but he slides his hand on my cheek and leans into my ear, ordering, "Breathe, pet. Just do what I say. I want you coming home with me after this is over."

It's another piece of reality. For the last ten days, all I've thought about is making sure I do whatever I have to in order to go home with Riggs. Even when he wasn't speaking to me, I still wanted to be his. I've never had a wavering thought about staying with him.

He points to the last remaining spot and orders, "Kneel."

I obey, and he attaches the leash to the wall. Then he crouches in front of me, lifts my chin, and studies my face, saying nothing.

My butterflies go crazy in a mix of nervous apprehension. Riggs demands, "Return to your position."

I bow my head, and his feet disappear.

Too many songs pass, with women on each side of me slowly disappearing until I'm the only one still chained to the wall.

More time passes. My body aches, but I continue holding my position, wondering why Riggs hasn't come to get me.

A man's shoes appear in front of me. He barks, "Look at me!"

I almost lift my head but hesitate. It's not Riggs. I fret about what to do, but all I hear in my head is Riggs saying, "You obey me and only me, pet."

The man reissues his order.

My pulse skyrockets. I stay in my position, silently willing the man to leave.

Riggs finally comes over and snaps, "Don't even think about touching my pet."

"She's beautiful," the man states. "Let's share."

My belly quivers. *Would Riggs put me in that position?*

Arrogance fills Riggs's voice as he asserts, "She's mine. Now, fuck off, Dooley."

The man grunts and leaves. Relief washes through me, and Riggs unlatches my leash. He wraps it around his hand, tugs me to my feet, and slides his hands over my cheeks. His hot breath hits my lips, and he praises, "Good girl."

I realize I just passed a test. Rage flares through me. He left me here for how long, chained like a dog, and for what?

But I can't dwell on my anger. He leads me to another room where there's a stage. A woman hangs, suspended in the air, her feet spread as wide as possible on raised blocks, her arms stretched and cuffed.

Two men surround her, whispering things. Her chest rises and falls faster. Her lips quiver, and her skin already glistens.

A song plays with no words, just multiple artists moaning in ecstasy. The air crackles with electricity, and everyone from the previous room is here.

Subs kneel at the feet of their Doms. Some of them get stroked by their Doms. Others suck their Dom's cock. Some haven't been released from their position and bow their heads.

I cringe, not wanting to kneel again, but Riggs surprises me, taking a seat and patting his lap.

I begin to straddle him, but he swings me around so my back is against his torso, my face toward the stage. He takes his hands and widens my thighs so they rest on the outer part of his.

The air hits my pussy. I move to cover it with my hands, and Riggs grabs them. He moves one behind my head, then pushes my fingers, lacing them into his hair.

I smile, happy he's allowing me to finally touch him.

He takes my other hand and holds it on my lap.

I glance at him, and he murmurs in my ear, "Your eyes stay on stage, open at all times, and you don't come without my permission."

Don't come? There's a room full of people. He doesn't have to worry about that.

A man in leather pants and carrying a black flogger steps on stage. He nods to the other men.

The chains lower by a few inches, releasing a tad of tension. A floorboard rises between the woman's feet.

The second man steps in front of her and drags his fingers down the inside of her thighs.

She shudders.

Riggs murmurs in my ear, "That's the Dom in leather. Those are all his subs."

My heart races. *How many subs does a man need? And why does he have men and women?*

The Dom snaps his fingers, and the music turns off. Silence ensues as new tension crackles through the air.

Riggs moves my hair over my shoulder and kisses the curve of my neck. Tingles erupt down my spine, traveling right to my core.

I squeeze my thighs together, and he moves our hands between my legs.

The Dom announces, "You've been a good girl, princess. You deserve a reward. Where do you want his cock?"

"My ass, Daddy," she breathes, then adds a desperate, "Please."

The Dom locks eyes with the man behind the woman. "Prepare her."

"Yes, Sir," he says, then slides his finger past her forbidden zone.

She cries out, her eyes fluttering.

"Don't make a sound," Riggs orders, then he shoves his finger and mine inside my pussy and pushes the butt of my palm on my clit, rotating it with the perfect amount of force.

I inhale sharply, trying to stay quiet.

He kisses my ear, murmuring, "No coming."

The Dom gives the woman on stage a minute, then questions, "And what about him, princess? Do you want his mouth or cock?" He points to the man in front of her.

She takes two anxious gulps of air, and her voice cracks when she says, "His mouth. Please, Daddy."

The Dom orders, "Kneel!"

The man in front of her obeys, replying, "Yes, Sir." He puts his face in front of her pussy, bows his head, and waits.

The Dom questions, "Should I go easy or hard on him for his punishment, princess?"

More excitement fills her eyes. She answers, "Hard, Daddy. Please flog him hard."

The Dom nods and instructs, "Wrap your hands around the chains, princess."

She winds them twice around her and locks eyes with the Dom.

"Good girl," he praises, then says, "No coming until I permit you. You don't have to stay silent."

Adoration fills her expression. She pins her gaze on her Dom, replying, "Thank you, Daddy."

He barks, "Now!"

The man behind the woman pulls out his finger and grips her hips, thrusting his cock inside her in one move.

She shrieks as the man in front laces his fingers between the other man's, gripping her hips, and latches his face on her pussy.

Ecstatic sounds fly out of her, and she grips the chains so hard her knuckles turn white.

The man behind her bites on her neck, and the Dom takes the flogger and slams it on the back of the man eating her pussy.

I gasp, unable to take my eyes off the scene.

The man being flogged grunts, his back arches, but his mouth stays planted between her thighs. The man from behind pins his hands over the other man and thrusts into the woman's ass faster.

Riggs moves our fingers inside me at the same pace, rubbing my clit with an intensity that pools adrenaline in all my cells.

I whimper, shift my hips, and Riggs orders, "Don't move, pet."

It takes everything I have to still myself.

Riggs kisses the curve of my neck and removes his hand from mine. I try to move my hand, and he demands, "Play with yourself."

I start to turn my head, but he moves his cheek against mine so I can't. He adds, "Eyes on the stage."

I obey.

He repeats, "Play with your pussy, now. Permission to move your hips. I want to see it, pet."

My heart beats so fast I think it's going to explode. I've never done anything like this in front of anyone, much less a room full of people.

"Now, pet," he demands and helps me start, then removes his hand from mine, stating, "Keep going."

I do as he says, continuing to watch the scene as the Dom slaps the man again.

The woman begins begging. "Please let me come, Daddy."

"No!" he declares.

"Please, Daddy, I need to come," she screams as the man behind her tugs her hair so hard her face parallels the ceiling.

"Not yet," the Dom orders, distributing another flog on the man's red back.

"Please, Sir," I beg, my body already trembling, needing to come and no longer caring who sees me.

"No," Riggs states, then adds in my ear, "If you come right now, it's over, pet. Rule fourteen will be enforced."

"Please," I plead, not understanding why he won't let me if he doesn't want rule fourteen enacted.

The scene continues, and the man behind the woman begins begging the Dom, "Please, Sir. Let me come."

"Not yet," he repeats and flogs the other man.

The room becomes an echo chamber of the man and woman on stage begging to come, the sound of other subs, including myself, pleading with their Dom to come, and the man getting flogged, grunting louder and louder.

The Doms are all ruthless, denying everyone's request.

Riggs is no different, making me bring myself to the edge, then putting his hand over mine and making me retreat. It's enough to stop me from flying into a full-blown orgasm before he makes me return to the same excruciating situation.

"Sir, I...please, I'll do anything," I cry out, still facing the stage, with Riggs's mouth all over my neck, ear, and cheek. And my body won't stop shaking, yet I'm not experiencing the high I need.

The Dom on stage orders, "Come!"

All three of the subs erupt in euphoria. The man eating her pussy shoots his load all over the stage. The other Doms in the room order their subs, "Come!"

"Please," I beg Riggs, expecting him to let me now that the scene is over and the room is full of women crying out in pleasure. But to my surprise, the Dom on the stage, as well as the others surrounding me, are nicer than mine.

Mine's just cruel.

Riggs moves my hand to my mouth and makes me suck off my arousal, then murmurs in my ear, "Turn to the left, pet."

I slowly turn my head, and horror fills me.

Another Dom is staring at me. His sub is sucking him off. He's controlling her head, but his eyes fixate on me, moving over my body and legs, then pinning them on my pussy.

I turn back to Riggs, trying to process all of this and close my legs, but he doesn't let me.

The darkness in his eyes scares me. I don't know what to make of them. Is he upset with me? Did I do something wrong?

He pushes me to my feet and rises. I'm unable to stand on my own, my knees too wobbly. He slides his arm around my waist, grabs my collar, and leans into my ear, "Your pussy is mine, pet. No one else's, do you understand?"

"I-I didn't—"

He puts his fingers over my mouth. "I think it's time for your punishment."

18

Riggs

"What am I getting punished for?" Blakely frets.

I lead her over to the corner and pull her closer to me so my mouth hits her ear, murmuring so no one else can hear me, "You didn't have permission to look at me."

"I-I didn't. I watched the stage," she claims.

"You just did. I told you to look to your left. I didn't permit you to look away. And I definitely didn't tell you to try and cover up your glistening pussy," I inform her.

She whispers, "Riggs—"

I tug on her hair, and she gasps. "Who am I?"

"Sir."

"Are you trying to get rule fourteen enforced?" I question, then study her.

Fear enters her eyes. "No."

I arch my eyebrows.

"No, Sir," she says, correcting herself.

"I need your full submission, pet," I remind her.

"You have it. I-I promise."

"Do I?"

"Yes."

"Yes, who?" I ask, hating myself for not training her the last ten days. What the fuck was I thinking? How could I have frozen like this? She's not ready. She can't even consistently address me as required, and that's the easier thing to do.

And she hasn't learned how to hold her orgasms. I had to interfere with her masturbation. And I can only do that so much before I get called out on it.

Blakely lifts her chin. "Yes, Sir."

My cock hardens. Her defiant confidence, even when she's scared, which there's no doubt she is, turns me on. But the defiance is also the thing that will get her a one-way ticket to the club's secret residence.

I've not broken her yet.

It has to happen now.

The board gave me more privacy than normal. I expected them to have me on the open stage, but instead, they chose other Doms. I shouldn't be surprised. Whenever you think you know what will happen on nights like these, the board throws a curve ball at you.

They assigned me to room seven. It's another stage, although Blakely won't know unless I tell her. It has a mirrored glass wall, with room for at least a hundred to observe. The seating outside the room has raised levels, so anyone viewing has a clear view. The room is also completely soundproof, but the microphone will pick up everything.

My mind's been reeling since I learned I was in room seven. The club has a strict no-electronics policy. There's no photos, video, or audio documentation allowed.

The only exception is room seven.

Every breath my pet takes will be mine forever. Within minutes of our session ending, the club will put our recording in a secure portal.

Maybe this is why I haven't broken her yet. Now, I'll always have access to watch it.

I couldn't have asked for a better scenario. Blakely will think we're alone. It'll help calm her nerves unless I find it useful to reveal it to her in our session. Tomorrow, I can chop up pieces of our session and use them to further irritate Hugh.

It's perfect. And I've never felt so hard with anticipation. There's no one I've wanted to break more than my pet. Staying away from her all these days only made my ache deepen, and nothing will be sweeter than tonight. My determination to have her fully submit and make sure she leaves with me only grows.

I reiterate, "I need your full submission from here on out, pet. Every rule must be followed. There's no room for deviation. Understand?"

The anxiety increases in her blues. Her pouty red lips part to speak, but she shuts them and swallows hard. Then she states, "I'm trying, Sir."

I place my hand on her cheek, tracing her lips with my thumb, happy she added her Sir. Maybe we are getting somewhere. I reply, "Don't try. Fully trust me."

"I do," she claims. Then adds, "Sir." She glances at my lips, then locks her gaze on my eyes. Then she glances at my mouth again.

My chest tightens. She's a temptress, even if she doesn't know it. Her constant desire to kiss me never wavers. I don't normally care to kiss any of my subs. But Blakley... I take a few deep breaths, trying to strengthen my resolve to avoid her mouth.

She gives me another silent, desperate plea and moves her face closer to mine, but I step back. I wind the leash around my fist a few times and order, "Time for your punishment, pet. Do not look at anyone as we move through the club."

Anxiety flares across her expression, mixing with defiance. I pin my most challenging gaze on her. She internally fights her desire to defy me. It's so obvious, my cock twitches.

"What's it going to be, pet? Rule fourteen or submission?" I taunt.

She takes a deep breath and asserts, "I'm going home with you, Sir."

Her answer couldn't be more perfect. I praise, "Good girl." I slide my hand around her waist, tighten the leash in my other, and command, "Lower your head."

She obeys, strolling next to me, but her defiance is still there. It burns through her veins. I'm sure of it. I've known her forever, and maybe it's what is making this more impactful for me.

I steer her through the club, knowing all eyes are on us. They usually are, as the board often puts me in positions to teach the other Doms. But tonight is different. Blakely is different. She stands out as more innocent than the other subs. And I can tell from the other Doms' expressions, they all know I haven't broken her yet. They're practically drooling to watch it happen, and the crowd following us to see what room I'm in grows larger.

I open the door to room seven, guide my pet inside, and shut the door. There's soft music playing, intentionally designed to help ease the transition into playtime.

Pride sweeps through me as I observe Blakely. She keeps her head bowed and hands folded. The only physical sign of her nerves is her thumb slightly tapping her hand. "You may look up and see your surroundings."

She slowly lifts her head, her eyes growing wider as she takes it all in.

I move my palm over her ass cheek, stroking it over the silk, trying to steady my heart from racing too fast. I've never been inside room seven, only observed others. Every Dom I know wants the assignment, yet few ever get it. And it's only used on nights like these.

It's like the board knew I needed this room for more reasons than one.

I study my pet as she takes in every inch of the medieval space. Even the mirror fits the decor. Worn, golden-brown hues start at the corners and eventually fade away. Cobblestone brick lines the floor and runs up a chimney. A real wood fireplace crackles, with logs stacked next to it. A wooden cage sits in the corner. Metal spikes are on the floor, ceiling, and bars, so the person inside can't move without getting poked. Heavy metal chains hang from the ceiling with thick cuffs attached to the ends. Tools hang on both sides of the fireplace, most of which I would never use on my pet. They're meant to draw blood, and I'm not into that type of sadism. Yet I'm not telling her that.

The heat from the fireplace contrasts with the cold room. Goose bumps pop out on Blakely's skin, but I assume it's more from nerves, especially since she's staring at the sharp blades.

I assess the space again, take off my shirt, then sit on an over-sized chair. I demand, "Pet, turn and take off your dress. And don't forget the rules."

She swallows hard, faces me, and says, "Yes, Sir." She slowly removes her dress and holds it in her hand.

"Toss it on the ground."

She drops it and waits.

I curl my finger in the air. "Crawl."

Her head jerks backward. She utters, "Crawl?"

I scowl at her.

She takes a deep breath. "Sorry, Sir." She glances at the ceiling, then drops on all fours. She moves a foot on the cobblestone.

"Ass in the air, face closer to the ground," I demand.

She glares at me.

I add, "I expect to hear your gratitude."

She lets out a pissed-off breath and utters, "Thank you, Sir." She lowers her face and raises her ass.

"Louder and like you mean it."

She shuts her eyes for a minute, then repeats, "Thank you, Sir." She slinks over to me, her leash scraping on the cobblestones.

"Kneel," I order.

She assumes the position and waits.

I caress her cheek and move my face in front of hers. I lift her chin up and ask, "Who do you hate most in this world?"

Surprise fills her expression. She freezes.

Let the games begin.

"I asked you a question. I want an honest answer," I assert.

Her voice turns flat. She admits, "My father."

I arch my eyebrows.

She clears her throat. "Sir. My father, Sir."

"Why do you hate your father?"

Her face hardens. She blinks hard.

I wrap the leash around her chin, so there's no slack, and gently tug.

Flames from the fire dance in her blues. She gasps, and I demand, "Tell me."

The sad truth comes out. She confesses, "He's never loved me. I'm just someone he wants for show-and-tell."

"What else don't you like about your father?"

Her lip trembles. She whispers, "Why are you asking me this?"

"The next time you ask me a question without seeking permission first, you'll be in the cage. Understand?" I warn.

Her eyes dart to the cage, then back to me.

"Well? Understand?" I push.

"Yes, Sir."

"Last time I'm asking. What else don't you like about your father?"

She clenches her jaw, and I give her a moment. She reveals, "He's selfish, a liar, and cruel."

"How is he cruel?"

She blinks, and a tear slides down her cheek.

I soften my voice. "Tell me, pet."

Her voice cracks. "He'll do anything to have full control over me."

I wait.

She adds, "Sir."

I lean closer to her lips, and my mouth waters. She glances at it, and I assert, "You don't like giving up control, do you, pet?"

She clenches her jaw, then admits, "No, Sir."

My adrenaline kicks in. I tug her head back farther, taunting, "But you agreed to let me have it."

She fires daggers at me with her glare.

I trace her collar, demanding, "Tell me why you agreed to let me have it."

She whispers, "You know why."

"Sir," I remind her, then pinch her nipple.

She gasps, shuddering, her blue orbs widening.

I lean into her ear and pinch her again but don't release the pressure on her nipple. I murmur, "Is it all for your pussy? Or is there another reason?"

Her body trembles. Defiance grows on her expression, lighting up every deviant desire I have within me.

I demand, "I want an answer, pet."

She stays quiet, continuing to focus her glare on me.

I rise, sliding my hands under her armpits and moving her to her feet.

"What—"

"I will not tolerate your defiance."

"Riggs—"

"Who?" I bark.

"Sir!" she grits through her teeth.

I move her across the room until she's standing on a metal square, facing the mirror. There's one metal bar at shoulder height, longer than her arms stretch. I order, "Stretch out your arms."

She obeys.

I attach a brown cowhide strap around her biceps. Then I add the same ones to her wrists. I walk around and cross my arms, studying her.

A deep flush fills her cheeks, almost matching the color of her lip stain. Questions swirl in her blues, mixing with fear, a desire to resist my authority, and something I saw the day we were in the shower and I lost control. And her leash hangs between her breasts, twinkling from the glow of the fire.

I've never witnessed anything so majestic.

I remind myself there can be no mistakes tonight. She's naive to everything in my world. It's another part of her reality that's testing me, causing me to debate what route to take for her punishment.

There's a masochistic part of Blakely, something I've barely tapped into and want to explore. Her pain, while different from Aria's, runs just as deep. Yet my gut tells me Blakely's masochism doesn't exceed or even meet Aria's.

My pet needs mental pain, maybe more than physical. I've witnessed the clues. I know it well, more than most Doms could ever begin to understand. And I trust in my ability to deliver it to her.

"Why did you agree to let me have total control over you? To own you and do whatever I please?" I push.

The room continues to flicker from the fire, and the longer I debate, the more Blakely's expression changes. The fear begins to subside, morphing into an insubordinate stare.

I chuckle inside. Her reaction is predictable. My lips twitch, and I warn, "Last chance. Why did you hand over all the control of your body and mind?"

Her eyes turn to slits.

I drag my knuckles over her cheek, and she moves her face.

"Wrong move, pet," I state, then lift a hook from the bar and lock her collar to it.

She inhales deeply, jerks her head, but it goes nowhere. A new, beautiful look of terror crosses her face.

"It's time for your punishment," I inform her, then go to the wall and study the shelf. I choose a gold, hands-free vibrator. It's egg-shaped with two tentacles. I slip the remote into my pocket and return to Blakely, placing it over her clit and then securing the tentacles against her labia. Once I'm confident it's secure, I hit the button on the side of the contraption that's restraining her.

The front of the bar lowers, moving forward until her upper body's suspended in the air, lower than her ass. I grab a brown cowhide flogger and drag the tails over her spine, then underneath her, teasing her nipples.

Her breath hitches. A slight arch forms in her back.

I slide my hand over her ass, longer than normal, reminding myself to watch her body language. There's a point of no return, and I don't ever want to pass it with any sub, but especially not Blakely.

The hairs on her arms rise. I press the remote, and a faint buzz hits my ears.

She clenches her jaw, closing her eyes, taking shallow breaths.

"Eyes stay open, locked on the mirror," I inform her.

She slowly obeys, meeting my gaze with a challenge so fierce I almost come in my pants.

"Not on me. On you," I assert.

She gives me a final glare and refocuses.

I lean over her, kiss her shoulder, then state, "You'll thank me every time the leather hits your body. When I ask you questions, you'll answer them. You'll get your reward when I'm confident you're ready to submit. No coming, or we start all over. It's up to you when this is over and your pleasure begins, understand?"

Her eyes stay focused. She swallows hard, shifts her lower body, and breathes through her nose.

I debate about increasing the speed on her vibrator but decide to hold off. I demand, "Answer me."

"Yes, Sir," she seethes.

"Ah, my little pet. So angry. Is it thoughts of your daddy that make you disobey?" I taunt, running my hand over her inner thigh.

She blinks hard.

"I expect answers," I bark, then step back and administer her first flogging.

She gasps. Her back arches.

I wait, then remind her, "Thank you, Sir." I smack her again.

She scrunches her face. "Thank you, Sir."

I give her five in a row, watching her in the mirror and listening to her tone change. There's still defiance in it but less.

I caress over the red marks on her ass, demanding, "Tell me who you hate."

She closes her eyes briefly, then answers, "My father, Sir."

"And what does he do to you that makes you hate him?" I ask.

She doesn't answer, and I add two flogs.

When she doesn't thank me, I assert, "Did you forget something? Or should I go harder?"

"Thank you, Sir," she quickly says.

"What do you hate about him most?" I increase the speed of the vibrator.

She whimpers, then grits out, "He tries to control me, Sir."

I drop my pants, pushing my throbbing erection against her thigh. I kiss the bottom of her spine, making my way up until I get to her collar, stating, "So we're here again. Why did you give me the authority to fully control you, pet?"

She blinks hard but can't stop a few tears from rolling down her cheeks. Her eyes meet mine in the mirror.

I smack her ass with my palm, barking out, "Eyes on you, not me. Now thank me!"

Her eyes dart back, and she croaks out, "Thank you, Sir."

I pick up the leash and graze it across her breasts, thrusting my finger inside her, murmuring in her ear, "I can smell your sweet scent, pet." I flick my tongue across her lobe and warn, "We can do this all night until your skin's bruised and juices pool at your feet. It's your choice."

She squeezes her eyes shut and more tears fall.

"Why did you give me control?" I repeat, curling my finger inside her.

She moans, and tremors race through her frame.

"You don't have permission to come, pet," I remind her.

Sweat pops out, glistening all over her body. Her chest heaves, taking in short bursts of air.

"Should I get another Dom in here?" I threaten.

Her eyes meet mine. "No! Please!"

"Why not?"

"Ri—Sir! Please! No one else!" she cries out.

"Why did you give me control, Blakely," I shout, inhaling her driftwood and sea salt scent mixed with her arousal, feeling a craziness begin to unravel my discipline.

Tears fall everywhere. She confesses, blurting out, "Because I've always wanted you to love me!"

I freeze, not sure what I thought she'd admit but not expecting her to say that.

She shuts her eyes, sobbing, her body convulsing, maybe from an orgasm or perhaps just from her anguish of what she admitted.

And for the first time in a session, I'm too shocked to know what to do next.

19

Blakely

I'm mortified about what I admitted to Riggs. Until it came out of my mouth, I didn't even know what I was hiding.

Why did I tell him that?

I should have lied.

Why?

He's going to hold it over my head. I know it. I've learned enough about him over the last two weeks to understand he'll take anything he can and use it against me when it suits him.

Is it even true?

I thought I agreed to all this to escape my father's grasp. But I can't lie to myself anymore. It was a convenient excuse for me to be with Riggs.

How fucked up am I?

I can't stop the emotions plaguing me. And I'm going to end up losing him anyway. Adrenaline's coursing through me, thanks to that damn vibrator having a field day with my body. I can hardly catch my breath to stop my uncontrollable sobs.

Somewhere amid the chaos, Riggs releases me. He carries me to the bed, then holds my head to his chest.

Is his heart racing, or is it mine?

"Shh," he murmurs.

It's all too much. I don't expect his affection. It's another example of how he's a master of confusion. He seamlessly morphs from cruel to kind, and my head constantly spins from it.

And I wish I didn't still want him. I wish I could somehow use his cruelty against him and walk away. Yet even in my distress, rule fourteen never leaves my mind. It tortures me.

I lift my head, blinking through my tears, but his face is blurry. I choke out in a whisper, "Let me submit."

His body stiffens. He slides his palm on my cheek, and I close my eyes, trying to regain my composure.

He glides his thumbs under my eyes and gives me a few minutes. When he finally comes clearly into view, I stare at him, scared this is it and I've screwed up beyond repair.

He keeps his voice steady, ordering, "Kiss me, pet. Touch me how you want."

Master of confusion does it again. I open my mouth to speak, but no words come out.

He repeats, in a firmer tone, "I said to kiss me."

My hands tremble. I slide them up his chest, then neck, until my fingers entwine his hair. My pulse beats wild. I push my knees next to his hips and slowly move closer to his lips.

His hot breath merges with mine. The blues in his eyes swirl, making me think about calm chaos. My mouth melts against his, our tongues rapidly creating an intense fire, blazing out of control.

His hand weaves through my hair, holding my head firmly to him. His palm grasps my ass, tugging me closer.

I lift my pelvis, and he repositions his hand on my hip, shoving me over his erection until I've taken all of him.

His groan competes with my moan. The pressure of the vibrator against his body makes it all more intense.

My tremors continue, and I already know I'm coming, but I still blurt out, "Please let me come!"

Maybe he knows I'm already there. Perhaps he's aware there's no stopping the earthquake within me. But he breaks from my lips, asserting, "As much as you want, pet," before coming back for more and spinning me until I'm lying on my back.

He cages himself over me, slowing down his thrusts, nibbling on my shoulder, sucking on my breasts, tugging on my hair, and squeezing my neck underneath my collar.

Every adjustment he makes creates a new frenzy within me. My cries are incoherent. He pins my wrists above my head, his chest heaving, locking his calm-chaos eyes on mine.

His body inside mine unleashes a euphoria I've never felt. At times, he thrusts so fast, I think he'll pound through me until another wave of adrenaline attacks my cells. Then he'll slow down, gritting his teeth, his breath flaring through his nostrils and into mine.

Sweat coats us. Our skin glides across the other. A drop rolls down his cheek.

"I can't take anymore," I claim, the sensations from the vibrator tearing through me again.

"You can," he declares, flips me on my stomach, then bites the nape of my neck next to the top of my collar. He thrusts his cock back inside me.

"Riggs," I moan, then catch my mistake. "Sir...oh, Sir!"

He pins my hands on the headboard, flips a cuff over each, and kisses my shoulder.

I wrap my fingers over the bars, closing my eyes.

"Look in the mirror," he instructs.

I obey, staring at our reflection.

He lifts my hips, rises on his knees, and locks his challenging gaze on mine. He slowly thrusts, asking, "Who owns you, pet?"

I don't hesitate. "You do, Sir."

"Who's the only one allowed inside your pussy?"

"You, Sir. Only you."

"And what about your ass?"

"You, Sir."

"And what do you want me to do right now, pet?" he questions, his eyes growing darker.

"Whatever you want, Sir," I reply.

He slaps my ass cheek hard.

I gasp, then blurt out, "Thank you, Sir."

"Don't lie to me, pet. What do you want me to do to you?" he growls, desperation mixing with craziness on his expression.

"Whatever you want, Sir," I yell again.

He slaps me harder, barking, "Say what you want!"

"Your cock in my ass," I reveal.

"Say please," he orders.

"Please, Sir."

"Say all of it," he demands, a wild look I've never seen overpowering him.

I cry out, "Put your cock in my ass. Please, Sir!"

He slides past my hard ridge, not stopping like he did the last time, gliding all the way in until his pelvis hits my ass cheeks.

"Oh!" I scream, arch my back, and grip the bars so tight my knuckles turn white.

"Is this what you want, pet?" he barks.

"Yes! Th-thank you, Sir," I reply, trying to catch my breath.

He reaches for my hair, wraps it around his fist, tugs it, and asks, "Who do you submit to?"

"You, Sir."

"Whose cock do you suck?"

"Yours, Sir!"

"Whose cock do you clench with your pussy?"

"Yours, Sir!" I scream. He slaps my ass and thrusts faster. "Thank y—" My body explodes with new sensations, my eyes roll, and all I see are stars.

"Fuck, pet!" he cries out. He pumps his hot fluid inside me, slapping my ass a few more times while convulsing.

When he stills, I'm still trembling. He unlatches the cuffs, rolls on his back, and tugs me against him. He reaches for the vibrator and tosses it across the room.

Exhausted, I wait for my heart to slow, processing everything that's happened, realizing I said his name a few times, breaking rule two. I force myself to deal with a new fear that the cruel Riggs might be back.

But he's not.

He slides his hand on my cheek and kisses me. It's tender and sweet. I return his affection until he breaks our kiss and holds my face a few inches from his. He murmurs, "Who do you want to go home with, pet?"

"You, Sir."

His expression remains hard. I worry I said something wrong when he questions, "When?"

I don't hesitate. "Now."

He nods and kisses me again. He rises, goes over to a closet, and removes a robe. He brings it to the bed and helps me get it on. He ties the belt and then puts on his pants and shirt. He drapes his sport coat over his arm, then guides me down a dark hall and into an alley.

His driver sits in the SUV. He sees us and opens his door, but Riggs makes a hand motion. He shuts the door and turns on the engine.

Riggs opens the back door. I slide into the backseat, and he follows. We don't speak on the way home. Riggs keeps his arm around me and murmurs, "Go to sleep if you're tired."

I cling to him, but too many thoughts are going through my head. I stay awake until we get home. Riggs leads me to the shower, and we take one together, but it's not a long one. He dries me off and puts ointment on my ass cheeks, stating, "It'll help prevent bruising."

I had forgotten about the flogging. I stay quiet as he rubs the cream on my tender skin.

He leads me out of the bathroom and, for the first time in ten days, motions for me to get into his bed.

I slide under the covers, then curl into his back. I kiss his shoulder, wrap my arm around him, and he covers it with his forearm, stroking my hand with his index finger.

I yawn, then ask in a whisper, "Did I pass?"

He picks up my hand and kisses it, replying, "Yeah, pet. You passed."

"So no more rule fourteen?"

He confirms, "No more rule fourteen. You're stuck with me now."

I tighten my arm around him and fall asleep, smiling. Even through my admission, I'm still here. And Riggs is mine, even if I'm on borrowed time.

When I wake up the next morning, it's almost ten. Riggs has already surfed, showered, and eaten. He's at the table, working on his laptop.

I sneak behind him and put my arms around his chest. "Morning," I chirp and go to kiss him.

He turns his head, moves my arms off him, and slides his chair out. He shuts his laptop and gives me a hardened stare, stating, "Make sure you eat breakfast. I'll be back later."

My chest tightens. I blurt out, "So we're back to normal, I see."

He clenches his jaw, leers down at me, and declares, "That's right. I'm in charge. Don't forget it, pet." He grabs his laptop, puts it in his bag, and leaves, never looking back.

I don't know why I expected anything different from him. I know he's like Jekyll and Hyde.

I finally conclude that he's always going to be like this. No matter what I do, he'll always revert to his need for control.

He's got some sort of deep-seated issues. There's nothing I can do to change him.

So why does it still hurt so much?

20

Riggs

One Month Later

$\mathcal{I}$'m in uncharted territory, and I'm unsure how to navigate out of it. The more I try to stick with my normal playtime activities, avoiding anything intimate with Blakely, the more I fail.

I can only go so many sessions without kissing her before I break. And once I touch her lips, it's like relief hits me.

I don't know what's happening to me. It's a vicious cycle, but it doesn't help that the only time I really feel like Blakely fully submits is when I allow her to kiss me. It's why I let her the night at the club. I didn't plan it, but it seemed like the only path to take after her admission.

We've had too many play sessions to count. Every night, some-times during the day if it's the weekend, or even the morning if I can't surf, leads to sessions.

The ones I get through without kissing her don't eliminate the chaos looming inside me. If anything, I feel more on edge. Nightmares always follow. Blakely always wakes me, giving me a pitiful expression, which I hate. But my past continues to terrorize me until I finally cave. The nights we kiss and my pet fully submits, I sleep peacefully, sometimes later than normal, and I miss the ability to surf.

It turns me into a bigger dick.

Blakely doesn't take my shit, talking back to me and standing up for herself, which only irritates me further. So I always revert to our sessions, trying to keep my boundaries until I fail again.

My secret plans to take down Hugh continue to evolve. I've become ruthless in sending him footage of my pet. Sometimes she's at the piano, belting out a tune. At others, on the beach, with the wind blowing her blonde locks all over. But then there are the times I really piss Hugh off. Like last night, I took a video of Blakely sucking my cock and looking at me with her glistening, doe eyes.

It was only a few seconds of coverage, but I didn't hesitate to send it. And I've been editing footage from our night at the club, using an app to hide the identity of my voice. Hugh's seen nothing of that footage. I'm saving that for public humiliation.

My pet stirs, a soft whine coming from her as she curls closer into my chest.

I curse myself again, stroking her hip. Last night was another example of my lack of discipline. Right now, I need to get away from her, but even that is getting harder. On these types of mornings, I want to kiss her some more and go at it again.

I'm turning into a pussy.

This has to stop.

She's learning how to fuck with my head to get what she wants.

I walked in the door after nine o'clock last night, and she was in a hot-pink lingerie set, kneeling next to her piano.

I had no idea how long she'd been in her position, but my cock got so hard, all I could think about was getting inside her. Within two minutes, I kissed her and carried her to the bedroom. We fucked, and talked, and fucked some more until the darkness started to break with a brilliant orange glow.

I internally groan, recalling how I admitted to her that my mother was a prostitute, alcoholic, and drug addict. It came out of my mouth before I realized it. And she pushed me for more info until I cracked further and confessed too many things.

Yep, I'm a full-blown pussy.

Unable to hide from my reality, I slowly move her off me, then sneak out of the room. It's close to eight, which usually means I missed my surfing window. But a storm is coming, making the swell higher and more dangerous to surf. It's the perfect morning for how I'm feeling.

I go outside, put on my wetsuit, grab my board, and enter the ocean, fighting to get past the break.

There's no calm chaos today, except for the image of my pet's blue orbs. It's a fight to stay on the board, and the challenge helps alleviate some of my stress.

Then her lips pop back into my mind.

Hours pass, and it begins to rain. I head to shore, shower, and go inside.

Blakely sits at the table, drinking coffee, looking lost in thoughts.

Panic grips me. I question, "What's wrong?"

"Nothing," she states, but she's lying. Her fingers tap her mug like she's playing a fast song on the piano. Her other hand is softly scratching her neck. If I didn't know her, I'd wonder if she's an addict, jonesing for a hit. It reminds me of my mother or hers, but I try to shake it off. Since the night Blakely drank that bottle of wine, I've never seen her anything but sober.

I sit next to her, grab her hand from her neck, and assert, "You're going to have scratch marks. Stop lying to me and tell me what's bothering you."

She cringes and sighs.

I wait for her to speak, but when a vision of my mother pacing our falling-apart house appears in my mind, I reach for her hand that's tapping the mug. I hold it flat against the ceramic and arch my eyebrows.

She blurts out, "I'm going backward."

"How?"

"My career. I should be on stage singing. I'm not developing."

"You're supposed to be working on material for your demo," I remind her.

She bites her lip.

"Isn't that what you said you needed? A demo?" I question.

She nods. "Yes, but that requires me to write something. I-I can't."

I release her hands and sit back in the chair, inquiring, "How many new songs have you written since you got here?"

She winces again.

"It can't be that bad," I assert.

She closes her eyes, shakes her head, and confesses, "None."

Shock fills me. I blurt out, "Surely you've written something. You've been here almost two months."

She covers her hands over her face and groans. "I have nothing."

"What have you been doing all day?"

She glares at me. "I've been trying to write. It's just not coming to me. It's not that easy, or everyone would do it!"

I put my hands in the air. "Hey, I'm not judging."

"Sounds like you are," she says.

I soften my voice. "I'm not, pet."

Silence ensues. I curse myself. I promised her she'd be farther along in her career after a year with me. It's time to make good on that.

My phone vibrates. I glance at the screen.

> Chainsaw: Ready for you.

Excitement fills me. I've been waiting for this longer than I ever expected.

> Me: Be there in an hour and a half.

I ask, "What do you need to write?"

She scoffs. "A new brain."

My lips twitch.

"This isn't funny," she claims.

I rise, bend down, kiss the top of her head, and declare, "Your brain is fine. In fact, it's impeccable. Stop worrying, and it'll come to you. I have to get to work." I go into the bedroom, change, and leave.

I fight traffic, finally get in front of the warehouse, and hit the remote. The garage door opens. I reverse the Porsche in, then close the door. I take an envelope out of the glove compartment and exit my vehicle. I step inside the large, almost empty space.

Chainsaw sits on the desk, his arms crossed. The man, who I assume is Snake, is tied to a chair, his wrists bound behind his back and ankles strapped to the metal legs. He's huge, not unlike anything I'd imagine for a bouncer at a high-end strip club in L.A. A white cloth fills his mouth. Several layers of duct tape circle around his head, securing the gag.

My phone buzzes. I read the text.

> Jones: Have an update, but I'm leaving in the next two hours.

I glance at my watch, determining what traffic will be like. I could wait, but I told Jones not to text me until progress was made. My patience has worn thin, so I'll have to cut my little session with Chainsaw early.

> Me: I'll be there before you need to leave.

I refocus on the current situation and toss the envelope on the desk. I glance at Snake's black eye and say to Chainsaw, "Looks like you started the fun without me."

"Nah. He's a pussy," Chainsaw says, as if bored.

Knowing I'm pressed for time, I go over to Snake, slowly rip the duct tape off him to intensify the pain, and toss the skin-and-hair-covered adhesive onto his lap.

His muffled cries echo in the room.

I tug the cloth out of his mouth.

"I didn't do nothing," he claims.

I yank his head back so fast he screams. I lean over him, keeping my voice calm, and ask, "How much did you get for tricking Blakely?"

He blurts out, "That skank is why I'm here?"

I snap and punch him so hard he falls to the ground. The metal chair bangs on the concrete floor. Blood spews out of his nose, and he yelps.

I grab him by the hair, yanking him back into a sitting position, and he shouts, "Stop it!"

"See, nothing but a pussy," Chainsaw interjects.

"How much?" I repeat, my spit hitting his face.

"Two fifty!" he cries out.

His answer makes me angrier. I tug his head farther and fight to reclaim control of my emotions. I seethe, "That's the price of your life, then."

His eyes widen. He tries to get out of my grasp, but he's not going anywhere.

I release him, turn to Chainsaw, and order, "Finish the job."

Chainsaw cracks his knuckles. "Gladly. No one's gonna be missing this piece of shit."

I point to the envelope. Cash and pictures of Roy and George are in it, along with their home addresses and family situations. The last thing I need is women or children getting hurt. Surprises aren't good for Chainsaw's line of work. I assert, "When you're done, I've got two more pieces of shit for you. Destroy it once you're clear on the targets."

"Got it," he replies.

I leave, cranking the music in the car. Hugh's going to have a fit when Roy and George go missing. Jones has something for me now, and it has to be good news. I get to Compton and reverse into his garage.

He doesn't shut the door, comes over to my window, and announces, "I cracked it. I just siphoned the first million from one of his offshore accounts. I'm taking smaller amounts from the legal ones he has here."

A rush of adrenaline almost makes me dizzy. I'm finally making progress to take Hugh down beyond pissing him off with footage of my pet. I ask, "It's untraceable?"

Jones furrows his brows as if insulted. "Of course it is. My system is bulletproof. However, I'll continue upgrading it, as things always move fast in the cyber world."

I fist-bump him, feeling giddy. "Good man. Keep me posted."

I pull out, turn my music up again, and fight more traffic, not even bothered by it. I finally veer off the exit, and a car pulls out of the space directly in front of Naked Pipe Entertainment, one of L.A.'s hottest recording studios.

"My lucky day," I mutter, sliding into the spot. I get out and stroll through the front door.

A woman with bright-green hair, obnoxiously chewing her gum, removes her earphones, and asks, "Can I help you?"

I demand, "Riggs Madden. Here to see Ears."

She glances at her screen and offers a fake smile. "Sorry. He's in a meeting. Can I give him a message?"

I toss a thousand dollars in cash down on her desk, repeating, "Tell him Riggs Madden is here. That's for your trouble."

She glances at the cash, clears her throat, then folds the bills. She stuffs it in her bra and chirps, "Let me see if he's on a break."

"Yeah, you do that," I state.

She isn't gone long before Ears steps into the lobby, grinning. "Well, I'll be damned." He slaps hands with me and pats me on the back, claiming, "Long time."

"Yeah. Got a minute for me?" I ask, knowing he'd give me the shirt off his back. He's another friend from Compton who made it out. I was in more fights than I can count with him. We've always had each other's backs.

He leads me to a private office. "You want a drink?"

"Nah. All good," I reply.

He sits on an oversized armchair and motions for me to sit on the couch. I obey.

Ears pushes his fingertips together, asking, "What the fuck are you doing in my studio?"

I chuckle. "Love how you never beat around the bush."

"Nor do you, as I remember."

"No, I do not. I need studio time for a demo. And I need the top agents in the room."

Ears whistles. "That's a hefty demand."

"But I'm sure you can get it done. For a nice amount of change, of course," I add.

Ears crosses his arms, declaring, "I can't mess with my relationships."

"She has the talent. I promise you," I state.

He narrows his eyes. "You fucking her?"

I don't answer, keeping my eyes on his and clenching my jaw.

Ears scoffs. "Of course you're fucking her."

"This isn't about that. I wouldn't come to you if she wasn't the real deal," I insist.

Ears sighs. "Okay. I'll bite. Tell me about her."

"She plays piano, has the voice of an angel, and writes her own songs," I inform him.

He huffs. "Sounds like most of L.A."

"She has talent," I firmly repeat.

A moment passes. He asks, "What's she look like? She a looker? If she's not a looker, it'll never work. This industry is rough."

"Like you said, I'm fucking her," I reply.

Ears scrubs his face, then nods. "I had a cancelation today. Two months out."

"Perfect. Send me the bill," I say and rise.

Ears stands, warning, "Riggs, if she's not the next Mariah Carey, don't have me call my contacts."

I grunt. "You still have a thing for her, huh?"

He grins. "She's my queen."

"Don't worry. You're going to love Blakely," I reinforce.

"What's her last name?"

I almost say Gallow, then stop myself. "Fox."

He repeats, "Blakely Fox. Well, at least she doesn't have to change her name."

"Nope. See you in two months. Have your girl send me the date," I order, wanting to get out before he asks any more questions or changes his mind.

I fight through more traffic, heading straight to the beach house. It's around three when I stroll through the door, still feeling giddy.

Today couldn't have gone better.

Lightning streaks through the sky as I step inside, momentarily lighting up the dark house. Blakely's at the piano, but she's not playing. She's staring out at the water, lost in her thoughts.

"Pet," I gently say, sliding my hand on her shoulder.

She jumps, then glances up. "Oh, hey. I didn't hear you come inside."

"I guess not."

She glances at the clock, then says, "You're home early."

I slide next to her on the bench, teasing, "Is that a good or bad thing?"

She smiles, but the worry doesn't leave her face. She answers, "Always good."

Damn, if her statement doesn't make me happier.

And she sees it. She asks, "Why do you look elated right now?"

I chuckle. "Elated? That's an interesting choice of words."

Her smile grows. "Guess one part of my brain still works."

I lean closer to her face. "I have some news for you."

"Oh?"

"You've got two months to get ready."

"For what?" she asks.

"Your demo."

She gapes at me, then questions, "Riggs, what are you talking about?"

I drop another bomb. "It's at Naked Pipe Entertainment."

The color drains from her cheeks. She stares at the piano keys.

My heart races. "I thought you'd be excited."

She swallows hard and locks her blues on mine. She asserts, "Naked Pipe Entertainment isn't just somewhere you go to demo, Riggs. Anyone charting right now records with them."

Arrogance flares inside me. "I'm aware."

She gets up and paces in front of the window.

My gut drops. I question, "Pet, I thought you'd be excited."

"I-I'm not good enough for that studio!"

"Sure you are."

She shakes her head. "No, I'm not. I've never even properly recorded anything. I'm an amateur! I'm... I'm nowhere near ready for their caliber."

"That's absurd," I state.

"You don't understand. I only get one shot. They'll never let me return if I screw it up!" she cries out.

I step in front of her. "Breathe, Blakely."

Her fear-laced expression intensifies. She taps her fingers on her thighs like she has a nerve problem.

I pick up her hands. "Calm down."

She takes a few breaths, then asks, "How did you even line this up?"

"I'm friends with Ears."

Her eyes widen. "You spoke to Ears? About me?"

"Yes."

She squeezes her eyes shut.

My chest tightens. This is going the entirely wrong way. I restate, "I thought you'd be excited about this. Isn't this what you were shooting for? A demo?"

She glances at the ceiling, then me. "Riggs, you don't just go up to Ears and tell him your girlfriend needs a demo and to let her record."

"Girlfriend?" I blurt out, shocked that she used the term.

Her face turns red. She shakes her head and shrugs out of my grasp, biting out, "No. Of course not. God forbid anything is normal in your world."

"What does that mean?" I snap.

"Exactly what I said. Thanks for setting it up," she adds, but she sounds anything but grateful. She moves toward the bedroom.

I ignore all the alarms going off in my head. I follow her and claim, "I don't understand why you're pissed."

"I'm not pissed."

"Could have fooled me."

She spins toward me. "Did you not hear me this morning? I have no content. I've stagnated."

I cross my arms. "Yes, I heard you. Maybe this is what you need to move forward. A bit of pressure."

"A bit of pressure?"

"Yeah."

She scoffs. "I have enough pressure in my life."

"Don't be dramatic."

"I'm not," she shouts.

"You have a safe roof over your head, no bills, and food in your stomach. What is possibly creating pressure in your life?" I question.

"You! You're the pressure in my life!" she cries out, her eyes blazing and cheeks flushing.

I jerk my head back. Tension rapidly builds between us.

She realizes what she said and tries to backtrack. She lowers her voice. "I'm sorry. I didn't mean—"

"Don't lie to me, pet. Just put it all on the table," I seethe.

She shuts her eyes. "Riggs..." She opens her lids, and they're wet.

My pulse beats hard between my ears. I keep my voice as neutral as possible and state, "You have two months. And I wouldn't go to Ears if I didn't think you were ready...if I didn't believe in your talent. One thing I thought you'd know about me by now is that I don't put my reputation on the line unless I'm convinced it's a sure thing."

She swallows hard.

I add, "But you're only a sure thing if you want to be. And it doesn't matter if I believe in you or not. You have to believe in yourself. Make a choice, pet. You either want to make it happen, or you don't." I walk out of the house, slam the door, and take off to my apartment in the city. If Blakely thinks I'm her root of pressure, then I'll eliminate it for her.

It's probably best for us anyway. She's confusing our relationship with her girlfriend comment. And I need to stop being such a pussy when it comes to her.

21

Blakely
Three Weeks Later

*R*iggs has been punishing me. No matter what I do, he won't come home. It's been almost three weeks. I've texted and called him, but he hardly responds. A few times, I've gotten a returned text, always with the same message.

> Riggs: Do your work, Blakely.

I've begged him to come home, but he doesn't.

It's not doing anything for my writer's block. I still can't put any lyrics together to save my life. I sit at the piano most of the day, hitting the keys, but nothing comes.

I shouldn't have told Riggs he's the pressure in my life, but I did, and he won't let me take it back. Nor should I have said I was his girlfriend. And I'd do anything to have him back, but he won't come home.

Another day passes, turning to darkness. I wait up until midnight, then take a shower. I dry off and slide into his bed, trying to inhale the remaining scent of him on the pillowcase, but it's fading.

I send him a text message.

> Me: Will you please come home? I miss you.

I stare at the screen, but a message never comes. I finally fall asleep with the window open, listening to the waves crash on the shore, wondering if Riggs has surfed somewhere else or not.

At some point in the night, I open my eyes and wonder if I'm dreaming.

Riggs sits on the armchair in the corner, staring at me, holding a crystal tumbler of scotch.

I sit up in bed. My voice cracks as I ask, "Why aren't you in bed?"

He remains silent, his eyes pinned on me.

I walk over to him and put my hand on his cheek, but he moves his head.

"Don't do this," I beg.

He scowls, questioning, "What do you think this is between us, Blakely?"

The smell of scotch flares in my nostrils. I peer closer, assessing him, then accuse, "You're drunk."

It surprises me. I know how much Riggs hates intoxication. He told me about his mother and why he also gets so disgusted by my mother and her addiction issues. And, of course, I'll never forget how he acted the one time I got drunk.

He clenches his jaw. A small twitch forms. He reaches around my body, palming my ass, then moves his hand down and slides it underneath my nightgown. He repeats, "Tell me, pet, what do you think we are?"

My insides quiver. I ask, "Does it matter?"

He chuckles and takes a large gulp of his scotch. "I don't know. Does it?"

"Come to bed?" I ask and squeeze his hand. I pull, but he doesn't budge. Instead, he squeezes my ass harder, tugging me toward him until I fall over him.

I tuck a lock of his hair behind his ear, suggesting, "Why don't you take a shower and then come to bed?"

He drops the glass, and it shatters on the floor. His hand fists my hair, and he tugs my head back. He leans over me, snarling, "Answer my question, pet. What do you think we are?"

Tears form in my eyes. Emotions I've been holding in for the past few weeks overpower me. I admit, "I don't know. Whatever you want us to be. You're the one who gets to make the decisions, remember?"

"That's not what I asked," he snaps.

"Riggs, drop it. Just come to bed," I say again, but I'm suddenly afraid. When I'm with Riggs, I trust him. But the look in his eyes right now is so unhinged. There's no control in it anywhere, and that's not the Riggs Madden I know. Plus, I've never seen him drunk before. I know from my mother how someone can change when under the influence.

He glances at my lips, and I think he's going to kiss me. There's no doubt in my mind it's what we need. When Riggs allows me to kiss him, he always softens.

I slide my hand over his hair and push his face toward me, but he freezes, pausing an inch from my lips. He declares, "You're a temptress."

"I'm not," I state.

He grunts, claiming, "You know exactly what you're doing. Don't you, pet?"

"What are you talking about?"

He looks at me with disgust and rises, pushing me to my feet. He moves toward the bedroom door.

I follow him. "Riggs, where are you going? You can't drive like this."

He chuckles. "I can do whatever I want. I'm in charge. Remember, pet?"

I pull on his arm. "Riggs, you're drunk."

"So what?" he mutters.

"Stop. You can't go outside," I insist.

He grabs his keys off the table, then spins toward me. Anger flares on his face. "And why is that, pet?"

"Because I don't want something to happen to you!"

He grunts. "Why? Do you really care?"

"Of course I care. Why are you saying this? You know I care about you!"

He moves toward me, and fear reignites inside me. I step back, and he continues lunging toward me until I'm up against the wall. His rage radiates over me. He slides his hand on my cheek and rubs his thumb over my lips, seething, "Tell me what we are, pet."

I say the only thing that comes to mind that I think he might want me to say. "You're my Dom, Sir, and I'm your sub."

His face hardens to stone, confusing me. *Isn't that what he wants?*

I reach for him, not wanting to anger him further and trying to show him I care about him.

He holds my wrists in front of us. "Did I give you permission to touch me?"

"Sorry."

"Sorry's not good enough, pet. You don't like rules, do you?" he accuses.

I stay quiet.

He drags his knuckles over my chest, squeezing my nipple between his fingers until I gasp, demanding, "I asked you a question, and I want an answer." He moves to my other breast.

I try to steady my breath.

"Answer me," he pushes.

"I like your rules."

He grunts. "No, you don't. You don't even like me."

"That's not true," I cry out.

He scoffs. "Then what do you want us to be, Blakely? What do you get out of this?"

I don't know why he's pushing this. There's no answer I can give him that will make him happy. He's made it clear he doesn't want me to be his girlfriend. My acknowledgment that he's the Dom and I'm the sub wasn't what he was looking for. No matter what I say, I can't win. So I firmly state, "I want you to come home."

"No. Wrong answer," he asserts and cups his hand over my pussy. His index finger slides across my slit.

The fire in my core lights up. It's been so long since he's touched me. But I don't want him like this. It makes me realize how much I appreciate the in-control-of-everything Riggs.

I beg again, "Come to bed. Please."

"Nope, not until you're honest," he states.

"I don't know what you want me to say," I admit.

"Sure you do. I want the truth. Why can't you just give me the truth, pet?"

"I have told you the truth."

"No, you haven't," he insists. He leans closer to my ear and repeats in a slow but firm voice, "What do you want from me?"

I keep my mouth shut, too scared about what might come out.

"Tell me the truth, and I'll stay," he adds.

I can't blink my tears away. They drip down my cheek. I cave and admit, "I want you to love me."

He sighs as if relieved, which surprises me again. Then his face turns darker. He studies me for a moment, and a sinister grin forms on his lips. "Sorry to disappoint you, pet. I don't love," he claims.

I turn my face away, trying to control my emotions. He mutters, "You're better off." He spins and walks toward the front door.

"Riggs, you're drunk," I repeat and grab the keys out of his hand.

It takes him by surprise. He turns on me. "Don't fuck with me, Blakely."

"You're not leaving," I declare.

New rage flares on his cheeks. The fear hits me again, but I'm not giving them to him. He's too drunk.

He orders, "Give me the keys, pet."

"No," I say, my voice and body shaking.

He yells, "Give me the keys!"

"No!" I run to the bedroom and slam the door, locking it.

He bangs on the door.

I go into the bathroom, open the exit to the side balcony, and step outside. I put the keys underneath one of the vases, then return inside.

Riggs is still pounding on the door. He shouts, "Pet, open this door now."

I unlock the door, then slide into bed.

"What are you doing? Where are my keys?" he slurs.

"I threw them on the beach. You're not going to find them. Sober up and stop being a hypocrite," I add, then turn my face on the pillow.

He stands over me for a long time. I close my eyes, unsure what he's going to do next. He finally stomps out of the room and slams the door.

I stay in the room, and when I finally get up the next morning, he's nowhere.

Oh God! He must have had another set of keys.

How could I have been so stupid?

I text him.

> Me: Riggs, please tell me you're okay.

I don't receive a response and try calling. It goes to his voicemail.

All day, I keep trying to contact him. I call him. I text him. But it doesn't matter. He never answers. I don't even sit at the piano. The last thing I can think about is my work.

It's late at night when he finally comes back into the house. "Where have you been?" I ask.

He has on a fresh suit and looks like he does every night when he comes home from work. He clenches his jaw and looks down at me, threatening, "Don't you ever take my keys away from me again."

"You were drunk," I state.

"Like I said, don't ever do it again," he warns, then walks into the bedroom.

I follow him. "Where did you go?"

"None of your business."

"Yes, it is," I claim, sick of this bullshit with him. I put my hand on my hip and add, "I may have signed a contract, but this is ridiculous. I'm not going to be somebody that you can just walk all over whenever you decide to have a mood swing."

He steps out of his pants and tosses them into the laundry basket. Then takes his jacket and shirt off until he's wearing only his boxers.

"Riggs, we can't keep doing this," I state.

He turns, pinning his eyes on me. "Did you write anything?"

My heart pounds harder. "No."

"I've been gone for three weeks, and you've not written anything?" he accuses.

"It's not that easy."

"Well, you said I was the pressure. I removed it. Why don't you have a notebook of songs?"

"Riggs, I said I was sorry and didn't mean it."

"Sure you did," he claims and slides past me.

I follow him and tug on his arm. "Riggs!"

He spins into me. "What, Blakely? Am I pressure whether I'm here or not? Am I your excuse if you fail?"

I stare at him for a minute. It hits me how broken he is, even though I'm the one he always tries to break. It saddens me. Riggs is more broken than any man I've ever met.

I soften my tone, admitting, "The only person whose fault it will be if I fail is mine. I'm sorry I acted how I did. It's amazing what you've done for me."

His face hardens further.

"I mean it. Stay. I need you. You can't keep staying away from me like this."

He steps closer, dragging his fingertip down my cheek. "What do you need me for, Blakely?"

I lift my chin and square my shoulders. "I need from you whatever it is you need from me," I declare, my voice shaking.

"That's a paradox," he states.

"One you know makes sense," I claim.

Silence fills the air, and tension burns through the room like a hurricane.

I cave, restating, "I need you. All of you. I'm not doing well without you."

The darkness deepens to the point I can see the shift. He takes my hand, leads me to the piano, then picks me up. He sits me on the crystal top, ordering. "Kneel."

"On this?" I ask.

He traces the skin above my collar, commanding, "Assume your position, pet."

It only takes me a few seconds of debate. If this brings Riggs back, I'll do what it takes. I obey, kneeling, my spine straight, my ass on my calves, my head bowed.

He leaves the room but isn't gone long. When he returns, he orders, "Get on all fours."

I reposition my body, and he takes a pair of scissors and cuts my sundress, bra, and panties. He drags the smooth part of the blades down my spine, and I shudder. He kisses my ass cheek, murmuring, "Do you think I could hurt you, pet?"

I answer honestly. "You scared me last night."

"Sir," he adds.

I take a deep breath, repeating, "You scared me last night, Sir."

He keeps his lips on my spine and widens my thighs with his forearms until my body is only a few inches off the crystal. He asks, "So the answer is yes?"

Is it?

I confess, "I don't know. I want to say no."

He takes a deep breath, as if inhaling me, and pushes something inside me.

I gasp, and it begins to hum.

He slaps my ass, and I yelp. Without thinking, I cry out, "Thank you, Sir."

"Ah, my pet didn't forget," he says, relief in his voice. He rubs the sting out of my ass cheek.

"No, Sir. I didn't forget."

He leans into my ear. "You say you want my love, well, this is it. This is all I have. Is this what you want?" he questions.

I close my eyes, wishing I hadn't admitted it to him again and not understanding why I even seek what I know he'll never give me.

"Answer me," he says, slapping my ass again.

Whatever's inside me grows hotter, intensifying faster than what Riggs normally allows at this point of our play.

"Thank you, Sir!" I grit through my teeth.

"Is this what you want?" he repeats.

"Yes, Sir," I state, making peace with the fact that this is the only way he knows how to love. And if it's going to bring him home, I'll accept it. Because even though Riggs is cruel at times, I can't deny my feelings. No matter how much I don't want to be in love with him, I am. And if this is all I'll ever get, it'll have to be enough. But he has to come home. Every day he's gone, I die a little more inside.

He asks, "You know what I missed, pet?"

"What, Sir?"

"Your pussy. Specifically, my tongue on it. And hearing you beg me for hours."

I close my eyes, trying not to squirm, almost feeling him flickering on my body.

He drags his hand over my spine and steps toward my face, leaning into my ear and challenging, "I bet you break rule three."

"No, Sir. I won't," I state, determined to be the sub Riggs needs.

"I'll make you a deal."

"What, Sir?" I ask.

Tingles erupt on my skin from his hot breath. He asserts, "You come without permission, and I leave. You survive, and show me you're a good pet, and I'll move back in."

My determination only grows.

"It's up to you, pet," he says.

"Yes, Sir. I won't break rule three," I insist.

He kisses under my lobe, ordering, "On your back."

I roll over.

He takes my feet and plants them flat on the edge of the crystal. Then he grabs my hips and slides my ass toward him. He stares hungrily at my body, holds a remote in the air, and pushes a button while giving me a challenging expression, stating, "Let's see how badly you want me back."

Whatever he placed inside me intensifies its movements. I swallow hard, realizing he's not going to show me any mercy. He leans over me, his tongue hits my clit, and I grip his hair, my back arching into the crystal.

He pushes my hands to the sides of my body, far away from me, demanding, "Palms down, on the crystal at all times, pet." He sinks back into my pussy.

I cry out, unable to stop the incoherent sounds. A tidal wave of adrenaline quickly forms, rushing through my blood at lightning speed.

He reaches up, covers my mouth, then flicks faster while sucking my clit.

There's no ability to hold anything back. My eyes roll, and I convulse hard against the crystal, squirting my juices, which I've never experienced before.

Riggs doesn't let up.

It's so intense, I can't keep my hands still and put them back in his hair. I cry out, "I can't take anymore."

"Then use your safe word," he taunts, sticking his finger up my ass and nibbling my clit.

"Riggs! Please!" I beg.

He sucks, and another rush of adrenaline annihilates my cells.

It becomes a vicious cycle. Riggs makes me come, and I tell him I can't take anymore. He reminds me I have a safe word, but I never use it.

When he finally stops, there's a pool of my juices all over the top of the piano. He rises, wipes his forearm across his mouth, then says nothing, leaving the room.

I slowly sit up, trying to catch my breath.

He returns with a pair of joggers and a T-shirt on. His keys are in his hand.

"Don't leave," I plead.

"A deal's a deal. If you're frustrated, dig into it for your inspiration. Time's running out, pet. Get your shit done," he orders, then leaves me naked and still quivering on the piano.

Something in me snaps. I barely sleep for several days. All I think about is Riggs, and I can't stop writing.

Somehow, it's like he knows when I'm done. Four days pass, and I have a notebook of lyrics, along with some of the chords. I get a text.

Riggs: How many songs have you written?

Me: Six. Will you come home now?

Riggs: Put on the blue dress. No panties.

Me: Why?

Riggs: I'll pick you up for dinner at eight. Be ready.

I don't ask any more questions. Riggs picks me up, and it's like nothing has happened, as if he never left. We go to dinner, and it feels like a date. He even lets me kiss him all night. Several times, he initiates it. But in the back of my mind, I remind myself to be careful.

There is no normalcy with Riggs. And eventually, this will all end. Somehow, I need to figure out how to let him go.

22

Riggs
One Month Later

"*I*'m being hacked! All my personal accounts and the bank freezes aren't working!" Hugh declares over the phone.

My grin grows wider. I utilize my most concerned voice. "Are the business accounts safe?"

"George confirmed there's no breach," he states.

Fucking liar.

I continue, "That's good to hear."

Hugh booms, "But I'm getting drained!"

I add, "That sucks. I'm sure the bank will figure it out though. Best to stay calm. Besides, the bank has to refund your money if it's a hack."

"They have. But as soon as they refund me, another hack occurs."

"Maybe you should move banks," I suggest, rolling my deodorant over my armpit.

"It's happening at all five places my accounts are at," he frets.

"Shit," I mutter, but I know he's in it deeper than he's stating. The offshore accounts don't refund your money in the event of a hack. Jones looked into it. When he confirmed, it only made everything sweeter. I guess that's the price you pay for screwing over your business partner and clients.

"Someone's after me!" Hugh claims.

"Sounds like it," I agree, knowing it'll only make him more paranoid.

"Who the fuck has the balls to come after me?" he barks.

I stare at my reflection, giddy. I answer, "Someone with big balls."

He grunts.

"I have to go. Stay calm. It'll all get worked out. If anything happens to our business accounts, notify me immediately." I hang up before he can say anything else.

I whistle as I get dressed, feeling like I just took a hit of a really potent drug. Hugh's call came after I sent him a picture of Blakely in a white bra and panty set. I wrote a little note to go with it.

> Me: Maybe I'll marry her and knock her up.

A slew of pissed-off texts followed.

Hugh: I know who you are, you son of a bitch.

Me: Sure you do.

Hugh: Deliver my daughter to me tonight. Or I'm putting a hit on your head.

Me: You'd have to know who I am to do that. And you don't.

He continued tossing texts at me, even though I stopped responding. Ten minutes later, I got the call.

"You're in a good mood," Blakely declares, stepping into the closet.

I tug her into me and kiss her.

She freezes, then kisses me back.

It's something that happens more often every time I kiss her. I don't know why she freezes. She never used to. I chalk it up that I'm taking her by surprise and don't linger on it like I sometimes do. Nothing is going wrong today. I proclaim, "I am. Today's your big day."

Nervousness floods her features.

I peck her lips and assert, "Don't be nervous. You said you were ready."

She takes a deep breath, smiles, and nods. "You're right. I am."

"That's my girl!" I praise, then pat her ass. "Get ready so we're not late. Traffic's going to be a bitch." I leave the room and reply to a few emails, continuing to feel like I'm on top of the world.

Blakely appears, wearing ripped designer jeans, an oversized lavender sweater, and brown ankle boots. She chose it when I took her shopping last weekend. Her hair hangs in her natural beachy waves, and she has minimal makeup on.

"You look great," I tell her.

She puts on a brave smile.

I chuckle. "Are you always nervous before a performance?"

"This isn't the same thing," she claims.

"But are you normally nervous?"

She hesitates, then shakes her head. "No."

"Then I have an idea."

"What's that?" she questions.

I rise, take off her gold collar, and drape an eggplant purple one around her neck. Diamonds sparkle around it, and there's only one ring. It's on the back, hidden. I bought it for her when she told me what she was wearing to record.

She reaches up and traces over it. She says, "I think I'm going to have the most expensive choker collection on Earth."

I grin. "You mean collar collection."

She rolls her eyes.

I suggest, "Why don't you just pretend you're on stage instead of in a studio."

Her face falls again. "It's not that easy."

"Try."

She blows out an anxious breath of air. "I will."

"Good girl." I slide my hand around her waist, then lead her to the front door and out to the Porsche. We get inside, and I head toward the studio. I turn the music up.

Blakely turns it off. "Sorry, but I need some silence right now."

I glance at her, and her face is pale. She has her hand over her stomach.

"You're going to kill it, pet," I reassure her.

She closes her eyes and leans back against the headrest.

For the rest of the ride, we don't speak. I take her hand and hold it, caressing the back of it with my thumb. She never opens her eyes until I park and turn off the engine.

I gently reassure, "Everything will go perfectly. Just sing your heart out."

She softly laughs. "Easy for you to say."

"Is singing still your dream?"

"Of course."

I point to the front doors. "Then your dream is waiting for you inside. You just have to do your thing."

She taps her fingers on her thigh and blurts out, "You might not like what I wrote."

"Sure I will."

She furrows her eyebrows and looks at her lap.

I turn her chin toward me. "I'll love whatever you sing. But I'm not part of this equation, pet. You need to do what you do and not worry about anyone else in the room. Understand?"

She doesn't look convinced but nods.

Another moment of silence passes. I wish she wasn't nervous, but the anxiety riddles her expression.

She gives me a small smile and says, "Okay. You can open my door now."

I chuckle. "I should spank you later for being bossy."

She mutters, "Maybe you will."

I chuckle again, then get out of the Porsche. I walk around, open her door, and reach in to help her out. I kiss her and then add, "For luck."

Her smile appears, but it doesn't light up her face like normal. I decide it's best to get her inside and into the studio. I've not told her about the dozen agents Ears lined up to check her out, and I pat myself on the back for keeping it quiet. I never expected her to be this nervous.

The woman at the front desk changed her hair from bright green to neon orange. She beams at us. "Welcome to Naked Pipe Entertainment. You must be Blakely?" She holds out her hand.

Blakely shakes it and confirms, "Yes."

"I'm Rhonda. With an h," she adds and winks.

"Nice to meet you," Blakely states.

"You too. He's quite the fan," Rhonda announces and motions toward me.

Blakley glances at me and nods. "So I hear."

"Let me get you settled. I put a bottle of water in the studio, but if you want something different, just let me know."

"Water's perfect. Thank you," Blakley replies, and we follow Rhonda down a hallway.

She leads us into a room with a lot of sound equipment, then opens the door to the recording booth. Several musicians tune their instruments, and Rhonda introduces Blakely to them.

"I'll be outside. Have fun," I state and kiss Blakley on the head.

"Thanks."

I go into the other room, and Ears enters. He goes inside the recording box and introduces himself to Blakely. The sound is off, so I can't hear, but he says something that makes her laugh.

By the time the musicians are ready, a dozen agents have arrived. Ears gives me the lowdown on each one, along with his top three choices to represent Blakely.

The sound tech flips a switch and announces, "Are you ready to start?"

Anxiety appears on her face again. She glances at me, and my pulse creeps higher.

Come on, pet.

You got this.

She tears her gaze off me and answers, "Yes."

"From the top, then," he orders.

She puts her headphones over her ears and sits at the piano. She declares, "I'm going to go solo on this one... If that's okay?"

Ears chimes in with, "Let's hear it how you envision it."

"This one's called 'Invisibly Broken.'" She takes a deep breath and begins to stroke the keys. A slow melody fills the air. She locks eyes with me and belts out, *"If you loved me, you'd see what you're doing to me."* More notes fill the air.

She doesn't tear her gaze off mine, singing, *"But you're broken... So broken... And you think I'm the one who stands there in pieces, but it's you who's shattered..."*

My chest tightens. The notes get faster and louder as she slams her fingers on the keys, blinking hard as her blues never leave mine. My gut slowly flips, and the hairs on my neck rise.

She continues, *"I'm in front of you, loving you, but you can't see me..."* A tear slips down her cheek.

I clench my fists at my sides, feeling exposed, the words sinking in so deep within me they slice through my heart.

She roars, *"'Cause you make me invisible. So invisible..."*

The notes vibrate in the air, matching the quivering in my belly.

Another tear falls, and her gaze never falters. She sings louder, *"You're broken in pieces and push me aside... The darkness of you always breaks through... You think no one sees, but I see the true you..."*

My mouth turns dry. I swallow hard, trying to calm the chaos inside me.

The notes turn slower. She softens her tone, and a full river of tears rolls over her cheekbones. *"And you make me invisible."* Another set of only notes passes. She adds, *"Invisibly broken."* She continues playing, lowers her voice, and sings, *"Yet I still love you."*

The music stops, her glistening eyes stay pinned on me, and deafening silence ensues.

Ears claps loudly, pulling me out of my trance. He turns to the sound tech, "Tell me you got it recorded."

"All of it," he replies.

"Fuck me," one of the agents mutters.

"She's the next Nora Jones," another one declares.

"Told you I wouldn't waste your time," Ears states, then flips on the microphone. He gushes, "That's a hit, superstar."

Blakley wipes her face, lifts her chin, and squares her shoulders. She redirects her focus on Ears. "Thank you."

"Are your other songs all on the piano?" he asks.

"Yes."

"Let's do a round with only the piano, then. Take a break, guys," he orders the musicians.

They leave the room and disappear.

For six hours, Blakely sings, stating she doesn't need a break. Food arrives, but she doesn't eat, nor do I. She drinks water between songs, insisting she doesn't need to rest.

She hurls everything she thinks about me, along with how much I've hurt her, never singing without her sad, sometimes angry, blues pinned on mine and voice to match.

Nothing's ever felt so painful. It's like taking a hammer and hitting me over the head without any mercy. As the day goes on, they bring the musicians in, attempting the songs with different instruments.

It doesn't matter how many times I hear the lyrics. The words always feel like the first time I'm hearing them, as if they're a scab and Blakely's ripping it off me.

"You got any other material?" Ears asks.

She states, "I'm in the process of writing something, but it's not done."

"You mind singing what you've got so far?" he questions.

"If you want."

"I do," he proclaims, then once again clears the recording box. "Take another break, boys."

"Three, two, one," the sound tech directs.

"This one's called 'The End,'" Blakely announces, then moves her fingers over the keys. She belts out more revelations.

This time, it's about how she's on borrowed time, how she's not wanted forever, and how she'll be tossed away.

Every note is heartbreaking. Every blast of her voice, soul crushing. And the constant stare into my eyes supplies a steady stream of chaos to my blood.

"We're not forever, our days fade before us, and it's all okay to you," she blasts.

Is that what she thinks?

She continues, *"There's no love from you."* Another tear drips down her cheek.

The air turns stale in my lungs.

She stops playing and says, "That's all I have for that one."

"How long until you can finish it?" Ears questions.

She shrugs. "A few days."

"Good. Do that. I think we have enough for today. Can you come back next week?" Ears asks.

"Of course," she responds.

He declares, "That's a wrap, then."

The room erupts in applause, but Blakely doesn't beam as she should. She forces a smile and leaves the recording box.

Agents swarm her, introducing themselves and handing her their business cards. Anxiety appears in her expression again, and it's clear she's overwhelmed.

I take the business cards from her and interject, "Thank you for your enthusiasm. We'll schedule meetings with those of you we're interested in dealing with. Now, if you'll excuse us, Blakely's had a long day." I steer her out of the room.

"Riggs," Ears calls after me.

I spin us, arching my eyebrows.

He steps in front of us and nods at Blakely, a huge grin overpowering him. He asserts, "You got the goods, girl."

For the first time all day, she beams. "You really think so?"

He chuckles. "When those agents fight over you, you got the world by the balls."

She glances at me.

I tug her closer, still shaken by her songs and processing it all while having no clue how to deal with the damage I've done.

"Get some rest, Blakely Fox. Your name is about to go global," Ears claims. He pats me on the back.

"I'll call you tomorrow," I inform him, then lead Blakely to the Porsche. I open the door.

She gets in.

I shut the door, go around to my side, take a deep breath, and slide onto the driver's seat. A few minutes pass, and I turn to her, trying to figure out what to say. But everything is jumbled.

She slowly meets my gaze.

I finally just admit, "You were amazing."

She says nothing and stares out the window.

I open my mouth, then snap it shut. What am I trying to say anyway?

I turn on the engine and pull out into traffic. We drive in silence, but time doesn't help my thoughts. All I know is I need to get my shit together and do better. For the first time ever in the history of my relationships, I'm not looking for an out. Yet I'm unsure what that means for either of us.

23

Blakely
Two Months Later

"Mmm," I utter, hugging my pillow tighter.

Riggs's hand slides over my ass. Tingles erupt on my skin under his hot breath. He kisses the back of my neck and murmurs, "We have twenty minutes."

"Until...?" I question, too sleepy to open my eyes.

He shifts on the mattress. The weight of his body presses over my back, his arms sliding under my hips. He lifts them, and the tip of his erection teases my entrance. He taunts, "You'll be calmer if I let you come before we leave."

My eyes flutter open. I rack my brain, wondering why Riggs thinks I'll be anything but calm.

More meetings.

I groan.

"Not the usual response I get when I'm on top of you naked," he teases.

"Can't we pick—"

He slides inside my pussy until his pelvis hits my ass.

"Oh God!" I breathe.

His tongue flicks my lobe. He keeps one arm under my hips and slides his other hand under the pillow. He pins my wrists to the mattress, slowly thrusting. He buries his face into the curve of my neck, asking, "How's that feel, pet?"

"So good," I admit.

He nibbles on my collarbone, thrusting faster. "And now?"

"Better," I confess, closing my eyes, enjoying every moment of Riggs's body in mine.

His fingers glide over my clit, circling it, and within seconds, he's ordering, "Come."

My body erupts into chaos. And I don't know what's happening between us anymore. Since my first day at the studio, Riggs has been different.

I thought he'd be upset with me after hearing my songs. Yet I rarely see him angry anymore. He didn't say anything about my songs, except for praising me for how well I did.

More and more, he's constantly asking me what I want or like. It took me by surprise at first. Now, I'm starting to get used to it, and it scares me. His actions only make me fall for him harder, and I'm already in over my head.

It's not that he's never demanding anymore. If anything, his need for control is stronger than ever. And his sexual desires are borderline insatiable. Not one day has passed where we haven't had sex, or he's not kissed me. Plus, I no longer have to think about touching him. I do it, and he never objects.

But he hasn't punished me since before that day. The longer I go without seeing his wrath, the laxer around him I become. And when I catch myself, I can't lie. Deep down, I know it's a mistake to think he's changed. At some point, Riggs is going to show his true colors. Our contract will be up, and I'll be replaced.

So I do everything I can to remind myself we have an arrangement. It's been a little over five months, and I'm almost halfway to the end.

The anxiety growing within me about leaving him won't fade. Yet I can't stop it.

"Christ, pet," he mumbles, holding me tighter to him, thrusting harder into me.

"Yes, like that, Sir," I cry out, not even realizing anymore when I call him Sir during sex until it rolls out of my mouth.

He loves it. I know he does, and pleasing him makes me happy.

He groans. "Fuck, you're perfect."

It's another thing he often says these days. The glimmer of hope I'll be his forever springs forward, and I try to push it away.

His palm slides up my arm and onto my neck. He glides it under my collar. There's no slack left, and his fingers sprawl around my skin, holding me in place. He thrusts harder until my body's out of control, convulsing underneath him, and he erupts inside me.

He stays on top of me, his heart beating into my shoulder, his sweat mixing with mine. His breath calms, and he rolls over, then slides his palm over my cheek. His eyes full of calm chaos meet mine.

"Do I really have to go?" I ask.

His lips twitch. "How many times have we gone over this, pet?"

"I don't like these meetings. Can't you just pick one for me?"

He shakes his head. "No. I'll interview and negotiate for you. But you need to feel comfortable with whatever agent you choose. This is important."

I crawl on top of him and trace his lips with my finger. "Or, I could stay home, work on some new music, and you could text me when you're on your way home. Then I could put on a mystery outfit and kneel for you until you come home and order me around all night." I beam at him, wiggling my eyebrows.

He chuckles. "A mystery outfit?"

"Yep."

He flips me onto my back.

I screech, laughing.

"Or, you can put on your big girl panties, attend a very important business meeting, and put on the mystery outfit when we get home."

"Aww," I whine.

He rises and pulls me off the bed. "Time to shower."

We get ready and leave the house.

"Who are we meeting today?" I ask.

"Phil Millin, then Jack Secroy, and after that, Noah Kingsley."

"We met with all of them last week," I point out.

"Yeah. They're the top three picks," he states.

I lean closer to him. "Sounds like you have this handled. Why am I here again?"

He sighs. "Blakely, you'll be tied to your agent for years. These aren't short-term contracts."

"Guess they don't have commitment issues," I blurt out, then immediately regret it.

Riggs's face hardens. He questions, "You have something you want to talk about, pet?"

Heat flies into my cheeks. "No," I lie.

"Seems to me you have something you need to get off your chest," he asserts.

"I don't have anything to discuss. Is there something you need to talk about?" I question, my heart pounding so hard I'm sure he can hear it.

He veers onto the expressway, then he briefly pins his eyes on me before accelerating and weaving in and out of traffic, grinding his molars.

Why did I say that?

I put my hand on his thigh. "Thank you for helping me. I'd be lost without your assistance."

His face softens. "You're welcome. But you'd be fine."

I shake my head, insisting, "No, I wouldn't. You ask questions I don't think about, and contracts make my head spin."

"Is that the real reason you never read mine until I made you?"

My chest tightens. "No."

"Then what was it?"

"My father—"

"The truth would be nice, pet," he interjects.

My pulse creeps up. His eyes dart between me and the traffic until I cave, confessing, "I wanted to stay with you. It didn't matter what was on it."

"And now?"

"What do you mean?"

"Knowing all the things you know about me, would you still sign it? If I handed you a stack of papers and said, 'This is a new contract, sign it,' what would you do?" he asks.

Goose bumps break out on my skin. "A new contract?"

"Hypothetically speaking. Humor me," he adds.

Is he asking me this because he wants to keep me longer? Or is it really hypothetical?

He pushes, "Cards on the table, pet. Would you sign without reading it? Or would you study it and then decide? Or, would you toss it back at me and tell me to fuck off?"

My mouth turns dry. The flutters in my stomach somersault.

In a hurt voice, he asserts, "I guess the answer is so bad you can't admit it."

"Don't put words in my mouth," I scold.

He glances over his shoulder, veers into the left lane, and accelerates past a semi. The Porsche rattles, and he replies, "Well, your silence says a lot."

I toss back at him, "Why are you asking me this?"

"Because we're talking about contracts."

"Really? You want my honesty but can't even be honest with me in return?" I accuse.

Tension fills the car. He keeps his eyes on the road, pulls off the exit, then speeds down several streets before parallel parking.

For the first time in weeks, I'm pissed. I reach for the door, and he grabs my arm.

"Did you forget my rule?" he questions.

I sneer, "Which one? You have so many."

"Why are you acting like this?"

"Like what? Someone who can open their own car door?" I seethe, internally cursing myself for expecting him to change when he never will. He'll always just be playing games. No matter what I mean to Riggs, he'll never let me in.

If I even mean anything.

"It's for your safety," he claims.

I roll my eyes. "My safety?"

"Yes."

"There's another lie," I mutter.

"How is it a lie?" he questions.

I insist, "It's so you can control me."

"No. It's actually not."

I scoff. "Can you at least not lie to my face like I'm a moron?"

His face turns red. He blurts out, "When you step out of your car and get shot—and for no reason—then you can decide if I'm being a control freak or actually give a shit about your safety."

My gut dives. "Did that happen to you?"

He grinds his molars, then shakes his head. He lowers his voice and says, "You live in a bubble, pet. You always have. And hey, I'm glad you do. But don't ever question what I do to keep you safe." He gets out and slams the driver's door.

Ugh! What have I done now?

He walks around, opens my door, and holds out his hand.

I take it, rise, and say, "I'm sorry. I didn't mean—"

"Change the subject, pet."

"Riggs—"

"We have a meeting to get to," he states, then guides me into the hotel. He goes to the counter and checks in.

I stay quiet, and he leads me into the elevator, down a hallway, and into a suite.

"Make yourself comfy. We're going to be here all day," he announces, then pulls his laptop out of his bag.

I slide my arms around his waist, hugging him from behind.

His body stiffens.

I blurt out, "I'm sorry. I would read the contract this time."

He spins. "Why?"

I swallow hard. "So I know what I'm getting into and ask for what I wanted."

Surprise registers on his expression. "What do you want that I haven't given you?"

My pulse skyrockets, and my stomach flips.

The doorbell rings. Too scared to tell him what I want, I turn toward the door and announce, "I'll get it." I walk a little too fast to the door and open it.

"Blakely, good to see you, babe," Phil Millin booms, stepping forward and tugging me into his arms. He kisses me on the cheek.

Riggs steps next to me. His disapproval radiates off him. He slides his arm around my waist, tugging me away from Phil, and dryly asserts, "Have a seat at the table."

Phil arrogantly glances at Riggs, then saunters over to the table. He pulls a folder out of his briefcase.

Riggs pulls my chair closer to his and motions for me to sit. I obey, and he takes his seat next to me.

Phil leans closer to me, gushing, "I'm excited to sign you, Blakely. With my connections and experience, you're going to top the charts."

Riggs interjects, "With Blakely's talent, she's going to top the charts. And we're not committing to anyone today."

Phil jerks his head toward Riggs. "Is this a joke?"

"No. There are issues with your contract, if—and this is a big if right now—Blakely decides to sign with you," Riggs asserts.

"What's the issue, darling?" Phil asks.

Riggs shifts in his seat.

I put my hand on his thigh and lean closer to him. Maybe Riggs is right to have me involved in this process. Something about Phil gives me the creeps.

Riggs's voice turns colder. "Let's start with her royalties. You're 8% lower than where you need to be."

"The royalties are fair. The cost of promotion to take Blakely to the top is more than you realize," he claims.

Riggs stares him down, keeps his voice calm, and asserts, "It's less than the industry standard, and you know it."

Phil gives Riggs a warm smile. "No offense, but I know the music business inside and out. While your reputation as a busi-nessman is impeccable, this isn't your area of expertise."

Riggs turns toward me. "Are you looking to get screwed?"

My stomach flips. I quietly answer, "No."

"Then if I were you, I'd tell Phil to take his deal and shove it up his ass."

I gape at Riggs.

He gives me a challenging stare.

"Ms. Fox, the deal I'm offering you doesn't come around very often. I suggest you think twice before listening to someone who doesn't understand how things work in the music world," Phil warns.

Riggs waits for me to speak, the blues in his eyes swirling, reminding me of the calm chaos he loves so much.

It's nerve-racking to turn anything down. I've struggled for years to sit at a table with Phil Millin. He's a legend in the industry. But I know Riggs has my best interests at heart. I trust him more than anyone. And there's no way I'd accept an offer if he advises me not to.

So I lift my chin and lock eyes with Phil. "Thank you for your time, but I won't be signing with you."

"You're making a mistake," he declares.

Riggs winks at me, then rises. "When Blakely's first song hits number one, remember that your greed ruined this deal."

Phil's cheeks turn red. He seethes, "This industry is a small world, Mr. Madden." He locks eyes with me, warning, "Having friends in high places is always better than burning the bridges with the same hands that feed those who are in power to make or break you."

Riggs slides his arm around my waist and declares, "Thanks for the warning. Now, let me give you one. You do anything besides sing praises for Blakely's talent, and you'll have a lot more to worry about than the lost opportunity to sign her. Thanks for your time." He points to the door.

Phil scowls, shakes his head, and drops his card on the table. "Blakely, if you come to your senses, call me."

"She won't be. She knows her worth," Riggs firmly declares and hands the card back to Phil.

He storms out of the room.

When the door's secure, I turn to Riggs and fret, "Phil Millin isn't someone we should piss off."

"He's trying to screw you," Riggs scoffs.

"I'm just saying—"

"Both Jack and Noah have fair deals on the table," he informs me, then adds, "And their client lists are more impressive than Phil's. Don't listen to a word he says."

"Then why did you invite him here for another meeting?" I question.

Riggs's lips twitch. "Because he's Phil Millin."

My chest tightens. "And?"

"And he's in the top three. It's your decision who you go with, and you deserve full transparency."

"You could have just told me his deal wasn't up to par," I state.

Riggs chuckles.

"What's so funny?" I inquire.

"One day, when you realize what an ass he is, you'll always have the memory of telling him to shove his shitty deal up his ass," Riggs declares.

I furrow my brows, deciding Riggs is officially crazy. But also adorable when he's negotiating or telling important people off, sweet to care so much about this when he has a busy company to run and could be doing a million different things, and sexy as hell when he's sticking up for me. Still, I remind him, "You're the one who told him that."

He grins. "You did in your own way."

The bell rings, and my stomach knots again.

Riggs wiggles his eyebrows. "Next."

Even though the first meeting went badly, the next two are both great. Jack and Noah both offer fair deals, and Riggs even negotiates a few more things into the contracts. At the end of each meeting, Riggs informs them that I'll get back to them soon.

Noah leaves, and my head spins.

Riggs only seems energized by the negotiations.

"You love this stuff, don't you?" I ask.

A boyish look appears on his handsome face. He questions, "Is it that obvious?"

"You're good at it. My father got lucky when he met you," I point out.

Riggs's face darkens.

"Sorry. Did I say something wrong?" I fret.

He shakes his head and tugs me into him. "No. You've done everything right."

Surprised, I reply, "I have?"

He strokes my cheek. "Yeah, pet. You have."

"Just in these meetings, right?" I blurt out, then my face heats.

Why did I say that?

He freezes, then slowly shakes his head. "No."

"No?"

He steps closer. "You've done everything right. And I'm not easy. I know I'm not easy, but you still managed to pull it off."

My butterflies go full force. Time seems to stand still. I open my mouth and then close it.

"Say whatever's on your mind, pet," he demands.

"What does that mean? I-I want you to clarify what that means so I'm not confused," I admit, then add, "about us. I don't want to keep being confused about us." My stomach dives so fast that I think I might get sick, but it's the question that's always on my mind.

He locks his blues on mine, his chest filling with air several times, his exhales steadied and controlled. He closes the small gap between us, tilting my chin up and studying me.

For the first time ever, I swear Riggs is nervous. It swirls all over him, and I'm sure he won't answer me.

But he does.

He lowers his voice, claiming, "It means I was wrong."

"About what?" I whisper, scared about what he will say.

"How I want to love you," he declares.

My emotions roll through me. I'm unable to escape the tears. I force myself to ask, "Meaning?"

"I need to do better."

I inhale sharply.

He presses his lips to mine, then vows, "I *will* do better."

"Why?" I ask.

He strokes my cheek, announcing, "Because you see me. And I don't want us to ever end."

24

Riggs
One Month Later

*J*ones is a genius. He's siphoning money from Hugh's accounts at record speed. His system truly does seem unhackable. But as he stated earlier, he makes sure that he upgrades it daily to keep it that way.

The banks informed Hugh he can no longer keep his accounts with them. I know because Jones gave me the email documentation of Hugh going back and forth. The banks have had to replace his money too many times, and slowly, over the last month, they've all fired him as a client. They paid him out in cash, cutting their losses.

He's their only client that's been hacked like this, and since he's a target, they can't take the risk anymore. Hugh's level of arrogance is just as high as ever, except now there's rage involved.

And the emails back and forth, well, let's just say they haven't been the nicest.

All my plans are coming to fruition better than I could have estimated. My patience has paid off, and it's time for the next step.

I know Hugh put his cash inside the safe at the office. I had a camera installed in the lights, and Hugh has no idea I'm watching his every move.

Thankfully, I observed him over the years, learning how he operates. I'm aware he doesn't trust his wife, so he wouldn't leave money at home. And he's underestimated me. He still thinks I'm clueless and loyal to him.

I called Jones yesterday and told him he needed to hack into my security system at work. I want him to loop the recording so it looks like the room's empty. I also need him to delete my keycard entrance so there's no proof when I empty Hugh's safe.

My moment is now. It's dark, and everyone's gone, including the janitors. I make my way into the building through the fire exit, bypassing the security guards at the front desk. Then I text Jones.

> Me: I'm in.

Jones: Two more minutes.

I wait in the corridor and then receive another text.

Jones: You're clear.

Adrenaline pumps through my veins. I climb the forty-five flights, hauling with me two empty suitcases until I get to the top floor. Then I go directly into Hugh's office suite.

Since Hugh's now paranoid, he often opens his safe and stares at his money. It only took a few days before the camera captured the code, since he's old school. He laughed when I told him years ago he should switch to an electronic safe that requires a handprint.

I push my gloved fingers against the buttons, and the safe opens. I take all the cash, a set of collector Rolex watches, and his passport. I open a folder and freeze.

My pet's picture stares at me. She's younger, and the issue date states it was around her eighteenth birthday. I add it to the case, then pick up two large yellow envelopes.

I open the first one, then thumb through the documents.

It's a trail of all the money he's stolen from our client accounts and me. I've seen it before when Jones gave me his report. I toss it in with the other items. Then I open the second envelope.

A fresh burst of hatred rushes through my blood. There are details on where Blakely lived, worked, and photos of her. She's singing on a stage or carrying trays of drinks in her cheap thong and bra she wore the night she arrived at my house. In one, she's getting out of a car, and I recognize the surroundings as the lot near Cheeks.

I force myself to stay focused, toss it in the suitcase, and zip both bags.

I roll them through the office, then carry them down the stairs, exiting the same way I entered. I put everything into the trunk of my Porsche. I drive several blocks, then text Jones.

> Me: I'm out.

A few minutes pass, and I get a reply.

Jones: Done.

Me: Perfect. I owe you a bigger bonus.

Jones: I'll happily take your money. Stop by
tomorrow morning. I have something for you.

I chuckle, feeling a buzz. Hugh's going to have nothing left. He's going to lose it when he realizes everything is gone.

I drive home to the beach house. Since it's so late, Blakely's already sleeping. I unpack everything into my office safe, then lock it. I take a shower, then slide into bed.

She stirs. "You're back."

I give her a kiss, then tell her, "I am. Go back to sleep."

She snuggles into me, and the warm feeling I can't escape fills me. It's something I've gotten more used to lately. I can't lie to myself anymore. I enjoy it.

I kiss the top of her head and peacefully fall asleep until the morning comes, waking up at my normal time.

Blakely's still asleep. I unpeel my body from hers, then sneak out of the bedroom. I get outside, put on my wetsuit, then take my board down to the water and hit the waves.

The sun's risen when I finally see the calm chaos. I stay in the water for a few more minutes, thinking about my pet.

She's the one.

I need to keep her.

Anxiety mixes with that warmth I can't escape. It gradually spreads throughout my chest until it seeps into my stomach.

This isn't the first time I've told myself these things, yet time doesn't seem to override my reaction.

I paddle to shore, shower, then venture into the bedroom.

Blakely steps out of the bathroom. She sees me and smiles, chirping, "Morning. How was the surf?"

I close the distance between us and kiss her. "Great. Were you up late?"

She nods. "I finished another song. At least, I think it's done."

I glance at the clock, debating if I have time to play, but I don't. I announce, "I have a ton of things going on today at work."

"Busy week, huh?" she says, and the tad of disappointment I hear in her voice makes my heart beat faster.

I state, "I'd rather stay here with you."

She beams. "You can make it up to me later."

I squeeze her ass and chuckle, knowing I intend to do just that. "Deal."

She rises on her tippy-toes, pecks me on the cheek, then snaps my towel off me. She glances down at my cock, then bats her eyes, pouting, "Oops. Sorry."

I resist the urge to back her against the wall. I warn, "I see a punishment in your future."

She shrugs, then leaves the room, glancing back at me over her shoulder.

Yep, she's it.

The uncomfortable tightness spawns again. I fight through it and go into my closet. I get dressed, then leave, driving to Compton.

I pull into Jones's garage. He comes to my window. "I have access to all the new accounts. Here's the data." He hands me an oversized envelope.

"What's this?" I question.

"New offshore accounts. I've already hacked into them though."

"Good man," I praise and fist-bump him. I ask, "And you're sure there's no evidence I was in the building last night?"

He scoffs. "Of course. I'm not an amateur. Not a trace of evidence exists."

I chuckle. "No, you sure aren't an amateur." I reach into the glove box and pull out an envelope of cash. "Your bonus."

He takes it from me, stating, "I'll work on the credit cards this morning. You should be good in a few hours."

"Perfect. Text me when it's ready," I order, then leave the garage.

I fight the thick smog and traffic, then grab a coffee at a local shop while returning some emails. I get a text.

Jones: Done.

Giddiness hits me. I go to the country club for lunch. Hugh scheduled lunch with his cronies and pointed out that I hadn't gone in a while. Every now and then, I go to make Hugh happy. He likes to have me there to confirm when he brags about how well our company's doing. But I'm only here for my own bene-fit. And I can't wait to watch what's about to happen.

My timing is impeccable, arriving at valet just as Hugh gets out of his car. I can tell right away something is off by his distracted expression. His jovial arrogance is nowhere to be seen.

"Hugh," I call out when he doesn't seem to notice me.

Red deepens on his face. "Riggs."

"Why do you look frazzled?" I ask innocently.

He shakes his head. "I'm not. I'm fine."

Sure you are, you lying, thieving, manipulative bastard.

We go inside to the check-in desk. Mabel pins her wide eyes on Hugh. She clears her throat. "Mr. Gallow, Amy needs to speak with you."

His eyes turn to slits. "Why?"

Amy from membership walks out. "Mr. Gallow, can you step into my office for a quick minute?"

"I have people waiting," he declares in his haughty tone.

Amy nods and smiles bigger, but it's a strained expression. "Yes, but there's an important issue I need to discuss."

He seethes, "What would that be?"

I chuckle inside. Witnessing this is priceless.

Amy puts her hand on his arm and says, "Mr. Gallow, I think it's better if we speak in private."

"Just give her a minute. I'll wait here for you," I assert.

Hugh huffs, follows Amy into the office, and she shuts the glass door but not all the way.

She motions to the chair. "Have a seat, Mr. Gallow."

"I don't have time for this. What's going on, Amy?" he demands.

Her nervousness is apparent in her tone when she informs him, "The check bounced for your annual memberships dues. Do you happen to have a check for another bank account?"

Hugh groans, announcing, "I've been the target of fraud. All my accounts have been hacked. But here, take this." He drops his credit card on the wood.

So predictable.

"Thank you. Just one moment," Amy chirps. A moment of silence passes, and she clears her throat again. "I'm sorry, Mr. Gallow, but your card's been declined."

He barks, "That's impossible. I have no limit."

"I'm sorry, but it says it's declined."

"Run it again."

"Yes, sir," she says. Another moment passes, and Amy gets even more uncomfortable. "I'm sorry, Mr. Gallow, but this isn't going through. Do you have another card?"

"Why would I need another card? Did you not hear me? I have an unlimited amount of credit," he booms.

"Mr. Gallow, you might want to keep your voice down. I'm sure that we can work this out."

"This is ridiculous. Figure it out, Amy," he demands, rises, and storms out of the room.

She follows him. "Mr. Gallow, we have to sort this out!"

I hand her my card. "Run it on this. He's got some issues going on."

She hesitates. "Are you sure?"

"Yes."

"Thank you, Mr. Madden."

"No problem. I apologize for his behavior. He's stressed," I state.

"It's okay." She runs the six-figure fee on my card, then hands it back to me, smiling. "All set."

"Thanks."

"No, thank you," she replies.

I nod and leave the room, moving toward the restaurant. I run into Hugh as he's leaving the restroom. His face looks damp. I inform him, "I had her run my card."

"I didn't need you to do that," he claims.

"Well, it sounded like you have a problem, partner. Only makes sense I would help you out. You'd do the same for me, right?" I add, knowing he wouldn't without holding it over my head.

He takes a deep breath and straightens his shoulders. Reminds me a little bit of when Blakely does it, except now, I can't stand it when he does it. Pride sweeps through me when my pet's confidence grows.

He replies, "Whatever we need to do. This is just ridiculous."

"Agreed," I respond.

Amy appears. She hands me a piece of paper. "I forgot to give you your receipt." She glances at Hugh and smiles. "You're all set for the year, Mr. Gallow."

He scowls at her.

"Thank you, Amy," I say, taking the receipt. I steer Hugh toward the restaurant.

He stomps along the tile.

We get outside the restaurant. I put my hand on his shoulder. "Hugh."

He spins. "What?"

"Take a breather. You look like you're about to have a heart attack," I declare, wanting him to be anything but calm when the next thing happens.

He hesitates, then nods. "You're right. It's just these hackers. I don't understand why they're targeting me."

"We'll figure it out," I assure him.

"How? The banks won't even let me keep my money there. I have all my cash in a safe," he admits.

"Shit. That sucks. Well, at least you know where it's at," I add, doing the happy dance inside. His fortune is mine. I've never been a thief until now, but he's earned all the misery that's coming to him.

"It's ridiculous," he claims.

I nod. "Can't do anything about it right now. Let's go eat. We're keeping everybody waiting."

The hostess leads us to a table with half a dozen of Hugh's cronies. I can't stand any of them but play my part.

We're halfway into the meal, and I'm so anxious with excitement, I'm trying not to tap my fingers on my thigh. It's a bad habit I'm picking up from Blakely.

I should have fucked her before I left.

The TVs in the restaurant all turn on. They're normally used for sporting events—specifically horse races, golf, or tennis matches. One thing the members love is betting absurd amounts of money. So the big screens fill the walls, and the members vote yearly to upgrade them to the newest technology.

Blakely's face appears, and Hugh's hand grips the table's edge. He snarls, "What the fuck is going on?"

A video flickers with her face. It's only her face. I didn't want to show any other part of her body to these country club assholes. And her hair is dark, with her blueish-purple highlights in it. I chose that photo since I know Hugh will hate it the most. He thinks anything but natural hair color is trashy.

A full minute passes with just her face flickering.

Hugh stands up, slamming his hand on the table, shouting, "Why is my daughter on the TVs? Turn this off."

Blakely's voice tears through the loudspeakers, declaring, "I hate my father." Then it intensifies as her emotion-filled voice repeats, "I hate my father."

My masked voice pushes her, and she admits everything I caught on video when I first tried to break her. She cries, "He's selfish... He's a liar... He's cruel," for another ten minutes, over and over.

Spit flies out of Hugh's mouth as he screams at the staff to turn off the TVs. But no matter what he does, the TVs won't shut down. Jones is the only one with control over them, and the video continues repeating itself at the loudest volume possible.

I pretend to look appalled, pointing at the staff and agreeing with Hugh. "Turn that off!"

When they finally shut down, the entire restaurant is staring at Hugh. The people who claim to be his friends look uncomfortable, and I know he's cracking.

His face is red. He's borderline sweating, and rage radiates from him. "Who did this? Heads are going to roll!"

Everyone in the restaurant avoids his accusing gaze. I chuckle inside. The gossip will fly, and Hugh won't recover from this embarrassment; his impeccable reputation will be tarnished.

And all those "friends" of his who've secretly wanted to see him fall will finally have their wish.

I let Hugh have a tantrum for a few more minutes, attempting to calm him, then maneuver him out of the club. We get to the valet, and Hugh seethes, "This is getting out of control, Riggs. Whoever this bastard is will pay!"

"It's going to be bad for business if this keeps up. We need to find out who the culprit is," I agree.

His eyes turn to flames. "Bad for business? My whole personal life is falling into the shitter."

"It'll all be okay. We'll find this guy, but maybe you should lie low for a while?" I suggest.

His car pulls up. He scowls, shakes his head, and storms over to his Mercedes, not tipping the driver.

I toss the guy a hundred, stating, "He's having a bad day."

"Thank you, Mr. Madden."

I nod, and my car pulls to the curb. I tip my valet a hundred, then get into my Porsche, feeling like I'm on top of the world.

I stop at the jewelers and text him.

> Me: I'm outside.

His employee comes outside and hands me two boxes.

I drive through town, pull up to the boutique, and text Isabella.

> Me: I'm here.

> Isabella: Coming right out.

She appears with two men. One carries dress bags and boxes. Another rolls two suitcases.

I roll my window down as Isabella approaches, asking, "Is everything ready to go?"

"Of course," she chirps. "Now, tell me about the lucky woman."

"You'll know soon enough. Thanks," I reply, then roll up my window, not wanting to discuss anything else.

My trunk slams shut, and I take off, driving toward Malibu.

When I get home, Blakely's on the piano playing, singing a new song, but there are only a few words. She looks up and stops. "Hey, what are you doing home so early?"

"Is that a complaint?" I tease.

She grins. "No, it's never a complaint."

More warmth fills me, confirming this is the right thing. I don't remember ever being so damn happy in my life.

She walks over to me, and I give her a kiss. Then I guide her toward the door.

"Are we going somewhere?" she questions.

"Yep. It's a surprise."

"Oh?" Excitement flares in her blues. "Do I get a hint so I can try to guess?"

I chuckle. "It's not a surprise if I tell you, pet." I lead her to the car, and we get in. I drive to the private airport.

She glances out the window. "We're flying?"

"Yep."

Once we're inside the plane and all the luggage, bags, and boxes are loaded, the plane lifts into the air. The flight is just shy of six hours, and when we land, I order, "Go ahead and open the window shade."

She does, gaping.

The sun sets over the water, with mountains highlighted in the brilliant pink backdrop.

She turns to me. "Where are we?"

"Maui."

She beams. "You brought me to Maui?"

"Yep. Let's get off this plane, pet." I rise and lead her onto the tarmac.

A private car's waiting for us. It takes us to the resort in front of Maluaka Beach. It's also known as the secret beach, on the south side of Maui. You can swim and snorkel right off it, and it's usually calm, so you don't have to fight the crazy waves Maui's known for.

I'll go hit some of the surf down the road, but I wanted a place for us to chill out for a bit. The beach is in a cove, so it's calmer most days, without the crazy undertow and waves that terrorize other beaches.

We check in. The bellman brings our bags to the room, and I pull a soft pink dress out of the garment bag. "Put this on, pet."

She runs her fingers over it. "It's beautiful."

"It's going to be more beautiful on you. Go put it on. We have dinner plans," I announce.

We both get ready. I dress in a pair of khaki linen pants and a pink linen shirt. I roll up the cuffs, displaying my ink, and we step outside.

"Where are we going?" she questions.

I point to a deck on the beach. There's only one table. Candles flicker in the darkness, and a team of servers stand in a line. I reply, "Over there."

She gives me another surprised look, and I lead her over to the deck. My stomach fills with nerves during dinner, and I barely taste the poke, sushi rolls, and wine.

Before dessert arrives, I rise and motion for the staff to leave the deck. They disappear, and I say to Blakely, "Let's dance."

She laughs. "There's no music."

Almost on cue, her song, "The End," from the demo, blares through the air.

Her eyes widen. I don't let her be shocked for too long. I tug her into my arms and start moving in a slow dance.

Her voice belts out, *"We're not forever. Our days fade before us, and it's all okay to you."*

"Why is my song playing?" she questions, giving me a worried, sad glance. It's the same expression she wore the day she sang it in the studio.

I tug her closer to me and murmur in her ear, "You're wrong. Every word of this song is wrong."

She freezes, holding her breath, her eyes glistening, and she pins her calm chaos of blues on me.

I study her, nervous, but I've never been so sure about anything. I slide a ring on her finger and say, "Marry me. Make us forever."

25

Blakely

*S*ince I woke up, I've stared at the ring on my finger, still in shock, wondering if I was dreaming. I've not moved except to pinch myself a few times.

Riggs's deep laugh tears me out of my trance. "Are you having second thoughts, pet?"

I turn over in the bed.

He sits back in an oversized chair, shirtless, his eyebrows arched.

"No, I'm just..." I glance at the radiant, flawless, who-knows-how-many-carats diamond shining on my hand. I admit, "I'm still in shock."

His lips twitch.

I sit up. "Why are you watching me sleep?"

"I always watch you sleep," he confesses, which is another surprise. I've only caught him once, the night he drank too much.

Flutters fill my stomach. I ask, "How long have you been awake?"

He shrugs. "Since around four. I went down the street to catch some waves."

I blurt out, "I would've gone and watched you."

He shrugs again, and it hits me how laid-back he's been since we got to Hawaii. I'm not used to this new Riggs, but I like it. He says, "Maybe tomorrow you can."

"How long are we here?" I question, never wanting to leave Hawaii. It's beautiful, and I haven't been here since I was a child. Like his normal style, Riggs has gone over the top to ensure our privacy, but I'm not complaining.

"A week, possibly longer. I have some business deals I might need to close next week, so we have to play it by ear, pet."

"That's okay. I should get moving. It looks like a beautiful day outside," I state, glancing out the window, then rising. The water twinkles from the morning sun. Two volcanic islands, Molokini and Kahoolawe, look like they're a swimmable distance, even though it's too far.

Riggs stands, then dangles a skimpy white bikini in front of me. He leans into my ear. "Put this on, future Mrs. Madden."

Flutters fill my belly. I bite my smile. He's been calling me that since he proposed last night. And I have to admit, I love it.

I slide my arms around his neck and inquire, "Should I change my stage name?"

He stares at me a minute and then shakes his head. "No, Ears said you had the perfect name. Leave it as Fox, but you're legally changing it to mine."

I softly laugh. "Is that so?"

His chest puffs out. He squeezes my ass and asserts, "Without a doubt. Now get your suit on. It's perfect weather."

"Yes, Sir," I say.

He winks and goes into the bathroom. I put on my suit. We leave the suite and walk across the grass until we get to the sand.

There's no one on the beach. Crystal-clear water gently laps on the shore. An oversized blanket covers the sand, and we sit. I stare at the water in awe.

"It's gorgeous, isn't it?" he asks.

"Yes."

He adds, "Makes my Malibu place look crappy, huh?"

I laugh. "I wouldn't exactly say that. And how is this beach not filled with people?"

Riggs grunts. "Easy. I paid everyone off."

I gape at him. "I don't even want to know how much that cost."

"Good thing you don't have to worry about it, then," he claims and lies down.

I assess the property again, then slide over him, drag my fingers over his chest, and innocently ask, "So no one's watching us?"

Mischief explodes in his expression. He flips me onto my back so fast that butterflies dance wildly in my stomach. His eyes twinkle, matching the water. I've never seen him look so happy, which makes my heart soar. I'd do anything possible to keep him looking like this.

He questions, "Are you sure you want to marry me?"

"Are you changing your mind?" I blurt out.

"No, I want to know if you're sure you want to marry me," he repeats.

"Yes, I'm sure," I reiterate.

"Good." He scoots me off him, grabs the snorkeling gear, then slings me over his shoulder.

I shriek.

He slaps my ass and carries me into the water until it's past my neck. He states, "There's a reef about 100 feet out from here."

"Really?"

"Yeah. Let's go see what we can find."

We swim to the reef and snorkel for hours. It's like being inside a fish tank. Brilliant yellows, oranges, purples, blues, and greens pop everywhere beneath us. Sea turtles swim so close we can touch them, but Riggs warns not to.

When we tire, we head back to shore. Riggs tosses our snorkeling gear on the sand, then pulls me back into the water. I secure my limbs around him, and he kisses me, then asks, "Are you sure you want to marry me?"

My stomach dives. I fret, "Why do you keep asking me? Are you trying to get out of it?"

His lips twitch. "Is that a yes, pet?"

"Yes, of course. Please stop asking me."

Approval lights up his expression. "Good. Marry me tonight."

I gape at him.

His lips twitch. "Is that a yes?"

"Tonight? You want to marry me tonight?" I question.

He chuckles. "Yeah. Let's do it at sunset, right here on the beach. You, me, the officiant, and no one else.

"Don't I need a dress?"

"It's hanging in your closet," he informs me with a self-satisfied smirk.

I gape at him again. Then laugh. "Of course it is."

His grin widens, then his face turns stern. "I still haven't heard a yes from you, pet."

I tease, "Why don't you kiss me and show me how much you want to marry me tonight? Then I'll give you my answer."

He doesn't hesitate. His lips meet mine, our tongues slide against one another as soon as possible, and he holds my head, dominating me into full submission.

I grind my lower body against his erection. He retreats, muttering, "How's that?"

"Sold," I chirp.

His lips grin against mine. He slides his palm over my ass and announces, "Okay, time's ticking." He pulls me up toward shore.

I laugh. "You're serious? We're going to get married tonight?"

"Unless you don't want to?" He arches his eyebrows, but there's a vulnerability in his expression.

It hits me that Riggs is nervous, which I find pretty cute. It's not a look I ever see on him. I slide my hands on his cheeks, repeating, "Stop asking me."

He closes the distance between us and palms my cheek. He softly states, "Don't wear a lot of makeup. I prefer you like this."

My butterflies go crazy. I nod. "Okay. If that's what you want, that's what you shall get."

He leads me into our suite and says, "I'll get ready in the other bathroom."

I open the closet. My heart races faster. A sleeveless, mermaid-style wedding gown with spaghetti straps, lace overlay, and a court train hangs in front of me. It's the most beautiful dress I've ever seen. It's backless and dips right before my ass with an elegant string to secure it.

A pair of silver-heeled sandals lie on the bed. Inside a glass box is a fresh, white lei, complete with a clip for my hair.

I shower, then dry my hair, leaving it in beach waves. Then I secure the lei on the side of my head. I apply a tad of eyeliner, mascara, and pale-pink lip gloss.

Riggs steps into the suite. He's wearing white linen pants and a matching button-down shirt with rolled cuffs. His ink peeks out on his lower arms and chest. He freezes, dragging his eyes over me in approval, and my butterflies go crazy again.

He steps forward and spins me slowly. "You're gorgeous, pet."

I glance back at him. "You're super handsome, Mr. Soon-to-be-Husband," I declare, but my voice shakes slightly. I add, "Can you tie my dress?"

"Of course," he replies, then laces the back. He steps in front of me, assesses me again, then states, "But there's something you're missing."

"What?" I fret.

He slides his hand over my gold collar and releases it. Then he pulls a platinum choker out of his pocket. It matches my ring perfectly. Diamonds the same size are laced all around the metal, and tiny rings are set around it, along with a few bigger ones. It's a work of art, and there's an engraving on it. It reads: *Forever owned. Love, Riggs.*

"It's beautiful," I gush.

He secures it around my neck. I go to the mirror and touch it, tracing the edges of the diamonds, then the rings, wondering what goes through Riggs's mind when he selects my collars. Does he think about what he's going to restrain me to?

I touch the bigger ring on the back, stating, "This is stunning."

He steps behind me. His lips hit my ear, and he claims, "My soon-to-be wife is stunning." He pecks me on the cheek, then picks up my hand and kisses the back of it.

He says nothing else and guides me out of the room and onto the deserted beach, except for one person.

A female officiant wears a purple flowing dress and a matching lei in her hair. She chirps, "Welcome. My name is Makayla."

"This is Blakely, and I'm Riggs," he states.

The sun begins to set. It's a clear night with no clouds anywhere.

Makayla goes through the process during the short ceremony. She recites the normal vows, which we're to each repeat after her, but at the end of his vows, Riggs adds, "I vow to prove you wrong and work on my faults."

It brings tears to my eyes.

Makayla turns to me and repeats the normal vows, and I take my turn saying them. At the end, I add, "I vow to always accept all of you, your faults and all."

A look I've never seen on Riggs's face forms. It's a mix between happiness and darkness, and I guess it's fitting since it represents all that's really him.

Makayla pulls us out of our trance, announcing, "By the power vested in me by the state of Hawaii, I now pronounce you man and wife. You may kiss your bride."

Riggs steps forward and holds my face in his hands for a moment, staring at me until I'm almost shaking with anticipation. Then he kisses me. It's raw, consuming, and everything I've ever wanted from him.

And I wonder if this is real or if I'm dreaming. I never thought I would see Riggs so happy or that I'd be able to say that he's truly mine, not just at this moment but forever.

All I want to do is keep us like this for the rest of our lives. And nothing within me believes anything could ever change the love I feel for Riggs or how I always want him to remain my everything.

26

Riggs
Two Weeks Later

The wheels screech on the ground, and the plane comes to a stop. I softly stroke Blakely's cheek. "Pet, wake up."

She stirs but snuggles closer to me.

I chuckle. "Come on, sweetheart. Time to wake up."

Her eyes flutter open. It takes her a moment to realize she's on the plane. She sits up, claiming, "Oh, I fell asleep."

I kiss her on the lips, replying, "Yeah, you were tired. We need to get going."

She rises, and we get off the plane and into my Porsche, which is waiting on the tarmac. It's only four in the morning, but I can't avoid reality anymore.

We stayed in Hawaii for two weeks. Hugh's been going crazy over the phone. He even told me about the safe and the rampage he went on. He fired the security team, and since he hired them, I didn't care. I don't trust anyone on his payroll.

He had the security footage reviewed. Our techs told him it had been tampered with but they were unable to trace the source. Still, Hugh's blaming somebody from the night security.

He spent the last ten days ordering me to get into the office and continuing to ask for my location. I kept it brief, telling him via text I was dealing with personal shit. Then I stayed in Hawaii longer to piss him off. But in all reality, I was enjoying my wife more than the joy I got from angering him further. Yet the time has come to finish Hugh off. Plus, I must ensure that Blakely gets her deal signed with one of these agents.

It's barely five when we arrive in Malibu. I debate about taking the surfboard out for a few rides but decide against it. There's too much to do today.

I shower, then go out to the kitchen.

Blakely pours a mug of coffee and hands it to me.

"Thanks," I say.

We sit down at the table, and she sips her coffee.

"Okay, pet, you have to make a decision. Which agent are you choosing?"

She groans and puts her hand over her face. "Can't you do it for me?"

"No, we've gone over this," I remind her.

I've done everything possible to steer her toward Jack Secroy over Noah Kingsley. Both are offering the same deals at this point.

Blakely wants complete freedom over her music, so I made sure both contracts clearly state she has full control. There's no doubt in my mind that Jack and Noah can take Blakely to the top. But something is telling me not to trust Noah.

It first happened when I caught him checking out Blakely's ass. It pissed me off. And then he had the guts to flirt with her in front of me. She was oblivious to it, but I'm sure as hell not. And while I won't trust any guy with her, something tells me that Jack is a better bet than Noah.

"Please just decide for me, Riggs. You're better at this," she whines.

I internally fight not to decide for her. I firmly answer, "No. Everything you said you wanted is in these contracts, and I've ensured you won't get screwed financially. But this is your career. So listen to your gut. What does it say?"

Please don't pick Noah.

She hesitates.

I wait, my heart racing.

She finally says, "Jack's really nice, but—"

"But what?" I question, my gut dropping.

She cringes, claiming, "He's a tad ruthless, don't you think?"

I grunt. "Yeah. I like that about him. What's wrong with ruthless? It gets you places in this industry."

She winces again.

I repeat, "What's so bad about being ruthless?"

She looks toward the window, tapping her fingers on her mug.

I take her hand and lace my fingers between hers, gently demanding, "Tell me."

She squeezes her eyes shut. She confesses, "Something about him reminds me of my father. I don't think I can work with him."

It's a bomb exploding inside me.

I should have picked for her.

No. It's wrong. This isn't my decision. This is her career.

For God's sake, she can't work with somebody who reminds her of her father.

But Noah...fuck.

"Okay, but you don't have any bad feelings about Noah? Nothing in your gut is saying that maybe he's the wrong one?"

She shakes her head. "No, and Noah's younger. I don't know if Jack will be alive my entire career. Won't he be retiring in a few years?"

I can't argue with her, nor can I say it hasn't crossed my mind. But I figured we'd deal with that issue when it happened. My pet is smart. I should have guessed she'd also be concerned about the same issue. Still, I don't like it. I stay silent, with my chest tightening.

"He can't work forever. Right? And how old is he?" Blakely fires.

I finally admit. "No. And you're right. He's in his late sixties."

She wrinkles her nose and cautiously declares, "If you're making me choose, I pick Noah."

I clench my jaw, counting to ten.

"You don't like my choice?" she asks worriedly.

I silently vow to have a little chat with Noah about the rules, as well as an extra clause I'm adding to the contract. I answer, "No. Noah's fine. If that's who you think you need to work with, then that's what you should do."

I can't believe I'm saying this shit.

"But you look upset," she says.

I rise and lean over her. She looks up, and I see the worry in her eyes. I assert, "Don't stress about this. I'll call Noah and give him the news. I have work to do at the office. I'll text you when I'm on my way home."

"Okay."

"What are you going to do all day?" I ask.

She smiles. "Sing."

I grin and kiss her again. "Write something nice about me."

She laughs. "Maybe I will."

I lightly tap her head. "I gave you a lot of material on our honeymoon, didn't I?"

She laughs again. "Maybe."

I kiss her again. "Okay, pet, I have to go. Have a good day."

"All right, you too."

I leave the house and call the attorney I use for personal matters. It's another contact Hugh doesn't know about.

Marco booms, "Riggs!"

"I don't have a lot of time to chat, but I need a sexual harassment clause added to Blakely's contract. The one that's with Noah," I relay.

"Okay. Has he done something?" Marco questions.

I keep it vague, replying, "Not yet, but I won't put it past him."

"All right. When do you need it by?"

"The next thirty minutes would be great."

He groans. "Jesus, Riggs."

"Can you not get it done?" I push.

"I'll get it done. Check your email in a bit."

"Thanks." I hang up and dial Noah.

He answers, "Riggs. I hope you have good news for me. I've been waiting."

I assert, "We have some things to discuss."

"What now? I thought we got all the details worked out?" he questions.

"There's one quick thing that we have to discuss. It shouldn't be a big deal. If you agree, Blakely is willing to sign with you," I inform him.

"Great. I'll be at the diner on 45th and 8th. Can you meet me in an hour?" he asks.

I internally groan. It's going to take me the entire hour to get through traffic. But I state, "See you then."

I fight through the smog and rush hour traffic and arrive at the popular breakfast spot. Noah's in the back corner, sitting in a booth.

I slide in across from him.

He sticks his hand out. "Riggs."

I take it, squeeze it hard, and shake it. "Noah."

He pins his eyebrows together. "What's going on?"

I announce, "Let's put it this way. We both know my wife's probably the most beautiful woman you're ever going to lay eyes on."

His eyes widen. "Your wife?"

"Yeah, my wife," I firmly state.

He stutters. "O-oh. Congratulations. When did this happen?"

"A couple of weeks ago."

He nods. "Right. So what do you want to discuss?"

I sit back in the booth. "There's a new contract in your inbox. Why don't you take a look? Section eighteen. My attorney just added it."

He picks up his phone, reads the screen, then glances back at me. "Why is there a sexual harassment get-out-of-the-contract clause in here? I've never done anything inappropriate with Blakely."

"Yeah, and you're going to keep it that way," I declare.

He crosses his arms. "Riggs. I want her for her talent. I'm going to take her to the top."

"You better, or I'll find another way to get out of this contract because that's where she belongs," I warn.

He affirms, "I'll get her there."

I grin. "Great. Then you won't have any issues signing that contract."

He huffs. "You can't be serious. I'm not an amateur. I'm not going to put the moves on her."

I rise. "Once again, it shouldn't be a problem signing it if you have no intentions of anything inappropriate happening." I lean down into his ear. "Also, if you ever touch her, the contract will be the last of your worries."

He turns his head. "Is that a threat?"

"No." I squeeze my hand on his shoulder until he winces. I add, "It's a solemn promise. Hands off my wife at all times. If I find out you've touched her, all of L.A. will be searching for your body. Understand me?"

He clenches his jaw, his face turning a tad red.

"Thought so." I release his shoulder and leave the diner. I go directly to work, and when I get to our floor, I go to Hugh's personal office.

He's drinking scotch, pacing the office, and growls, "Where have you been?"

"I told you I was taking care of personal business," I calmly state.

"My life is falling apart, and you skip town? Don't you care about our company?" he accuses.

I pretend to look concerned. "Why? What's happened with the company? Has money been stolen from our bank accounts?"

He snaps his mouth shut and spins toward the window. Then he runs his shaking hand through his hair. He quietly states, "No, the business accounts are fine."

I offer, "You might want to lay off the booze. It's ten A.M."

He angrily spins back to me. "Do you have any idea what I'm going through?"

"Do you need a loan? I've got plenty of money if you need it," I taunt.

His face turns purple. He spits, "This isn't a joke, Riggs."

I hold my hands up in the air. "Never said anything of the sort. I'm only trying to help my partner and friend."

He peers at me, interrogating, "Where were you for the last two weeks?"

"Sorry, but none of your business. You know my personal life is off-limits," I remind him.

His eyes turn to slits. "That's convenient for you."

"Meaning?" I challenge.

There's a knock on the door. My assistant has a nervous look on her face. Her eyes dart between Hugh and me.

I ask, "What's going on, Connie?"

She clears her throat. "The CEOs from Windemere are here in the conference room."

"Is the paperwork in order?" I question.

"Yes. I sent it to you last night."

"I reviewed it on the plane. Please tell them I'll be right in."

She gives me a tentative smile. "Okay, thank you." She leaves.

I watch her walk away, then turn back to Hugh.

He finishes his drink, then states, "Let's go."

I step between him and the door. "No."

"What do you mean no?"

I declare, "You're in no state to go into that conference room."

"This is my company," he claims.

I cross my arms. "It's *your* company? The last time I checked, we were fifty-fifty partners."

"The last time I checked, I had the final say," he throws in my face.

"So what? Your personal life's blowing up, so you're going to blow up our company as well?" I accuse.

He scowls.

I add, "Do you think if you go in there drunk at ten in the morning, they'll sign the paperwork, trusting their life's work to us?"

Hugh squeezes his eyes shut, then rubs his forehead.

I soften my tone. "I know you're in the shitter here, but you need to be smart. You are not going into that conference room. Now, sober up." I shut the door and go into the meeting.

I shake hands with the CEOs. We get into all the details, and while they're signing the paperwork, I pull out my burner phone under the table. I send Hugh a photo of the back of Blakely in her wedding dress. It's one of my favorite pictures of her. She's turning her head and blowing me a kiss.

I also send a message with it.

Me: She's mine. Forever.

He replies with a slew of messages, but I don't look at them. I turn off my phone, slide it back into my pants pocket, and finish the meeting.

Once everything is secure, I see the clients to the elevator, then go to my office.

Hugh storms into the room, seething, "That bastard's at it again." He shows me the text messages and photo.

I pretend to look shocked. "She's married?"

"Motherfucker," he utters.

"You better figure out who that is."

"Like I don't know that. What do you think I've been trying to do?" he barks.

I sigh. "Hugh, you need to go home. You're not in any shape to stay at the office. The last thing we need is business going down or the staff scared."

He shakes his head and starts pacing in front of my window.

I reiterate, "Hugh, this isn't the time to be here. Go home."

He finally gives up and leaves.

I sit back in my chair, staring out at the L.A. skyline, thinking about how sweet revenge is when karma bites those who have it coming to them.

I pick up my phone and text Blakely.

> Me: Put on the black leather one-piece and garter. Wear your wedding collar.

> Blakely: Where should I kneel, Sir?

Me: On top of the piano.

Blakely: Yes, Sir.

Another text comes in from my pet. It's an emoji face with heart eyes.

My cock grows harder. My pet loves playtime as much as I do.

Yep, life is perfect. Nothing could ever break us.

27

Blakely
One Month Later

"*I*t's worth a try," Ears states.

Noah nods and slides onto the piano bench next to me. He hits a couple of piano keys and directs, "Try it lower."

"Lower?" I ask in doubt.

"Yeah, just humor me," he replies.

I shrug. "Okay."

He hits the notes, and I lower my voice, singing, *"Love you."* When I'm done, I turn to him. "Like that?"

He grins and pats my leg. "Yes, exactly like that." He glances at Ears. "You hear the difference?"

Ears grins. "Yep. Can you sing it like that on the next go-round?"

"Sure," I agree. It's a bit strange getting instructions on how to sing my lyrics. I've never had anyone give me suggestions, but everything Ears and Noah propose seems to make my songs better.

We go through another take, and I sing it how they want me to. I decide I like it better, as well.

Noah leans closer, asking, "How's that feel?"

I nod. "Good. I think you guys are right."

Ears chuckles. "I usually am, darling. I usually am."

I roll my eyes. I've gotten used to Ears's ego, and I spend lots of time laughing over some of the things he says.

The buzzer rings, and the recording box door opens. I turn, and Riggs steps inside. He pins his glare on Noah.

Noah stiffens, jumps up, and praises, "Good work, Blakely."

"Thanks," I say, wondering why he's acting so weird and why Riggs is staring at him like he wants to kill him.

Noah crosses his arms and asks, "Riggs, can we help you with something?"

Riggs demands, "We need to go through Blakely's schedule."

Noah's jaw twitches. He keeps his gaze on Riggs, then slowly grabs his phone out of his pocket. He swipes at the screen and states, "I have a dozen interviews lined up for her to promote her first single, 'Invisibly Broken.'"

"Did you decide on a release date?" Riggs questions.

"Next month," Noah affirms.

My butterflies take off. I'm still shocked this is happening. It's like all my dreams are coming true, and I have to give all the credit to Riggs.

My husband.

I study him grilling Noah, and my heart soars. He's taking care of all the issues I don't want to be bothered with so I can focus on my music. It's perfect.

Noah informs Riggs about the places around the country where he's scheduled me to do interviews or sing, and my head spins. Even with Riggs handling the business side of things, it's overwhelming to me.

Noah states, "She has a radio interview in Atlanta, and I booked her to open a concert two days later. I can stay there with Blakely, and she can meet some of my contacts over there."

Riggs shakes his head, "No. She must be back on the plane immediately after the radio interview. I'll fly her back to Atlanta in time for the concert."

Noah shifts on his feet, declaring, "It's Atlanta. It's known for its music scene. Surely you know this."

Riggs stands his ground, asserting, "Blakely has an important charity event that she has to come to with me."

I groan. "Riggs, you know I hate those events. It's just a bunch of rich people wasting money on their fancy food and $1000 bottles of champagne. They should take that money and donate it to the charity if they care. It's super hypocritical."

Arrogance fills Riggs's face. "Exactly. That's why everything has been donated to this event. Not a penny will be wasted."

"How's that possible?" I ask, not believing it. I've been to too many of these events with my parents. I know how they work and what these people expect.

"Because I've been planning it," he announces.

"Oh. I-I didn't know."

"Now you do. So why don't you ask me what it's for?"

"Okay, I'll bite. What's the charity?"

He briefly studies me, then lowers his voice. "It's for the L.A. Center for Addiction's new Blakely Fox-Madden Wing."

My heart pounds harder. I finally stutter, "A-a wing in my name?"

He nods. "Yes. And I've been planning this charity event for months—four, to be exact. And you can sing that night, as well. Give more people in L.A. a sample of your music. But you don't have to if you don't want to."

"No. Of course I want to," I blurt out.

Noah interjects, "This sounds great, but I can assure you the contacts in Atlanta we could meet with are going to be better than any new fans in L.A."

I raise my chin. "Noah. I'm coming back to attend the event with Riggs. I'll have to meet the people in Atlanta at a different time."

He huffs. "You don't just meet people on a whim, Blakely. They have schedules."

"It's not open for discussion," I state, holding my ground. It's something I've gotten better at executing. I blame Riggs.

Noah opens his mouth again, but Riggs interjects, "You heard her."

I rise, but I then reach for the piano cover as a rush of dizziness hits me.

"Pet, you okay?" Riggs mutters, putting his hand on my back.

I sit back down and grow dizzier, then put my hand on my belly as a wave of nausea rolls through me.

Riggs crouches in front of me, peering at me and fretting, "Sweetheart, what's wrong?"

My vision returns, and my belly calms. I shake my head. "Nothing. I'm fine."

"Have you eaten today?" he questions.

"I had breakfast."

"That one piece of toast? That's all you've had?" he accuses, his voice rising.

I shrug. "We were working, and I wasn't hungry."

Riggs glares at Ears and Noah, asserting, "From now on, Blakely takes mandatory food breaks."

"We offered her food," Ears informs him.

"Not good enough. Make sure she actually eats," Riggs says in a very firm and upset voice.

"I will from now on," I assure him.

He gives me a look like he doesn't trust me.

"I will," I insist.

He sighs, then takes my hand and pulls me up. "Let's go eat."

"But I think we have more work to do," I state.

Riggs says to the men, "See, this is why it's mandatory."

"Sorry!" I cringe.

"You're good, Blakely. Get something to eat. We can do more songs tomorrow," Ears states.

I glance at Noah, not wanting him to be upset with me about the charity event or leaving too soon. "Is there anything else you need from me today?"

He shakes his head. "No. Go eat."

Riggs guides me out of the recording box, then leads me out of the studio and down the street. There's a small sandwich shop, and he takes me inside. We order Italian subs and sit down. He hands me a bottle. "Drink some water."

I obey to appease him, then inform him, "I had four bottles today."

"Well, at least you won't be dehydrated," he mutters.

I grin. "Nope!"

A server sets our sandwiches on the table. "Need anything else?"

"No, we're set," Riggs answers. He motions to me. "Eat."

I pick up the sandwich and move it toward my mouth. A foul smell fills my nostrils. I cringe and drop the sub on the paper.

"What's wrong?" Riggs inquires.

"I think I'm just tired," I say.

He feels my head. "You don't have a fever."

"I don't. I'm just tired," I insist again.

He stares at me, and I can tell he isn't buying that I'm just tired. He nods toward the sub. "You still need to eat."

I push the sandwich away. "I can't eat this. It smells rotten. Smell it!"

Riggs picks his sandwich up and sniffs it. "No, it doesn't."

"It does," I insist.

He grabs my sub, holds it to his nose, deeply inhales, then declares, "This is fresh."

The thought of taking a bite makes me wince.

"Let me get you another sandwich," he says.

I glance at the case of desserts. "I'd rather eat a piece of that double chocolate fudge cake."

He arches his eyebrows, and his lips twitch. "You haven't eaten all day and want a piece of cake?"

"Yeah. If you're good, I'll let you smear it all over me, then lick it off later tonight," I tease as I lean closer and wiggle my eyebrows. I admit, "I'm suddenly feeling a little needy."

Riggs chuckles. "I guess I'll get a couple of extra pieces of cake, then."

"Can we get it to go?" I ask, then add, "I'm sorry. Are you starving?"

He holds his hand up. "No, I'm fine. We can take it home, but at least eat the chips." He hands me the paper container.

I shove one in my mouth and chew it. "These are good."

"Glad you approve. Have some more," he orders, then wraps up the sandwiches and goes to the counter. He orders three pieces of cake.

The staff boxes everything up.

Riggs leads me out to the Porsche.

I get in the car and don't make it very far before I fall asleep. When I wake up, Riggs is carrying me into the bedroom. I stroke his cheek and say, "Hey."

He kisses me on the forehead. "Hey. Go back to sleep. I'll tuck you under the covers."

My stomach growls. "I think I want my chocolate cake."

He sets me on the bed, removes my shirt and pants, and pulls the blankets over me. He states, "I'll go get your dessert."

"Thanks."

A few minutes pass. He carries a TV tray into the room. It has a plate and a piece of cake on it. There's a bottle of water, one fork, and two napkins.

Riggs takes a forkful and holds it near my mouth.

I bite into it and groan. After I chew and swallow, I declare, "This is so good."

He grins. "Glad you're enjoying it."

He picks up another forkful of cake, but I move his hand toward his mouth. "Try it. It's delicious."

He bites into it and nods. I take a sip of water and then he does as well. "You're right. It's pretty good. Good call making me get this for you."

I wiggle my eyebrows. "You can still spread it all over me if you want."

He chuckles. "Maybe after you get some rest. I don't recall ever seeing you so exhausted. If Noah and Ears are working you too hard—"

"They aren't!" I interject, then yawn and say, "Tell me about the charity event. How did you get everything donated?"

The ego that I love so much washes over him. He leans his face toward mine, claiming, "Because your husband knows how to get things done."

I laugh, confirming, "I'm aware of this."

His face falls. "You and I have the same opinions on these events. I hate them just as much as you. But, if we can do something good with our status, then we should. So let's be the couple that does better."

Everything about his statement makes me happy. It's just another reason I love him so much. I curl into him and lean up to kiss him.

He returns my affection.

I retreat. "Hey, I-I wanted to ask you something."

He arches his eyebrows.

My pulse increases. I inquire, "Have you told my father we're married?"

A brief moment of anxiety fills his face. It disappears quickly, and he replies, "No, I haven't. Why do you ask?"

I should have considered it long before now. We've been married for over a month. But I've been so engrossed in Riggs and my career that it didn't occur to me. I admit, "Today, it crossed my mind that you and my father are business partners. At some point, he's going to find out. How is that going to work for you? Plus, once my singles get released, and the promotion begins, it won't be hard for him to figure out how to find me."

Surprise registers on Riggs's face.

I blurt out, "We should have thought about this."

"Why? Are you regretting marrying me?" he questions.

"No! Of course not! I hate for you to have to deal with my father's wrath, but I also don't know how we avoid it."

Riggs chuckles.

"What's so funny?" I question.

Arrogance washes over him. In his most confident tone, he answers, "One, your father and I aren't going to be partners much longer."

Shock fills me. "You're not?"

His eyes darken so intensely, a chill runs down my spine. He tightens his arm around me and affirms, "No. And two, there's nothing your father can do to hurt you or me. He's weak."

I don't doubt Riggs's strength, but I also know my father.

Riggs sees my worry. He strokes my cheek, insisting, "You have nothing to worry about, pet."

I hesitate, then ask, "What did he do to you? Will you please tell me?"

A few moments pass, with tension building between us. Riggs finally rolls onto his side, strokes the curve of my waist, and says, "This is between us."

"Of course," I reply.

Riggs studies me, then announces, "Your father stole from our client accounts and me."

I gape at him, speechless. My father is a lot of things, but a thief?

He adds, "It's hundreds of millions of dollars."

My mouth turns dry. I inquire, "Will he go to jail?"

A sinister smile lights up Riggs's darkened expression. "No. I'm taking care of things, so it's not public, but your father will soon have no money. It's better than doing hard time. All the things he takes for granted and waves in everyone's faces will disappear."

I swallow hard, asking, "How?"

He kisses my lips. "Don't worry about it. I have everything under control."

My belly quivers. I hate my father, yet he's still my blood. A moment of sympathy hits me.

"You don't like the thought of your father suffering?" Riggs questions.

Visions of all the bad things my father did to me over the years, including kidnapping me twice and ordering me to choose to marry a man who disgusts me, fill my mind. And stealing, screwing over Riggs and his clients, adds to my disgust. I softly admit, "He deserves to lose everything."

While I believe in my statement, something about Riggs's admission nags at me. I can't put my finger on what bothers me about it.

Riggs palms my cheek, insisting, "He can't harm you, pet. Don't fret over this. Plus, I'll go to my grave protecting you."

I convince myself Riggs has everything under control. I smile at him. "I know you will."

I fully believe my statement. He'll always protect me. He's my husband. No matter what my father tries to do to retaliate, Riggs will make sure I'm protected.

I snuggle into him and fall asleep in his arms; safe, warm, and happy in the belief Riggs would never hurt me.

28

Riggs

*a*s soon as I close the latest deal, I leave the office and pull out of the parking garage.

A black Charger veers into my lane a few cars behind me. My gut says something is off. I'm unsure why, but I don't ignore my gut feelings.

I detour through a few L.A. side streets, and the black Charger is still there.

Am I being followed?

I speed up, weaving in and out of heavy traffic for a few blocks. The Dodge stays far enough behind, and it could be a coincidence, but I'm not taking any chances.

I turn on my blinker to go right, and at the last second, I cut across the intersection in the opposite direction.

Horns blare at me. I accelerate, passing traffic as fast as possible. I wait until I haven't seen the Charger for several miles before I feel confident I've lost it. I'm still unsure if I was being followed, but it's got me rattled.

Is Hugh onto me?

No, he can't be. He's clueless, and his life falls apart more and more every day.

This will be over soon.

Hugh doesn't have the resources left to pay anyone to follow me.

It's only a matter of weeks until he's completely out of his money. Jones has drained the last of the offshore accounts. I alerted the banks we use for our business accounts about the hacks on Hugh's personal accounts. Most already knew since Hugh had banked personally there as well. I asked them how we could add additional layers of security to play it safe, even though Jones is always watching.

After the bank meetings, I informed Hugh that we would get alerts for any transfers in the accounts. Normally, those things are on statements and George reviews it all. But now, he and Hugh can't hide anything.

Hugh didn't like it, but there wasn't much he could say without blowing up his secret regarding all the stolen funds. And it's stopped him from taking any more.

Hugh declared I should have spoken with him first before speaking with the bank. I innocently asked him again why it was a problem.

He stayed silent, still unable to give me a good answer.

I offered to lend him money when he complained that he was out, but Hugh was too proud. This past month, he's offloaded personal items, selling several cars and other valuables to cover his cash flow issues.

But tomorrow's the big day. He'll have nothing after I force him to sign his shares over to me. Then, once I transfer the funds to buy him out, I'll steal the payout back.

It crosses my mind again that he might already know I'm behind all this. But I shrug it off, convincing myself that it's impossible. I've done everything I can to cover my footsteps. There's no trail, but I make a note to be extra vigilant.

My phone rings, tearing me out of my thoughts. Madelyn's name appears on the screen.

Why is she calling me?

I hit the button on my screen. "Madelyn."

She slurs, "Riggs, Riggs. You have to come over. Hugh's... He's out of control."

"What are you talking about?" I question. Normally I'd think she was being dramatic, but not with everything going on.

She begs, "Please come over! He's unstable!"

I bite my tongue. Madelyn chose an interesting word since she's been unstable for years. I play the part, obliging, "It's going to take me about an hour, but I'll be there as soon as possible." I hang up.

The smog in L.A. is the thickest I've seen in months. I drive through it, trying to stay calm in the crowded lanes, and eventually arrive at their Beverly Hills mansion.

The place is a disaster. I've never seen it in such a state. The gates are open, and the security guards are gone. Weeds flourish in the flower beds, and the grass is several feet high.

This is what happens when you have no funds to maintain your lifestyle.

Another wave of excitement flies through me. I turn off the Porsche and climb up the front steps.

Madelyn opens the door before I get to the top. It's the first time I've ever come to the house where a staff member hasn't greeted me.

She looks smaller, so tiny you can see her bones. The typical booze smell wafts around her, and I assume she's been hitting the bottle and pills for days. She throws her arms around me, and I feel like I might break her if I hug her too tight.

She slurs, "Thank God you're here."

I gently push her off me, feeling nostalgic about my mother. God, I hate the memories. The thought of my poor pet growing up with this woman as her mother only irritates me further. I can only imagine what it was like for her. And while Blakely had some things better than I did, our situations aren't that far apart.

Blakely lived in a house without affection and where addiction was common. She may have had money, but the neglect can't be erased.

I curtly ask, "What's going on, Madelyn?"

"My baby," she cries.

The hairs on my arms rise. Did something happen to Blakely? Does Madelyn know something I don't? I try to stay calm, inquiring, "What are you talking about?"

She shrieks, "She's married. Hugh knew and didn't tell me." Tears stream down her face.

Hugh appears in the doorway, his hair disheveled, shirt rumpled, and a ragged beard growing on his face. Red burns his cheeks, probably alcohol induced since a crystal tumbler of scotch is in his hand.

I can't help myself and dig, "If you need me to send some yard people over, let me know. You can't let your place go like this."

It infuriates Hugh. He snarls, "You want to send some of your staff as well? Ungrateful cocksuckers. You employ them for years, miss a few paychecks, and they desert you."

I assert, "Yeah, they have families to feed. You can't expect them to stay without payment."

Hugh scowls at me.

"This is your fault," Madelyn accuses, pointing at him.

He scoffs. "Madelyn, go cry somewhere else."

She pushes him, claiming, "You know where she is. Stop hiding her from me."

He downs the rest of his scotch, declaring, "I've told you I have no idea. Now stop this nonsense."

She reaches her arm back and slaps him, the sound of it echoing in the air. It shocks me. I've never seen Madelyn become violent.

Anger flares in his eyes as hot as his cheeks. He steps toward her, and she backs up until she's against the wall.

I lunge across the room and pull Hugh away from her, ordering, "Settle down."

He shrugs out of my grasp and threatens Madelyn, saying, "Your time in my house is limited."

She screams, "The house we're going to lose?"

I pretend to feign innocence. "What?"

"He hasn't paid the property taxes," she yells, her bloodshot eyes glaring at him. She adds, "They sent us a tax foreclosure."

"It's not my fault, you witch," Hugh spits out. It flies from his mouth and hits her arm.

She glances at it, wrinkles her nose, then whines, "How could you put us in this situation? You promised you would always take care of us."

He seethes, "You ungrateful woman. I paid for your sorry ass and your ungrateful daughter all these years."

Madelyn's eyes widen. She snarls, "You mean *our* daughter. Not that you've done anything to get her back."

Hugh shakes his head in disgust and stomps over to the bar. He pours more scotch and turns. The alcohol sloshes out of the glass, hitting the marble floor. He pins his wrath on his wife, insulting, "If you weren't such a lousy mother, she wouldn't have run away."

"Me?" she mocks. "Now, that's calling the kettle black."

Having seen enough of their shit show, I interrupt, announcing, "I'm going to let you two deal with your family matters alone."

Madelyn spins, begging, "Take me with you, Riggs."

"What? No. Sorry, but I'm not getting involved in this," I state.

"Fucking whore," Hugh blares.

"Oh shut up, you pig!" she screams.

Hugh tosses another mouthful of the scotch back.

Madelyn grabs my arm, pleading, "Riggs, please. Don't leave me with him." She bats her lids, but she's so intoxicated she can barely stand up.

I pry her off me and lead her to the chair. "Sit down, Madelyn."

She obeys.

I order Hugh, "Take care of your wife."

He shoots me a sharp look.

"Riggs, don't go," she says and leaps off the chair, trying to come after me.

I open the front door and step outside.

"Riggs," Madelyn shouts.

"Stop embarrassing yourself," Hugh demands.

I walk faster, slide into my driver's seat, and rev the Porsche. I speed out of the driveway. I look in my rearview mirror, and Madelyn's dropped to the ground, sobbing.

Part of me feels sorry for her and Hugh, but then I remind myself what he's done and how she's been a horrible mother to Blakely all these years. She doesn't deserve any mercy either. They deserve everything they're getting and all the wrath that's still to come.

I turn up my music, ecstatic this is almost over. It's been a huge test of my patience, and I know I'm playing a dangerous game, even though I've covered my tracks.

I race home, ready to announce Blakely to the world at the charity event tonight. Things couldn't be more perfect between us. I've kept the name of her wing under wraps, but all of Hugh's friends will be there, and more gossip will fly once they find out I've married her.

But it doesn't matter if he finds out tonight. Tomorrow, he'll know I'm the one who's taken him down. The company will be mine, and his daughter is mine. She loves me, and I love her. We'll do good things together, and nothing will ever break us.

Things couldn't be better in my life.

29

Blakely

*W*arm air hits me as I step out of the plane. Riggs stands at the bottom of the steps, and I bounce down them, leaping into his arms.

He squeezes me tight, then kisses me, asking, "How was your interview?"

"Awesome," I gush.

Noah clears his throat behind me, adding, "She did great."

Riggs locks eyes with him. "I don't doubt it. See you tonight. Make sure you bring your checkbook." He leads me over to his Porsche and opens the door.

I slide inside.

He gets in the driver's seat, starts the engine, and asks, "So, what was it like?"

I shrug. "It was the same as all the others." This month, Noah's kept me busy with interviews. They're fun, and my single is climbing the charts. It's currently at number five, which is beyond my wildest dreams for my first single. Ears and Noah claim it will hit number one, but I'm grateful for all the initial success I'm having.

"Something happened while you were in the air," Riggs claims.

"What?"

His grin widens. He kisses the back of my hand and declares, "You're at number four."

I gape at him. It only hit number five yesterday.

He chuckles. "Don't look so shocked. You're going to the top, pet."

"It's just surreal," I mutter.

He squeezes my hand and veers into another lane. "Well, get used to it, Mrs. Madden. Your album is amazing."

My butterflies kick off. It happens every time he calls me Mrs. Madden.

He turns down another street, then pulls into a parking garage, stating, "We don't have a lot of time to get ready."

"We're not going home to Malibu?" I question.

He stops at a concrete wall, rolls his window down, then puts his hand on the screen. The wall lifts, displaying a tiny area. He drives the car into it.

My goose bumps break out. "Are we at Apartment Thirteen?"

"No. This is my L.A. apartment."

"How many do you have?"

He shrugs. "A few dozen. But this is where I stay if I need to be in the city."

"Is this where you were for all those weeks?" I ask, my voice dropping at the memory of how bad it felt to not know where he was and worry about whether he would ever return home.

"Yeah," he replies, then the concrete wall shuts. The lift moves up.

"Are all your places locked up like this?" I question.

"Only the ones I use. The ones I rent aren't as secure."

We stop moving and the doors in front of us open.

Riggs maneuvers the car forward and then reverses into a spot. He turns off the Porsche, gets out, then opens my door. He reaches in and states, "Our driver will be here in an hour and a half."

I rise, and he leads me through another secure door, a small entryway, and into a penthouse. I freeze, gushing, "Wow."

The entire L.A. skyline glimmers through the penthouse's windows. It's one of the most incredible views I've ever seen.

He slides his arm around my waist. "Glad you approve."

"How did you find this place?" I question.

"Years ago, I stumbled on it."

"It's breathtaking," I claim.

He kisses me on the head. "Let me show you around."

He gives me a tour, then leads me back into the main suite. "We should get moving so we aren't late."

"I assume I have a dress here?" I ask.

He wiggles his eyebrows. "Of course." He slides his fingers around the hot-pink collar around my neck. He unclasps it, then kisses the curve of my neck. He squeezes my ass and then states, "Get in the shower."

I obey. After showering, I dry and then curl my hair. I ask Riggs, "What do you think about my hair if I do something like this?" I twist it up to show what I'm thinking about doing.

His eyes light in approval. He affirms, "Go for it, pet."

I secure my hair with pins into a messy updo, then apply my makeup.

I debate about what lip color I should use, then question, "What color is my dress?"

He rolls his deodorant over his armpit and answers, "Deep red."

I pick up my red stain and apply it. Then I enter the closet and find a gorgeous, floor-length dress hanging up. I open the lingerie drawer, but Riggs shuts it.

He asserts, "Nothing underneath tonight."

I fight to hide my smile but can't. When Riggs tells me not to wear panties, it usually involves something dirty in public. I often wonder if it's challenging for him to tease me while no one else knows what's happening.

He leans into my ear. "I wouldn't want you to be bored this evening."

I softly laugh. "Okay, then. Nothing underneath." I unzip the dress and step into it. It's sleeveless, backless, and has a built-in push-up bra. I close the zipper under my left arm and spin.

Riggs dangles a pair of red, six-inch stilettos in front of me, stating, "I'll be out in a minute."

I take the shoes, go to the bed, and sit down. I slide into them.

Riggs walks out of the closet, wearing his tux pants and buttoning his shirt, with a jacket and bow tie slung over his arm. His ink quickly disappears.

My heart pounds harder. My husband is beyond gorgeous. I kind of like the fact most people don't get to see his tattoos.

He steps to the dresser, removes the lid off a box, and hands me a pair of oversized, black-and-white diamond chandelier drop earrings.

"Wow!" I exclaim, taking them from him.

"Glad you like them," he says.

I put them on and glance in the mirror, declaring, "They're perfect!"

He slides a matching choker around my neck. His fingers trace the spaces between the diamonds, and he claims, "The setting is strong enough for me to slip anything through here. I could keep you restrained for hours."

My pulse skyrockets. I squeeze my thighs, stating, "I've been a good girl."

He chuckles and kisses the back of my neck. Tingles erupt underneath his lips. He murmurs, "I'll be the judge of that."

I spin into him and slide my arms over his shoulders. I ask, "What do you think people will think? When they find out we're married?"

He grunts. "I could give a shit what they think, but the men will all be jealous."

I bite on my smile.

He pecks me on the lips, and his phone vibrates. He pulls it out of his pocket, glances at the screen, and then announces, "Driver's here."

I step back, and he slides the bow tie through his collar. I reach forward and tie it.

His lips twitch. "When did you learn to do this?"

I shrug. "Every girl in Beverly Hills gets taught to tie a man's bow tie."

"Is that so?"

"Yep." I finish securing it and rise on my toes, but I'm only a few inches shorter than Riggs in the heels.

He puts on his jacket and leads me to an elevator. We get in and when it stops, it opens into a lobby. He nods to the security guards as we pass, then steers me outside toward an SUV.

The driver opens the back door, and I slide into the vehicle. Riggs follows and shuts the divider window. He tugs me closer to him and says, "I forgot to tell you. I scheduled a meeting with the designer on Tuesday."

"For?" I question.

"Your wing."

I arch my eyebrows, surprised. "You want me to meet the designer?"

"Yeah. Your name's on it. The final design should be something you approve," he asserts.

"Really?"

"Of course."

I kiss him. "Thank you. For all of this. It..." I swallow the emotions climbing up my throat. I manage to admit, "It means a lot to me."

Sadness flares in his blues. He says, "Hopefully, it'll help a lot of people."

If only it would save my mother.

I try to push the thought to the back of my mind. I can't afford to go down that rabbit hole this evening.

The event isn't far. The driver parks in front of the red carpet, and Riggs gets out. He reaches in for me, and camera lights flash as soon as I step out. Reporters scream questions, and Riggs leads me through the crowd, answering questions with brief responses, then stops at the top of the steps.

"How long have you and Blakely Fox been dating?" a man hollers.

Riggs tightens his hand around my hip, securing me next to his body. "We're not dating."

The crowd laughs.

He announces, "Let me introduce all of you to my wife, Blakely Fox-Madden."

There's a brief moment of stunned silence before the shouting chaos reignites. Riggs spins me and leads me inside. He murmurs in my ear, "Now everyone knows you're mine."

My flutters reappear. I tilt my head and smile at him, stating, "And you're mine. You're off the market, Mr. Madden."

He asserts, "I was off the market the minute you stepped on that stage, pet."

My heart soars. I open my mouth, and Ears's voice tears through the air. "Blakely! You look stunning!"

We turn, and Ears embraces me, then kisses my cheek. "I heard Atlanta went well?"

I nod. "It was great."

We make small talk, and more people from the studio arrive. Riggs excuses us, stating we need to make our rounds. He leads me through the room, saying to each group of guests, "You know my wife, Blakely, correct?" or "Let me introduce you to my wife, Blakely."

The look on those who know me through my parents is always the same. Pure shock. But something else registers on the faces of some of my parents' friends. I can't put my finger on it, and it makes me a bit uncomfortable. I eventually realize that the common denominator is all of them are country club members.

I chalk it up to the fact I've never enjoyed any of them and push it out of my mind, standing tall next to Riggs, feeling loved and powerful.

After a glass of champagne, I tell Riggs, "I need to use the restroom."

"Excuse us," he tells a group of people and then guides me to the restroom.

I go inside, do my business, then reapply a coat of lip stain to ensure it stays fresh. One of my mother's friends comes inside and says, "How have you been, Blakely? It's been so long."

I nod. "Yes, it has. I'm great, Cheryl."

She scans my face, then asks, "Have you talked to your parents recently?"

My face heats. I lift my chin. "No."

She opens her mouth and then snaps it shut.

I need to get out of here. No need to give her any other ammo for the gossip.

"Nice seeing you," I state, then exit the bathroom and freeze.

My heart pounds hard against my chest. I grip the wall to keep my balance.

My father and Riggs are in a heated conversation. My father has never looked so disheveled. He appears to have aged at least thirty years. It makes him seem small and weak.

My father seethes, "Blakely Fox-Madden!"

Riggs boasts, "She's mine, and you're going to stay away from her. I don't know how you got in here, but you aren't welcome. Leave."

My father's eyes turn to slits. He snarls, "Does she know you sent all those pictures of her to me? Or what about the porn videos or audio clips?"

Goose bumps pop out of my skin. *What is my father talking about? Surely Riggs wouldn't do something like that.*

My father threatens, "You'll pay for this if it's the last—"

"Don't you threaten me. One call and you're spending the rest of your days in jail," Riggs warns.

"Over what?" my father spits.

"I know about the offshore accounts," Riggs informs him.

My father's eyes widen.

Riggs snarls, "Game's up, Hugh. Tomorrow you're signing your shares of the company over to me."

"Bullshit!" my father blurts out.

"Blakely, my baby!" my mother's voice shrieks.

I turn my head, and she lunges through the hallway, tugging me into her arms.

I gape over her shoulder.

My father and Riggs stare at me. Both my father and mother are intoxicated, my father more than I've ever seen him, but my mother reeks of alcohol.

My stomach churns. Her body is way too thin. I can feel her bones.

She slurs, "Did he force you to do those things?"

"What things?" I question, tearing my eyes off hers and locking them on Riggs.

"Shut up, Madelyn!" Riggs orders.

My belly quivers. I lock eyes with him, demanding, "What are they talking about?"

"Nothing. They're drunk."

"Don't lie to me, Riggs."

My father shoves his phone at me. "Have a look yourself."

Riggs snaps it out of my hand. "I'm calling security. Neither of you are staying."

Anger fills me. My voice shakes, and my eyes fill with tears. "What did you do?"

"Everything's under control. I'm sorry they're here. I'll have them removed," he replies.

Rage tornadoes through me. I try to control my wavering voice, insisting, "Tell me now what you've done."

"Pet—"

"Did you send footage of me to my father?" I interrogate.

His eyes fill with guilt. He tries to hide it, but I know him.

I brush past him, warning, "Stay away from me." I walk as quickly as possible in the stilettos toward the main door.

"Blakely!" Riggs shouts, following me.

"Baby," my mother shrieks again.

The entire room turns quieter, and eyes follow me. I push through the crowd and step outside.

"Blakely," Riggs calls again.

I tear down the steps, past the media, who scream at me.

Noah's getting out of his car. I call out, "Noah!"

He assesses the situation, then meets me a few steps from the car. He ushers me into the backseat. "Get in."

"Blakely!" Riggs shouts again.

I slide into Noah's backseat, and he follows.

Riggs pounds on the window, and the driver takes off.

We weave in and out of the L.A. streets as more shock fills me.

I need to find out what Riggs sent them.

How could he do this?

No. My father has to be lying.

Riggs is capable of anything.

My gut flips faster.

Noah quietly asks, "Blakely, what's going on?"

I stay quiet, fighting tears.

"Blakely?" Noah asks again.

I blurt out, "I need you to take me to Malibu."

"Why there?"

"I need to go home before Riggs gets there. Can you take me?"

"Sure," he agrees and pushes the button for the divider. He tells the driver, "Malibu. Blakely, what's the address?"

I state it, then Noah puts the divider window up.

"What did Riggs do?"

I don't answer, just shake my head and turn toward the window, doing my best to hold in my tears.

When we pull up to the gate, I order, "Stay here, please." I get out, put my hand on the screen, and the side door opens. I get through the gate, then put my hand on the alarm for the house and go directly to the bedroom.

I grab a suitcase out of the closet, open it, and toss a few outfits inside. I go into the bathroom and gather my toiletries. Then I slide it into the zippered pocket of the suitcase.

My hand hits something. I pull it out, and the hairs on my arms rise. It's a burner phone, similar to the one Riggs gave me.

My gut tells me to turn it on. I push the button, and my stomach pitches. There's only one number on it. It's my father's.

I scroll through the text messages, feeling more ill with each one. My voice fills the air, and my face and body appear in multiple audio and video clips.

How could he?

My father's angry, threatening messages and Riggs's taunting ones all become blurry.

"I can explain everything." Riggs's voice tears my eyes off the phone.

I feel nauseous. My voice shakes, and I seethe, "Don't you dare."

"Pet..."

"Don't ever call me that again."

He shuts his mouth. For the first time, I see fear in his eyes.

I swallow down bile, toss the phone in the suitcase, and zip it up.

He closes the gap between us and tugs me into him.

I push him away. "Do not touch me!"

"Blakely, let's discuss this!"

I shove him as hard as I can. Tears stream down my cheeks.

He stumbles back, and I bolt past him. He follows me, demanding. "Blakely, wait!"

I carry the suitcase out of the house, and he grabs my arm.

"Stop!" I scream.

He keeps his grip on me.

I hiss, "I said stop. At least abide by my safe word."

He freezes. Shock fills his features.

I retreat, walking backward, claiming, "I trusted you."

"You need to let me explain."

"Explain? Explain what? That you sent intimate things to my father? That you used me for revenge? Is that why you married me?" I accuse, my heart breaking at the thought.

"No, of course not. I love you," he declares.

A sad laugh bursts out of me. I assert, "You don't know what love is, Riggs. Stay away from me." I step through the gate door.

"Blakely." He grabs my arm again.

I angrily spin and jab my finger into his chest. "I said stop."

He clenches his jaw, then quietly begs, "Don't do this, pet."

My vision turns blurry. "You did this, Riggs. Not me. And you know what?"

He swallows hard, waiting. More tears fall. I add, "You're just like my father."

Pain fills his expression. "No, I'm not."

I wipe my tears.

Noah grabs my suitcase, ordering, "Get in the car, Blakely."

"Stay out of this, Noah," Riggs warns.

Noah puts the suitcase in his trunk.

I get into the car.

"Blakely," Riggs tries again, in a desperate tone that kills me.

Noah slides next to me, slamming the door. Riggs pounds on the window. "Blakely!"

The car pulls away.

We get several blocks before I ask, "Can you find me a place to stay tonight?"

He shakes his head. "No. I'm taking you to my place. You can stay as long as you need."

I don't argue. I'm too distraught to even come up with any other plan. I always knew Riggs had a dark side, but I never believed he would use it to hurt me.

He used me to get at my father. I should have put two and two together about why he wanted me in his life.

The truth flares, breaking my heart into millions of pieces.

Riggs isn't capable of love. He's only capable of pain and revenge.

30

Riggs

$\mathcal{T}$he sun comes into full view. Its blazing rays begin to blind me. I grunt, pick up the empty tequila bottle, and step inside the house.

I check my phone again, but there's no response from Blakely or Noah.

I'm going to kill him for getting involved in our dispute.

This isn't a dispute.

She left me.

She'll come back.

She has to come back.

I can't shake the fear that clings to me. It grown more intense as the night went on, morphing into the morning.

I call Blakely's number, but she still has her phone turned off. I call the burner phone I used to text Hugh, but it's off too.

I toss the empty bottle into the trash and stare out the kitchen window. Calm chaos sparkles across the sea, and everything inside me tears further apart.

What have I done?

I never expected Blakely to see her parents again. They weren't on the guest list, but I shouldn't have been so careless.

I text her again.

> Me: I love you. I married you because I love you. Call me so I can bring you home.

I finally get a response.

> Blakely: I'm never coming back, Riggs. It's over. Don't contact me anymore.

> Me: Don't say that. We need to talk.

She doesn't respond. My insides quiver harder. I grip the phone, reread her message, and make a new vow.

I've never been more motivated to take Hugh down. This is his fault. If he had been the father Blakely deserved, or a loyal business partner, none of this would have happened.

But there's another thing I'll relentlessly do.

I text my pet.

> Me: It'll never be over between us. And you will return home. To me. Forever.

She still doesn't respond, but it doesn't matter.

I shower, sober up, and get dressed to go to the city. First, I'm taking Hugh's shares today. Then my wife's coming home. She's mine. We're unbreakable, and I will get her back.

I return to the bathroom, open the cabinet, and look for a fresh bottle of mouthwash. I reach for it, then freeze.

My pulse skyrockets.

How long has it been since her last shot?

I only gave her one.

I stare at the box of pregnancy tests and then pull it out. It's unopened.

I dig through the trash, looking for evidence of other tests, but there aren't any.

She can't be pregnant.

She didn't get her shot.

All the times Blakely's been exhausted or unable to eat recently fill my mind. Her beautiful glow I assumed was from the happiness we both felt. I lean against the counter, and shock rolls through me. I try to remember when she last got her period, but it's been months.

Why hasn't she said anything to me if she thinks she's pregnant?

I stare at my reflection in the mirror, vowing for the hundredth time since she left that somehow, I'll make this right. She'll see how much I love her. I promise myself out loud, "No matter what, I'll get my pet back."

**Ready to find out what happens to
Riggs and Blakely?**

Click to get your copy of The Vow,
The final book in the Club Indulgence Duet.

THE VOW

CLUB INDULGENCE DUET: BOOK TWO

I made a vow... and he won't let me escape it.

Riggs is possessive and cruel, twisted beyond all measure.

I knew it, yet still trusted and loved him.

Then he betrayed me.

I can't forgive what he did.

So I try to break what's between us...to exit his dark world without a second thought.

Yet the lonely nights torture me, reminding me what it felt like to be his, proving he's right. Once you're in his world, there's no getting out. It becomes ingrained into your soul.

And Riggs' obsession with winning me back doesn't help. Nor does my weakness to visit the club.

Each of our encounters hurt more, leaving unanswered questions.

How can he love me and do what he did?

Why do I keep returning to his arms?

It's a cycle I'm terrified will never end—part of me doesn't want it to.

The Vow is the second and final book of the Club Indulgence Duet. It's a second chance, age gap, forbidden love, dark billionaire romance.

Click to get your copy of The Vow,
The final book in the Club Indulgence Duet.

MAFIA WARS IRELAND SPINOFF SERIES

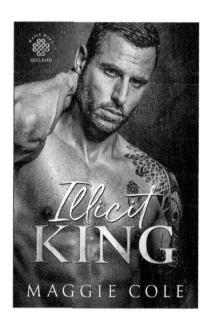

**Are you ready for the O'Connors in
Mafia Wars Ireland?
Cover Reveals and Titles Coming Soon!**

Illicit King (Brody)- May 1, 2023
Illicit Captor (Aidan) - June 1, 2023
Illicit Heir (Devin) - July 15, 2023
Illicit Monster (Tynan) - Sept 1, 2023

CAN I ASK YOU A HUGE FAVOR?

ould you be willing to leave me a review?

I would be forever grateful as one positive review on Amazon is like buying the book a hundred times! Reader support is the lifeblood for Indie authors and provides us the feedback we need to give readers what they want in future stories!

Your positive review means the world to me! So thank you from the bottom of my heart!

CLICK TO REVIEW

MORE BY MAGGIE COLE

Mafia Wars Ireland

Illicit King (Brody)- May 1, 2023

Illicit Captor (Aidan) - June 15, 2023

Illicit Heir (Devin) - Sept 1, 2023

Illicit Monster (Tynan) - Oct 15, 2023

Club Indulgence Duet (A Dark Billionaire Romance)

The Auction (Book One)

The Vow (Book Two)

Standalone Holiday Novel

Holiday Hoax - A Fake Marriage Billionaire Romance (Standalone)

Mafia Wars New York - A Dark Mafia Series (Series Six)

Toxic (Dante's Story) - Book One

Immoral (Gianni's Story) - Book Two

Crazed (Massimo's Story) - Book Three

Carnal (Tristano's Story) - Book Four

Flawed (Luca's Story) - Book Five

Mafia Wars - A Dark Mafia Series (Series Five)

Ruthless Stranger (Maksim's Story) - Book One

Broken Fighter (Boris's Story) - Book Two

Cruel Enforcer (Sergey's Story) - Book Three

Vicious Protector (Adrian's Story) - Book Four

Savage Tracker (Obrecht's Story) - Book Five

Unchosen Ruler (Liam's Story) - Book Six

Perfect Sinner (Nolan's Story) - Book Seven

Brutal Defender (Killian's Story) - Book Eight

Deviant Hacker (Declan's Story) - Book Nine

Relentless Hunter (Finn's Story) - Book Ten

Behind Closed Doors (Series Four - Former Military Now International Rescue Alpha Studs)

Depths of Destruction - Book One

Marks of Rebellion - Book Two

Haze of Obedience - Book Three

Cavern of Silence - Book Four

Stains of Desire - Book Five

Risks of Temptation - Book Six

Together We Stand Series (Series Three - Family Saga)

Kiss of Redemption- Book One

Sins of Justice - Book Two

Acts of Manipulation - Book Three

Web of Betrayal - Book Four

Masks of Devotion - Book Five

Roots of Vengeance - Book Six

It's Complicated Series (Series Two - Chicago Billionaires)

My Boss the Billionaire- Book One

Forgotten by the Billionaire - Book Two

My Friend the Billionaire - Book Three

Forbidden Billionaire - Book Four

The Groomsman Billionaire - Book Five

Secret Mafia Billionaire - Book Six

All In Series (Series One - New York Billionaires)

The Rule - Book One

The Secret - Book Two

The Crime - Book Three

The Lie - Book Four

The Trap - Book Five

The Gamble - Book Six

STAND ALONE NOVELLA

JUDGE ME NOT - A Billionaire Single Mom Christmas Novella

ABOUT THE AUTHOR

Amazon Bestselling Author

Maggie Cole is committed to bringing her readers alphalicious book boyfriends. She's an international bestselling author and has been called the "literary master of steamy romance." Her books are full of raw emotion, suspense, and will always keep you wanting more. She is a masterful storyteller of contemporary romance and loves writing about broken people who rise above the ashes.

Maggie lives in Florida with her son. She loves sunshine, anything to do with water, and everything naughty.

Her current series were written in the order below:

- All In (Stand alones with entwined characters)

- It's Complicated (Stand alones with entwined characters)
- Together We Stand (Brooks Family Saga - read in order)
- Behind Closed Doors (Read in order)
- Mafia Wars
- Mafia Wars New York
- Club Indulgence Duet
- Mafia Wars Ireland

Maggie Cole's Newsletter
Sign up here!

Hang Out with Maggie in Her Reader Group
Maggie Cole's Romance Addicts

Follow for Giveaways
Facebook Maggie Cole

Instagram
@maggiecoleauthor

TikTok
https://www.tiktok.com/@maggiecole.author

Complete Works on Amazon
Follow Maggie's Amazon Author Page

Book Trailers
Follow Maggie on YouTube

Feedback or suggestions?
Email: authormaggiecole@gmail.com

twitter.com/MaggieColeAuth

instagram.com/maggiecoleauthor

bookbub.com/profile/maggie-cole

amazon.com/Maggie-Cole/e/B07Z2CB4HG

tiktok.com/@maggiecole.author

Printed in Great Britain
by Amazon

22391565R00229